PERFIDY

A CIRCLE CITY MYSTERY

M. E. May

*To Lorraine,
Thanks so much
and enjoy!
MEMay*

True Grit Publishing
(an imprint of Weaving Dreams Publishing)

Copyright © 2012 by M. E. May

ISBN # 978-1-937148-20-1

Library of Congress Control Number
2012908105

ALL RIGHTS RESERVED

Cover Art by Julie Kukreja, Pen and Mouse Design

Printed in the United States of America
10 9 8 7 6 5 4 3 2

PERFID

A CIRCLE CITY MYS

M. E. May

8.7.15

True Grit Publishing
(an imprint of Weaving Dreams Publ
Watseka, IL

Th
inc
use
dis
me
rec
exp
bri
per
P.

Dedication

To my husband, Paul,
the first man who truly believed in me.

And to my children, Brian and Marie,
for always loving me no matter what.

Acknowledgements

First and foremost, I want to thank my publisher, L. Sue Eggerton, for giving me the opportunity to see my words in print. Thank you for your trust, for believing in me, and for making my dream come true. It's truly an honor to be part of the Weaving Dreams family.

I want to acknowledge those who serve and protect the great city of Indianapolis — the men and women of the Indianapolis Metropolitan Police Department. They are a big part of what makes me so proud to call Indianapolis my hometown. I am especially grateful to those in the department who have been willing to answer my technical questions about the IMPD's policies and procedures. Your assistance is very valuable and greatly appreciated.

I would also like to acknowledge David Mann from Hellyer Security and Investigations in Columbus, Indiana. David gave me invaluable information regarding Indiana laws pertaining to a private investigator's rights concerning client confidentiality.

A special thank you goes to my editor, Brittiany Koren of Written Dreams Editorial Services for holding my hand through the editing process and teaching me so much. I appreciate all of your hard work and patience.

To my daughter, Marie; my grandson, Kodey; my niece, Annette; and my friends, Ann, Claire, Janie, Barb, Judi, and Maricella: thank you so much for reading my drafts and sharing your critique with me. Your feedback served to keep me on my toes, help me keep my facts straight, and encourage me to make *Perfidy* the best it could be.

Last, but not least, a very special thank you to my fellow author and dear friend, Tricia, for spending the last four years poring over my prose and encouraging me when I wanted to give up. Thank you for your help, your love, and your encouragement. I couldn't have done it without you.

"Before you embark on a journey of revenge,
dig two graves."

Confucius – 504 B. C.

Prologue

The full moon and stars sparkled atop the dark surface of the lake. The air was unseasonably cool. A sign autumn was coming soon. The engine purred as he maneuvered the boat around a small, tree-filled island. He knew this was where the water was deepest and well hidden from view of the lake houses. This was the perfect disposal spot.

"I think this is a good place," he said to her, cutting the engine. "It's really dark on this side of the lake. There aren't any houses for miles so no one will see us. Let's dump our, uh ... cargo and get the hell out of here."

"Why so nervous?" she asked in a calm, smooth voice caressing his cheek. "The worst is over. No one will ever suspect you or I had anything to do with this. All we have to do is stick to the plan."

"There's just one little hitch," he said. "Mandy."

Chapter 1

Mandy Stevenson leaned back, her auburn curls spilling over the back of the chair. Her gaze was fixed on an intricate spider web in the corner of the ceiling. It appeared to have a morsel of last night's dinner still hanging from it. "Circle of life," she said aloud, closing her pale green eyes. Mandy couldn't stop herself from thinking the worst. She shuddered as her thoughts were compounded by the fear she felt for her mother. Studying the room to distract herself from her feelings of foreboding wasn't working.

She stood and walked to the window. His office was devoid of decoration except for a few plaques and citations. However, the view from the north window of the City-County Building was a picturesque Indianapolis skyline.

Mandy took a deep breath and turned, nearly running into his metal frame desk. Or at least she assumed there was a desk under all of those papers and files. She could not imagine how he kept anything straight. The nameplate sitting on the desk which read "Lieutenant Thomas Melrose" was barely visible.

Lieutenant Melrose had been in Mandy's life since the day she was born. She and her brother, Charlie, had always called him Uncle Mel. He started his career as a rookie patrol officer with the Indianapolis Police Department as her dad's partner and eventually became her dad's best friend. It was natural for her dad to think of Mel when it was time to choose Mandy's godfather. Mel and his ex-wife had never had any children so he was thrilled to take on the responsibility.

Five years ago, her dad was promoted to Captain and Commander of the Homicide and Robbery Branch, and Uncle Mel accepted an investigating position in Missing Persons. Now he was the head of the department and the perfect person to help her.

Feeling anxious, she paced, peering out into the department. Amidst a sea of metal desks, she spotted her Uncle Mel, tall and muscular with bright red hair and freckles. He looked up from his conversation and held up his index finger.

Nodding and feeling a little embarrassed, she turned and sat down in a chair trying her best to wait patiently. She couldn't understand why he would take so long. Didn't he realize she wouldn't be here unless it was very important?

A few minutes later Mandy heard the click of the door handle. She rose to see him standing there with his most welcoming smile. Facing her, Uncle Mel put his hands on her shoulders. "Mandy, I haven't seen you in ages," he said. "What was so urgent you felt you had to come all the way downtown to see me?"

Mandy blinked a few times, then took in a deep breath determined to get through the next few moments without crying. Looking straight into his eyes, she said as calmly as she could, "Mom has disappeared. She hasn't been home for two days now. She didn't call; leave a note, or anything. I know she's gone on last minute trips before, but something's not right. Please, Uncle Mel, you have to help me."

Lieutenant Melrose's face went from pleasant smile to concerned frown. "Okay, Mandy, hang on a minute." He walked to his door and opened it. "Jacobs, Mayhew, in my office!" Mel stepped aside as two men entered the office. "Mandy, I'm going to assign this case to two of my best investigating officers, Detective Tyrone Mayhew and Detective Benjamin Jacobs. Gentlemen, this is Mandy Stevenson. She's Captain Robert Stevenson's daughter. It appears her mother, Cassandra Stevenson, is missing."

Detective Jacobs sat in the chair beside her while Detective Mayhew scooted some papers over and sat on the edge of the desk. Both Jacobs and Mayhew appeared to be in their mid-thirties, but were polar opposites in looks. Detective Mayhew was dark skinned, about six foot-two and muscular with a shaved head. He might have been very intimidating except for his friendly, dark smiling eyes. Detective Jacobs was shorter, about five-eleven, with sandy blond hair and serious slate blue eyes.

Mandy glanced at Uncle Mel as he took his seat behind his desk.

"I thought you would be the investigator," she said, disconcerted by this assignment.

"Basically, Mandy, I'm in the position of an administrator now. These very talented detectives will do most of the legwork. But don't worry. I'll be keeping a close eye on this investigation."

Afraid she had insulted them, she said, "No offense."

"None taken," said Detective Jacobs, opening his notepad.

"Now, Mandy, give us the whole story beginning with the last time you saw Cassandra," Uncle Mel said, looking serious and official.

Mandy adjusted herself nervously in her chair. "Tuesday morning," she began. "It must have been around 10:00. I had an interview for a part-time job at Le Françoise Boutique. Mom was giving me a few pointers on salesmanship. Tuesday being her day off, I asked her if she had plans for the day. She said no and told me she'd be there when I got home."

"Do you remember what she was wearing?" asked Jacobs.

"Yes. She was wearing a pair of blue jeans and a mint green pullover tee shirt."

"So what time did you get home after your interview?" asked Uncle Mel.

"It must have been close to 1:00 in the afternoon because I'd stopped for lunch. Mom's car wasn't there, so I assumed she was running an errand. When she wasn't home by late afternoon, I thought maybe she'd received a call from the real estate office and was showing a house."

Although Mandy was trying her best to appear cool under stress, she couldn't control those facial expressions her godfather knew so well.

"I can see you're very upset over all of this, Mandy," said Uncle Mel. "Take a moment if you need it, and then tell us what happened next."

Mandy nodded, collecting her thoughts and continued. "By about 7:00 that evening, I was beginning to worry. I decided to call Dad to see if he'd talked to her. He was at a seminar in Detroit."

"Yeah," Uncle Mel confirmed. "He told me he was going up there. What did he advise you to do?"

"You know Dad," she said rolling her eyes. "He never gets *excited* about anything. He told me not to worry because Mom has done this so many times before. I tried not to let his lack of concern bother me. Actually, I was hoping he was right, that she'd just gone off to be alone for a few days, because she *did* do that sometimes...," Mandy paused gulping back a sob, "...after Charlie...."

"I know, sweetie."

The urgency to find her mom began to swell inside her. "But this time it's different, Uncle Mel. Mom *always* leaves us a note or a voicemail letting us know she needed some time away, but she didn't do it this time. I went to bed that night and didn't sleep well. I kept waking up thinking I had heard her. I got out of bed around 7:00 the following morning hoping I'd find her in her room. She wasn't there.

"That's when I really started to panic. While I was in her room, I looked around. I noticed her makeup pouch on the vanity. She would never leave *it* behind. I looked in her closet. The overnight bag she normally uses was still there. Even her toothbrush was in the bathroom. She would have taken all of these things with her."

"That *is* very strange," Jacobs said, frowning.

"I called Dad to tell him and he told me we'd discuss it when he got home."

"Did you?" asked Uncle Mel.

"Yeah, but I got the same old reaction. I also spoke with Michelle, the receptionist at Mom's office, on Wednesday. She said Mom came to the office on Tuesday to get her laptop. She assured me Mom didn't have any scheduled appointments on Tuesday."

Mandy felt the tears coming. She couldn't hold back any longer. "I'm sorry, Uncle Mel. I'm trying not to think the worst. It doesn't help when Dad acts like it's no big deal."

Uncle Mel got up and went to Mandy placing his hand on her shoulder. "There's no need for you to apologize, Mandy. I don't think your dad means to be hurtful; he's just not very diplomatic."

"You can say that again," she laughed nervously.

"So he got back from Detroit last night?" asked Jacobs.

"Yes. He's in his office this morning," she said, feeling a twinge of anxiety. "I know he won't like it when he finds out I'm filing this report."

"You have every right to be concerned about your mother *and* to file this report," said Uncle Mel.

"Something which will help us get started is a list of all of your mother's contacts; family, friends, people at work," said Jacobs. "We'll need their names, addresses, and phone numbers if you have them. You can do this from home and either send them to me by email or give us a call with the information."

"I don't want to put any undue pressure on you, Miss," said Mayhew, "but the sooner we get those the better. When a person goes missin' it's important to get started before the trail runs cold."

"I'll start collecting the information as soon as I get home," she said, stung by the fact she hadn't filed the report sooner. "Thank you."

"Here is my business card with my contact information," Jacobs said, rising from his chair. "You can call me anytime."

"Here's mine, too. We'd better get out there and start callin' the folks we know about," said Mayhew. "It was a pleasure meetin' you, Miss Mandy."

"Same here, Detectives," she said, standing and offering to shake their hands. Both detectives nodded and smiled on their way out.

"I know it will be hard to talk to your father, so if you want me to tell him, I will," said Uncle Mel.

"Thanks, but no. I'd better do it myself," she said.

"If he gives you a hard time, let me know. Okay?" He lifted her chin peering into her eyes. "I'm as convinced as you are that we need to pursue this."

"Deep down in my gut I know something is terribly wrong. No matter how Mom and Dad feel about each other, she wouldn't intentionally hurt *me* like this."

She looked at him with deep affection. He was the father she wished she had. Squelching a burning desire to hug him, she simply said, "Thanks, Uncle Mel. I knew I could count on you."

"Just stand your ground with him. He may not like it, but he'll respect you for it." Uncle Mel gave her his best toothy smile, but she knew beneath the surface, he was just as worried as she was.

"I know." She laughed nervously. "I'll go talk to him right now. Thanks for your help."

"Shall I walk you to the elevator?"

"Thanks, but I'm a big girl. I'll manage."

As she headed for the elevator, Mandy felt the dread of having to face her father. Inside the elevator car, she turned to press the button and saw Uncle Mel watching her. Forcing one more smile and a little wave, she saw him disappear as the door slid shut.

Mandy stood in the elevator twisting the strap of her purse. She'd thought about waiting until her Dad came home from work, but decided it was a bad idea. It wouldn't be pleasant, but he might be more likely to hold his temper in the office than he would at home. He wouldn't want to lose control in front of his detectives. He was a strict, 'by the book' kind of guy, and very stubborn — the latter being an attribute Mandy had unfortunately inherited.

She looked up at the elevator numbers — one more floor to go. Her heart was racing. Surely her father didn't expect her to just sit around doing nothing. He'd been married to her mom for twenty-five years. Mandy hadn't been able to understand how her dad could think her mom would leave without saying a word to anyone, or without taking any of her things.

By the time the elevator stopped, she had mustered enough strength through her anger to face him. As the door slid open, she took a deep breath and turned to her right towards the homicide unit. The floor was full of filing cabinets and metal desks which looked like they'd been there since the early 1960's.

Scanning the area, she saw Brent Freeman, an old friend of her brother's, pecking away at his keyboard. He had come by the house with Charlie several times. Charlie had once told her Brent was one of the most brilliant students at the academy. He looked up at her, smiled then turned his attention back to his computer. To Mandy's surprise, the brief encounter had sent an inexplicable, but delicious chill down her spine.

There were a few other people she recognized, but she didn't have time to stop and chat. She saw her dad pacing in his office, talking on his cell phone. He didn't notice her until she was directly across the glass from him. Once he hung up, he gestured for her to enter.

"What brings you here?" he asked, frowning at her.

She was sure he already knew so she got straight to the point. "I just finished filing a missing person report." Then quickly added, "It's not like Mom to disappear and not take any of her things with her, so I decided to take action. Besides, Uncle Mel thought it was a good idea."

She was hoping adding Uncle Mel's opinion would soften her dad's reaction. Instead, he rolled his eyes at her in the same way he'd done when she was a child and he was about to tell her she'd done something stupid.

"You know how it is in that house," he said in a soft, but stern tone. "She ran off to punish me. She didn't tell you because she knew you'd do something like this and embarrass me in front of the whole police force."

As Mandy had anticipated, he was thinking about himself, about how this was going to make him look. It took a minute for her to recover. "Oh, so this is all about *you* and how embarrassed *you'll* be!"

"Calm down and lower your voice," he said through clenched teeth.

"I will not calm down! I'm not a child anymore," she shouted. "My mother would not use me that way!"

He'd taken a step toward her but she stood her ground, growling at him in anger. "Don't come near me. I know you and Mom have become bitter toward one another, but she wouldn't treat *me* this way. She wouldn't put our family through this agony just to get back at you!"

"I don't agree," he said, nostrils flaring. "You've been away at school for four years, only seeing her during breaks. She's changed. Cassandra is getting more spiteful as the years go on. She would definitely do this, if for no other reason than to try to put a wedge between you and me."

"She can't do that unless you let her, Dad," Mandy fumed. "You haven't exactly been father of the year lately, have you?"

She turned, practically running from his office. She didn't care that everyone was watching as she stormed toward the elevator. In her fury, she'd muttered curses at the elevator for not being there, while pushing the button frantically until it finally arrived. She entered and pressed the button for the first floor. She and her father glared at one another until the elevator doors broke the connection.

On the first floor, she moved quickly towards the parking area, face flushed with anger. She finally found her car after passing it twice. Getting into her bright red Mustang convertible, she slammed the door and pounded the steering wheel with her clenched fists. She raved about her father's unyielding stubbornness until the tears took over.

As she cried, her mind wandered to Alex, her best male friend since their freshman year at college. How she wished he hadn't chosen to go to Michigan this week to fish with his father. He wouldn't be back until Sunday. She desperately needed to talk to him, but he'd told her he would be out of cell range.

Hands feeling bruised and sore, she wiped the last tear away then started the car. Putting on sunglasses to hide her swollen eyes from passersby, she started the drive home. She had a lot of work to do.

Chapter 2

Mandy arrived at home feeling like she'd been in a fistfight. She felt lucky she hadn't broken any bones during her temper tantrum. Why had she let herself get so out of control? Physically drained, all she wanted to do was sleep. However, it was more important to complete the list of her mom's contacts for Detective Jacobs.

When all else fails — eat! She decided a sandwich and a diet soda would be just the thing to get her energy level up again. As she prepared her lunch, she considered who she should place on the list. She would need to add Mom's boss, Paul Benson, leaving it to the detectives to obtain the names of her co-workers. Friends would be easy, because her mom had very few of them. Then there was the family — Uncle Frank, Aunt Karen, and, of course, Gran. A sudden pang of dread came over her. How was she going to tell Gran? She'd contact her Aunt Karen first in hopes she would volunteer to call Gran.

Mandy sat down at the table, staring at her ham sandwich. Her thoughts strayed to the moment her family started its slow disintegration. A moment she would never forget.

She was seventeen-years old that hot summer day in August. It was her senior year at North Central High School. She had been out all day shopping with her best friend, Marie, for clothes to complete a special wardrobe to make her senior year perfect. While showing her purchases to her parents, the doorbell rang and her mom went to answer it.

She remembered hearing her mom scream, "No, it can't be! No, please God!" Sometimes Mandy still heard those screams in her sleep. She and her dad ran to the front door to find two police officers, one trying to keep her mom from collapsing. Mandy still couldn't remember the officers' names, but one of them said, "We're sorry, Captain Stevenson. Your son was shot in the line of duty and he died at the scene." That was the first time she'd seen her dad falter. He was usually so strong and in control. He'd tried to console her mother, but was immediately met with anger. She said if Charlie had listened to her and gone to college, he'd still be alive. She ran up to her room and slammed the door. Her dad instructed Mandy to wait for him in the living room while he went outside to speak with the officers.

That was the most horrible day of her life. Her brother, her protector, her friend, gone. Thinking about the moment still brought tears to her eyes. Would she ever really get over his loss?

Choking back her tears, Mandy remembered how she'd tried to comfort her mom in the following days only to be rejected. She'd always known Charlie was her mother's favorite, but Mandy had always handled it well knowing how much Charlie had loved her. Charlie could calm their mother with a smile and often took the blame for things Mandy did because he'd known their mom would forgive him faster.

Her aunt had been Mandy's only solace after Charlie's death. Although she knew how difficult it was, Aunt Karen had encouraged her to get on with life. She helped Mandy prepare for her SATs and fill out her final applications for college. If it hadn't been for her Aunt Karen's encouragement, she might have given up on the idea of even going to college.

She recalled how Aunt Karen had stood up to her dad that evening, telling him Mandy was old enough to hear the truth about what happened. He hadn't liked it much, but agreed. When Mandy had been told a man had shot Charlie in the face during a domestic violence call, she nearly passed out. At the time, she wished Aunt Karen had stayed out of it, but she was right. Cop shootings are always front-page news. Mandy would have heard about it anyway.

Her mom's heart was broken and she blamed Mandy's father for Charlie's death. No matter how many times Charlie had tried to explain his reasons for his decision to become a police officer, their mom was sure it was due to their father's influence.

She took a bite of her sandwich, barely able to swallow. These recollections were so painful. She hadn't been even remotely close to her mother since Charlie's death. Her dad was affectionate towards her at times, but he worked long hours. Mandy was on her own most of the time. College had been a major relief for her.

Picking up her napkin, she wiped away at her tears. The first thing on the agenda was to call Aunt Karen. She went to the counter and rummaged through her purse for her cell phone, then entered the number.

"Hello," she heard the sweet relaxed voice of her aunt trill.

"Aunt Karen, it's Mandy," she said, feeling guilty for interrupting her aunt's well-deserved vacation.

"Well, that's what it says on the caller ID. What's up?"

"I'm afraid I have some news which may or may not be bad."

"Your dad's okay, isn't he?"

Mandy was surprised by this question. However, she quickly justified it since her father's job made it possible bad news was more likely to be about him. "No, Aunt Karen, it's not Dad."

"Then what is it? You're okay, aren't you?"

"Not really," Mandy admitted, choking up. "Mom is missing."

"What do you mean, missing?"

"Tuesday I came home after my interview and she was gone."

"Mandy," said Karen sounding relieved. "She's done this so many times, it's hard to keep track."

"Not like this," insisted Mandy. "None of her things are missing. Not her suitcase, her clothes, toiletries; she didn't take anything with her. Don't you find it odd?"

"Oh my. That is odd. I'm sorry, Mandy," she apologized. "I didn't mean to make light of it. Have you talked to anyone else about this?"

"Dad, of course, but he won't even consider it a problem. So, I took it upon myself to file a missing person report with Uncle Mel's help. When I told Dad about the report, we had a big fight. He was more concerned about his reputation than about his wife being missing."

To Mandy's surprise, her aunt came to her dad's defense. "Mandy, I'm sure you know your parents have been at odds for a long time now. Try to look at this from his point of view." She paused. "You know, you and your father would probably get along better if you weren't so much alike."

She knew Aunt Karen was right. Mandy and her father had very similar personalities.

"So have you talked to Gran or Uncle Frank?" Aunt Karen asked after a short silence.

"No, Aunt Karen," she said, dropping her voice. "I was hoping you'd do it for me. You're so much better at handling this sort of thing than I am."

"Of course, I'll help you. You're my favorite niece, aren't you?"

"I'm your only niece," Mandy laughed half-heartedly.

"That's right, I keep forgetting," Aunt Karen quipped. "I'll make those calls then I'll pack and check out. I should be back in Indianapolis by early evening."

"Thank you, Aunt Karen," Mandy said in relief. "I appreciate it so much. Give me a call when you get in. I want to know how Gran is taking the news."

After they said their goodbyes, Mandy took a swig of her diet soda. Relief filled her. She was so thankful for Karen's help. She grabbed her mother's address book, some paper, and a pen. In order for Detectives Mayhew and Jacobs to get started, she had to complete the list.

Chapter 3

Mandy awoke hoping it had all been a really bad dream. Once the fog lifted from her brain, she knew it was all too real. She sat up in bed checking her alarm clock. It was after 9:00 and her father had already left for work. Mandy had given up on apologizing to him the night before. She was too tired to wait up until he came home.

Throwing on a robe, she went downstairs to find a bowl of soggy corn flake crumbs sitting in the sink. There was a half cup of coffee still in the coffee pot and she was glad to see he'd remembered to turn it off before he left.

Mandy sighed, knowing she would have to wait all day now in order to get the chance to talk to her dad. After the big scene the day before, going by his office again was definitely not an option. Calling him wouldn't work either. He hated being disturbed at work with personal issues. Besides, she really wanted to talk to him face-to-face.

Her conversation with Aunt Karen the evening before had been very difficult. Apparently, Gran hadn't taken the news well. Mandy knew Gran would be upset, her daughter was missing. She just hated to think of her elderly grandmother all alone in Tampa with no one to comfort her. Gran had been ill lately and couldn't travel; otherwise, she'd be on Mandy's doorstep.

Mandy pulled the refrigerator door open. Although she wasn't really hungry, she should eat breakfast in order to keep her strength up. After some orange juice, corn flakes, and coffee, Mandy went straight to her computer. She checked her email to find a note from Detective Jacobs letting her know he'd received the contact list. A sense of relief wafted over her as she rose from the chair satisfied she was able to help in some small way.

Mandy showered, dressed, then went into her mom's room

hoping for something — a clue, a vibe, anything which might give her comfort. Sometimes when she was little and scared of a noise she'd heard in the middle of the night, she'd sneak into Mom's room trying to snuggle up next to her. Her dad had worked the night shift in those days. Her mom would wake and ask her what the hell was wrong. When Mandy told her she was scared, her mother grudgingly allowed her to hop into bed with her, cautioning Mandy not to kick or she'd put her right back into her own bed. Her mom's resentful attitude hurt, but she was scared. Getting yelled at was better than going back to her own bed.

Sadness crept into her heart as she looked at the photo of Charlie sitting on the vanity. "Oh, Charlie," she said aloud, voice cracking with emotion. "I miss you so much. I need you now more than ever." Renewed tears welled up in her eyes as desperate need over took her. She knew if Charlie were here, everything would be so much better. No fighting. No hateful snipes.

She never understood why God would take such a wonderful person when there were so many horrible people in the world. Gran tried to explain it away by saying God needed another angel, but Mandy was too old to buy into an explanation meant for children. Mandy didn't blame God. He was not the one who put the gun in the killer's hands.

She shook her head as anger began to swell in her. She thought when Charlie's murderer was put on death row her relationship with her mom would get better. But it didn't. Her mom had become so much more withdrawn. Everything just seemed to wilt and die along with Charlie.

Dad had been sleeping in the guest room for years now. Mandy wondered why they hadn't divorced. Was Mom hanging on so she could torture him for the loss of her only son? Or, was Dad punishing himself for the loss? As she glanced around the room once more, she realized how cold and uninviting it was in this room. Why on Earth did she think she'd feel better coming in here?

To Mandy's knowledge, there were only two people her mom truly loved — Charlie and Great Grandma Irene. The vanity in the corner had once belonged to her great grandmother. She sat down on the short vanity stool running her hand over the silky fabric cover. She pulled open the drawer and found the only items missing were the watch and diamond earrings her mother had been wearing the last time she saw her. In the center of the drawer was a box, which she knew held a very special pearl necklace. It was a family heirloom which Gran had instructed Cassandra to give to Mandy on her wedding day. It might not happen now.

She closed the box placing it back in the drawer, then slammed the drawer shut and leapt from the stool knocking it over. She couldn't spend one more miserable moment in that room. Running into her bedroom, she slammed the door behind her and fell on the bed sobbing uncontrollably.

Chapter 4

"Excellent," said Jacobs, gazing at his computer screen. "I guess Mandy Stevenson takes after her father. Usually it takes a couple of days to get a list like this from someone."

"She may have her father's flare for bein' organized, but I see a lot of pain in that child's eyes. Not just because she's missin' her mama either," said Mayhew.

"You a psychotherapist now?"

"Jacobs," he said. "You know I have good instincts about people. Don't say you don't."

"What? You gonna hold me in a full body bind until I agree with you?"

"Real funny!" Mayhew retorted, shaking his index finger at his partner. "You'll be singin' another tune when you see I'm right."

"Can't wait," Jacobs responded with a hint of sarcasm in his voice. "Let's take a look at this list. I've already spoken to the captain's mother-in-law, Ella Johnson. The only thing she could tell me was her daughter stopped calling her about two weeks ago."

"Did Miss Mandy say she talked to Captain Stevenson?"

"Yeah, she mentions it in the email," Jacobs answered, crinkling his nose. "I suppose we should get the captain's interview over with next. At least it will be out of the way. Since I talked to Mrs. Johnson, I think...."

"Oh, no you don't!" Mayhew interrupted. "You're not gonna take all the easy ones. We'll flip for it."

"That's a little childish, don't you think?"

"No," Mayhew answered furrowing his brow. "It's the best, most civilized way to decide such controversial matters."

"You can be so dramatic!" Jacobs said, pulling a quarter from his pocket. "Heads or tails?"

"Heads," Mayhew said, crossing his arms.

Jacobs tossed the coin into the air and they both watched as it came down on the desk and spun a couple of times, finally flattening to a stop.

"Ugh," Jacobs whined.

"Man up, Jacobs!" said Mayhew, a hint of laughter in his voice. "You can handle the big, bad captain. Who's on the list I can call while you're doin' your interrogatin'?"

"Here," his partner tossed the printed list at him. "Figure it out for yourself."

"You're such a sore loser!" Mayhew cackled.

Jacobs had given his partner one last disdainful glance before sitting down to call Captain Stevenson. The captain had agreed to meet him in the interrogation room in about ten minutes, so he made some last minute notes in preparation, while listening to his partner continue to chuckle at his expense. No police officer ever wants to question the integrity of a fellow officer, but it had to be done.

Jacobs entered the small interrogation room feeling almost claustrophobic. The grey fabric walls seemed to close in on him. He sat down in the beige vinyl chair placing his notepad and a recording device on the table. When Captain Stevenson arrived he was quite surly and took the seat opposite Jacobs.

"Captain," Jacobs began, "your daughter has some concerns your wife's disappearance may not have been voluntary and has filed a missing person report. As you know, we have to interview all of your wife's family, friends, colleagues, and acquaintances to get a full picture of where she may have gone."

"Yes, I understand," answered Captain Stevenson. "But I'm going to tell you right now, I think Mandy was wrong when she decided to file this report. Cassandra has taken off for God knows where many times before."

"I'll keep it in mind," said the detective. "Of course, you are aware we will be recording this interview."

"Yes, Jacobs. I'm well aware of police procedure," he snapped.

Jacobs started by recording the date, time and other pertinent information regarding who he was interviewing and why.

"Captain Stevenson, when was the last time you saw your wife before her disappearance?"

"On Sunday morning, just before I left for Detroit," he replied, glancing around the room.

"What was Mrs. Stevenson's mood like that Sunday?"

The captain shifted in his chair again. "Actually, she and I didn't talk much Sunday morning. Cassandra isn't much of a morning person," he said. "But to answer your question, she didn't seem to be any moodier than normal."

Jacobs scribbled a few notes before asking his next question. "Captain, your daughter has implied you feel your wife left of her own accord. Why would you make this assumption?"

"Life is complicated at my house," the captain replied. "From the day my son died, there has been nothing but tension between Cassandra and me. She's never forgiven me for Charlie's decision to become a cop. She claims she takes these little hiatuses to get away from the stress in her life."

"Do you have any idea where Mrs. Stevenson goes during those periods of time?"

"No. That was the point. She wanted to get away from me. Letting me know where she was would ruin it for her." The captain paused for a moment, looking thoughtful. "Actually, Mandy is right about one thing. Although she didn't share her destination with us, Cassandra usually left a note or a voice mail telling one of us she was going away for a while."

"Did you argue often?"

"Not really," he replied. "Like I said, the relationship had become rather ambivalent. We rarely spoke to one another. You can't argue if you aren't talking."

"I'm sorry I have to ask this, but did you and your wife ever have a physical altercation?"

There was silence. The captain looked anxious. He seemed reluctant to answer the question.

"Captain, did you hear the question?"

"Yes, I heard you," he snapped. "Well, if you're asking me if I beat my wife. No." Captain Stevenson paused momentarily, pursing his lips. "However, there was one incident a year ago when Cassandra was very angry about some trivial matter. She attempted to strike me. I swung my arm around to defend myself, accidentally knocking her off balance and she fell to the floor. I wasn't trying to hit her. Besides, she didn't get hurt, just got angrier. I left the house and stayed out until I knew she would be asleep."

"I didn't ask about accidents. I asked if you hit your wife. A slap, a punch, a kick?"

"I'd never hit a woman. But to answer you more *clearly*, I've never assaulted Cassandra in any way for any reason."

"Thank you, Captain," said Jacobs. "You said you left for Detroit on Sunday. Is that where you were this past Tuesday, the day your wife disappeared?"

With a hint of sarcasm in his voice, Captain Stevenson answered, "Yes. I was with a few thousand other cops in Detroit, Michigan, attending a forensics seminar which lasted until Wednesday."

"Can anyone in particular corroborate your whereabouts?" asked Jacobs.

"I spent most of Tuesday with Detectives Kramer and Reese from our Narcotics division. I had drinks with a couple of guys from Houston PD, a Miguel Rodriguez and Tyson Maddox, both homicide detectives."

"I'll need your hotel information, Captain, so I can verify your stay."

"Sure. I'll get my online reservation info to you as soon as I get back to my computer."

"Is there anything else you would like to add that might aid us in this investigation?"

"No detective, I can't think of anything."

Jacobs thanked the captain then told him he was free to go. On his way out the door, Jacobs saw Mayhew coming towards him with a plump auburn haired woman. He thought he could see a bit of Mandy in her face.

"Miss Johnson, this is Detective Jacobs," said Mayhew. "He and I are investigatin' your sister's disappearance."

She held out her hand to Jacobs. "It's nice to meet you, Detective. Thank you so much for helping my niece during this terrible time."

"You're welcome," replied Jacobs.

"Miss Johnson and I were about to have a little chat about her sister."

"Excellent," said Jacobs. "Can I offer to get you a cup of coffee, a soda or water?"

"You're very kind Detective, but I'm fine. Has there been any progress in locating my sister?" she asked, brow furrowed with worry.

"No, I'm afraid not," answered Jacobs. "I did speak to your mother this morning. I tried to keep it brief as I'm sure she is very upset by this ordeal."

Karen gave him a modest smile. "Yes, she is," she said. "Thank you for your sensitivity."

"I have a few more calls to make, so I'll leave you in my partner's capable hands."

"Please have a seat, ma'am," offered Mayhew. "What do you do for a livin'?"

"I'm a social worker in Adult Protective Services. I specialize in the prevention of elder abuse."

"It must be tough."

"It can be. I tried to tell Mandy how tough it is, but she insisted upon pursuing a career as a social worker. She is supposed to start her Master's program this fall."

"I'm sure you're very proud of her," he said, watching Karen Johnson's mouth turn up in a grin. Then he veered the conversation back to the case at hand.

"I must ask if you know of anyone who might have wanted to harm your sister."

"No, Detective Mayhew," she answered. "My sister didn't have very many friends, but if she had any enemies, I'm certainly not aware of them. Of course, she and I weren't particularly close. Even when we were kids, she never confided in me."

"Miss Johnson, it's come to my attention her marriage to the captain was rather...," he paused as though struggling for the right word, "...strained. How would you describe their relationship?"

"My sister can be very vindictive and unforgiving. She blames Robert for their son's death."

"Why would she do that?" he asked.

"Because Cassandra thinks Robert talked Charlie into becoming a police officer," she explained. "She thinks if Robert hadn't done so, Charlie would still be alive."

"Do you believe she was correct?" he asked.

"I think it was more along the lines of Charlie watching a very worthy role model in his father. I don't believe Robert consciously tried to influence the boy. As a matter of fact, I recall Robert trying to talk Charlie out of it. Lots of boys grow up wanting to be just like their fathers. Of course, Robert wasn't the only police officer Charlie admired, you know. Lieutenant Melrose made quite an impression on him as well.

"Cassandra just wouldn't accept that Charlie seriously thought this through, making this decision on his own. When he died, everything went downhill.

"She hasn't really been close to anyone since Charlie died. She doesn't even spend time with her best friend anymore. She used to call our mother at least once a week, but since the tragedy she very rarely calls her. It's as though Charlie was her only reason for living."

Karen's eyes started to tear up.

"Miss Johnson," he continued, "Mandy told us your sister had left for long periods of time in the past. Would you have any idea where she would go when she left town?"

"Like I told you before, my sister didn't confide in me."

"Just one more thing, Miss Johnson," Mayhew interjected. "Can you tell me where you were the day your sister disappeared?"

"Why, yes, Detective," she answered with an air of confidence. "I was vacationing in Holland, Michigan. I stayed at a lovely bed and breakfast there. As soon as I got Mandy's call about Cassandra, I checked out and came home. I can provide you with any information you may need to check my story."

"I appreciate your willingness to come see me today, ma'am," he said. "That's all I need to ask for now. Please try to get your vacation information to us as quickly as you can. If you can think of anythin' that can help us with this investigation, please give us a call." He gave her one of his business cards.

"I will, Detective Mayhew," she said. "Again, thank you for your hard work in looking for my sister."

"You're welcome," he said as she rose from her chair. He watched as she made her way to the elevator without looking back.

"Hey, Jacobs. Interviews went pretty well, don't you think?" asked Mayhew, when he returned to his desk.

"Captain Stevenson's interview went better than I expected," commented Jacobs. "I just spoke to Mrs. Stevenson's brother, Frank

Johnson. Lives up in some suburb near Chicago. Has a wife and two sons. Said it's been at least three months since he's spoken to his sister. He doesn't really know much about where she would go except she showed up in Chicago a few times, told him she was staying in a friend's condo downtown."

"Guess I should start checkin' out Miss Johnson's alibi," said Mayhew, a curious look on his face.

"What's up?" asked Jacobs, seeing his partner's expression.

"Not sure yet," he answered. "Just a hunch."

"You and your hunches!" Jacobs retorted.

"Name one time one of my hunches failed us."

"What about that bouncer you thought might be dealing?" Jacobs shot back.

"Hey, you've got to admit he had a slinky-eyed look about him."

"Whatever!" said Jacobs shaking his head. "I called Benson Realty so we can go over and interview Mrs. Stevenson's co-workers. We've got an appointment with Mr. Benson at 1:00 this afternoon."

"What you do that for?"

"What?"

"You do this all the time, Jacobs," he snorted. "Make appointments right at lunch time. You know I need my sustenance."

"There's a White Castle on the way," quipped Jacobs.

"Oh, no," Mayhew said emphatically. "I'm not gettin' in a car with you after you have them things. Nuh, uh! You better be findin' an Arby's or somethin,' or you're goin' to be walkin' back here."

"Tyrone, you are way too intense," smiled Jacobs. "You need to learn to relax, buddy."

"I ain't your buddy. Now get off your ass and let's get to gettin' so we can grab somethin' before this meetin'."

Chapter 5

Detectives Mayhew and Jacobs arrived at the Benson Real Estate office right on time. The office was in a small building on 96th Street. Upon entering, they found a receptionist behind a cherry wood counter. The waiting area looked comfortable. There were two dark brown leather wing back chairs and a dark blue love seat facing them. The cherry wood coffee table had several select magazines on top of it and the Tiffany floor lamp standing between the leather chairs created a look of elegance.

Detective Jacobs approached the receptionist, "Hello, Miss Danson."

She looked up at him in surprise. "How did you know my name?" she asked batting her long dark lashes. "I don't believe we've ever met. I'd remember you."

"It's on your nameplate," Jacobs replied, pointing at it, "Michelle Danson."

"Oh, I do that all the time!" she giggled. "I forget the thing is there."

The woman was young and thin with short spiky black hair. "How may I be of service?" she asked.

Both detectives pulled out their badges, Mayhew taking the lead. "Miss Danson, I'm Detective May…."

"Oh!" she interrupted. "You must be here about Cassandra. Isn't it awful? I hope she's okay."

"As do we," Jacobs assured her. "Could you tell Mr. Benson Detective Jacobs and Detective Mayhew are here for our 1:00 appointment with him?"

"Why yes," she said enthusiastically. "You officers sit right over there and I'll let him know you're here."

Jacobs picked up one of the Multiple Listings magazines from the coffee table, flipping through it as they waited. Both detectives looked up as they heard footsteps coming from the hallway. They saw a tall, slender man with thinning brown hair and a neatly trimmed mustache. He wore a charcoal gray pinstripe suit with a lavender shirt and deep purple silk tie.

"Hello Detectives. You're right on time. I like that. Cassandra's daughter, Mindy, called yesterday to let us know what happened."

The officers glanced at one another. "You mean *Mandy*, don't you sir?" asked Jacobs.

"Oh, yes of course," Benson said, not missing a beat. "Would you like to come back to my office?"

They both nodded. They followed him down the hallway past several offices before entering the last office on the right. The cyan blue walls held several spectacular seascape paintings. The office was very orderly, with cherry wood furnishings and rich brown leather chairs. In the center of Benson's credenza was a photo of him standing next to a sailboat with three other people.

"That your family, Mr. Benson?" asked Jacobs.

"Why, yes it is," he answered with a smile of pride on his face. "That's my wife, Ciara; my son, Sean; and my daughter Whitney. She just graduated with honors from Northwestern this spring. She's taking a year off to go to Europe before she starts her graduate work."

Benson motioned for them to sit down. "Please have a seat, Detectives. How can I be of assistance to you?" he asked. "It's so sad. Cassandra was the best sales agent I've ever known."

"I'm sure she *is*, Mr. Benson," said Jacobs. However, Jacobs' correction of verb seemed to go right over Benson's head as he didn't react to the modification.

"Mr. Benson," Jacobs began. "When was the last time you saw Mrs. Stevenson?"

"It was Monday, as I recall," he answered in a confident voice, without looking Jacobs in the eye. "I heard she was here on Tuesday, but I was out of the office at the time."

"So, what were you doin' on Tuesday?" asked Mayhew.

"That's my day off," he answered. "I was running errands, puttering around the house. You know the usual stuff."

"Then you weren't here when Cassandra Stevenson came by on Tuesday?" Mayhew said more as a matter of fact than as a question.

"I just told you Detective Mayhew," said Benson tensely, "it was my day off."

"Funny," Jacobs said. "It was Mrs. Stevenson's day off as well."

"There's nothing funny about it," Benson said, squirming in his chair.

"There's no need to get worked up about it, Mr. Benson," said Mayhew, scowling.

"If you don't believe me," Benson spouted indignantly, "you can ask my wife."

"We will, Mr. Benson," said Jacobs, eyeing him suspiciously. "Now, tell us about the last time you saw Mrs. Stevenson. Did she seem nervous or anxious about anything?"

"Not that I could tell," he answered. "I don't recall anything being out of the ordinary."

Mayhew jumped in. "Mr. Benson, were there any clients who may have been angry with Miss Stevenson? Anyone threaten her because they were unhappy with her services?"

"No. No one," Benson emphatically stated. "She was an excellent employee, outselling everyone. You don't accomplish that with a bad reputation."

Mayhew watched Jacobs eyeing Benson. "Did Miss Stevenson have any problems with any of her co-workers?" Mayhew asked.

"Absolutely not," he snapped. "My staff works well together. I don't believe there is any animosity amongst them. As a matter of fact, the others seemed to admire her."

"Well, Mr. Benson," said Mayhew. "I think that's all we need from you right now. We'd like to see Miss Stevenson's office, if you don't mind. Then we will need a private place where we can interview the rest of your staff."

Benson seemed more than happy to show them Cassandra's office. His facial expression changed to one of instant relief as soon as Mayhew told him they were finished.

When Benson left them in Mrs. Stevenson's office, Jacobs commented, "He sure was happy to get us out of his office, don't you think?"

"Yeah, suppose so," answered Mayhew.

"That's odd," said Jacobs after a quick sweeping look at the desk.

"What?" Mayhew said, frowning.

"Mrs. Stevenson has a picture of herself and a young man in an IMPD uniform I assume is her son, Charlie."

"Spit it out Jacobs. What's so *odd* about it?"

Jacobs frowned at Mayhew. "There aren't any pictures of Captain Stevenson or Mandy. Don't you think it's peculiar?"

"I think the captain already established he and his wife weren't exactly in wedded bliss," said Mayhew.

"But what about her daughter? Usually people have photos of all their children on their desks."

"Sounds like when her son died she lost interest in the rest of her family. Besides, it doesn't have anything to do with what we need to be lookin' for."

They searched the desk drawers and files. Mayhew found an appointment book and bagged it as potential evidence. There were a few CD's which probably contained work files, but they decided to take them so the forensics lab could take a look at them.

"I'll be right back," Mayhew said to his partner. He went to Benson's office and rapped on the door.

"Come in."

"Pardon me, Mr. Benson. We're wonderin' if you might keep a computerized appointment schedule in your office."

"Why yes, we do. Michelle keeps an office calendar on her computer of everyone's appointment schedule so I know where everyone is at any particular time. Would you like for me to ask her to print a copy for you?"

"That would be great, sir," Mayhew answered. "Also, we're ready to talk to each of your employees."

"Of course, Detective," Benson answered. "You may use the private conference room across the hall from my office. We often have client conferences in there, but no one is scheduled in there this afternoon."

Jacobs was coming towards Benson's office when he saw Mayhew emerge. "We got the conference room over there for interviews with the staff."

David Quinn was interviewed first. He was very pleasant, young, and had only worked at Benson Real Estate for two months. He didn't know Mrs. Stevenson very well, but said he'd always gotten along with her. He had seen her come in on Tuesday to pick up her laptop, but hadn't spoken with her. He had very little to offer.

Felicia Hernandez was next. Age thirty, she was married and the mother of four. She had obtained her real estate license a year ago and started working for this office in March of this year. She said she really liked Mrs. Stevenson's style and wished she was just like her. Felicia told them she pretty much ignored office politics and concentrated on her job. She couldn't think of anyone who would want to harm the missing woman.

When the detectives interviewed Pamela Cartwright, she said Cassandra seemed to be in a hurry that Tuesday. "She didn't speak to anyone until I asked her if she had an appointment," said Pamela. "She abruptly told me 'no', but of course she was huffy sometimes."

"What do you mean by abruptly?" asked Mayhew.

Frowning slightly, she turned to Mayhew. "Of course, I suppose all of us are abrupt from time-to-time, you know snapping at people for no reason. There's a lot of pressure in this job."

"I'm sure there is, Mrs. Cartwright," said Jacobs. "How long have you worked with Mrs. Stevenson?"

"About four years now," Pamela sighed.

"I hope we're not boring you, Mrs. Cartwright," Jacobs said sarcastically and she stiffened.

"How would you describe your relationship with Miss Stevenson?" asked Mayhew.

"Everyone got along with her," she answered. "She was our top sales person you know."

"So we've heard," said Mayhew, giving her a stern look. "So you didn't have any problems with her?"

"No, officer, I've learned not to make waves," she said turning away from his gaze.

"Okay, Mrs. Cartwright," said Jacobs. "You're free to go, but we may have more questions later."

Pamela rose from her chair and left the conference room. When the door closed behind her, Mayhew turned to his partner. "There's somethin' funny goin' on with her. Did you notice how she didn't give us any straight answers?"

"I sure did," his partner responded. "She's hiding something."

The last employee interviewed was Michelle Danson. When she entered, she handed the copy of the last month's appointment schedule to Jacobs.

"Miss Danson, did Miss Stevenson come by the office on this past Tuesday?" asked Mayhew.

"Oh, yes," Michelle confirmed. "Just for a short while though. All she did was get her lap top. I was kind of surprised when Cassandra stopped in. She didn't have any appointments scheduled, so I assumed she was taking it home to do some work. You know, set up appointments for the rest of the week."

"I understand. Do you know of anyone in the office or of any clients who might have had a problem with Mrs. Stevenson?" asked Jacobs.

"Well," she said in a very quiet voice, causing the detectives to lean in to hear her. "I don't want to cause any trouble for anyone, but Pamela Cartwright was a bit upset with Cassandra this past month. Pamela claimed Cassandra stole a couple of her clients and three of her sales."

Michelle glanced nervously over her shoulder at the door. "The thing is," she paused looking directly into Jacobs' eyes. "Cassandra sells a lot of property. As long as she's raking in the bucks, Mr. Benson tends to look the other way."

"Then Mrs. Cartwright must have been pretty angry with Mrs. Stevenson," Mayhew interjected.

"You can say that again," she snorted. "Her husband lost his job three months ago, so they really depend on Pamela's income — no sales, no money. She was really angry when Mr. Benson chose to ignore her complaint. I overheard him tell Pamela she didn't have enough proof the sales were hers.

"She probably would have quit," Michelle whispered, "but like I said, she's the only breadwinner right now. They have two kids to think about."

"Do Mr. Benson and Mrs. Stevenson seem to be close?" asked Jacobs.

"Well, Mr. Benson is married," she said with some hesitation, "but at times I've wondered about those two."

"What do you mean?" inquired Mayhew.

"Sometimes I would see him getting a little too close to her, physically I mean. You know, like rubbing up against her when she's at her desk." Michelle was squirming at this admission, but continued. "Sometimes they would spend a really long time in his office. I'd hear them laughing. I don't know. Something about it just didn't seem right."

"I would agree with you, Miss Danson," said Jacobs, evoking a bright girlish smile from Michelle. "Do you remember anything else unusual about Mrs. Stevenson's behavior?"

"Oh, wait," she said excitedly. "There was also this guy who called a lot the past couple of months. Since he wouldn't give me his name, I doubt he was a client. Clients always want you to know exactly who they are so you put them through right away."

Jacobs' eyes widened and he sat forward, asking, "Do you remember anything about his voice or something he said?"

"No, not really," she replied. "But I did notice Cassandra seemed to lower her voice whenever she was talking to him. A few times she left the office right after she got one of his calls and was gone for at least a couple of hours. I mean, she just left without saying anything and she didn't have an appointment with anyone. I guess Mr. Benson didn't care, because Cassandra made the sales."

"Thank you, Miss Danson," said Jacobs.

She smiled at him. "You're welcome," she said brightly.

Before leaving, the detectives thanked Benson for his time and the use of his conference room. As they left the building, Michelle made sure to get their attention. She said goodbye to them looking straight at Detective Jacobs.

"I think she likes you," Mayhew chuckled when they were on the other side of the door. "I thought there for a minute she was gonna ask you out."

"Whatever!" Jacobs snapped. "You do have to admit what she had to say was very interesting. Sounds to me like Mrs. Stevenson may have a few secrets."

"Yeah," Mayhew said thoughtfully. "*And,* I guess we know what Miss Cartwright meant when she said she'd learned not to make waves. It didn't do her any good. It was also funny Benson didn't bother to mention there was a problem between Miss Cartwright and Miss Stevenson."

"We need to bring Mrs. Cartwright and Mr. Benson in for further questioning. Get them out of their environment and into ours," said Jacobs. "Let's go grab some coffee on the way back."

"Sounds good because we're goin' to need it," said Mayhew. "I sure don't want to be the one to tell the captain his wife may have been foolin' around."

"Neither do I, pal. Neither do I."

Chapter 6

On Saturday, Mandy woke at around 10:00 a.m. feeling almost as weary as she had when she went to bed the night before. Every rustle of leaves or creak of the floorboards made her jump, thinking her mother had come home, only to be disappointed.

The only thing holding Mandy's sanity together at the moment was the fact she knew Alex would be back from his fishing trip tomorrow. She'd met Alex during their freshman year at Indiana University. They never had the physical chemistry a relationship demanded, but definitely clicked as friends. They'd found they had a lot in common, which unfortunately included losing a loved one at a young age.

Mandy had surprised herself in trusting Alex so quickly. She hadn't been sure she could ever trust another man. Not after her high school sweetheart, Todd Sleezak, had burned her. She'd started dating Todd in the second semester of her junior year, losing her virginity to him later that spring. After Charlie's death, Todd was never around. It turned out he was much too immature to handle Mandy's grief.

The break up with Todd, plus watching her parent's marriage crumbling, had compelled Mandy to think twice before getting involved with anyone again. Alex was different, like a brother. Without Charlie around, she needed Alex in her life.

Alex's mother died when Alex was six, so he understood the feeling of loss. His dad had married again when Alex was eight. His stepmother, Gloria, was much younger than Alex's father and full of herself. Two years after the marriage, Alex's half-sister, Lana, was born. He told Mandy it had been a tough adjustment after being an only child for nearly ten years.

As Mandy rose from her bed, heading toward the bathroom and a nice hot shower, her cell phone rang. She caught it on the third ring. "Alex, I am so glad you're home. I didn't expect you until tomorrow." She paused. "You're not going to believe what's happened." She told him about her mother's disappearance.

When she finally stopped to take a breath, Alex exclaimed, "Oh, my God, Mandy! She didn't even leave you a message telling you she'd be gone?"

"No, she didn't," she said. "I can't talk to Dad about it. He's sure she left of her own accord."

After a moment's silence and with a hint of hesitation, he asked, "Mandy, are you sure your dad isn't right about her going off for a few days? People do weird things when they're angry, and you've told me she's gone off on her own before."

Mandy felt her temper rising, but tried to keep her voice pleasant. "Alex, I was with her that morning. She was fine. She hadn't argued with Dad, he was in Detroit. She told me she'd be there when I got home. Even if she'd been angry enough to go somewhere without leaving a note she would have calmed down and called by now. Besides, I had Uncle Frank check out the place where she normally goes and she's not there. I could really use your support right now."

Alex fell silent and she knew she'd made her point.

"Alex, I really need someone to talk to you about this," she pleaded, worrying she had offended him. "I've been going crazy waiting for you to get back."

"Okay, let's go to lunch. I'll be by to pick you up at noon and take you to your favorite Italian restaurant," he suggested.

"Sounds great," she agreed. One of the things Mandy liked about Alex was his punctuality. When she answered the door at precisely noon, there he was, tall, lean, and handsome with his light brown hair shining in the sunlight. He flashed that sweet, toothy smile of his at her, and she couldn't contain herself at the relief she felt at seeing him. She threw her arms around his neck, hugging him tight. Mandy always felt safe with Alex nearby.

When they arrived at the restaurant, they were led to their seats by the hostess and then greeted by their favorite waitress, Liz. She was middle-aged, with dark hair and a quick wit.

"Long time, no see you two," Liz said with a glowing smile.

"Where've you been hidin' out?"

"Fishing!" answered Alex.

"Guess I shoulda known," said Liz. "What about you Mandy? What's happenin'?"

"Nothing much, just looking for a part-time job."

"I can hook ya up here, if ya like," offered Liz.

"Thanks, Liz, but I'm way to klutzy to be a waitress," Mandy said. "First time I tried to carry one of those big trays, the food would wind up on somebody's head and they'd send me packing. I admire anyone who can do this job."

Liz grinned at her. "Thanks, honey. The usual for you two?"

"Sound good to you, Mandy?" asked Alex.

"Sure does," answered Mandy.

"Okay then. Lasagna, cheese bread and two diets comin' up."

As Liz walked away to place their orders, Mandy turned to Alex. He looked tired and somehow sad. "So, did you and your dad catch your weight in fish?" she asked.

"Nah," he answered. "Fish weren't biting like usual. I wasn't feeling too good part of the time, so I missed out on a few days."

"I'm sorry to hear that," she said as Liz brought their sodas.

Alex took a big swig of his soda. The silence was a bit uncomfortable. Something she felt was unusual. She got the feeling he didn't want to talk about his trip. "You know, I've had a really hard time these past few days. That's why I'm so glad you're home. My dad just doesn't get it."

"Dads can be like that sometimes," Alex agreed.

"Not your dad," Mandy replied. "He's great. He's so funny, and he never acts like he's the only one who knows anything."

"Sorry to disappoint you, but he's not as perfect as you think he is."

Mandy looked at him curiously. He'd never spoken about his father this way before. "You and your dad have a fight this week?" she asked.

"No, he was great," he said.

She still wasn't sure he was telling her the whole story, but chose not to push the subject. She knew he would tell her about it eventually. Besides, she was still anxious to talk about her mother.

"Anyway, the first forty-eight hours in any missing person case is critical. Mom's been missing now for four days."

"You said your Uncle Mel's got people looking for her," Alex said. "I'm sure he'll find her."

"You're probably right, Alex, but I'm a mess. I can't sleep, I'm stress eating, and I can't talk to Dad about it."

"Yeah, I know. You said that already," he said, glancing down and tapping his fork on the table.

Mandy was a little taken aback by the sharpness of his comment, but chose to ignore it and carry on. "Dad's very stubborn. I think he's in denial. We've been fighting ever since I filed the report." She bit her lower lip trying not to cry, but the tears started to fall.

"Come on, Mandy, don't cry," he said, touching her hand.

"I can't help it. Detective Jacobs checked her cell phone records and there weren't any calls made or answered since Mom disappeared."

"I know it looks bad, but maybe it's not as bad as you think," he said. "Maybe she went someplace where her cell doesn't work, or the battery's dead. Did she take her charger?"

"I'm not sure," she said. She smiled her thanks when Liz showed up with a plate of cheese bread.

"It's about time," Alex said testily.

"Lasagna will be right up," Liz said, looking as though she wanted to give Alex a smack on the back of the head.

"Let's talk about something else," Alex said, grabbing a slice of cheese bread. "You ready to start classes Monday?"

"I have to put grad school on hold," she said. "I don't see how I can concentrate on school work under these circumstances. I'll just put it off until January. Maybe things will be back to normal by then."

"Are you sure you should do that?" he asked, meeting her eyes. "I guess I was hoping to see you on campus, that's all. We *were* a great study team down in Bloomington."

"Believe me, if things were different and I had any other choice...." A lump formed in her throat and she couldn't speak. She took a drink of her soda to ease the frustration she was feeling.

Liz was back with the lasagna in hand. "Good, I'm starving!" exclaimed Alex.

"What's up with you, hot shot?" Liz said, finally having enough of his attitude. "You seem a little cranky today."

Alex didn't say a word but dove into his lasagna with a vengeance. Mandy smiled at Liz and shrugged, feeling embarrassed by his behavior. Maybe she shouldn't have pressed him to go out today.

They finished their lunch in silence. Alex paid the bill then they walked out into the late summer air. Closing her eyes, Mandy could feel the warmth of the sun on her face. "Summer is almost over, but I do love fall," she said. "It's not too hot or too cold. Soon all of the trees will be bursting with color. Too bad winter has to follow."

"Winter isn't so bad. There's lots of good ice fishing," Alex chuckled, seeming to get back a little of his humor.

"I'm scared, Alex. I believe Mom would have contacted me by now, if she could." She noticed how gloomy Alex's face had become again. This finally convinced her he just wasn't in the mood to deal with this right now. Maybe it made him think about his own mother.

She cleared her throat. "I'm pretty tired. Could you take me home now?" she asked.

"No problem," he said, as they reached the car.

They drove to her house without speaking. Mandy leaned back in her seat closing her eyes. She found his behavior this afternoon very disconcerting. When they arrived in her driveway, she turned to Alex. "Thanks for lunch. Will you call me tomorrow?"

"Of course," he replied. "I'll call you when I get my lazy behind out of bed. I should be up before noon."

Mandy started to exit the vehicle when suddenly Alex grabbed her arm. "Wait," he said. "Please."

Mandy turned to face him. "What?" she asked, noticing Alex avert his eyes.

"I'm sorry I've been acting so shitty today. I lied to you, Mandy."

"What about?"

"I didn't have a great time with my dad," he stated. "As a matter of fact, we had a pretty nasty blow out. I've been staying in a hotel in South Bend for the past few days, thinking about things."

"Your dad's usually so congenial and happy," she said. "What did you fight about?"

"I can't talk about it right now," he said looking away. "I need to work this out with him. I'd tell you if I could, I just can't."

"It's okay, Alex," she assured him. "I understand your need for privacy."

"Thanks, Mandy."

"I'm the one who should be apologizing to you."

"Why?" he asked.

"You come home from a rough trip, and here I am practically demanding you listen to all of my woes."

"Well, your *woes* are pretty serious. I'm sorry. I've not been much help."

"I feel better just being with you," she told him, rubbing his shoulder. "I wish you could stay."

"I know, Mandy, but I need to get home. I haven't unpacked yet and I should probably do some laundry."

"Okay," she said. "Don't forget to call me."

"I won't."

Mandy got out of the vehicle and watched as he drove away. Alex and his father had always been so close. She couldn't imagine what could have caused them to have such a terrible fight. Maybe he'll tell her tomorrow.

Chapter 7

Lieutenant Melrose sat pondering the case file lying open on his desk. It had been four days since Mandy reported Cassandra missing and nearly a week since she'd disappeared. He checked over Cassandra's most recent bank, credit card, and cell phone reports for any activity. There was none. "Surely Robert will have to admit Cassandra is in deep trouble now," he said aloud.

The lieutenant looked up as Jacobs and Mayhew entered the room. "Okay, give me all you know about this case so far," said the lieutenant. "Any leads yet?"

"Nothing substantial," Jacobs answered. "But we have learned a lot of background on the family dynamics and about some of Mrs. Stevenson's relationships."

"Go ahead," Lieutenant Melrose urged as he leaned forward resting his arms on his desk. "We all know it's not a good sign she's been gone this long without communicating with her family and with no financial activity."

"Of course you know Captain Stevenson's alibi is rock solid," said Jacobs. "We confirmed he was at the hotel with the people he indicated. We can definitely rule him out as a suspect."

"Karen Johnson's story checked out as well," said Mayhew. "She had time and date stamped receipts from several shops in Holland. The owners of the bed and breakfast said she was there every mornin' for breakfast and saw her in the sittin' room every evenin' socializin' with the other guests."

"What about the phone records, Jacobs?" Lieutenant Melrose said, tapping his foot. "Find anything interesting?"

Jacobs leafed through his notes. "The only calls I discovered for the period of time since Mrs. Stevenson disappeared are calls from

Mandy and from current clients which appear to be unanswered."

"I can see that," said Lieutenant Melrose, tapping the file of reports he'd read before they arrived.

"However, when I checked her records for the past three years, I found a number that had been dialed pretty consistently. The guy's name is Jonathan Richmond. He's an attorney — just opened an office in Carmel four years ago. I checked with Michelle Danson at the real estate office and discovered Richmond and his wife, Savannah, were clients of Mrs. Stevenson. She worked with them three years ago to find a house in Carmel. Previous address was off 75th Street near Spring Mill."

"How long did it take them to find a house?" asked Lieutenant Melrose, frowning.

"I asked myself the same question. Three months," answered Jacobs. "We're going to his office at 1:30 tomorrow afternoon for a little chat. He needs to explain why these calls continued for two more years."

"Excellent," said the lieutenant. "Anything new come out of the interviews you conducted at the real estate office? It was my understanding you wanted to bring in Pamela Cartwright and her husband as well as Paul Benson for second interviews."

"Mayhew and I interviewed Mrs. Cartwright again on Saturday," continued Jacobs. "This time she admitted she was pissed at Mrs. Stevenson and had filed a complaint. When we asked her why she didn't mention this in the first interview, she just shrugged. Said she didn't think it was important."

"Whatever," the lieutenant mumbled. "People never think things are *important* when they know it might be incriminating."

"I hear you, Lieutenant," Mayhew agreed. "In the second interview, Miss Cartwright claimed she'd worked 'til 6:00 the night Miss Stevenson disappeared. Says she went home to spend a romantic evenin' with her man. Kids were with her mother-in-law for the night."

"So what's your impression?" asked Lieutenant Melrose.

Jacobs glanced at Mayhew who shrugged. "We're not sure her alibi is all very solid, sir," Jacobs responded. "The rest of the office personnel were gone by 5:00 that night, so they can't corroborate her claim she was there until 6:00. Of course, her husband told us she was home by 6:30."

"We also think the alibi sucks because the husband, Patrick Cartwright, dropped the kids off at his mother's house at 10:00 in the mornin'," Mayhew added. "He could have snatched Miss Stevenson in the afternoon then met his wife later on. We bet he was just as pissed off as the wife about losin' all those proceeds — $15,000. Man's out of work. This amount of money could have paid their mortgage for almost a year and put a lot of grub on the table for his wife and three kids."

"Sounds like motive and opportunity to me," commented the lieutenant. "I'm going to assign somebody to keep an eye on those two. Don't want them taking off on us. Jacobs, check their finances, phone records — all the usual stuff.

"Mayhew see if the Cartwrights will come back in voluntarily to give us their prints and a DNA swab. Tell them we want to rule them out as suspects. If they don't do it, then we'll know they have something to hide."

"Miss Danson corroborated everybody's claim Miss Stevenson was at the office in the afternoon before she disappeared," Mayhew continued. "Miss Stevenson took her laptop then left."

"Too bad she took the laptop," the lieutenant grunted. "There might have been some contacts, emails or Internet searches which could have given us a clue as to her whereabouts."

"We do have her appointment book," said Jacobs handing the book to the lieutenant. "We checked it against a copy of the appointment schedule the receptionist keeps. We couldn't find any discrepancies."

"Then there's the boss," stated Mayhew. "Benson's a pretty slick character from what we could tell. Two kids and a beautiful wife, but accordin' to the receptionist, there were some mighty cozy moments between Benson and Miss Stevenson."

"In our interview with him, we ascertained he wasn't working at the office that Tuesday," said Jacobs. "He claims to have been running errands and doing things around the house. We haven't had a chance to confirm this with Mrs. Benson yet. She's conveniently been out of the country and, according to her housekeeper, should be back today. Mayhew plans to call her this afternoon."

"Get a time off schedule from Miss Danson," Lieutenant Melrose directed to Jacobs. "They surely keep track of time off for payroll purposes. Check out how many times Benson and Cassandra were out of the office at the same time. Then we can check credit cards for both of them to see if they were ever in the same place at the same time."

Detective Jacobs looked at his boss with concern. "Lieutenant, I know the Stevensons are your friends, but do you think Mrs. Stevenson could have been having an affair with Benson or this Richmond character?" he asked. "Michelle Danson told us Mrs. Stevenson was receiving calls from a man who wouldn't identify himself. After the calls, Mrs. Stevenson would leave the office for a few hours without explaining herself."

Lieutenant Melrose stroked his chin in contemplation. He closed his eyes briefly. "We can't rule anything out," he said with a note of sadness in his voice, "but with the length of time she's been gone, with no recent cell phone or card activity, it's not looking good. If she was having an affair and tried to break it off, her lover may not have taken it well.

"You two need to get Benson in here A.S.A.P. Give him a call today," said Lieutenant Melrose. "If he gives you any grief, tell him he can come in here on his own or we'll have to send someone to his office to pick him up. Doubt he wants any of his clients to see him hauled off in a cruiser.

"Oh, and Mayhew, make sure you talk to the wife before he comes in. Might give you more ammo, if you know what I mean."

"I know exactly what you mean," Mayhew said with a smirk.

"I think I'll stop by Robert's house tonight," said Lieutenant Melrose. "Perhaps there's something he isn't telling us."

Chapter 8

Mandy and her father had just finished a pleasant dinner, which she was sure was thanks in part to her Uncle Mel. He'd been working on her father daily to get him to realize this wasn't Mandy's imagination. Her father had been home for dinner the last two nights and there seemed to be a cease fire for the moment. Mandy also suspected her Aunt Karen had a hand in her father's apparent change of attitude. Aunt Karen seemed to have a way with her dad no one else had.

Mandy was clearing the dishes when she heard the doorbell. Wondering who was stopping by this time of night, she peered through the peephole discovering Uncle Mel. As she opened the door, she noticed a big bouquet of daisies in his hands.

"Hey you," she said. "Since when do you have to ring the bell?"

"First of all, these are for you," Uncle Mel said handing the bouquet to Mandy. "I thought you might need something cheery around here. And second, I always ring the bell when I am on official business. Where's your dad?"

"He's in the family room drinking a beer and watching the ballgame," she said. "White Sox versus the Twins."

"Right. The big game."

"Enough chit chat," she said. "Is there any news about Mom? Is that what your *official business* is all about?"

"I don't have anything new on her location," he said. The disappointment she felt must have been evident on her face because he quickly added, "Mandy, don't forget this also means nothing bad has been discovered either."

"I know," she said unable to muster a smile. "It's just hard to hold onto hope when she's been gone so long."

"I understand," he said. "Why don't you put those in some water and I'll grab a soda."

"Sure," she said, then led the way to the kitchen. Quickly she put the flowers into the first pitcher she could find. She didn't want him going into the family room without her.

Mandy put her arm around her Uncle Mel and they headed for the family room.

Her father was sitting in his recliner sipping his beer when Mandy and Mel entered the room.

"Hey, Mel, what brings you here this time of night? You should be home with your feet up, beer in hand, watching the game," he said. "This one could make or break the Sox's chances for the playoffs."

"Business, Robert," Mel said.

Her dad's face took on a more somber expression. "It must be pretty serious for the head of the department to make a house call."

Mel grinned, "I have some questions of a rather sensitive nature for you. You may not want Mandy to be in the room while we are talking."

"Look Mel, if it pertains to Cassandra's disappearance, Mandy has every right to hear anything and everything. She's twenty-two years old and is more than capable of handling whatever it is you have to say. Besides, she's the one who filed the report."

"So, what's going on Uncle Mel?" asked Mandy nerves on edge, terrified of what he may have to say.

Mel smiled, but she could see the sorrow in his eyes. "Well, it's been six days. There's been no trace of Cassandra. It's as though she just vanished. We have a couple of suspects with flimsy alibis, but no concrete evidence to prove they were involved. As your friend, Robert, I told my team *I* wanted to approach you this evening with our latest suspicions."

Her father motioned for Mel to get on with it. Mandy knew her dad wasn't a very patient man and wanted Uncle Mel to get to the point. Mel provided them with a quick update of all of the information they had to this point.

"Do either of you know where Cassandra might have gone on those occasions when she wanted to be by herself?" Uncle Mel asked. "Was she in town, out of town? Did she have a particular hotel where she liked to stay?"

Mandy looked at her father timorously. "I know a couple of

summers ago when I was home on break, I found out her boss had been letting her use his condo in Chicago," she said, watching her father's reaction of surprise. "I called Uncle Frank to see how his family was doing and I told him Mom was on one of her adventures. He told me she'd come by to visit him the day before.

"I was curious about her going there, and I thought maybe Michelle Danson had been in touch with her. It seemed like Mom never stopped working. Michelle told me she didn't know where Mom was exactly, but she'd seen Mr. Benson give Mom a set of keys and heard him tell her to enjoy the condo.

"When Mom came home, I asked her about it. She told me Mr. Benson had been very understanding and kind to her since Charlie's death."

"Humph," Robert growled. "I'll just bet."

Mandy saw Mel give her father one of those looks she'd often seen pass between them when Mel thought her dad was being unreasonable. Then Uncle Mel turned his attention back to her.

"Why didn't you mention this to me before?" he asked. "We should really have someone up there check it out."

"I'm sorry, Uncle Mel," she said. "It slipped my mind until Saturday. I called Uncle Frank to ask him to go see if she was staying there. He checked twice and each time no one answered the door. He contacted the owner of the building to ask if he could get access to the condo. Uncle Frank designed this particular building for him.

"The owner, Mr. Pace, checked with Mr. Benson who said Mom hadn't asked for the keys lately, but they were welcome to look. They didn't find any sign she'd been there. The parking lot attendant hadn't seen her vehicle come through either. I thought it was a dead issue. I didn't think it was important."

"It's okay, Mandy," Uncle Mel said, giving her a reassuring smile. "Just remember, *nothing* is insignificant. I want you to promise to tell me everything from now on. Okay?"

Feeling foolish, she nodded.

"Have either of you ever suspected Cassandra might be having an affair?" Uncle Mel asked.

Mandy looked at her father, searching his face for some sign of awareness. He looked puzzled for a moment, until the initial shock wore off.

"If she was having an affair, I certainly didn't know about it," he began. "Where did you get this idea? Is there more you want to tell me about Paul Benson? Do you think he actually met her up there?"

"I'm not sure about Benson. There were some discrepancies in his initial discussions with Jacobs and Mayhew so they've scheduled another interview with him. The information Mandy just provided about the condo is very helpful.

"We should be getting copies of the employee time off schedules from the real estate office first thing tomorrow. We'll see if Benson and Cassandra were ever gone at the same time other than the day she went missing."

Mandy saw Uncle Mel fidget in his chair. "We do have two other possibilities. Jacobs found several calls made over the past three years to an attorney, Jonathan Richmond. Cassandra helped him and his wife find a home in Carmel three years ago. Could be she was just seeking some sort of legal advice. Jacobs and Mayhew are going to meet with him tomorrow afternoon.

"There could be another man involved," he continued. "Cassandra was apparently getting strange phone calls at work from a man. The receptionist was certain he wasn't a client. Cassandra would be gone from the office for hours after receiving his calls."

Uncle Mel paused for a moment glancing in Mandy's direction. She could see the pain in his eyes. It was obvious he hated what he was doing. "I'm sorry I have to go into this with you," he continued, "but you know I'm right when I say nothing is insignificant."

"I know," her father said, his eyes flashing. Standing, he walked toward the window, running his fingers through his thick brown hair. He turned abruptly looking straight at Mel. "You, of all people, know things have been strained in this house for quite some time. Since I haven't actually noticed anything Cassandra has been doing lately, I certainly wouldn't know if she was fucking around."

Blushing with embarrassment, Mandy looked to Uncle Mel to stop this before she lost her temper. Things had been more peaceful between her and her father lately, so she didn't want to say something she would regret.

"Look," Mel addressed her dad in a very serious tone. "I don't believe Cassandra left willingly, otherwise there would have been a trail and contact of some kind. The boys are double-checking all her records for the past three years. We're hoping there's something she's done in the past which will give us a clue as to what happened to her. Maybe this mystery man is our culprit."

"Yeah, I'm afraid I have to agree with you," her father conceded. "I don't believe she left willingly."

Mandy hung her head staring at the floor. She didn't want to give up hope. However, the length of time her mother had been absent only made the possibility of them finding her alive remote.

After another moment of uncomfortable silence, Uncle Mel said, "I need to get home and feed the cat. If either of you find anything that might confirm or dispel the idea of an affair, give me a call." He stood up and clapped his old friend on the shoulder. "See you at work tomorrow."

Her father grunted his affirmation, returning to his recliner.

Mandy walked with Mel to the door. "I didn't know you had a cat," she whispered.

"I don't," he said furtively. "I just wanted to talk to you alone for a moment." He stopped at the door, turned, and smiled at her. "Don't let the old bear get you down. I think he's more worried than he lets on. He loves you, Mandy, even if he doesn't always show it."

"Thanks, Uncle Mel," she said. She threw her arms around him, hugging him tight. In that moment, she wished he was her father. She backed away from him, feeling the same old pang of guilt she always felt when she allowed this thought to seep in. He gave her a quick peck on the forehead and opened the door.

"Don't forget," he told her as he crossed the threshold, "*nothing* is insignificant."

Chapter 9

The phone was ringing as Mandy stepped out of the shower the next morning. She wrapped a towel around her body and went dripping through her bedroom to answer the phone. The caller ID indicated it was someone from IMPD.

"Miss Stevenson, this is Detective Jacobs. We've found your mother's car."

"Where?" Mandy said, feeling both excited and terrified.

"We found the vehicle in the parking lot of the airport in Westfield. It's a couple of miles just north of State Road 32 on Spring Mill Road. We would have called Captain Stevenson, but all of the department heads are in some kind of important meeting this morning."

"You say you found the car, but what about my mother? Was there any sign of her?"

"No," he said, "I'm afraid not. We have a search team out here right now. They are using dogs to canvass the fields around the airport."

"How do you know it's her car?" asked Mandy, her throat tight with worry.

"The plates and registration are missing. Stupid criminal trick in my opinion, because we were able to ID it by the VIN number."

"I'm coming down there!"

"Miss Stevenson, I don't think you should…."

"I'm not going to argue with you, Detective, and I'm not going to sit here and do nothing. I know I can't enter the area around the car, but I can certainly join in the search."

Mandy hung up the phone, quickly dried herself, and pulled her wet hair back into a ponytail. She found clothes and dressed quickly. Heart pounding with anticipation, she grabbed her purse and ran downstairs to the garage.

She reached the tiny airport in time to see news teams from all of the stations setting up cameras. The reporters were primping, getting ready to report the big news of the day. She felt a twinge of panic as she contemplated how she could dodge them. She hated the way reporters treated crime victims' families on the news, and she didn't relish the idea of being asked a million questions she couldn't answer.

Mandy parked her car and scanned the area to see if there was someone she recognized. Getting out of her car, the first thing she heard were the deep melodious tones of hounds barking in the distance mixed with the voice of a reporter asking a man who she was. Spotting the tall dark figure of Detective Mayhew, Mandy walked swiftly towards him trying to avoid being stopped by the inquisitive reporter.

"Miss Mandy," he said as she approached. He took her by the arm. "Girl, we'd better get you over to a no admittance zone before these vultures figure out who you are."

"Thanks," Mandy said looking up into Mayhew's kind, dark eyes.

He took her straight to where his partner was standing. "I'm going to leave you with Detective Jacobs here while I check on our search party."

"Detective Jacobs," Mandy said. "Is it all right if I see my mother's car?"

"I'm afraid we can't let you enter the taped off area," he replied. "We need to make sure no one but our forensics staff gets near it. We don't want the evidence compromised. I will tell you we found a small amount of blood in the car."

Mandy's heart was racing at this latest news. As they approached the area where the blue Toyota Camry was parked, she could see a tall, thin man with dark hair searching the vehicle. He was wearing crime scene investigator coveralls and vinyl gloves.

"Mark!" Detective Jacobs shouted, motioning for him to come over by where they were standing. "This is Mandy Stevenson, Captain Stevenson's daughter. Miss Stevenson, this is Mark Chatham, Supervisor of our Crime Scene Unit."

"Sorry to meet you under these circumstances, Miss Stevenson." Chatham said to her as he pulled off his gloves and shook her hand. "We take care of our own," he commented. "This will get top priority."

"Chatham is one of our best forensic experts," said Jacobs. "If there's a clue to be found, he'll find it."

Mandy nodded at Detective Jacobs then watched as Mark Chatham returned to the vehicle and completed his search. She heard him call over a couple of his colleagues and told them to "wrap it" and get the truck to take it to the lab. Then he approached her again.

"I've collected all of the evidence I can here," said Chatham. "We'll be taking the vehicle to the lab processing bay in a few minutes. I'll have one of my team members go over it again in case I missed something."

"I understand," said Mandy. "Detective Jacobs told me there was blood in the car."

"Yes, I'm afraid so," he replied.

A rush of panic pulsed through her veins. "How much?" she asked, her stomach churning.

He looked at her with sympathetic eyes. "There were a few droplets of blood on the carpet and some smearing on the passenger door on the inside and outside door handles. Someone may have cut their hand. Lab tests will help us determine whose blood it is."

Dizzy, Mandy stumbled. Detective Jacobs helped her regain her balance.

"Are you alright?" he asked.

"Yes, Detective. Just overwhelmed." Directing her attention back to Chatham, "How will you know if it's *her* blood?"

"If you have anything at home, like a toothbrush, razor, or hairbrush belonging to her, we might be able to find some of her DNA on them. Also, we can take a DNA swab from you."

"How will that help?" she asked.

"Your DNA would give us a familial match. You and your mother should have several points in common in your DNA. This would at least tell us if the person is related to you."

"I'll be glad to provide whatever you need. If you've got a swab, I'll do it right now."

Chatham put on a new pair of gloves and pulled a DNA swab from his kit. He turned to Jacobs. "There were also several sets of prints on both sides of the car and a couple of short brown hairs on the driver's seat headrest."

"Do me a favor and run those fingerprints against the prints we just got from Patrick and Pamela Cartwright," Jacobs requested.

"Will do," Chatham responded as he gathered his kit. "I'll meet you at your house in about an hour, Miss Stevenson," he said before heading for his vehicle.

Scenarios were running through Mandy's mind fast and furiously. She wasn't sure what to think. She could still hear the dogs barking in the distance. What should she do? Join the search? Go home?

"Miss Stevenson, I know this is very hard for you," said Jacobs, "but we really don't know for sure the blood on the door is your mother's."

"I appreciate the fact you want to make this as painless for me as possible. But I'm not a naïve child," she said fighting back tears. "What do we need to do now?"

"You should go home now, Miss Stevenson," Jacobs suggested. "You'll want to be there when Mark Chatham arrives."

"But I want to stay and help," Mandy insisted.

"No offense, but you are a civilian. I've got a dozen of our best officers and dogs searching. It would be more helpful for you to go home and wait for Mark."

"So why didn't you and Detective Mayhew ask me for something with Mom's DNA on it before now?" she asked, glaring at him.

"Until now, we had no evidence of foul play," he answered. "I don't mean to sound insensitive, but these types of tests are very expensive so we can't order them for every case that comes across our desk. Money's been really tight lately."

"I see," she said. There was no point arguing with him.

"Those reporters over there have probably already figured out who you are," he said. "Being naturally curious beasts, they've most likely talked to their connections and found out about this case. Sooner or later they're going to corner you. Let's make it later."

"Okay, I see your point," she said, glancing at the increasing number of reporters. "How long before we get the results from these tests?"

"Although Chatham said he would make it a priority, it will take several days, perhaps as long as two weeks," he responded. "We'll contact you and Captain Stevenson as soon as we get the results."

"Hey, you two. Need some back up?" She heard the deep,

welcomed voice of Detective Mayhew and turned to see him coming toward her.

"That would be great," said Mandy.

"Ready?" asked Jacobs as they looked at the reporters swarming much too close to Mandy's car. Mandy took a deep breath and nodded.

Mayhew took the lead. His huge muscular stature was quite intimidating to most people, but not to determined reporters. Jacobs put an arm around Mandy and Mayhew stretched out his long arms to keep the wolves at bay. Mandy could hear them shouting her name, asking her what happened. Was her mother in the car? Where was her father? Mayhew kept shouting, "No comment!" as Jacobs helped her get into her car.

"Thank you for everything!" she yelled over the din.

"We'll make sure nobody follows you out of here Miss Mandy," said Mayhew. "Just pull out nice and slow. Jacobs will promise them a statement or somethin' to get them off you."

Mayhew closed her door, and sure enough, Detective Jacobs was shouting for the reporters to back away and he would give them a statement. They followed him like rats following the Pied Piper.

As she drove away, she could imagine seeing the blood smears on the door of the sedan. Were they really as minimal as Mark Chatham had said, or did he just say that to keep her from freaking out? Since her mom's disappearance, Mandy knew there could be the possibility she wasn't alive, but this made it all too real.

Before she knew it, she was pulling into her driveway. She peered around to make sure Detective Mayhew had kept his promise. No reporters had followed her. There weren't any in sight, but she decided to pull into the garage rather than take the chance of someone jumping out of the bushes blasting her with questions.

When she walked into the kitchen she saw it was 11:30 already. How could so much time have elapsed? She had just pulled a diet soda from the fridge when she heard the doorbell ring. She looked through the peep hole and found a familiar face.

She opened the door and Mark Chatham greeted her. "Thought since there were so many reporters at the scene you might appreciate seeing someone at the door whose face you recognized."

"Absolutely," she said in relief. "Please, come in."

Chatham was still in his CSU coveralls and was carrying a forensics kit. She guided him to her mother's bedroom and bathroom. Chatham donned vinyl gloves, carefully collected Cassandra's hairbrush, razor and toothbrush placed them into individual evidence bags.

It had been so quiet they both jumped when they heard the front door slam. Mandy and Chatham went out to the landing and saw her father in the foyer.

"What were the two of you doing up there?" her father asked.

"They've found Mom's car out by the little airport in Westfield. There's blood in it. He needed to collect a couple of things that might have her DNA on them."

Mandy's father looked away. "Oh, I see," he said, then walked toward the kitchen.

Mandy showed Chatham to the door, thanking him for being sensitive to her situation. She closed the door behind him and set off toward the kitchen.

Her father was sitting at the dining table with a can of unopened diet soda in front of him. He seemed to be studying it as though he'd never seen one before.

"Dad, are you okay?"

He said nothing but continued to stare at the unopened can.

Exasperated, Mandy went to the opposite side of the table, pulled the can away and took his hands in hers. "You realize what this means, don't you?"

"Mandy, it's not that I don't care about what happens to her," he said. She saw him searching her eyes as though begging for understanding. "After the first few days, I knew you were right, but I just couldn't accept it. Even after Mel came by last night, I still didn't want to believe it — but now."

Mandy squeezed his big strong hands then raised them gently to her lips kissing them. "Dad, I know this is as tough on you as it is on me, but the glimmer of hope is fading. We may be the only family we have left, so we've got to stick together. Okay? I love you…"

"I love you, too," he said.

A sudden rush of joy filled her heart. She hadn't heard those words from him in years.

"Dad, we'll need to tell Gran and Aunt Karen about the car

before they see it on the news. There were reporters from every station at the airport and they tried to question me and…."

Her father pulled his hands away suddenly and hopped up from his chair. "Good idea," he said. "I'll go call Karen right now. Could you make me some lunch? A ham sandwich would be great." Then he rushed out of the room.

Mandy was stunned at how anxious he was to make that phone call. Those two had certainly been talking a lot in the past week.

Curious, she decided to sneak around the corner to listen at the door. As she approached, she heard her father speaking softly, giving her the impression he didn't want to be overheard.

"They found the car, Karen." Then after a short pause, he said, "I know what you mean, but try not worry."

Aunt Karen must have had a lot to say because there was a long pause before her father spoke again. "I understand, but we can't tell her. Promise me."

Who could they be keeping in the dark?

"Okay," she heard him say, "just stay cool and stick to the plan. I'll talk to you later."

Mandy realized he was about to hang up. She quietly returned to the kitchen as she heard him say goodbye. She couldn't stop thinking about what the plan might be, or even more interesting, from whom they were hiding this secret information.

Her father came into the kitchen and frowned. "I thought you made lunch."

"No, Dad. I haven't made lunch yet," she answered bristling.

"Something wrong?" he asked.

"What's going on between you and Aunt Karen?" she blurted.

"What are you talking about?"

"I just heard you talking and…."

"You listened in on my phone call!" he shouted.

"I didn't pick up the extension," she angrily retorted. "I only heard your end of it and thought…."

"Doesn't matter what you thought!" he bellowed. "You've got no right to spy on me! That conversation was private!"

"Apparently!" she said, her temper boiling. "You told her to promise not to tell someone something. What was that all about?"

"None of your damn business!" he shouted. "Forget lunch! I'll grab something on the way back to the office!" He stormed out the door.

She threw the glass she was holding at the door and it shattered. She then shouted at him even though he was too far away to hear. "Fine! Fine! I'll find out sooner or later!" Then she sat down at the kitchen table, broke down and let the tears fall.

Chapter 10

The search by the K-9 crew had not resulted in finding Cassandra Stevenson. The dogs had stopped at a service road to the north of the airport where the trail seemed to disappear. It had taken the majority of yesterday to gather all of the evidence and write up the reports. Jacobs met with Lieutenant Melrose to go over the most recent crime scene information.

"It's evident there were at least two people in the car. Looks like whoever she was with took her by foot to another vehicle," stated Detective Jacobs. "At least we can be relatively certain she was alive at that point. It was quite a walk from where her car was parked, so why bother if she was dead? Besides, he'd have had a hell of a time carrying a dead body that far."

"I guess that's a little good news," said the lieutenant. "We'll have to wait for the DNA results to confirm whose blood it is, though. Might not be hers."

"In reference to the blood, Chatham said there were sparse amounts along the trail. Droplets here and there, indicating the bleeder wasn't bleeding heavily. Probably just a minor injury," said Jacobs. "Oh, and they found some tire tracks which might help identify the type of vehicle along with some size ten men's footprints."

"I spoke with Robert and Mandy last night," the lieutenant interjected. "It seems our Mr. Benson's condo is in Chicago and he let Cassandra use from time-to-time." Lieutenant Melrose gave Jacobs a piece of paper with a name and telephone number on it. "I want you to call the building owner, Connor Pace. See if he has any info about the goings on up there."

"I'm on it," said Jacobs. As he approached his desk, he saw his partner typing away on the computer.

"'Sup?" Mayhew asked.

"Apparently, Mandy told the lieutenant Mrs. Stevenson used to go to a condo in Chicago, owned by guess who?"

"Oh, please Detective Jacobs, sir," he said sarcastically. "Please don't make me be a guessin?"

"You're such an ass," Jacobs said, frowning at him. "Mr. Benson."

"Oh, ho," Mayhew laughed. "Well, now. This does make things interestin', doesn't it?"

"Lieutenant wants me to call the building owner to see if he's heard of any incidents at the condo."

Mayhew handed Jacobs a tissue. "You got somethin' on your nose. Best wipe it off before anyone else sees it."

"You're a laugh a minute, Mayhew," he said tossing the tissue back and dialing Mr. Pace's number. "Listen and learn," he said as he put the call on speakerphone.

"Connor Pace."

"Hello, Mr. Pace. This is Detective Jacobs along with Detective Mayhew. We work with the Indianapolis Metropolitan Police Department in the Missing Person Division."

"Ah, yes, Detective," said Mr. Pace. "I spoke with Frank Johnson about his sister not too long ago. Is that why you're calling?"

"Yes," said Jacobs. "I was hoping you might have some information you hadn't divulged to Mr. Johnson. Some gossip from your staff perhaps."

"I'm afraid I haven't any other information for you," he replied. "However, it might be more productive for you to talk to onsite personnel. The manager, Carlton Hester, might be of some help. Also, our garage attendants see people coming and going daily. One of them might have seen something. I'll give you Carlton's number."

Jacobs thanked him for his time. He made a few notes before calling Carlton Hester. He used the speakerphone so Mayhew could listen in.

"Good day, this is Carlton Hester speaking. How may I be of assistance?"

"Hello, Mr. Hester," Jacobs began. "My name is Detective Jacobs and I'm here with Detective Mayhew. We're investigating the disappearance of Mrs. Cassandra Stevenson. I understand she frequently visits the condominium owned by Mr. Paul Benson."

"Well, sir, we are usually very discreet about our residents and their guests."

"Mr. Hester," Jacobs sternly replied, "this is a missing person investigation. Mr. Pace assured me you would be most cooperative."

"Oh, well, certainly Detective," he stuttered. "Let's see now. There was one report on an incident involving Mrs. Stevenson and Miss Benson. Let me find the file."

"Do you mean Mrs. Ciara Benson, Paul Benson's wife?" asked Jacobs.

"No, Detective. I meant precisely what I said, I was referring to Miss *Whitney* Benson." Mr. Hester paused momentarily and Jacobs could hear the rustling of papers. "Ah, here it is. Yes. Several witnesses saw the two aforementioned ladies having quite a row near the concierge desk. Our concierge reported the incident to me."

"What happened exactly?"

"The report indicates Mrs. Stevenson had just exited the elevator, when Miss Benson approached her yelling for Mrs. Stevenson to quote 'get out of our lives' end quote. Mrs. Stevenson told Miss Benson she didn't know what she was talking about. Miss Benson then slapped her and told her if she didn't stay away from her father, Mrs. Stevenson would get worse next time. Then Miss Benson stormed off and out the front doors. The concierge asked if Mrs. Stevenson wanted to call the police and file a complaint. She told him no, the girl didn't know what she was talking about and it would all blow over."

"Is that the only time you can recall any incidents involving Mrs. Stevenson?"

"That's all I am aware of, Detective," Mr. Hester replied. "Of course, it's all that has been reported. I'll check with the staff to see if there's something I haven't been told. We have maid service and valet parking, so maybe one of them saw something."

"Could you fax a copy of the report to us, please," asked Jacobs.

"I'll have to get approval from Mr. Pace first," he said smugly.

"I understand," replied Jacobs giving Mr. Hester his fax number. "Please give me a call if you find out anything further."

"I certainly will," Mr. Hester agreed.

Jacobs put down the receiver then turned to Mayhew. "I believe we have a new suspect to interview."

"Benson's daughter," Mayhew said, shaking his head.

"It would appear so," replied Jacobs. "She may have suspected her father and Mrs. Stevenson were having an affair."

"We're interviewin' her slimy daddy around 4:00, right after we get back from Richmond's office. Think we should interview her before we talk to daddy dearest?"

"Nah," replied Jacobs. "Let's try to get her in here tomorrow morning. We just have to be careful not to indicate to Benson we suspect his daughter. Let's see if we can get the truth out of him first. That could give us more leverage with the daughter."

"How so?" asked Mayhew.

"When she comes in here tomorrow, she'll assume we want to talk to her about her dad. She won't have any idea we're looking at her as a suspect."

"Good thinkin'," said Mayhew. "I guess that's why you'll be makin' sergeant before long."

"Very funny, Mayhew," stated Jacobs grinning slightly. "I'll give Miss Benson a call and set up something for first thing tomorrow morning."

Chapter 11

Right after lunch, Jacobs and Mayhew headed for Carmel and the law office of Jonathan G. Richmond, Esquire. He had consented to meet with them at 1:30 in his office. The office was located on the sixth floor of the Marks Building.

Exiting the elevator they saw a huge reception area with rich mahogany furnishings, large well-kept plants, and plush forest green chairs in the waiting area. A well-dressed woman with graying hair and reading glasses on the tip of her nose sat at the receptionist desk.

"May I help you?" she asked.

"Yes you may," Mayhew quipped, but the woman gave him a stern look. He and Jacobs pulled out their badges and Mayhew continued. "We have an appointment with Mr. Richmond at 1:30 today. Would you be so kind as to tell him we are here?"

"Of course," she said then pointed to the waiting area. "Please have a seat and I'll be back directly."

"What a tight ass," Mayhew whispered to his partner. "Usually when I speak so elegantly to a lady, I at least get a smile."

"I guess not everyone is sucked in by your charm."

The receptionist returned. "Mr. Richmond will be with you in a moment, Detectives."

"Thank you, ma'am," said Mayhew, trying hard to remember what his mama taught him about being nice to people even when they aren't nice to you.

Jacobs sat in one of the plush comfortable chairs and started thumbing through the latest edition of *Indianapolis Monthly Magazine*, while Mayhew sat and stared at his nemesis. A buzzer sounded and she picked up the phone receiver, "Yes, sir."

She stood and looking stiffly at the detectives straightening her suit jacket. "If you gentlemen would, please follow me to the conference room."

The detectives followed her into a huge room with a large dark wood conference table and a dozen black, leather chairs. She told them to have a seat and Mr. Richmond would join them shortly.

"Didn't even ask us if we was thirsty," protested Mayhew.

"Chill out Mayhew. These guys don't get rich giving handouts to just anyone who walks in off the street."

"Well, you'd think they'd be nicer to us seein' we might have one of their clients in tow some day."

"This guy's a corporate attorney," said Jacobs.

"Like I said," Mayhew said, raising an eyebrow. As far as he was concerned, corporate attorneys got rich off of helping the wealthy stick it to everybody else.

They turned as they heard the conference room door open. In walked a tall gentleman, with dark brown wavy hair, blue eyes and a neatly trimmed mustache. He was wearing an expensive looking navy blue silk suit, with a light blue shirt and a navy silk tie. He looked the part down to his highly polished shoes.

"Mr. Richmond?" Jacobs said extending his hand.

"Yes," he said, shaking Jacobs' hand.

"I'm Detective Jacobs and this is my partner, Detective Mayhew." Mayhew also shook Mr. Richmond's hand. "As I told you when I set up this appointment, this inquiry is in regards to Mrs. Cassandra Stevenson. She has been missing for a little over a week. We're talking to people who knew her."

"Well, detectives, I can tell you right now I didn't know her all that well. Besides, it's been a long time since I saw her last."

"Really?" asked Mayhew, giving Mr. Richmond one of his most intimidating stares. "Accordin' to Miss Stevenson's phone records, you've been callin' her a lot over the past three years. Seems to me you were pretty chummy. I'm not sure why, but you don't seem even a little concerned she's disappeared."

"She was our real estate agent. We weren't *chummy*."

"Mr. Richmond, do you honestly think my partner and I would come all the way out here if we didn't know there was somethin' more to it?" Mayhew inquired.

"Come on, Mr. Richmond," said Jacobs. "Just tell us everything about your relationship with Cassandra Stevenson. From the beginning, please."

Richmond looked at each of the detectives then sat back in his chair looking defeated. "My wife and I met Cassandra three years ago when we decided to buy a house in Carmel. I wanted to be closer to the office. She wanted the kids to grow up in a nice neighborhood and go to the best schools."

"According to the real estate office records, you found a house within three months," stated Jacobs. "But according to her phone records, the two of you have kept in touch for three years."

"Okay, I admit it. Cassandra and I had a fling, but that was all it was. My wife was always busy and Cassandra was available."

"Not really, Mr. Richmond," said Mayhew. "The lady was married."

"It was just fun," said Richmond. "Haven't you ever wanted more than one woman, or at least thought about straying."

"Jacobs here isn't married, but I can tell you with utmost certainty, Mister, I'd never cheat on my wife."

"I didn't mean to offend you, Detective," said Richmond. "I guess there are some good marriages out there."

"Damn straight," said Mayhew glaring at him.

"Let's get back to your relationship with Mrs. Stevenson," said Jacobs, getting the conversation on track. "You had a 'fling' lasting at least two and a half years. So what happened? Why did you stop if you were having so much fun?"

"My wife got suspicious. She hired a private investigator to find out what I was doing. When Savannah told me she knew about the affair, I broke it off."

"Just like that?" Mayhew asked, snapping his fingers.

"Have you seen how much a nasty divorce costs these days?" Richmond asked. "Of course I broke it off. Savannah gave me an ultimatum. Break it off or pay the price. Since it wasn't important to me to continue seeing Cassandra, I did what Savannah wanted."

"So who was this P.I. she hired?" asked Jacobs.

"His name is Niccolo Rosini. He's got an office on East 82nd Street," answered Richmond.

"Where did the two of you rendezvous?" asked Mayhew. He really didn't like this guy's attitude.

Richmond turned around to the credenza and pulled out a tablet of paper. "Here, I'll make a list. It's actually rather short. We didn't see any reason to switch locations every time we met." He scribbled down some locations, tore off the page and handed it to Jacobs.

"Thank you, Mr. Richmond," Jacobs said. "That's all we need to ask for now. Please don't leave town without notifying us in case we need further information from you."

"I've got nothing to hide Detective," said Richmond.

"Good to hear," said Jacobs. "Let's go partner."

Jacobs and Mayhew walked back through the reception area, receiving yet another stern look from the woman at the front desk. Apparently unable to resist the temptation, Mayhew turned to her and smiled. "Bye. It was a pleasure makin' your acquaintance."

She just shook her head and went back to working on her computer. Still no smile.

"Do people who work in corporate law take a class in how to be emotionless assholes?" asked Mayhew.

"If they do, I think our friends in there passed with flying colors," replied Jacobs.

"Isn't Rosini the guy who gave us so much trouble on the Parsons case a few months back?" Mayhew asked Jacobs.

"One and the same," answered Jacobs, rolling his eyes. "I'm really looking forward to seeing *him* again."

"Then maybe you can take care of this one on your own," sniggered Mayhew. "I know you thought I was out of line in there, but I just got no respect for some man who thinks cheatin' on his woman is fun. And, he doesn't show any respect for the fact someone he was seein' for more than two years is missin'."

"Aren't there enough social wrongs to be pissed about without adding cheating husbands to your list?"

"Watch it, Jacobs. Just because you're my partner doesn't mean I won't kick your ass if I think it needs kickin'."

"Whatever," Jacobs replied. "I just found it interesting Richmond folded so quickly."

"Yeah, like a damn bed sheet. We didn't even put any pressure on," Mayhew noted, pursing his lips in thought. "Most attorneys are hard nuts to crack."

"Guess he knew there wasn't any point lying about it," Jacobs added. "Oh, and just for the record, I find your loyalty to your wife one of your few admirable qualities."

"Come on now. You're gonna make me blush. Besides, if Jada ever caught me foolin' around, she'd be the one kickin' ass."

Jacobs laughed.

Chapter 12

Lieutenant Melrose had been correct in assuming Mr. Benson would consent to come to headquarters for a second interview rather than being picked up at his office by a police cruiser. Jacobs readied the interrogation room while his partner was waiting at the front desk for Mr. Benson to arrive.

At 4:15, Detective Mayhew came into the room with Paul Benson. "I was just tellin' Mr. Benson here I was beginnin' to worry about him since he was supposed to be here by 4:00."

"I run a real estate office," said Benson indignantly. "Clients don't understand that there is anyone else in the world but them."

Jacobs directed Benson to have a seat. He explained the session would be recorded, and asked the usual identifier questions. Jacobs then went right to the heart of the matter.

"Mr. Benson, when we met in your office last week, you told us your day off just happened to be the same Tuesday Mrs. Stevenson vanished," Jacobs began.

"Yes, I did," Mr. Benson replied.

"And you suggested we call your wife to confirm your whereabouts on that Tuesday," Jacobs reminded him. Mr. Benson didn't respond, so he continued. "Detective Mayhew spoke with your wife yesterday afternoon. She said she saw you in the morning, but then she had lunch with friends. After lunch she went to a spa for the afternoon."

Jacobs paused. Benson tensely pursed his lips. "Then, she claims to have come home to get ready for her trip to Paris. She doesn't recall seeing you at all in the late afternoon or evening. Mrs. Benson said she didn't see you again until she woke up the following morning and heard the shower running."

"Well," Benson responded, "we often have different schedules. Sometimes we don't see one another for days."

"Mr. Benson," Mayhew said, "it's come to our attention there might have been some inappropriate behavior in the office between you and Miss Stevenson."

"Why ... what ... how dare...," Mr. Benson spluttered. "I've never heard something so ridiculous. Who told you that?"

"Mr. Benson, you need to be answerin' our questions, not the other way around," Mayhew reminded him firmly, but politely.

"Of course there wasn't anything going on!" he exclaimed. "I'm a married man!"

"You wouldn't be the first man to cheat on his wife, Mr. Benson," commented Mayhew.

"Look here young man," Benson said pointing his finger at Mayhew. "I've been married for 30 years. I love my wife."

"You still haven't answered Detective Mayhew's question, *sir*," Jacobs repeated. "Did you and Mrs. Stevenson have more than an employer-employee relationship?"

"Well," he said, beads of sweat seeping from his forehead. "I was very fond of her. She made a lot of money for me, but I'm sure I don't know what you mean by inappropriate behavior."

Mayhew's face showed his patience was wearing thin. "Are you shittin' me, mister? Do I have to explain this to you? Okay, fool, let me give you a list — fondling, rubbing up against her, keepin' her alone in your office for way too long givin' people the impression there might be somethin' of a sexual nature goin' on!" he said raising his voice with each phrase. "You understand my meanin' now, Mr. Benson?"

"Of course," Jacobs interjected, "maybe you saved the actual sex stuff for those little trips to your condo in Chicago."

"What?" Benson exclaimed practically falling out of his chair in shock. Obviously, he didn't think Cassandra would ever tell anyone about his little hideaway.

"Apparently, Mrs. Stevenson told her daughter she went to your condo in Chicago from time-to-time to get away from the stress at home," Jacobs smirked. "Are you denying it?"

"Uh, no," Benson said, his calm demeanor fading. "I just wanted to help her. Like I said, I was very fond of her. I felt sorry for her after her son died. She was a basket case for a while. But the last three years she's been fantastic."

"I bet she was," Mayhew said.

"That's not what I meant!" Benson said his eyes as big as saucers. "I meant she was a fantastic sales agent. I didn't go to the condo with her. I just gave her the keys so she could stay there whenever she needed to get away."

"Well then, it should be easy enough to prove, shouldn't it?" asked Mayhew. "Do you have someone who can vouch for your whereabouts durin' those periods when you loaned out the condo to Miss Stevenson?"

Jacobs pulled a piece of paper from the file in front of him, sliding it across the table for Benson to see. "Computers are marvelous, aren't they?" He looked Benson in the eye, watching him gulp nervously and adjust himself in his seat. "Mr. Benson, I think you'll recognize this report. You did say Miss Danson should give us whatever we needed, didn't you?"

"Yes, I did," answered Benson starting to rock a bit.

"As you can see, this is a list of dates going back three years on one of your Employee Time-Off Reports. It shows all of the time off you and your employees took during that period, doesn't it?"

"Yes," Mr. Benson said barely able to speak.

"Oh, how rude of us," Mayhew said smiling at Benson when it had become apparent they were getting to him. "Can I get you somethin' to drink, Mr. Benson?"

"If I could just have some water, please," Benson requested.

"Sure thing," said Mayhew. He called the assistant from the doorway asking her to bring a bottle of water for Benson.

"If you look at this list closely, sir," continued Jacobs, "you will see that on the majority of occasions you were not in the office — surprise, surprise — neither was Mrs. Stevenson. I'm sure if we get a warrant for your credit card records, phone records, etc., we will find these weren't all family sailing trips."

Benson finally broke, "Alright, alright! We had an affair, but she ended it in May. She apparently found another chump to bed."

"And how did that make you feel?" asked Jacobs.

"Used," he admitted, "but I got over it. Like I told you before, she was my top moneymaker."

"So you're tellin' us you've forgiven her because she makes you lots of money?" asked Mayhew. "Sounds like a pimp, doesn't he Jacobs? Got any idea who this new guy was?"

"No idea and I don't care," said Benson. "It was fun while it lasted."

"Jacobs. Where did we hear that one before?" Mayhew commented, shaking his head and pacing.

"You know a guy named Jonathan Richmond?" asked Jacobs.

"He was one of Cassandra's clients. He and his wife bought a house through Cassandra a few years ago. Two-story brick in Carmel. It brought in a $40,000 commission."

"You always look at everything in dollars and cents, Mr. Benson?" Mayhew asked.

Benson didn't answer; he just stared at Mayhew with a look of contempt.

"Back to your naughty behavior, I take it your wife doesn't know about your little indiscretion?" asked Mayhew sarcastically.

"She either doesn't know, or doesn't care. We have a summer home in the Hamptons, a winter home in the Caymans, and she has a closet full of the best clothes. She likes her comforts. She can do whatever she pleases, so she ignores what I'm doing as long as it doesn't come back to embarrass her."

The assistant knocked on the door delivering the bottle of water wrapped in a paper towel. Mayhew took it by the lid passing it along to Benson who opened it, taking a deep pull from it before turning his attention back to the detectives.

"Well, Mr. Benson, we can't guarantee we'll be able to keep this out of the public eye," Jacobs said. "You will let us know if you plan to leave the state. Oh, and you should definitely *not* make any plans to visit your place in the Caymans. You'll continue to be considered a suspect until this case is solved or another suspect is identified."

"But I told you. I hold no grudge against her," Benson pleaded. "I didn't have anything to do with Cassandra leaving this time."

"Well, we might actually have believed you if you had told us the truth from the beginning rather than waiting until we pried it out of you," said Jacobs raising one eyebrow. "You also lied to us when we first met you. You do remember us asking you about any animosity in the office, don't you? You neglected to mention the accusations Mrs.

Cartwright made against Mrs. Stevenson — accusations of which you were very well aware."

Benson was obviously not going to volunteer any further information, so Mayhew told him he was free to go for now.

Benson set the bottle of water on the table. He stood using the tabletop to brace himself then exited the room in a fury. Mayhew turned off the recording device.

"Slimy snake!" Jacobs commented sharply. "Acting like we're the assholes for daring to call him a suspect. People crack me up."

"Do you think he's involved?"

"Let's get Forensics in here to try to lift his prints off of the table. Did you notice how he put both of his hands firmly on the table when he got up to leave? I think there should be some nice ones there."

"Then we can compare them to those prints found in the car," said Mayhew.

"You bet," said Jacobs. "The lab should be able to swab the water bottle for DNA. Have you and Emily been practicing that method of handing off water bottles to suspects? Good move!"

"Thanks, shorty," said Mayhew. "I figure there should be enough DNA on that bottle for Chatham to compare to the hair he found in the car."

"You're a genius, partner," Jacobs chuckled.

"I know," smiled Mayhew.

Chapter 13

Lieutenant Melrose, Detective Jacobs, and Detective Mayhew stood behind the one-way glass waiting for Whitney Benson to arrive. Jacobs and Mayhew had done a superb job of rattling Mr. Benson yesterday. Now they'd have their chance to do the same with his daughter.

"Jacobs, you said Benson confessed to having an affair with Cassandra. Did he happen to mention how long this was going on?" asked the lieutenant.

"Not exactly. He did say he'd been letting her use the condo since Charlie Stevenson died," answered Jacobs. "It sounded like the affair started not too long after that. I'm going to get copies of his credit card records and crosscheck them with hers. Then I'll see how they correspond with the time-off schedule."

"Excellent. I wonder when his daughter found out," commented Lieutenant Melrose. "She was attending Northwestern so you'd have thought she would've been living in the condo while she was there."

"We'll make a point of askin' her, Lieutenant," said Mayhew.

They turned to see Emily escorting Whitney Benson into the interrogation room. She was even prettier in person than in her photo. She was at least five-foot seven-inches tall and lean with long straight blonde hair, crystal blue eyes, and full red lips.

"Okay fellas," said the lieutenant. "Go do your thing."

Mayhew and Jacobs left Lieutenant Melrose in the observation room. "Do try to keep that charm of yours under control," Mayhew said to his partner.

"Shut up," Jacobs said rolling his eyes.

As they entered the room, Whitney stood and extended her hand. "Hello, Detectives. I'm Whitney Benson."

"Miss Benson, I'm Detective Jacobs and this is Detective Mayhew. I believe you spoke with him yesterday."

"Yes, I did," she said taking her seat again. "I also understand you interrogated my father yesterday, so I assume that's why I'm here today."

"In a manner of speaking — yes," replied Jacobs as he and Mayhew took seats across from Whitney. "We need to ask you some questions in regards to the disappearance of Cassandra Stevenson."

Whitney stiffened a look of disgust on her face. "I can assure you, my father had nothing to do with that woman's disappearance!" she said.

"I'm sure his DNA will provide the answer to the question, Miss Benson," said Mayhew. "However, we didn't bring you in here to ask your opinion on whether your daddy's capable of doin' such a thing. We need to talk to you about *your* attitude towards Miss Stevenson."

"My attitude!" she huffed. "I don't have an attitude one way or the other about her."

"Actually your body language and tone of voice thus far have indicated you don't like Mrs. Stevenson very much," stated Jacobs.

"Look," she said leaning toward the detectives. "My father screwed around on my mother all the time. She just let it go. I don't know how she could just turn a blind eye to it, but she did. I tried to do the same."

"Didn't work out too well for you though, did it?" asked Mayhew.

"I don't know what you mean," she said, shifting in her seat.

"Your father has a condo in Chicago, doesn't he?" asked Jacobs.

"You obviously know he does," she sneered.

"Well, then you probably know we've talked to the staff there and found out about your little disagreement with Mrs. Stevenson in the lobby in front of at least a dozen people."

"I was angry," she said. "I went to the condo because Mom told me Dad was in town on business. I wanted to surprise him. Instead, I was the one who got surprised."

"Go on," said Mayhew watching her.

"The night before I confronted her, I'd gone to the condo. When I rounded the corner, I saw them right outside the building — kissing. I turned and walked away hoping they hadn't seen me. I knew he fooled around, but it never seemed real to me until I actually saw it with my own eyes."

She paused for a moment. "I went back to my apartment and the more I thought about it, the angrier I got. I decided to go there the next day and confront them."

"May I ask, since you attended Northwestern University, why you didn't live in the condo?" Jacobs asked.

"I talked my dad into letting me live somewhere closer to campus. Most of the students live in Evanston. It was just more convenient."

"Makes sense," Mayhew confirmed. "So tell us what happened the day you confronted Miss Stevenson."

"I went to the condo building and saw my father getting into a cab. I'd just missed him, but I decided to go up to see if his whore was still there. Unfortunately, she got off the elevator just as I was about to go into it. I remember yelling at her, but I'm not even sure what I said. She called me a silly little girl and I slapped her. Then I got the hell out of there."

"There were about a dozen witnesses who heard you threaten her," said Mayhew.

"They're lying!" she declared. "I would never do such a thing."

"'Imagine that, Jacobs. A dozen people want to lie about our little girl here."

"I'm not a little girl!" she snarled, glaring at Mayhew.

"Did you have any contact with Mrs. Stevenson after the…encounter?" inquired Jacobs.

"No, and she obviously didn't say anything to my dad, because he would have been furious with me."

"Miss Benson," Jacobs said. "Mrs. Stevenson disappeared the second week of August. We need for you to tell us your whereabouts during that period of time."

"I went back to my apartment in Evanston," she said in an haute tone.

"Then I'm sure you can prove it," Jacobs said, impatience permeating from his voice. "Did you fly and keep your boarding pass? Anybody see you there?"

She sighed deeply and then pursed her lips as though she'd just sucked on a lemon. "No, I drove up. And nobody saw me because my roommate had gone to her parents' house in Michigan for the summer. She wasn't due back until the following week. I just went up there to get the rest of my clothes and a few personal items I'd left."

"Oh, I see," said Jacobs.

"You see what?" Whitney spewed. "I went up there by myself. Since Fran wasn't back, I decided to take advantage of some quiet time and stayed the whole week. Is there something wrong with it?"

"Nothin', as long as you can prove it," said Mayhew.

"Are you calling me a liar?" she screamed, standing and glaring at him.

"Why, Miss Benson," Jacobs said calmly. "You do have quite a temper, don't you?"

"I didn't do anything to Mrs. Stevenson!"

"Then you won't mind givin' us a DNA sample and fingerprints," said Mayhew, standing as well. "If you're innocent, then neither of those things will show up in any evidence we might find, will they?"

Mayhew's large stature was ominous. She finally sat back down.

"Fine, fine. Do what you have to do," she seethed. "But my father is going to be very unhappy about this."

"He'll get over it," retorted Mayhew.

"We'll get someone from Forensics down here to take care of collecting the prints and DNA. You just sit tight while we go get him," said Jacobs.

Jacobs and Mayhew left the room and headed straight for the observation room. Lieutenant Melrose had already called the Forensics Evidence Section to have someone come down. They all looked at the beautiful blonde as she fidgeted with her purse retrieving a cell phone. She tried to text a message to someone, but found she had no reception. That seemed to frustrate her more. She threw it back into her purse and slammed it on top of the table.

"She does have a nasty temper, doesn't she?" Lieutenant Melrose observed. "She might have had something to do with Cassandra's disappearance. She certainly has motive."

"I agree, Lieutenant," said Jacobs. "Problem is we don't have any solid evidence linking her to it. Our only hope is her prints match some of those prints found in Mrs. Stevenson's car."

"Even if they're not a match, it doesn't mean she wasn't involved," said Mayhew. "I don't like her attitude. If my child showed a temper like that one, Lord have mercy."

"There's the lab tech," said the lieutenant. "You two better get back in so there are witnesses to the evidence collection."

Jacobs and Mayhew went back into the interrogation room. "Glad to see you didn't change your mind about cooperating with our lab tech," Jacobs directed to Whitney.

"Like I had a real choice," Whitney simply stated.

When the lab tech was finished and left the room, Mayhew turned to Whitney. "Miss Benson, we understand from your father you're plannin' a trip to Europe."

"Not until January," she said. "What does that have to do with anything?"

"'Til you're cleared as a suspect, you won't even be allowed to leave the state, so definitely no outta the country trips," Mayhew explained.

"Are you serious?" she blurted.

"*Very* serious," Mayhew answered, staring at her.

"Doesn't matter," she sneered. "I'm sure this will be cleared up long before January."

"You're free to go for now, Miss Benson," said Jacobs.

"Thanks," she smugly retorted. She rose and Mayhew held the door open for her then escorted her to the elevator.

When Mayhew returned to the interrogation room, he found Jacobs sitting there with Lieutenant Melrose.

"Do you think she's a flight risk?" asked Jacobs.

"Possibly," answered the lieutenant. "Assign a couple of Patrol Officers to keep an eye on her for a few days. If she doesn't run away soon, then she probably won't."

"I'll get on it," said Jacobs.

"While you're running credit reports," the lieutenant said to Jacobs, "check out Ms. Benson. If she used her cards in the Chicago area that week, at least we'll know she was telling the truth about that."

"By the way, Lieutenant, we got an appointment with Nic Rosini this afternoon regardin' his work for Savannah Richmond," said Mayhew.

"The asshole!" said Melrose. "He probably won't give anything up without a warrant. If he doesn't give you anything, then question Mrs. Richmond. If she refuses to permit you to see the files, we'll contact Natalie Ralston in the Prosecutor's office and get a warrant for Rosini's records."

"Okay, let's go Jacobs," Mayhew said jovially. "We've got some harassing to do!"

Chapter 14

Jacobs had set up a late morning appointment with Niccolo J. Rosini, P.I., who preferred to be called Nic. He moved to Indianapolis from a quaint Italian neighborhood in the Chicago area. Nic was average height, with dark hair and eyes, and would have been quite handsome if it weren't for his very crooked nose. Seems more than one person hadn't taken kindly to his snooping.

"I wish we hadn't had to warn Rosini we were coming," Jacobs told Mayhew. "But suspects seem to be multiplying now. I didn't want to waste time trying to surprise him just to find him out of the office."

They walked through the door of his outer office into a clean, but not overdone reception area. They spotted Rosini talking to his young, rather busty, red haired receptionist.

"Ah, if it isn't two of Indy's finest," said Rosini. "Come on into my office, fellas. Patty, hold my calls."

Mayhew and Jacobs followed Rosini into his office. Like the reception area, it was neat but not nearly as plush as Benson's or Richmond's offices. Filing cabinets were metal instead of wood. The oak desk looked like it had been around for a while. Rosini did have a nice view of the traffic on 82nd Street and of the buildings' parking lot. The latter could come in handy if an unwanted visitor came.

"Detective Jacobs, your phone call was pretty vague," he said, leaning back in his chair with his fingers laced together, resting on his chest. "Who do we have in common now?"

"Savannah Richmond," said Jacobs. "She apparently required your services a while back to spy on her husband."

"Now, now, you know I can't talk to you about a client without her permission," Rosini smirked.

"Look, Rosini, we got a missin' woman here, and it's startin' to look like foul play," Mayhew seethed. "Don't fuck with me!"

"Detective Mayhew, I've been in this business long enough to know the tough cop routine and it doesn't work on me."

"Okay, let's calm down," said Jacobs glaring at his partner. "Nic, we are way past forty-eight hours on this one. I'm sure you've seen the Cassandra Stevenson case on the news. We discovered her abandoned car. You also know Cassandra Stevenson is the woman who was fooling around with Richmond. We know it because he told us when we talked to him. That's how we got your name."

"Jonathan Richmond wasn't my client, so all this doesn't mean jack to me."

"Yeah, we know how you work." spat Mayhew. "You don't give a shit about anybody but yourself."

"I'm just trying to make a living, Detective," Rosini sighed. "If I go around telling you guys everybody's business, then I'm going to be out of business. You feelin' me?"

The expression on Mayhew's face gave the impression he was about to feel Rosini, all right. Jacobs jumped up from his chair to position himself in case his partner decided to go for it.

"Okay, Rosini. You win," Jacobs conceded. "We're going to interview Mrs. Richmond this afternoon. We'll either get her permission or a warrant. Either way, we'll get what we want." He turned to his partner. "Let's get out of here, Mayhew."

"Yeah, I'm needin' some fresh air," Mayhew replied.

"Have a nice day," Rosini gloated.

Outside, Mayhew turned and poked Jacobs in the shoulder. "You should have let me break his fuckin' nose again. Nobody would have known the difference. Why you treatin' him like fine china?"

"Number one, don't poke me," Jacobs growled. "I'm not the enemy here! I probably saved your ass from an assault charge. Number two, we won't get anywhere with this guy by bullying him, and you should know that by now. He knows all the rules and he'll use them. We have to do this by the book. We've got to do what Lieutenant Melrose said, interview Savannah Richmond first. Maybe she'll give us permission to look at the file. If she doesn't, then we get a warrant."

"All right, I'm sorry about the poke. But I'm tellin' you right now,

I better never find the S.O.B. walking down my street in the dark, or he and I are gonna have a little talk!"

"Whatever, Mayhew," Jacobs said. "Let's get back so we can get started on this report before Mrs. Richmond arrives."

Savannah Richmond was tall, blonde, and pristine from head to toe. She was wearing a navy blue pantsuit with a white silk blouse, pearl necklace, and earrings. Her nails were long and manicured with bright red polish which matched her lipstick. Definitely the type of spouse one would expect Jonathan Richmond, Esquire to have.

Jacobs was seated in the interrogation room across from her. Mayhew would join them later as he and Lieutenant Melrose were observing on the computer in the lieutenant's office. The plan was to have Mayhew come in late in hopes of intimidating her if she were being uncooperative.

"Mrs. Richmond, I'm going to get right to the point of this interview."

"That would be most appreciated, Detective Jacobs," she said with a gentle smile. "I like for people to be direct and honest."

"We spoke with your husband yesterday, and he told us about his personal involvement with Cassandra Stevenson. He said he discontinued seeing her after you hired Nicolo Rosini to check on his activities."

"That is correct," she affirmed.

"How long has it been since this affair ended?"

"As far as I know, it ended about a year ago."

"And you are absolutely sure about that, Mrs. Richmond?"

"As sure as I can be," she said, maintaining her placid demeanor.

"Did you ever confront Mrs. Stevenson about the affair?"

"I really didn't see any reason to do that, Detective," she said showing the first signs of impatience. "My husband assured me it was over, so I believed him. I didn't have to do much persuading. He knows what it would have cost him if he hadn't complied with my wishes."

Jacobs looked at her for a second and then jotted down a few notes. "You don't appear to be too upset about your husband's infidelity."

"Why should I be?" she answered. "I told you the affair was over."

"We have some doubts about that. Mrs. Stevenson was getting calls at work from a man who refused to identify himself."

"And you think it was my husband?"

"We are looking at it as a possibility," said Jacobs. "The calls were made during office hours. He could have called from his office phone instead of his cell."

Mrs. Richmond bit her lower lip and looked away from Jacobs. She either hadn't thought of that before or she was a great actress.

"Mrs. Richmond, we also visited Mr. Rosini's office earlier. We'd like to have your permission to look at the files on your case."

"What on Earth for?" she asked.

"There might have been something Mr. Rosini observed he put in his notes that would give us a clue into Mrs. Stevenson's disappearance. Maybe someone she met with other than your husband or someone Rosini saw her having a disagreement with."

"I've seen those files. There's nothing of the kind in them."

"But you weren't looking for anything like that. You just wanted to find out what your husband was doing."

"No," she said sternly, her brow wrinkled.

"Sorry, I'm late," Mayhew said as he entered the room. "Did I miss anything?"

"Mrs. Richmond doesn't see any reason for us to look at the files Mr. Rosini created during his investigation of Mr. Richmond and Mrs. Stevenson," stated Jacobs.

"Oh, she doesn't," said Mayhew, stroking his cheek and pacing. "You know, Mr. Rosini was stubborn about this, too. Do you have somethin' to hide, like maybe you're involved in what happened to Mrs. Stevenson?"

"How dare you imply such a thing!" she exclaimed, sitting up straighter and scowling at Mayhew. "I should have my husband sue you for defamation of character!"

"Humph," Mayhew grunted. He looked at Jacobs and said, "Like I haven't heard that one before."

"You leave us with no choice but to get a warrant," said Jacobs. "If you have something to hide, we will find out about it."

"Then get your warrant," she said, becoming aloof once more. "If there's nothing else, I'd like to leave."

"Certainly," said Jacobs. "Please don't leave the area without checking with us first. We'll be in touch."

Mrs. Richmond rose from her chair and glided from the room with an air of dignity. They walked out behind her and watched as she entered the elevator.

Lieutenant Melrose came out of his office. "Well, I guess I'll get the paperwork started for the warrant and call the prosecutor to see if she can push this through for us."

"It's Thursday. I bet she won't get it 'til Monday," said Mayhew. "The slime ball could get rid of anything incriminatin' by then."

"Mayhew, I know he can be an ass," said the lieutenant, "but I've worked with him several times. I don't see him destroying evidence. He wouldn't want to lose his license for the few extra bucks."

"I bet you're right, Lieutenant," said Jacobs. "Patience, partner. We'll get those files. We'll discover what she's trying to hide."

Chapter 15

Alex had invited Mandy to meet him at his dad's and Gloria's for a family cookout. She had the feeling he had invited her as a buffer. He still seemed uncomfortable talking about his father.

Alex's childhood home was in an older section of Carmel. There were lots of lovely brick ranch homes and huge maple, oak and tulip trees. As she pulled her car into the driveway, she saw Alex and his twelve-year old sister, Lana, sitting on the front step.

"Hey, you two," Mandy said as she walked up the drive. "Thought all the fun was out back."

Lana leapt to her feet, ran to Mandy and threw her arms around her. "I'm so glad you're here. Alex is in a crabby mood. Maybe you can cheer him up."

"I'll do my best," Mandy told her as they stepped back from one another. "Let's go see what I can do about it."

"I'm going to go tell Daddy Mandy is here so he'll put the burgers on," Lana announced. "I'm starving!"

"Good," said Alex. "You're getting on my nerves."

Lana stuck her tongue out at him, smiled at Mandy, and ran inside.

"Sour mood today, huh?" Mandy remarked. "What's going on? You and your dad still at odds?"

"Mandy, I want to tell you about it. I just…." He stopped, rose from the step and walked into the yard.

Mandy ran to catch up with him. "Alex, wait up. It's me. Mandy." She grabbed his arm and he stopped walking. He looked into her eyes with such a pained expression it stung her.

"Alex, you know you can tell me anything. But I hope you know you can also keep things to yourself. I'm only asking because you seem so torn and unhappy. If you can't tell me, it's okay. Just know

I'm here for you."

He shook his head. "You are the best friend I've ever had," he said to her. "Even better than Jay." His eyes watered.

"Wow, that's quite a compliment."

"The thing is, Mandy…" He hesitated. "The thing is… I just can't tell you — not right now anyway. I need to think things through. It could affect a lot of people."

"Sounds serious," she said, trying not to let her curiosity overwhelm her into pushing him for details.

"It is," he responded.

She could see this was tearing at him, but continued to try to respect his need to keep it secret. "I'm sorry you feel you have to carry this burden on your own. I can see it's eating you up inside."

"You know me better than I know myself," he said, taking her into his arms, hugging her.

"No big deal, amigo," she quipped, hugging him tightly. "That's what friends are for, right?"

"What's going on out here?" The deep baritone voice of Bradley Phelps resonated across the yard. "Burgers are ready!"

They parted and she slipped her arm through the crook of Alex's arm. "Let's get back there. I'm starving!"

Before they could even reach the door, Lana came bounding out. "Come on, you guys. Dad won't let anybody eat 'till our guest is there. I'm soooo hungry," she whined.

"We're coming already!" Alex exclaimed.

Mandy and Alex followed Lana through the ornate oak front door into the foyer. Mandy's arm was still securely hooked into Alex's as they made their way through the house to the patio.

"Hello Mandy," Gloria simpered. Her five-foot-seven frame was well-toned and tan. "We haven't seen much of you this summer."

"I've been looking for a job and have been busy catching up with family."

"I'm so sorry to hear about your mother," Gloria said a little too sweetly. "Is there any news yet?"

"Come on, Gloria," said Alex. "I brought Mandy here tonight to get away from these types of questions. I want to cheer her up."

"Seems to me you could use a little cheering up, too," she said patting his backside and turning to join her husband.

"Gloria looks great," Mandy commented derisively. "Guess she's still got her personal trainer."

Alex gave Mandy a sideways glance. "That and her massages, manicures, and whatever else."

"Food's getting cold you two," said Bradley. "Better get over here and grab something before Lana eats it all."

"Oh, Dad," cried Lana. "That's not funny."

Once their plates were full and they joined the others at the patio table, Bradley turned to Mandy. "So, Alex tells me you aren't going to start your graduate program this fall as planned."

"There's just a lot of stress at my house right now. I thought it best to wait until next semester," she answered, hoping he wouldn't delve further. No such luck.

"How's it going? Do they have any leads on your mom?" Bradley asked. She found it interesting that he wanted to ask about the investigation instead of how she was holding up. Actually, she was a bit hurt by it as Alex must have seen.

"Dad! I don't think Mandy wants to talk about it," Alex protested. "She came here to relax and get away from all that crap."

"Well, you two sure had plenty to talk about out on the front lawn earlier," Bradley retorted, anger stirring in his voice.

"We weren't talking about *her* situation," Alex countered.

Mandy saw Lana look at her mother with a hint of fear in her eyes. She wondered if this had been happening a lot lately.

"Oh, for Christ's sake!" shouted Gloria. "You two haven't had a civil word to say to one another in the past two weeks! Can't you see you're upsetting Lana?"

"I'm just wondering what *situation* my son needed to talk about," said Bradley, his face turning red and his eyes narrowing.

"That's it!" Alex bellowed, standing up so quickly his chair fell over with a crash. "I'm going home...to my home where I don't have to put up with this shit!"

"Alex!" shouted Gloria.

Alex turned and stormed through the house. Mandy excused herself and darted after him. "Alex! Alex! Please stop!" she called after him.

Alex stopped just short of his car and started to pace. His breathing was so erratic Mandy was afraid he might hyperventilate.

She stood there watching him, hoping his pacing would slow him down and he would put his anger in check. He certainly shouldn't be driving in this condition.

"He is such a hypocritical ass!" he shouted as he stopped to look Mandy in the eyes. "I don't care if I ever see him again!"

"Alex," she said, in disbelief. She didn't want to set his temper off again, so she continued in her most soothing voice. "I know you want to leave, but please calm down first. I could drive you."

"No!" he barked. He shrugged. "I'm sorry, Mandy. I didn't mean to yell at you. If I leave my car, I'll have to come back tomorrow. I really don't want to do that."

"I understand," she said. "Do you need another hug?"

He started to laugh, "You are something else! You think a hug is a cure-all for everything."

"Tell me a time when I gave you a hug which didn't make you feel better," she said smiling at her ability to calm the savage beast.

"Can't think of one," he said. "Okay."

They held each other a moment and hugged.

"Thanks, Mandy. You're the best. I've got to go. I'm better now. Really, I am, so don't worry about me."

"Call me when you get home so I know you got there okay," she insisted.

"Okay, Mom!"

After she watched Alex pull away, she realized she'd have to go back inside to face the rest of the family again. She'd gone after Alex so quickly she'd left her purse in the house. She turned and slowly walked back, tensing with each step.

Opening the front door, she heard the clanking sounds of dishes and silverware being abused. It was pretty evident Gloria was not happy.

As Mandy was about to turn the corner to the kitchen, Lana came around it. They nearly collided, but when Lana saw Mandy she threw her arms around her.

"Oh, Mandy. Isn't it awful?" she said her voice cracking.

"So your dad and Alex have been fighting like this for a couple of weeks?"

"Yeah, and neither of them will tell us what's wrong," Lana said, tears welling in her eyes. "We were at Grandma and Grandpa's.

When we came back, they were mad at each other. I don't understand."

"I don't either, sweetie," Mandy told her. "But I plan to find out. Go hide out in your room. That's what I always did when my folks were in a bad mood."

Lana flashed a smile, hugged her again, then ran upstairs.

"Oh, it's you!" Gloria said, making Mandy jump. "Forget something?"

"My purse," Mandy said timidly. "Can't get home without it."

"Fine. You know your way out, I'm going to bed."

Wow. She hadn't expected this type of cold reaction from Gloria. Mandy had known tension within her own home, but her parents just didn't speak to one another. People yelling, screaming and throwing things weren't something she'd been around before. She slipped into the kitchen to retrieve her purse when Bradley came in through the patio doors.

"He gone?" he asked.

"Yes, but he was pretty calm before he got into the car."

"You seem to have that affect on him," he said.

"I'll take that as a compliment," she said getting the uncomfortable sensation Bradley was about to interrogate her. "I'll just get my purse and be on my way."

"I'll walk you to your car," he offered.

Knowing he made an offer she couldn't refuse, she picked up her purse, walking ahead of him through the house and out to her car. She opened the driver's door and with keys in hand tossed her purse to the passenger's seat. Turning to say goodbye to Bradley, she realized he was standing uncomfortably close.

"Sorry you had to get into the middle of this thing between me and my boy," he apologized. "Did he tell you what's eating him?"

"As a matter of fact, he didn't, Mr. Phelps. But I can tell he's upset about something."

"Yeah, I guess he is. He'll get over it someday," he said a little too matter-of-factly for Mandy's taste. "You be careful driving home."

He backed away from the car door and Mandy slipped into the driver's seat. Something about his questions gave Mandy the chills. What could have happened between them in the past two weeks? She thought about the tears in Lana's eyes and remembered her promise.

She would discover what the secret was for her own sake, as well as Lana's.

Chapter 16

Mayhew was right. It wasn't until Monday morning that they got the warrant for Rosini's files on Jonathan Richmond. Jacobs and Mayhew had picked them up by 10:30 a.m. and were back in the office an hour later. They began scanning the files, newest dates first.

"Well, looky here," said Mayhew. "Seems our Mr. Richmond wasn't bein' very truthful with us."

"What is it?" asked Jacobs.

"This file is from March of this year. Accordin' to Rosini, he spotted Richmond goin' into a hotel on the northwest side with Miss Stevenson. And, they didn't come back out for two and a half hours. Sounds like a bootie call to me!"

"Yep," agreed Jacobs. "Wonder what else he lied about."

Mayhew flipped a few more pages, looking for key words which might give them some answers. He finally found something else of interest. "Don't know if he's told more lies, but Miss Richmond forgot to tell us somethin'."

"Well," Jacobs pressed.

"Hold your horses, I'm gettin' to it," Mayhew said. "Remember how she told us the affair had been over with a year ago and she never had to confront Miss Stevenson? It seems she *did* have a confrontation with her in late March. A week after the day the Mister met up with Miss Stevenson."

"Read it out loud," Jacobs requested.

"How about you read it. You have such a beautiful voice," Mayhew said.

Jacobs snatched the file from Mayhew scowling at him then began to read aloud.

"*It's Wednesday, the day of the week Cassandra Stevenson and Jonathan*

Richmond normally meet at the hotel for their weekly rendezvous. I witnessed Cassandra entering the hotel at 1:00 p.m. At this point, Jonathan Richmond hadn't shown. Immediately, afterward I saw Savannah Richmond getting out of her car and going towards the entrance of the hotel. I left my vehicle to try to stop her from doing something foolish. By the time I reached the lobby, Savannah Richmond had already engaged Cassandra Stevenson in an argument. One of the desk clerks was asking them to please go outside, but they ignored him. Then I saw Savannah pull a gun out of her purse, holding it with both hands pointing it at Cassandra. She told her if she came near her husband again, she would kill her. Savannah heard one of the desk clerks calling the police and decided to put the gun back in her purse and left the hotel.

I stuck around to see what would happen when the police arrived. Cassandra told the police that she'd never seen this woman before and had no idea who she was. She thought the woman might have mistaken her for someone else, so she didn't want to press charges. The description the clerks gave the police wasn't very good, so I don't think they'll figure out who she was. Not sure why Cassandra decided not to turn her in.

NOTE: Jonathan Richmond never showed up. Maybe he saw Savannah leave or maybe she told him he'd better not show up today. I hope she didn't do anything stupid."

"Sounds like a confrontation to me," said Jacobs. "So, Savannah Richmond knew her husband was still cheating. Rosini must have told her about the weekly Wednesday afternoon rendezvous. Rosini was probably right. She must have told her husband he'd better not go and decided to try to scare Mrs. Stevenson with the gun."

"Did you find anythin' in your files?" asked Mayhew.

"According to Rosini, Cassandra and Richmond met for lunch on April 3rd. About a week after the incident I just read to you. He didn't catch their conversation, but by the looks of them it was pretty tense. I'm assuming that's when they ended it because the rest of the entries show Richmond being a good boy. He closed the case the end of April."

"I guess havin' a gun stuck in your face gives you a little different perspective on things," commented Mayhew.

"That'd make me think twice," said Jacobs. "Well, I guess I'd better get on the horn and call those two in."

Jacobs arranged for Jonathan and Savannah Richmond to come to headquarters at 3:30 in the afternoon. His plan was to question the wife while Mayhew questioned the husband. However, when they arrived they came fully armed with respective attorneys.

Percy Van Gordon the Third, one of the best criminal attorneys in the state, represented Mrs. Richmond. Bringing in the 'big gun' could only make one wonder about her innocence.

"Mrs. Richmond, we have evidence you not only knew your husband and Cassandra Stevenson were still having an affair as late as March of this year, but you threatened her with a gun," said Jacobs. "Would you please explain what happened that day?"

"I'm sorry," began Van Gordon, "but unless you have evidence linking my client directly to Mrs. Stevenson's disappearance then this interview is over."

"I believe the incident in question shows Mrs. Richmond had motive to want to *dispose of* Mrs. Stevenson in order to keep her marriage intact."

"As I said, my client will not be answering any questions," said Van Gordon more aggressively. "My understanding is you don't even know if there's been any foul play. I also understand Mrs. Stevenson has a tendency to leave the city to 'clear her head' from time-to-time."

"If your client has nothing to hide," Jacobs said, guiding the conversation away from Mrs. Stevenson's actions and back to Mrs. Richmond's, "then neither you nor she should mind if she answers a few simple questions."

"Are you going to arrest her?" Van Gordon said appearing quite bored with Jacob's persistence.

"No," said Jacobs. There was no way Jacobs could get anywhere with Mrs. Richmond while Van Gordon was attached to her hip. "If she doesn't want to cooperate with us at this time, she's free to go. However, please advise your client she is a suspect in this case and therefore is not to leave the state of Indiana without talking to us first."

"No problem, Detective," Mrs. Richmond said smugly. Then she and her attorney rose from their chairs and left.

Jacobs slammed his fist on the desk. He joined Lieutenant Melrose in Mayhew's observation room to see if he was having better luck with Mr. Richmond. His attorney was Gregory Saxson. Saxson had a good reputation, but wasn't as ruthless or well publicized as

Van Gordon.

"Look, Greg, I don't mind answering these questions," Richmond said, as Jacobs entered the observation room.

"Get anything out of the wife?" asked Lieutenant Melrose.

"No. She lawyered-up right off the bat."

"Too, bad," said Lieutenant Melrose.

"So, Mr. Richmond, it appears you didn't tell us the truth when you said you'd stopped seein' Miss Stevenson?"

"Actually, I believe I said I quit seeing her about a year ago. I guess I lost track of the actual amount of time."

"By about six months!" declared Mayhew.

"Jonathan, I must advise you to say no more," said Saxson.

Richmond waived him off. "What difference does it make when I stopped seeing Cassandra? I already confessed to having the affair. We were both in unhappy marriages and wanted some release. To feel good. Nothing serious."

"Did you know your wife pulled a gun on Miss Stevenson?" asked Mayhew.

"No way! That's impossible!" blurted Richmond. "She doesn't even own a gun."

"I beg to differ," said Mayhew. He then produced a print out showing a Glock 23 registered to one Savannah L. Richmond. "Not only did she pull the gun on her, she did it in a hotel lobby in front of several witnesses. So you're tellin' me, Miss Stevenson didn't tell you about the gun incident?"

"Detective, I had no idea Savannah even knew how to use a gun," he said, obviously baffled. "And, no, Cassandra didn't tell me anything about a gun."

"Oh, really?" Mayhew asked voice dripping with skepticism. "Then why did you stop seein' each other the following week?"

"Cassandra said she wanted to stop," Richmond replied. "She didn't give me any good reason; just that she thought it was time to end it."

"Uh, huh."

"Detective, I don't believe my wife had anything to do with Cassandra's disappearance, if that's what you're implying. When I saw Cassandra the beginning of April she said she wanted to stop seeing me. She said things had gotten too complicated."

"A gun in a woman's face would definitely complicate things," said Mayhew.

"The last Wednesday in March, Savannah told me she knew I was still seeing Cassandra and told me not to go or she'd be calling a divorce attorney."

"That's when she did it, you know, pulled the gun on Miss Stevenson," stated Mayhew. "Funny part was the private dick she hired saw it happen."

"Okay, Jonathan. That's enough," stated Saxson sternly. "I must insist you stop talking now. Detective, unless I'm mistaken, infidelity isn't a crime. Charge my client or let him go."

"You have anything else you want to tell me, Mr. Richmond?"

"No. I've already told you everything I know."

"Okay," said Mayhew. "Oh, but Mr. Richmond, before you go I got just one piece of advice for you. Now that you know your wife has a gun — I'd stop screwin' around if I was you."

Richmond's eyes widened and his attorney said, "Point taken, Detective Mayhew. Let's go Jonathan."

Once they were gone, Mayhew turned, looking at the two-way glass grinning.

"Well," said Lieutenant Melrose with a chuckle, "Mr. Richmond looked a bit pale after Mayhew told him about the gun. I guess he'll be a little more attentive of his bride from now on, won't he?"

"I think so, Lieutenant," said Jacobs. "I think so."

Chapter 17

Mandy had been waiting anxiously for the test results on the evidence found in her mother's car. Uncle Mel had called early and woke her at about 8:00 in the morning. He asked her to come down to headquarters around 10:30. With the backlog in the forensics lab, Mandy was sure they had pushed this testing to the top of the list. If her father and godfather hadn't been such respected members of the IMPD, it would have taken weeks to get these results.

She sat down to a light breakfast of toast and tea despite the protestations of the knots in her stomach. She wasn't stressed as much over what the test results might be as she was by the constant intrusion of reporters. It was as if they knew her every move. She could barely step out of her own front door without having a microphone shoved in her face. The missing wife of the Commander of IMPD's Homicide and Robbery Division was big news. They were even dredging up Charlie's death.

"Has tragedy stricken the Stevenson household once more? Was it fate or something more sinister?" Phil Flack had reported on last night's news.

"They always blame the spouse," she said aloud. Her father had been in Detroit when her mother vanished. There was no way he could have been involved. Of course, she'd heard on one talk radio program they were asking listeners what they thought happened to Cassandra Stevenson. One listener said she thought Captain Stevenson had lured his wife to Detroit and disposed of her there. Then there was the guy who said her father had obviously hired someone else to 'whack her'.

On her way out to the garage, she sighed wondering who might be waiting when she tried to pull out of her driveway. She had started putting her car in the garage all the time to avoid reporters' questions. This didn't mean they wouldn't fling themselves in front of her car though. As she pulled out, she was astonished to find there weren't any reporters in her yard this morning. Where could they be?

On her ride downtown, she marveled at the beautiful old mansions along North Meridian Street. It was always lovely through here, but soon the cool September air would cause the leaves on all of those huge old trees to change color. Crimsons, yellows, and browns would burst into dazzling displays. Her mother had loved the fall. When she and Charlie were young, they would make leaf bouquets for her. Why had life become so complicated?

When she arrived at the City-County Building, she got the answer to her earlier question. There were TV crews and cameras all along the front of the building. She pulled around to the public parking area hoping they wouldn't recognize her, but her bright red vehicle was hard to miss.

Mandy jumped out of the car, trying to make a run for it before anyone saw her. However, reporter Andrea Atkins seemed to come out of nowhere.

"Miss Stevenson," she called, trotting along with her cameraman in tow. "Miss Stevenson, we'd like to ask you a few questions."

Mandy just shook her head and moved toward the entrance. Then she saw him. Her father was coming toward her with two uniformed officers. He put his arms around her and told Ms. Atkins, "My daughter and I have no comment."

"Captain, we understand you'll be getting test results today from the evidence in your wife's vehicle. Do you believe she's been murdered?"

Her father didn't answer. "Don't listen to them, Mandy," he whispered pulling her closer. The uniformed officers were shielding them. Several other reporters had seen what was going on and had caught up to them.

"Captain Stevenson, did you have anything to do with your wife's disappearance?" Mandy heard a male voice asking.

Her father turned his head towards the reporter, but didn't stop walking. "No comment," he said, picking up the pace.

Once they were safely inside with the two officers blocking the entrance, her father turned to her. "I'm sorry about that Mandy. I had a feeling this would happen once word got out. You know I didn't hurt your mother, don't you?" he asked.

"Of course, I don't think you had anything to do with this," she said emphatically.

"Good," he said, relief showed on his face. "Everybody always suspects the spouse first, so be prepared to hear more of this. I wish I could protect you from it, but it's that *freedom of speech* thing, you know."

"I'm early so I think I'll go get a cup of coffee after I get through the security line," she said. "Do you want some?"

"Don't think my stomach could handle another cup right now," he answered. "You go ahead. You'll be safe from those buzzards in here. I'll come get you when they're ready."

She wasn't sure her stomach could take another cup of coffee either, but it gave her something to do. She watched him as he walked away from her, his head bowed, looking at the floor. She knew he had been under a lot more stress since the discovery of her mom's car. He'd discouraged her from watching the news, but sometimes she wanted to hear what they were saying.

After passing her security check, she found the break room on her father's floor. With coffee in hand, Mandy perused the vending machine trying to decide whether or not to purchase a cherry pastry. Hearing the door open, she turned to see Brent Freeman enter the room. His warm hazel eyes penetrated her, causing her heart to race. He was six foot tall, more handsome than she remembered, and his smile was intoxicating.

"Hey, Mandy, it's been a while. I heard about your mom. How are you holding up?"

She realized she'd been staring at him. "Umm, they're giving us the results today," Mandy said.

"I heard."

His eyes were intense as he looked her over. Mandy shifted her weight feeling self-conscious. When he smiled at her, warmth flooded her cheeks.

"Mandy, if you ever need someone to talk to, I'm here," he said. "Right now, however, I'd better get my cup of coffee and get back to work or your dad will have my hide."

She watched him pour his coffee. Just before he walked through the door, he turned his head to look back at her giving her a smile sending chills down her spine.

She was contemplating her reaction to Brent's smile when the door opened again. This time it was her father.

"They're ready for us," he said.

Serious once again, Mandy disposed of the remainder of her coffee and followed him to Uncle Mel's office.

Lieutenant Melrose sat behind his desk while Detectives Jacobs and Mayhew stood nearby, looking glum. They offered the chairs to Mandy and her father. When Mel looked at them, she knew it was bad news.

"Robert, Mandy, I'm afraid this isn't good," he said. "The blood in the vehicle is Cassandra's. I don't want you to panic," he said when he saw Mandy's face drop. "She may only be injured. However, we must be prepared in case it is worse." He paused, picking up a file from his desk and opening it.

"We found her fingerprints on both sides of the vehicle as well as another unidentified set on the driver's side of the vehicle. We've compared them to the prints we collected from both of you, and to those we collected from the Cartwrights, the Richmonds, and the Bensons. We also ran them through IAFIS. There were no matches found." He turned the page.

"There were a couple of brown hairs on the driver's seat. The DNA results on the hair came back male. Again, this DNA did not match any of the DNA collected from our suspects nor was it found in the CODIS database. Of course, this only rules out the other suspects as being the driver of the vehicle. We don't know if there may have been another person involved. There was another vehicle waiting at the airport to take her away. For this reason, we'll continue to keep an eye on our group of suspects." He closed the file and placed it back on his desk.

"Robert, I think we need to involve a couple of officers from Homicide to assist us with this investigation."

"I've got two officers who are free right now, Erica Barnes and Brent Freeman."

Mandy's heart leapt at hearing Brent's name.

"They're two of my best detectives." Although her father's voice sounded very straight-laced and professional, she could see the anxiety in his face.

The lieutenant then suggested they all meet in a conference room in thirty minutes. He told Mandy she didn't need to stay, but she maintained she should be there in case she remembered something which would help.

Mandy took advantage of this break to go to the ladies room to splash cold water on her face. She also needed the privacy to come to terms with the fact that the worst was probably true. What was left of her composure was slipping away. She started to cry, she couldn't help it. Letting it out now would be better than losing control in the meeting.

She thought about all of the dead ends. Every time the police had a possible suspect, they didn't have enough hard evidence to make an arrest. They still had no clear idea of who might have been calling her mom at the office. Now, even though they kept saying her mother may only be injured, Mandy knew they didn't really believe it themselves. Otherwise, why would they bring in detectives from Homicide?

When she stopped crying, she splashed cold water on her face in order to remove some of the red blotches from her cheeks. Then rummaging through her purse she found a compact, some eyeliner, mascara, and luckily, some eye drops. She glanced at her watch. The meeting would start in ten minutes. It only took five to make herself presentable. Mandy took one more look in the mirror, breathed deeply, and headed for the conference room.

Captain Stevenson was already in the room with his detectives. He introduced them to her as she entered. She shook Erica's hand, then turned to Brent as he said, "I've already had the pleasure of meeting your daughter, Captain. Charlie brought me over for dinner a couple of times."

"Oh, yes. I remember," her father said, not reacting to the fact Mandy and Brent were looking steadily into one another's eyes.

The two of them didn't break eye contact until they heard the door open again. Mandy very quickly glanced down at the floor then took a seat next to her father. She tried not to look directly at Brent again for fear she would be exposed. Mandy could definitely feel some powerful chemistry with this guy. However, she admonished herself for even thinking about Brent in this way with her mother's life at stake.

The missing person team went over all of the evidence uncovered by the investigation thus far. Detective Jacobs reported the blood evidence indicated Cassandra was injured before she got into the vehicle.

"The blood is smeared on the interior and exterior door handle. The positioning of the hand print indicates she opened the door with the exterior handle and pulled the door shut with the interior handle," stated Jacobs. "If she had been injured while inside the vehicle there would have been specific blood spatter patterns to indicate this. The only blood spatter found was on the floor of the vehicle near the door. Mostly drops of blood as though the blood was dripping.

"We found no gun powder residue on the car's interior or exterior, so we don't believe a gun was used. Of course, we can't rule it out, but we feel there would have been gun powder residue left on the steering wheel by the perpetrator."

Captain Stevenson addressed the group. "I do not wish to be directly involved in this investigation since it involves a member of my family. Freeman and Barnes, you will report to Lieutenant Melrose during the course of this investigation," he instructed. "If this is all right with you, Lieutenant."

"Of course," said Lieutenant Melrose.

"If you find this is a homicide," said the captain, "then Major Lewis will need to become involved. He will have to decide whether or not he should supervise the homicide investigation and how much Missing Persons should be involved."

Captain Stevenson then looked at his daughter. "Mandy, we've done all we can here. Let's go. We need to let these officers do their job. Thanks everyone," he said as he and Mandy rose from their chairs.

In the hallway, her father put his arm around Mandy's shoulders.

"Are you all right?"

She nodded, grateful for his concern.

"All we can do now is wait," he said. "It's been a tough morning. Let's go. I'll walk you out to the car in case those reporters are still lurking in the parking lot."

Chapter 18

Mandy decided not to go straight home. She needed someone to talk to about this frightening discovery and who better to talk to than Alex. Today he had no classes and wouldn't have to work until evening. She was sure he wouldn't mind if she stopped by.

Since Alex was doing his graduate work at IUPUI this year, he'd decided to get an apartment in the city close to campus. He had moved to this apartment complex right before his last fishing trip with his father in early August — just before they had their mysterious quarrel.

She saw his apartment building straight ahead. It was a nice gated community only about five years old, with limestone walls, and a well-kept courtyard. The apartment was a one bedroom, one bath, living room-dining room combo with a small galley kitchen. Everything was very masculine. Black lacquer tables, black lamps, and a black leather couch and chairs. A little too dark for Mandy's taste, but she didn't have to live with it.

She told the guard at the gate she was there to visit Alex Phelps. He called Alex to confirm it was okay to let her in. Mandy drove to the visitors' parking area then hurried up the sidewalk to Alex's building. He met her in the hallway.

"What's up?" he asked. "You look anxious."

"Let's go inside and I'll fill you in," Mandy said.

"Can I get you a diet soda?" Alex offered as he closed the door.

"No, thanks. I just came from the police station," she said, heart thumping. "I needed to talk to someone. I hope you don't mind."

"Of course not," he said offering her a spot on the couch. "What happened?"

"The DNA they found from the blood in Mom's car is hers," she began.

"That's impossible!" exclaimed Alex.

Mandy was startled by this declaration. She eyed him curiously, but decided he must be trying to keep her from losing faith. Then she continued to give him all of the details of the test results.

"There was a man in the car with her at some point. The brown hairs they found belong to a male, but the DNA testing didn't match them to anyone they've been looking at, including Dad."

"So, are you okay, Mandy?" Alex asked, looking a bit shaken. "I don't like what this is doing to you."

Mandy touched by his apparent concern, said, "I was pretty shaken up at first, but I'm doing all right now. Thanks for letting me spill my guts."

"Hey, no problem. So what are they going to do now?" he inquired.

"Well, the only thing they can do is keep looking for her. The search dogs they used didn't find any trace of her in the field near the airport," she said, her feelings mixed between relief and disappointment. "There was evidence she'd been taken to another vehicle. Uncle Mel's concerned about foul play now, so they've involved a couple of homicide detectives — Erica Barnes and Brent Freeman."

"Didn't you tell me Brent was one of Charlie's friends?"

"Yes," Mandy said blushing. She turned to look out the window so Alex wouldn't notice. But it was too late.

"What's this?" he asked with an impish grin. "Do you have the *hots* for Detective Freeman?"

"I hardly know him," she said still looking out the window. "However, he is very nice."

"Really? Hmmm. Sounds to me like he has some potential," he teased.

"Drop it, okay?" she retorted, blushing a deeper scarlet.

"Mandy, I don't know what to say. Maybe she just cut herself or something. It doesn't sound like there was a lot of blood."

"I guess so," she said. "Everything is just so messed up!" she shouted in frustration. "When I graduated, I moved back home hoping it would help Mom and Dad work things out and we could be a *real* family. Mom just never got over losing Charlie."

She practically leapt off the couch and began to pace. "I understand why she misses Charlie. God knows *I* do. What I don't understand is why I'm not enough for her! Some people who've lost siblings complain because their parents become overprotective. I wish *I* had that problem. Sometimes I feel like she thinks I died with Charlie or maybe I just never existed in the first place."

"I'm so sorry, Mandy," Alex said.

She noticed he was looking at the floor, rubbing his hands together in a nervous gesture.

"It's not *your* fault," she assured him. "This mess started long before you came into my life. If anyone should be sorry, it's me. I shouldn't keep running to you with all this crap."

"Hey, what are friends for?"

"Want to go grab a burger or something? My treat," she said, hoping to make up for popping in on him like this.

"Wish I could," he said walking toward the door, looking dejected. "I've got some homework I've got to get through this afternoon. Plus I'm working tonight."

"Alex, you seem upset," she noted. "Have you and your dad been arguing again?"

"No, we aren't talking right now," he said. "Believe it or not, he can be just as stubborn as your dad when he thinks he's right about something."

"Is that the only thing which has you looking so glum?"

"Grad school is tougher than being an undergrad," he explained. "Lots of papers to write, which means lots of research, which means lots of time in the library and on the computer. That, plus my job, doesn't leave me much time to socialize. Kind of bums me out."

"College was tougher than high school, and you adjusted to it. I'm sure you'll adjust again," she reassured him.

Alex pulled her into a bone-crushing hug. "You're the best, Mandy Stevenson. You know I'd never intentionally hurt you, right?"

"Of course," she said, hugging him tighter. "I don't know why you'd say something like that."

"I don't either," he said. "Ignore me."

"I guess I'd better go home and let you study. Besides, I need to buck up the courage to call my Aunt Karen. This will be very upsetting for her, but I hope she volunteers to call the rest of the family again. I definitely don't want to face telling Gran."

"We'll talk tomorrow," he said as he let her out of his grasp.

"Sure. Thanks for listening," she said, stroking his cheek. She turned away and went to the door. Glancing over her shoulder, she threw him a kiss on her way out.

Chapter 19

Despite her constant worry about her mother, Mandy couldn't stop thinking about Brent Freeman. She couldn't imagine why such a handsome man was still unattached. Would he even give her the time of day? Maybe. He had been a little flirtatious with her the last couple of times she'd seen him. It couldn't hurt to give him a call. He'd said if she ever needed to talk he'd be there for her. Before she could talk herself out of it, she called the IMPD switchboard asking to be transferred to Detective Freeman in Homicide.

"Homicide, Detective Freeman. How may I help you?" said the warm deep voice at the other end of the line.

It took Mandy a moment to speak. "Hello, Brent. It's Mandy."

"Mandy Stevenson, I presume?" he said with a smile in his voice.

"Yes. Sorry, I guess I thought I was the only Mandy you knew," she said feeling the embarrassment she'd been hoping to avoid.

"You are," he said with irritating smugness. "What can I do for you today, Miss Stevenson?"

"Well, I was hoping you could give me an update on my mother's case," she said. It was the first thing which popped into her head.

"Not much has changed since yesterday."

There was a long pause making Mandy feel self-conscious. Finally she went for it and said, "Well, it would be nice to get together and catch up. It's been a while since we spent any time together."

"That's true," he said. "That would be nice. Perhaps we can get together for dinner soon. Let me check my appointment book."

She was beginning to question her sanity when Brent's voice came back over the line.

"Ah, yes, how about...tonight. Say around 6:30. Casual, of course. Does Tijuana Flats sound good?"

"Sure. Sounds great," she said trying not to appear too overzealous.

"All right then, I'll be at your place to pick you up at 6:30 sharp. I've got to get back to the grind now though," he said.

"I'll see you tonight," she said before hanging up. Her head was spinning. She actually had a date tonight. Not a friendship thing, a real date! This was the best thing that had happened to her in weeks.

She headed for the closet and started rummaging through every sweater and pair of jeans she owned. She decided on a conservative light blue cable knit sweater and a pair of her best designer jeans with a pair of short brown leather boots. She didn't want to appear she was overly anxious to please him, but she also didn't want to drive him away.

She felt giddy, like she was sixteen again going on her first date. There was something about Brent Freeman, something she couldn't quite put her finger on that she liked about him. Then another thought occurred to her. What would her mom think? Would she approve of Mandy dating a cop? She decided not to think about it right now.

That evening, Mandy was putting the last minute touches on her makeup when she heard her father come home. A tuna casserole and salad were waiting for him in the kitchen. She headed downstairs to make sure he ate before Brent arrived. Then she realized she hadn't warned her father she and Brent were going out to dinner.

"Mandy," she heard him call. "Mandy, are you here?"

"Yeah, Dad, I'm coming," she called from the stairs. "Go ahead and get ready for dinner, it's all set."

When she reached the kitchen, her father was washing his hands at the kitchen sink. "Table for one," he noted. "Am I dining alone tonight?"

"Yes," she said casually. "I have a date this evening."

"Oh, really," he replied. "Do I know this young man?"

"Well, yes, actually you do. It's Brent Freeman," she said, waiting for his objections, least of which would be the fact Brent works for him.

But he didn't say anything of the kind. Instead he replied with just a hint of sarcasm, "You're dating a cop? At least he's a fine young man. I've no reason to doubt he will be a perfect gentleman with the boss' daughter."

"Dad!" she exclaimed. "Please be nice. I like Brent. He's a really good guy."

"Of course I'll be nice," he said indignantly. Mandy wasn't sure whether she could believe him.

She pulled the casserole from the oven, the salad and dressing from the refrigerator, and served it all with a freshly brewed cup of coffee. "Okay, here you go," she said. "I need to go finish getting ready."

He waved her off dismissively. "Go."

Brent arrived at 6:30 on the dot as promised. When she heard the doorbell ring, Mandy hurried to answer it. Her father had already settled himself into his favorite chair to watch television. To Mandy's relief, he had apparently decided not to check out her date.

Brent had a huge grin on his face and a single pink rose in his hand. He looked handsome in his brown leather jacket, denim shirt, and tight jeans. It made Mandy shiver with excitement.

"For you, my lady," he said, bowing as he presented the rose to her.

She laughed. "How gallant," she said. "Stay right there. I'll put this in a vase then we'll go."

She went to the kitchen; put the rose in the first container she could find then hurried back to the front door.

"I'm leaving, Dad!" she shouted.

"Okay!" he shouted back.

"Are there any reporters out there?" she asked.

"Not that I saw," said Brent. "I'm sure there's something more exciting going on so they've headed for the latest, greatest tragedy."

Mandy grinned as Brent opened the front door offering her his arm. She took it glad it was getting dark so Brent wouldn't be able to see her blushing.

On the way to the restaurant, they made small talk about her time at IU and about his career in homicide. They arrived at the restaurant, placed their order at the counter, and then found a private table in the corner.

"Well, Mandy, you've certainly grown up."

Mandy sensed a blush coming on.

"Don't be embarrassed," he said. "I meant it as a compliment. I mean, you're hot!"

She smiled, feeling a tingle again, astonished by his boldness. "Why, thank you, Brent. It's about time you noticed."

He laughed heartily. "Actually, I noticed a long time ago, but you were much too young at the time," he disclosed. "Then circumstances put us out of touch. I'm just sorry similar circumstances have brought us back together."

"Yeah, me too." This was true. When Charlie died, Brent no longer had a reason to come to Mandy's house. Now her mother's case had brought them back together.

Brent finally broke the silence looking at her with those warm hazel eyes. "Let's not talk about the bad stuff tonight. I have a feeling you need a break from all of that. Tonight, let's talk about you and me."

She was no longer the awkward teenaged sister of his classmate. He was no longer the young police cadet. They spent the next two hours talking and getting to know one another all over again. They talked about everything except the case.

"You know, you remind me of Charlie," he said.

"How so?"

"Charlie was really loyal and took care of the people he cared about," said Brent. "You do the same thing. I can't imagine you ever giving up until you find your mom."

"Funny you should say that," said Mandy. "I don't think I'd know what real love is if it weren't for my brother. He'd always take the fall for me when Mom would lose her temper. He seemed to calm her somehow."

"I remember him coming to my rescue a few times," said Brent. "Some of the *tough guys* used to bully me because I was always top of the class."

"What did he do?" she asked.

"He told them they'd better think about how they were treating me because the smart ones usually wind up being their bosses."

"That definitely sounds like something Charlie would say," she said, laughing.

"Oh my gosh, it's 9:00 already. I've got to call it a night. I've got to work tomorrow."

Just as they were leaving the restaurant, Alex came in with his friend, Jay Sumner.

"Hey, Alex," Mandy said.

"Hey, yourself," he replied, giving Brent a strange look.

"Oh!" she exclaimed, suddenly realizing no one knew Brent. "Alex, this is Brent Freeman. Brent, this is my friend, Alex Phelps, and this is Jay Sumner."

"Glad to meet you," Brent said, offering to shake each of their hands in turn.

"Jay and I were about to have a drink," Alex said to Mandy. "Want to stick around? I'll make sure you get home safely."

"Thanks, but no. Brent has to be up bright and early tomorrow and I'm a bit tired," she said giving Alex a curious look.

"Don't let us keep you then," Alex said snidely, turning away abruptly.

"I'm not sure your friend likes me much," Brent observed as they walked toward his car.

"Don't be silly. It's not you. He's been having a rough time lately," Mandy explained, although Alex's rudeness upset her.

"Well, I don't know him very well, but I think he likes you as more than just a friend," Brent said as he opened her car door. Mandy rolled her eyes as she slid into the passenger's seat.

When they arrived at Mandy's house, Brent escorted her to the door.

"I had a wonderful time," he said. "I hope we can do it again soon."

"That would be great," said Mandy. She looked into his eyes, anticipating a good night kiss. He leaned forward and she closed her eyes, her heart thumping fast in her chest. Then he planted his warm lips on her forehead, said good night, and left her at the door.

Mandy couldn't help but be disappointed. Perhaps Brent was trying to be a gentleman. Of course, maybe he was afraid her father might see them.

As she entered the house, her thoughts wandered back to Alex and his strange behavior. Just days ago, he seemed pleased she was ready to date again. Why was he so rude to Brent?

Chapter 20

Mandy was still disturbed by Alex's behavior of the prior evening. She couldn't believe how rude he had been to invite her to stay for a drink and not ask Brent. Could he be jealous? No. Just a few days ago he was teasing her about Brent. He must be upset about something else.

Alex had classes until mid-afternoon and should have been on his way home by now. She decided to give Alex fifteen minutes to get home and get settled. However, she was disappointed when she tried to call and it went straight to voicemail. She tried his cell as well with the same result.

A half an hour later, Mandy still hadn't received a return call from Alex. This was odd. She tried his home and cell numbers again leaving new messages on his voicemails. She started to fear something might have happened to him. It wasn't like him to do this. It reminded her too much of the day her mother vanished.

By 4:00, she was angry. Mandy had decided to go to his apartment and confront him when her cell phone rang.

"Alex, are you upset with me?" she asked.

"No, Mandy, I could never be upset with you," he said.

She wasn't sure what to say. Before she could answer, however, Mandy heard a knock in the background.

"Do you have company?" she asked.

"Yeah, Mandy," he said. "Somebody's at the door, so I can't really talk right now. Why don't you come by at about six tonight? I have something I need to tell you."

"Sure," she agreed. This fueled Mandy's curiosity. Was he finally going to tell her what had been going on between him and his father?

When Mandy's dad arrived home at 5:30, she had his dinner all prepared for him — Gran's famous curry chicken.

"Going out again tonight?" he smirked.

"Just over to Alex's," she replied. "He and I need to have a talk. He seems to be upset about something. I shouldn't be gone very long. Just leave the dishes. I'll clean up when I get back." She gave her father a quick kiss on the cheek, grabbed her purse and keys, and set out.

She arrived at Alex's apartment complex a few minutes early. Alex had apparently already told the guard at the front gate he was expecting Mandy because the man hadn't bothered to call Alex before allowing her to drive through.

As she approached Alex's apartment, she noticed the door wasn't completely closed. She pushed it open with her fingertips, thinking he must have left it open anticipating her arrival. Mandy called out his name, but there was no answer. Slowly she walked through the short foyer passing the galley kitchen on her left. Cautiously entering the living area, she noticed a bare foot at the edge of the couch. There was obviously someone lying on the floor.

Mandy felt her blood pressure rise. The hair on the back of her neck prickled. She called Alex's name again, but the foot didn't move. Icy fingers of dread and fear were spreading through her body as she approached the end of the couch. She saw legs wearing navy blue sweatpants, then a shirtless pale chest. When she reached his face, she saw Alex's lifeless eyes and a hole in his forehead. He was lying in a pool of blood. There were spatters of blood everywhere.

She opened her mouth in a silent scream as shock took charge of her body. She had to do something. She had to call someone to get some help. Her heart was pounding so hard she thought it would burst through her ribcage. Hardly able to breathe, she was afraid she was going to vomit.

Alex was dead. This couldn't be. She'd just talked to him a couple of hours ago.

Finally regaining enough control of herself, she found her cell phone in her purse. She called the first person she could think of…her father.

"Hello," answered her dad's deep gruff voice.

"Daddy," she said, her voice trembling. "Daddy I need you."

"What's wrong, Mandy? Did you have an accident?" he asked.

"Are you hurt? Do you know where you are?"

Mandy told him she had just arrived at Alex's and she found him on the floor. "Daddy there's so much blood, and his eyes are open and blank. He doesn't respond to my voice. I didn't touch him, but I'm sure he's dead. What should I do?"

"Try to stay calm, Mandy. Don't touch anything in the apartment," he told her firmly. "Move out into the hallway. I'll send a squad car out there right away. Got that?"

"Yes, Dad," she said.

"I'm going to leave the house as soon as we hang up," he said. "Just don't answer any questions until I get there. Do you understand me, Mandy? Just point to where he is and don't let the officers interrogate you."

"Okay, Daddy, please hurry," she said frantically.

Mandy was shaking as she placed the phone back into her purse. She looked at Alex's lifeless face one more time, turned and left the apartment.

As she waited in the hallway, she paced back and forth trying to breathe deeply enough to get her heart rate back to normal. Her whole body shook uncontrollably. She couldn't believe this was happening. It had to be a nightmare. She would wake soon and this would all go away.

Tears came rushing from her eyes as she allowed herself to realize this was no nightmare, Alex was dead. She felt dizzy. She stopped pacing, and leaned her back against the wall. Then she sank to the floor, sobbing into her hands.

Within a few minutes, two police officers entered the hallway. The female officer approached her. "Miss Stevenson, I'm Officer Angela Sanchez and this is Officer Gavin Lloyd," she said. "Your father called the station and said there was a dead body at this address. Are you the one who found the deceased?"

Unable to speak, Mandy nodded and pointed a shaking finger at the apartment door just as her dad had instructed.

"It's okay," Officer Sanchez said. "Officer Lloyd will secure the scene. I just have a few questions for you."

"I can't," Mandy squeaked between sobs.

"Look," Officer Sanchez said tersely, "someone has been killed here and you say you found the body. I need to know your side of the story."

"I don't have a side," she said suddenly feeling like a suspect. "I came to visit my friend, Alex. I found him on the floor," said Mandy choking back tears. "I called my father, and..."

"You called your father!" snorted Officer Sanchez. "Why didn't you call 911?"

"I don't know. I panicked," Mandy stated indignantly. "I don't go around finding dead bodies every day."

"Well, we do," said Officer Sanchez pointedly.

Mandy's head was spinning. She had stopped sobbing again as she realized Officer Sanchez meant business. When she started to look in her purse for a tissue to wipe her face, Officer Sanchez stopped her.

"Don't do it, Miss Stevenson," commanded Sanchez.

"Do what?" said Mandy.

"Do *not* reach into your purse. Give it to me," Sanchez said tersely.

"No!" Mandy shouted. "I just need a tissue."

Officer Sanchez drew her weapon. "I told you to give me the purse, Miss Stevenson. Don't make me ask again."

Terrified, Mandy did as the officer instructed.

Just then, she heard heavy footsteps approaching. Mandy looked up to see her dad coming off the stairway closely followed by Brent Freeman and Erica Barnes. The captain rushed over to his daughter, immediately noticing the officer's drawn weapon.

"Sanchez, what the hell are you doing?" growled the captain.

"Just following procedure, sir," Officer Sanchez replied. "I was questioning her when she reached into her purse. I was going to search it for a weapon."

"I'll take care of it from here," he said glaring at her. "You should be helping your partner secure the scene and getting a log started."

"Yes, sir," she said stiffly, leaving to find Lloyd.

Her father helped Mandy stand. She threw her arms around him sobbing again. "Dad, she thinks I did it. How could she think that?"

"She doesn't know you, Mandy," he said holding her close, "but that's the reason I told you not to talk to anyone. We are trained to treat the person who finds the body as a suspect."

"I'm sorry, Dad." She glanced at Brent who smiled at her.

"Mandy, I'm going to take you out to the car," her father said. He turned to his detectives. "Barnes, I want you to scan the scene, see if there's a weapon, but don't touch anything until forensics gets their photos and gives the okay. Freeman, I want the security guard questioned to find out who besides Mandy came to see Alex this afternoon."

"Come on Mandy," her father said, guiding her towards the stairway. "Let's go down to the car. I need to ask you a few questions." He put his arm around her shoulders, squeezing her close to him.

Finding a box of tissues in the back seat of his vehicle, Mandy's father handed them to her. He waited for her to wipe her tears and her nose then lifted her chin so their eyes met.

"God, I'm so sorry you had to see that. I wish I could protect you from all the ugliness in the world." Her father's eyes glinted with tears of his own, causing her to look away so she wouldn't burst into tears again. "When you're ready, tell me everything."

Mandy told him about her phone conversation with Alex earlier in the afternoon. She told him she'd heard someone knocking on his door, but Alex didn't say who he was expecting. He simply asked her to come by at 6:00. He had something he needed to tell her.

"Dad, I can't imagine anyone wanting to hurt Alex. He's so sweet. He doesn't do drugs or anything else illegal. I just can't believe he's gone," Mandy said choking on the last few words, trying not to break down again.

"Dad, what am I going to do if Officer Sanchez puts in her report she suspects me? I was home alone most of the day."

Her father touched her hand. "If Officer Sanchez puts it in her report, there are a couple of things which will prove you were home," he assured her. "Time of death and phone records. Did you use our home phone or your cell to call him?"

"I used the home phone," she answered.

"Then all I have to do is ask for our phone records of today's outgoing and incoming calls from the phone company. That will prove you made the call from home," he assured her. "Did you call anyone else?"

"Yes," she answered. "I talked to Gran for about fifteen minutes at around 4:10 pm. I asked her how to make the baked curry chicken you like so much. I used the home phone then, too."

"That's good, Mandy. There's no way you could have made those two calls, had time to run down here, commit murder, and be back home in time to greet me with a home cooked meal."

He paused, looking thoughtful. "There are a couple of other factors which will prove you're innocent. I know you couldn't have had time to leave our house at 5:30, come here, shoot Alex then change your clothes and get rid of the gun before you called me at 6:05. Our cell phone records will show the time of the call. Also, I'm sure the first responders were here within ten minutes of my call out to them."

"I wouldn't know. I have no idea how much time elapsed."

"You know, Freeman and Barnes are two of my best detectives. I've assigned them to this case. I'll be keeping a close eye on it, but can't be directly involved since you're the one who discovered Alex's body. The forensics team will dust for prints. They'll collect anything that might give us a DNA profile, such as a hair. Did you touch anything when you went in?"

"No, I did exactly what you told me to do," she said, "but I've been there a lot. I did touch the front door when I entered the apartment."

"Excellent," he said as he saw Mark Chatham and his team pull up. "Right now I want to have Chatham test your hands for GSR."

"For what?"

"Gunshot residue," he explained. "That will be one more way to prove you didn't have anything to do with killing Alex."

Mandy and her father exited his car. He stopped Chatham and asked him to test Mandy for GSR since she was the one who discovered the body.

"Negative, Captain," Chatham declared as he showed the captain his results.

"Make sure it's recorded, bagged, and tagged, because we have a very enthusiastic first responder in there."

Chatham snorted, "Sanchez must be here." Then he headed for the crime scene.

Her father then asked her if she felt she could drive home on her own. She said she thought so. He walked her to her car, took her face in his hands and looked into her red, swollen eyes. "Take your time, please. You've had a terrible shock. I don't want you having an accident on the way home.”

“I’ll be careful, Dad. I promise.”

He smiled at her, stroking her cheek. “I’m going back to the apartment,” he pointed behind her. “I’ll make sure he’s given the respect he deserves.”

“Thank you, Daddy,” she said. She hadn’t called him daddy since she was ten. The shock must have sent her back in time, because she’d called him *that* several times since her discovery.

“Make sure you eat something, okay?”

“Okay,” she said, getting into her car. She sat there for a moment wondering why and who could have done this to Alex. After a few minutes of deep, calming breaths, she decided she could manage the drive home. When she passed by the guard shack, she saw Brent still questioning the nervous looking guard. Brent’s warm eyes met hers. She smiled feebly then drove away.

Chapter 21

Freeman was writing down the guard's description of the only other visitor Alex Phelps had that afternoon. The guard said she was Caucasian with medium length blonde hair wearing sunglasses and black clothing.

"The weird thing about her was the black leather gloves. It's 60 degrees out today," the guard said. "I couldn't tell what her eye color was because of the sunglasses. She didn't get out of the car until she was out of sight, so I'm not sure of her height."

"Could you tell how old she was?" Brent asked.

"Not really. These days the young ones look older and the older ones look younger. If I had to guess, I'd say she was somewhere in her mid-thirties to mid-forties."

"She give you a name?"

"Of course. I don't let people go in unannounced," he said indignantly. "Her name was Savannah Richmond."

"Are you sure?" asked Freeman.

"Oh, yeah," said the guard, "I always write it down in the log. Mr. Phelps must have known her, because he told me to send her in. If the tenant says it's okay, I don't question it."

"Did you notice the car?"

"Only that it was a white Infinity. Tan interior."

Freeman scribbled this information down on his notepad then asked, "Did you get a plate number?"

"Not a job requirement," the guard answered. "I didn't even look, so I don't even know if it's an Indiana plate."

"Shortly after Savannah Richmond pulled through," the guard continued, "Mr. Phelps called to let me know Mandy Stevenson would be here at about 6:00 p.m. He said I could let her in without calling him. That was the last time I talked to Mr. Phelps."

"Did you happen to notice when Savannah Richmond left?"

"It was about 4:35 p.m. I remember because I had just looked at my watch then saw the car go by. Ya know that was weird too, because she'd only been in there about ten minutes."

"Thanks for the info," Freeman said. "We would appreciate it if you could come down to the station to meet with one of our sketch artists to create a drawing of the woman you saw."

"Sure thing, Detective," he said. "I get off at 11:00 tonight."

"Here's my card," said Freeman. "Call me when you get up tomorrow morning. I'll arrange an appointment for you. I'll make sure you're scheduled early."

Freeman walked away from the guard station and over to the parking area near Alex's apartment. He searched the area for something — a piece of paper, a matchbook, a cigarette — which could have been tossed. It could be anything that might have had a fingerprint or DNA on it. Scoping the path *the visitor* would most likely have taken to Alex's apartment, he found nothing.

As Freeman ascended the stairs, he met Captain Stevenson in the hallway. The captain had just completed questioning the neighbor across the hall.

"Captain," he said, "I've finished my interrogation of the guard. He'll come by the station sometime tomorrow to meet with one of our artists. She told the guy her name was Savannah Richmond."

"Wait a minute, I've heard that name before," he said as his brow furled in thought. "You've got to be shitting me," said the captain shaking his head in disbelief. "Are you sure he said that?"

"Yes, sir," said Freeman. "That's what he wrote on his log. He said Alex told him it was okay to let her in."

"Did he at least get a plate number?" asked Captain Stevenson.

"Negative," Freeman replied. "He wasn't even sure what state it was from. He just knew it was a white Infinity. Do you know this woman, Captain?"

"Not personally," grunted the captain. "However, she is on the list of suspects Mayhew and Jacobs have questioned in my wife's disappearance."

"Now I remember," said Freeman. "She's the one who hired the

P.I. and gave the guys such a hard time."

"One and the same. Mel told me she lawyered up on them. She's got that dick head Van Gordon representing her."

"Great." Freeman said. "Dealing with him is always fun."

"The one thing which might get us a warrant though is the fact she was seen waving a gun at Cassandra in the middle of a hotel lobby. Turns out she owns a Glock 23. From the bullet they found in the wall, Chatham's sure it came from a Glock. The injuries are consistent with this weapon, too."

"I guess I'll have my work cut out for me when I get back then," Freeman frowned. "Is it really bad in there?"

"I've seen worse," said the captain. "But Mandy hasn't. I'm very concerned about her. Alex was one of her best friends. This combined with Cassandra's disappearance..." He sighed, shaking his head again.

"Mandy seems like a very strong person, Captain Stevenson. I'm sure she'll be okay. If there is anything I can do to help..."

"Thanks, Freeman," Robert said abruptly. "If there is, I'll let you know."

Freeman blushed, then turned and walked down the hall towards Alex's apartment. As he entered, his partner came toward him. Barnes started spewing facts as soon as he was within hearing distance.

"We didn't find the weapon, but Mark found a bullet lodged in the wall," she said. "Looks like a .40 caliber and there's a mark on the bullet indicating a silencer was used. That would explain why the neighbors didn't hear anything. Dr. Patel says the bullet wound suggests it was fired from about two feet away. At that distance, the perpetrator would have considerable back spatter on his or her clothes."

"Her clothes," Freeman said. "The guard said the only visitor Alex had besides Mandy was a female. She was dressed in black so it would be unlikely people passing her in the hallway would have seen any blood spatter on her clothing."

Barnes shook her head. "That confirms the story Mandy told her father about hearing someone knocking at his door when she spoke to Phelps earlier this afternoon," she stated.

"Hopefully the fact Mandy didn't have a weapon nor any gunshot residue or blood on her will get our enthusiastic first responder off her case," she said nodding toward Officer Sanchez.

"Plus the guard said he'd been working since 3:00 and hadn't left his post. He only saw Mandy the one time this afternoon, just before 6:00."

"Mark's got Sanders dusting for prints," she said steering the conversation back to the crime scene.

"She was wearing gloves," said Freeman. "I doubt they'll find any prints."

"This killer's smart," said Barnes. "Let's hope she dropped a hair or something."

"Actually, we might be in luck there," Freeman replied. "The guard said her name was Savannah Richmond and if you recall, she's a suspect in the Stevenson case."

"You know it's not going to be *that* easy, don't you?" Barnes asked.

"Probably not, but I can hope, can't I?" Freeman asked with a goofy grin.

Barnes punched him in the arm. "They're done photographing the desk area. We should start there."

"We need to make sure they get the laptop over to Kodey Marshall," Freeman said pointing toward the desk in the corner. "It might have some sort of email or list of friends we can question. There also may be an address book or files in the desk."

As they approached the desk, Freeman slipped on a pair of vinyl gloves. He opened the drawers to search for anything which might be relevant, while Barnes unplugged and bagged the laptop. She also took the CDRs which were next to it. Freeman found a flash drive in one of the drawers giving it to Barnes to bag and tag.

"Maybe he put some of his secrets on these," commented Barnes as she bagged the flash drive. "Poor Mandy," she added. "The news media will have a field day with this. How can someone her age have so much tragedy in her life already?"

Freeman simply shook his head, shrugging his shoulders.

Chapter 22

Since Alex had died on a Friday evening, Freeman and Barnes were unable to obtain a search warrant for the Richmond home until Monday afternoon. That morning, they had spoken at length with Mayhew and Jacobs about the interview they'd conducted with Savannah Richmond.

As Captain Stevenson had predicted, Mrs. Richmond had brought her attorney with her to the interview, so they hadn't made any progress with her. They had checked out the alibi her attorney had provided. She claimed to have been home alone the afternoon Mrs. Stevenson disappeared and her children were home from school at 3:00. So far, she had checked out, but they theorized she could have hired someone to do it for her. They just had to prove it.

"I say we take our warrant and go over there," said Barnes. "There's nothing like the element of surprise to get people to talk."

"After listening to Jacobs and Mayhew, I'd have to agree," he said. "She's going to be a tough one to catch off balance."

They pulled into the driveway of the Richmond house with a patrol car and two officers behind them. It was a two-story brick home which was beautifully landscaped with Autumn Blaze maple trees whose leaves were just beginning to turn a lush dark red. There were neatly trimmed junipers along the sidewalk and pots of bright yellow mums on the porch. They rang the doorbell, but there was no answer so they decided to park across the street and wait. Freeman instructed the two patrol officers to park around the block and they'd call them as soon as Mrs. Richmond arrived.

They sat in their car for what seemed like hours before Mrs. Richmond's black SUV pulled into the driveway. Barnes quickly called for their backup team. Savannah Richmond was pulling groceries from the back of her vehicle when the detectives walked up behind her.

"Mrs. Richmond," said Barnes, causing Savannah Richmond to twirl around in surprise. Barnes and Freeman had their badges out, showing them to her. "This is Detective Freeman and my name is Detective Barnes. We are from the Indianapolis Homicide Department."

"Homicide?" she exclaimed. "What does that have to do with me? Did they find the Stevenson woman in a ditch somewhere?"

"No, ma'am," said Freeman.

"Look, I'm very busy and I don't want to talk to you without my lawyer present," she said as she headed for her front door.

"Did you know Alex Phelps, Mrs. Richmond? He's been murdered," shouted Barnes.

Savannah Richmond stopped and stood still. She dropped her bags of groceries and started to tremble. Barnes and Freeman looked at one another. She collapsed into hysterics going down on her knees. This would not have been a normal reaction for a suspect in a murder investigation.

"Mrs. Richmond, where are your keys?" asked Barnes, while Freeman helped Savannah to her feet.

Savannah didn't answer, she was sobbing so hard.

"Move her, Freeman, so I can look under those bags," Barnes suggested.

Barnes found the ring of keys and rushed to open the door. Then she and Freeman took Mrs. Richmond inside. Barnes directed her to a couch in the living room. Freeman went to find the kitchen to get some water. Savannah leaned to the side and lay down on the couch, crying as though her heart were breaking.

"Mrs. Richmond," Barnes said gently stroking Savannah's arm. "We're sorry, but it's been all over the news. We thought you knew."

Savannah sat up abruptly. "What happened? This can't be true. He can't be dead!"

"He was murdered Friday evening," Barnes said. "The person who did this used your name to gain access to his apartment. That's why he told the guard it was okay for her to enter."

"It wasn't me!" she shouted, just as Freeman entered the room holding a glass of water, two patrol officers at his side. "My husband came home early on Friday. We left at 3:00 in the afternoon. He wanted to take the kids to The Dells in Wisconsin. We were gone all weekend. I haven't seen the news or read the paper yet. I needed to get groceries."

"I'm sorry, Mrs. Richmond," said Barnes, "but I'm a little puzzled. Why are you so upset? Did you know Alex Phelps?"

"My husband is Bradley Phelps' lawyer," she said gulping back tears. "We socialize with the Phelps family quite often."

"And you were particularly fond of Alex?" asked Freeman.

"Oh, God," she said, rubbing her eyes. "I guess you'll find out eventually. I'm in love with Alex. I've been seeing him for a little over a year now. It started last summer when he was home from college."

"Do you think your husband could have found out about it?" asked Barnes.

"No, I think he was too busy banging Cassandra Stevenson to pay any attention to what I was doing."

"Speaking of Mrs. Stevenson," said Barnes. "We read the report Detectives Mayhew and Jacobs obtained from Nicolo Rossi. He claims to have seen you pull a gun on her."

"The gun I showed Cassandra wasn't even loaded. I just wanted to scare her and make her think I'd do it. It's never been fired, to my knowledge."

"I see," said Barnes. "If it was that simple, why didn't you just tell them about it?"

"My father is a very influential man in Indianapolis," she said wiping the tears from her cheeks. "He's the one who brought in Percy Van Gordon and insisted I let him do all of the talking. Daddy always makes things more complicated than they need be."

"We found a record which shows you own a Glock 23," said Freeman.

"I suppose that's what it is. I didn't really pay attention," said Savannah. "Why is this important?"

"We suspect the person who shot Alex used a Glock 23. Since his last known visitor before he was killed said she was you, we obtained a warrant to search your home for the gun," said Freeman. "It would go a long way for you to tell me where to find it."

"I keep it in my bedroom closet," she said. "Top of the stairs, turn left, last room on the right. It's in a blue box on the shelf of the closet."

Freeman excused himself taking one of the officers with him. Barnes took the water from the table and offered it to Savannah.

"Thank you, Detective Barnes. You're very kind."

Barnes nodded.

"Found it." Freeman announced, coming down the stairs with the Glock already securely sealed in an evidence bag. "We'll be taking this with us for testing. If it's not the weapon involved in the shooting, we'll return it."

"I understand," she said, looking away. "Actually, I hope I never see it again."

"Mrs. Richmond, would you like for us to retrieve your groceries for you?" asked Barnes.

"Oh my, I forgot about them," she said, tearing up again. "The ice cream will melt."

Freeman locked the Glock in a security box in the trunk of his car. Then he told the patrol officers they could leave. He and Barnes retrieved the groceries and brought them into the house.

Once they had placed all the grocery bags in the kitchen, Barnes addressed Savannah. "Are you going to be all right, Mrs. Richmond? Would you like for us to stay for a while, or is there someone we can call for you?"

"No, thank you," she said quietly. "I'll be fine." She walked to the front door and closed it behind them.

The two detectives sank into their respective seats in the car and stared at one another. Freeman broke eye contact and started the car.

"Can you freakin' believe this?" Barnes exclaimed. "Here we're thinking we're going to surprise her and we're the ones who get surprised."

"Guess Alex was into older women," commented Freeman.

"No way she whacked Alex. Of course, it doesn't get her off the hook for Stevenson," Barnes observed. "But maybe Mrs. Stevenson found out about their little fling and was blackmailing her. Would have been sweet revenge after Mrs. Richmond's little scare tactics."

He nodded and pulled out into traffic. "It'll be interesting to see if this is our murder weapon," said Freeman. "Guess we'd better get back to the office and write this up. Wished I'd had a video camera. You know Mayhew and Jacobs are never going to believe us."

Chapter 23

Twenty-four hours ago, Mandy's dad sat down with her to go over the facts in the Alex Phelps case. These were things the news media and Alex's family already knew, but he wanted to explain everything to her personally.

The autopsy confirmed the cause of death was one gunshot to the forehead which tore straight through his brain and out the back of his head. When he fell, he hit his head on the coffee table. The blunt force trauma from hitting the table caused massive bleeding in the brain. The forensic pathologist estimated he'd only lived for fifteen minutes or so after sustaining these injuries.

The forensics team had found no trace evidence on Alex's body or in his apartment that would identify his killer. The only thing the police had to go on was the bullet taken from the wall and the incomplete description of the alleged assailant given by the guard.

Ballistics had confirmed the bullet was a .40 caliber fired from a Glock 23. However, tests on the Glock belonging to Savannah Richmond found it was not the weapon used.

The coroner's office released Alex's body to his family four days after his death. The funeral would take place at 11:00 this morning.

Stunned and heartbroken, Mandy was frustrated by the haunting questions that kept creeping into her mind. Why would someone want to kill Alex? Was he into something illegal and been afraid to tell her? He hated drugs, legal and illegal. He didn't drink alcohol very often, and he wasn't a gambler. She desperately wished he had confided in her about his situation. Maybe she could have helped him. Prevented his death.

Mandy was really dreading the funeral. She hadn't spoken to Alex's father since the day Alex was shot, and she wasn't looking forward to answering a lot of questions. There wasn't any information she could provide he hadn't already heard from the police. Still, Mr. Phelps had always been very kind to her, so she felt obligated to be there to support him. And how could she not pay her respects to Alex? She already missed him so much. She couldn't imagine life without him.

She was disappointed Aunt Karen couldn't get away from work to go to the funeral with her. She'd always found comfort in Karen's arms. But her father had agreed to go and sit with her during the services. She suspected more to help Freeman and Barnes keep an eye on the crowd than to support her. Still, she was glad she wouldn't be alone.

She and her father took their seats in the sixth row. She was so overwhelmed with grief she didn't even realize when she began to cry. She felt her father clumsily put an arm around her shoulders.

The music began to swell and the service began. It was a beautiful service. Mandy noticed many of Alex's favorite songs were played. The chapel was full to capacity. Everyone who knew Alex loved him. At the end, friends and family filed past the casket to pay their last respects--one more final goodbye before he was gone forever.

He looked so peaceful in his mahogany casket as if he were just sleeping. The mortician had done a remarkable job of covering the place in his forehead where the bullet had gone through. Tears flowed freely as Mandy saw the blue suit he wore. The color would have made his eyes sparkle. She kissed the tips of her fingers and placed them on his cheek realizing this would be the last time she'd ever see his face or touch him. It wasn't fair. He had so much to live for. Why, Alex, why you?

She tried to compose herself but she couldn't stop staring at him. Hoping, waiting for his eyes to open. This was all a bad dream. But she knew deep inside this was reality and her best friend was gone from her forever.

Her dad gently pulled her from the casket. Like someone in a trance, she allowed him to lead her away. She hadn't realized she'd lingered there so long.

She and her father went to the parking lot waiting to start the long, slow journey to the cemetery. The tears came freely and she let them flow. Her father didn't say a word, just placed a hand over hers.

After the burial service, Mr. Phelps found Mandy and Robert. "Mandy, I hope you and your father can come by the house. I have something special I want you to have."

"I wish I could, but I have to return to work," said her dad. "But it doesn't mean Mandy can't come."

"Of course I'll be there," said Mandy. "I want to make sure Lana is okay. She loved Alex so much."

"I'll see you there then," said Mr. Phelps.

Once he was out of sight, Mandy turned to her father. "Dad, can't you take the rest of the day off? This would be so much easier for me if you came along."

"I'm sorry, Mandy, I can't," he said. Although she could see the sincerity in his eyes, his refusal stung her. "Barnes and Freeman are waiting for me. I'll see you for dinner tonight."

"Okay, Dad," she said.

As she watched him walk away, she couldn't help but miss her mom. "I bet mom would have found a way to take a day off," she mumbled to herself. Tears trickled down her cheeks, not for Alex this time, but for the yearning to know her mother's whereabouts. Was she dead or alive? Did she have enough to eat? Was someone abusing her?

Wiping her face and regaining her composure, she drove to the Phelps' home. It took a few minutes for Mandy to find a parking place on their street, but she finally found one about a block from the house. Despite the sad occasion, it was a beautiful, sunny, and unseasonably warm late September day, so she didn't mind the walk.

As she walked toward the house, Mandy looked up just as the breeze caught a cluster of leaves pulling them from their branch and carrying them off into the neighbor's yard. Thinking of the leaf bouquets she and Charlie used to make for their mom, she didn't see the woman in the navy pantsuit approaching her.

"Miss Stevenson," the woman said, making Mandy jump in surprise. "Miss Stevenson, may I ask you a few questions?" It was Andrea Atkins, the newswoman who had harassed her at the police station.

Mandy had been reclusive since Alex's death. Her father and Brent had been keeping an eye out for reporters. The media hounds knew she'd found Alex's body. Again, they were playing up the angle of the losses she'd suffered…brother, mother, and now a dear friend.

"No comment," Mandy said stiffly.

"Oh, but surely you want the world to know your side of what happened, Miss Stevenson."

Mandy turned abruptly, staring into Andrea Atkins' dark brown eyes. "Look! I just came from my best friend's funeral. Focus on trying to help the police find who did this instead of harassing me on a daily basis. Okay?"

Seeing the Phelps' red brick ranch just ahead, she ran as fast as she could. Luckily, Alex's childhood friend, Jay, had seen who was chasing her and ran interference. She heard Jay shouting, "Have a little respect people! Let us grieve in peace!"

Panting, Mandy entered the house. She immediately recognized several people she knew to be Alex's aunts, uncles and cousins. Then she spotted Alex's sister, Lana. She looked lost. Mandy knew just how devastated Lana was feeling. She too had lost a brother tragically. Then she was horrified to realize like Charlie, Alex had died from a gunshot wound to the face. Shaking her head to rid it of the similarity, she went to Lana and hugged the girl. Lana held her as though her life depended on it.

"I can't believe he's gone," she said, releasing Mandy from her grip.

"I know, sweetie, but Alex would want us to be strong." She tried to smile, but it came out more of a half-smile instead. How could she tell this child to be strong when she felt so weak? "Your dad wanted to see me when I got here. Do you know where he is?"

"I think he's in the den," said Lana. "Don't leave without saying goodbye, okay."

"Of course." Mandy turned from Lana and noticed Gloria playing the perfect host. Mandy wondered if she actually cared about what had happened to Alex, because she hadn't seen her shed a tear all day. Wouldn't want to ruin your makeup would you, Gloria? The thought of Alex's last blow up with his father crossed her mind. She wondered how this was weighing on Mr. Phelps' conscience.

Mr. Phelps came out of the den catching sight of her. "Mandy, I'm so glad you're here." He hugged her then burst into tears. She let him hold her, patting his back until he regained his self-control. As he let go and took a step back, he asked her to come into the den. He offered her a seat in a large overstuffed brown leather chair. Then he pulled out a desk drawer and retrieved a small black box.

"Mandy, you are the best thing that ever happened to Alex," he said grinning at her. "I confess I was hoping you might be my daughter-in-law some day, but I understood about the friendship. How horrendous it had to be for you to find him."

"Yes, it was awful," she whispered. "I'm so sorry this has happened to your family. If Lana ever needs someone to talk to, I'll be glad to help. I know what it's like to lose a brother at such a young age."

"Yes, you do understand, don't you? It's very sweet of you to volunteer to help my daughter," he said with a weak smile that couldn't mask the sadness in his voice. "Mandy, this is something I wanted to give to Alex one day. You know, when he finally decided to settle down." He offered the little black box to Mandy. She opened it to find a beautiful gold necklace with a sparkling teardrop diamond pendant. "I gave this necklace to Alex's mother when he was born. When she died, it was to be passed along to him. But now that he's gone I want to give it to someone who was special to him."

"Oh, Mr. Phelps, I couldn't," she protested. "What about Lana?"

"Victoria wasn't Lana's mother. I meant for this to go to someone who was special to Alex. I've decided it should go to you."

Tears welled up in Mandy's eyes. "This is so unexpected. It's beautiful. Thank you so much."

"You are welcome, my dear," he said. "My only regret is that Alex and I were still at odds when he died."

"He told me you'd had an argument when he met you in Cassopolis," Mandy ventured.

"The last time Alex and I were at the summer home was in June, and we didn't argue," said Mr. Phelps.

Mandy blinked in surprise. She wondered if she'd heard him correctly. "June? I thought Alex joined you in Michigan in early August."

"What are you talking about, Mandy?" Mr. Phelps asked, sounding defensive. "Alex and I haven't been fishing since June. Business has been crazy this summer, so I haven't been able to get away. He has his own set of keys. Maybe he wanted to get away one last time before school commenced but I didn't go with him."

"I guess I misunderstood," she said. She knew she hadn't, but she wasn't going to worry Alex's grieving father with this. However, she definitely wanted to know why Alex would tell her he had gone to Michigan with his father if he had not done so. Worse yet, why would he tell her he'd had a horrible argument with his father if it never happened? They certainly weren't getting along a few weeks ago when she came here for that fateful cookout. Besides, Mr. Phelps had just admitted they were still at odds when Alex died.

"As I recall," Mr. Phelps added, "that was during the time Gloria and Lana were visiting her folks in Toledo. It was the last chance for Lana to see her grandparents before school started." Mr. Phelps looked at the door and sighed. "I should probably get back out there."

Mandy rose from her chair, following Mr. Phelps out into the crowd of mourners. She thanked him again for the generous gift stowing it in her purse. Before she could walk away, Gloria suddenly appeared with a very handsome couple in tow.

"Bradley, I thought you'd run off," said Gloria glaring at Mandy. "Look who's here to pay their respects."

"Thank you for coming," said Bradley taking Mandy by the arm. "Mandy, I would like to introduce you to Jonathan and Savannah Richmond. Jonathan is my attorney and…."

"And I hope you count me amongst your friends as well," Jonathan interrupted.

"Of course I do," said Bradley.

"I think I'll go see about Lana," said Mandy looking at Mrs. Richmond's red-rimmed eyes. She wondered why the wife of Mr. Phelps' lawyer would be so upset over Alex's death. "It was very nice meeting you both."

She walked through the living room speaking briefly with other mourners, asking if they'd seen Lana. No one seemed to know where she might be. Going back to her own experience, she went to the stairway and found Lana sitting there alone.

"Hi, there," Mandy said, plopping down beside Lana on the step. "How are you doing?"

Lana didn't say a word. She looked into Mandy's eyes, burst into tears and flung her arms around Mandy as she sobbed. Mandy pulled Lana onto her lap and held her, rocking back and forth while she cried. She rubbed Lana's back as silent tears rolled down her own cheeks. They sat there together for a very long time, lost in one another's grief.

"Mandy," Lana croaked.

"Yes, Lana."

"Is Alex in heaven with your brother?"

"Yes. I believe he is," Mandy lied, since she wasn't so sure about it any longer. However, she wasn't going to let Alex's alleged sins cause his sister more pain.

Lana looked exhausted. "Mandy, I'm really tired. Do you think Mom and Dad would be mad if I went to my room now?"

"There are so many people here, I doubt they would notice," Mandy answered. "You should get some rest. It's been a very long day."

Mandy watched as Lana ascended the stairs. At the top, Lana turned and smiled at her one more time before heading for her bedroom. Then Mandy joined the other guests, letting one of Lana's aunts know she'd gone to her room to rest. She felt she'd been there a respectful amount of time, but was afraid the reporter was still outside. It would have been so much better had her father accompanied her.

"Hey there, Mandy," came the welcome voice of Jay Sumner. "Need an escort to your car?"

"Thank you for keeping the beast at bay earlier," she said.

"My pleasure," he quipped. "I've got to leave, too. I told those cops at the funeral I'd come down after I left here to talk to them about Alex. They seemed okay."

Stepping out into the afternoon sun, they walked close to one another down the pathway leading away from the house and to the street. "Yeah, the detectives are cool. Just tell them everything you know," said Mandy. "Jay? Do you know of anything Alex was doing could have contributed to his murder?"

"What do you mean?"

"Well, I know he and his dad weren't getting along," she said.

"Yeah, I thought it was kind of weird," said Jay, rubbing his chin. "They always got along so well. Did everything together."

"Alex told me he went up to the summer house to meet his dad in early August, but his dad just told me he had to work and wasn't up there. I don't understand why Alex would lie to me."

"I don't know Mandy. He told me the same thing," said Jay looking puzzled. "You ready to get out of here?"

"Sure," she said.

Mandy wondered if Alex was watching her right now. Did he know what she was thinking? Did he know how angry she was with him at this very moment? Angry because he left her questioning her ability to judge who she could trust. Angry because he lied to her and betrayed her. How would she be able to forgive him for this? She needed to know what he had been doing that got him killed. Did he know someone was going to kill him?

"Yo, Mandy. Scum bag at 3:00," said Jay pointing at Jack Flack. "Let's go around these trees and hope the wicked witch who was bothering you earlier isn't hiding behind one of them."

They managed to make it to her car without running into any reporters. If they hadn't just come from a grieving household it might have been a fun adventure trying to dodge the reporters.

"Thanks, Jay. You're my hero."

"Any time," he said. "Mandy, did Alex ever mention Whitney to you?"

"I think I remember the name," she said, furrowing her brow in deep concentration. "Now that you mention it, I do. But it was a long time ago, probably when we first met. Old girlfriend or something. Do you think she had something to do with this?"

"Nah. She was there today."

"Oh. I never met her, so I don't even know what she looks like."

"I knew her back in high school. She had a bad temper, but I can't imagine her hurting Alex."

"Then why did you even mention it?"

"I heard the chick who showed up at his place was a blonde, that's all," he said. "Ah, shit!" he said, grabbing the car door handle. "It's the Crapton dude from News 8."

"You mean Cramden," she laughed. Man it felt good to laugh.

"Whatever!" he exclaimed. "Better get out of here before he gets any closer."

She got into her car then rolled down her window. "You're a wonderful friend, Jay Sumner."

"Thanks," he said, smiling. "Now get outta here!"

She looked in her rear view mirror, and could hear Jack Flack and a few others running towards them, shouting her name. She took one more look at Jay as he started running towards his own car before she sped away.

Chapter 24

As soon as they had arrived in the office after the Phelps burial, Captain Stevenson asked Detectives Freeman and Barnes to meet him in the conference room to go over their observations. The room was set up with a white board, corkboard with photos of the crime scene and all of the lab and coroner reports.

"This case is a real pain in the ass," the captain complained. "No good prints, no DNA, no murder weapon, no reliable description. Did either of you at least see anything of interest at the chapel or the cemetery today?"

"I didn't see anyone who shouldn't have been there," Barnes reported. "It was mostly family and close friends. There weren't very many blondes attending and only three matching the guard's description. There was a girl who looked to be Alex's age, a Whitney Benson, who was a blonde, Caucasian and about five seven. Very stoic kept staring at the casket. Reminded me of a zombie."

"Seen many zombies lately, Barnes?" Freeman smirked.

Barnes frowned at him. "Benson's a suspect in the Stevenson case. From what I understand, Whitney was angry with her for being a home wrecker." She looked up realizing what she'd just said. "Sorry, Captain. I didn't mean to be insensitive."

"Don't worry about it," he said. "Let's move on."

"Savannah Richmond was there. She's in her early thirties, a very classy dresser," said Freeman. "We interviewed her the Monday after Alex's death. She confessed to having an affair with him and voluntarily gave us the Glock for testing. Turns out it wasn't the weapon used to kill Alex."

"Last but not least, Mrs. Gloria Phelps," Barnes stated. "Of course, I doubt she had anything to do with it."

"Barnes!" Captain Stevenson barked startling her. "We never assume anyone is beyond reproach. Check out her alibi!"

"Yes, sir," Barnes said, cheeks turning red. "The one thing I did notice about Mrs. Phelps — she didn't shed a tear. Even if she didn't like her step-son, you'd think her own daughter's tears would have conjured up some emotion from her."

"I noticed, too," said Freeman. "Maybe we'd *better* keep a close eye on step-mommy dearest."

Barnes gave Freeman a dirty look. "I took some photos at the cemetery. Jackie is processing the photo card as we speak," she concluded.

Detective Freeman looked at the crime scene photos shaking his head. "I can't believe the killer left the place so clean. I know she was only there for a few minutes, but it just seems like we should have found something."

"We interviewed some of the family members last week," Barnes went on. "You'd think this guy was a saint. No drugs, very little drinking, helped little old ladies cross the street — just your average all-American Boy Scout."

"Mandy couldn't think of anyone who would want to hurt Alex," the captain finally said. "She said basically the same things about him." He paused appearing deep in thought. He finally turned to his detectives.

"Jay Sumner will be here in about an hour," stated the captain. "According to Mandy, Jay and Alex have been friends since grade school. This is the first summer they've spent much time together because they had attended different colleges."

He pulled a report from his stack and passed it over to Freeman. "Tomorrow morning I want both of you to go talk to Alex's neighbors again. Find out if anyone saw Alex with a blonde at any time since he moved in. They may not have seen her the day of the murder, but she might have been there before. After you're done, go to the campus. Get his school schedule and names of his professors. Find out if he had any problems with anyone there."

"You got it, Captain," said Freeman.

"Oh, and set up appointments with the three blondes from the funeral," ordered the captain. "Find out how the Benson girl knew Alex and if she was close to him. I'm sure you get my meaning."

"Yes, sir," Barnes and Freeman said in unison.

Approximately an hour after their meeting with Captain Stevenson, Barnes and Freeman were in an interrogation room with Jay Sumner.

"Nice to see you again, Detective Freeman," said Jay extending his hand.

Freeman introduced him to his partner then began the interview. "Mr. Sumner, as I understand it, you have known Alex Phelps since the two of you started grade school. How would you describe Alex?"

"Wow, this is weird. No one's ever called me Mr. Sumner before," said Jay, apparently nervous. "Oh, yeah. Uh, I met Alex in first grade. He was pretty happy then. He got along with everybody, until just before Christmas when his mom died suddenly. He changed a lot after that. It had to be pretty hard losing your mom when you're only six. He got pretty depressed."

"I see," said Freeman writing in his notepad.

"I always liked Alex, because he was a good friend. He never made fun of me for wearing glasses like the other kids did. He used to tell me his mom wore glasses and she was the most beautiful woman in the world."

"So you said Alex had been depressed over the loss. Did he seem to get better after his dad remarried?" asked Barnes.

"No, not really," Jay said, a vivid sadness in his eyes. "The dude got worse. He was real pissed after Mr. Phelps married Gloria. He got into a lot of fights. Everybody, except me of course, teased him about his young step-mom. Just like my glasses, kids always seem to find something to torment other kids about. Alex didn't take any crap off of anybody though."

Jay paused a moment, then sighed. "Alex and I were a pair of loners for the most part. We had each other's backs, like you two do."

Barnes smiled. "He seemed pretty together for a kid who had such a hard childhood."

"After his dad insisted Alex go to counseling, he seemed to get better. By the time he started high school, he was more interested in his studies and started making A's and B's. He loved history and had decided he wanted to be a high school history teacher. He got accepted to Indiana University and I got accepted to Northern

Illinois University. We didn't see much of one another until this summer."

"Did he talk to you about any other friends, especially girlfriends?" asked Barnes.

"He dated a girl in high school for a while. Her name's Whitney Benson."

The detectives exchanged knowing looks.

"Seemed like they were pretty tight for a while, but her dad didn't approve," added Jay.

"Really?" Barnes replied. "Why was that?"

"Her dad didn't think she and Alex were in the same *social class*," Jay sneered. "Sure we all lived in Carmel and went to Carmel High School, but not everyone there is rich."

"But Mr. Phelps has a very successful business, a nice home, plus his summer home in Michigan," said Barnes.

"Yeah, but his business is in construction. Just because he owns his own business doesn't mean snooty people like the Bensons will accept him as an equal."

"What does Mr. Benson do?" asked Freeman.

"He's in real estate," Jay said. "I'm surprised you didn't know. Mandy's mom worked for him."

"So she's the daughter of Paul Benson?" asked Freeman.

"Yes, sir."

"To your knowledge, have Alex and Whitney kept in touch?" asked Barnes.

"Not while he was in school. When he went to IU, the only woman he talked about in his emails was Mandy, and the occasional female prof. They never had any romantic chemistry. He was just thrilled to have another friend who understood him and accepted him the way he was. I don't remember him ever saying anything about Whitney."

"So you don't think he and Whitney got together again?" Freeman asked.

"I didn't' say that," he said. "I saw him at the mall back in July and he was walking with Whitney. They were walking arm-in-arm, laughing."

"And you didn't suspect they might be involved again?" asked Barnes.

"At first, but I asked Alex about it and he said he'd just run into her there. He said they were just catching up and joking around. You know, like old friends do."

"So what was he like this summer?" Freeman inquired. "Was he dating anyone to your knowledge?"

Jay shrugged. "I remember asking him if he was seeing anyone. He laughed and told me he doesn't kiss and tell. I teased and prodded him trying to get him to tell me. In the beginning, he wouldn't budge. Then I guess he needed somebody he could trust to talk to about it. He told me he had to be discreet because he was seeing a married woman. Sounded like she might be older than him."

"So, he didn't give you a name?" asked Barnes.

"I think he would have eventually. He just didn't want it getting out. Not sure I really wanted to know," Jay confessed.

"Did anything else happen this summer which seemed odd?" Barnes inquired.

"In August, he told me he stayed with his lady friend at Lake Shafer for a few days. When she had to go home, he decided to join his dad in Michigan for the weekend to get in a little fishing. When he returned he was all moody, said he and his dad had a big fight. I'd known him long enough to know not to ask because he'd tell me about it eventually."

"Did he?" Freeman asked.

"No," Jay said shaking his head. "He got sort of withdrawn. Even seemed miffed with Mandy the night we saw the two of you at Tijuana Flats. You know, the night before he…got shot."

"Did Alex confide any details about their argument," asked Freeman.

"No. As a matter of fact, I just left the Phelps' house and spoke to Mandy before I came," recalled Jay. "She said she'd talked to Mr. Phelps and he wasn't up at the summer house in August, so there couldn't have been an argument. She's really upset thinking Alex lied to her. I'm not too happy about it myself."

"Can you think of anyone who might want to harm Alex?" asked Freeman.

"No, Detectives," Jay said shaking his head. "Alex was squeaky clean as far as I knew. I can't think of anyone he had any problems with. I definitely didn't know anyone who might want him dead. Of course, if the killer had been a dude, you could check out the girlfriend's husband."

"Thanks, Mr. Sumner. You're free to go," Barnes said as she stood up. She showed Jay to the elevator then returned to the interrogation room.

"Well, what do you think?" she asked.

Freeman ran his fingers through his hair, sighing heavily. "Sounds like Alex was keeping secrets. But why the hell would he keep this relationship a secret from Mandy?"

Chapter 25

The following morning Freeman and Barnes prepared to interview Whitney Benson regarding her relationship with Alex Phelps. Since Mayhew and Jacobs had interviewed Miss Benson in the Stevenson case, Barnes and Freeman met with them to discuss their insights into Miss Benson's temperament.

"The woman has a flamin' hot temper," Mayhew began. "She blew up durin' our interview with her."

"She admits she assaulted Mrs. Stevenson in Chicago when she caught her with Daddy," said Jacobs. "She tried to come across as sweet, but there was a definite undertone of hatred there."

"So do you think she could be involved in what happened to Mrs. Stevenson?" Barnes asked.

"She's definitely got motive," Jacobs answered. "Her alibi sucks, but without evidence that links her to the car, we're stuck with a theory."

"Do you think she could lose it enough to kill someone?" asked Freeman.

"Damn straight she could!" exclaimed Mayhew. "I thought she was goin' to come across the table and kick my ass when I asked her about her alibi. I just wanted to know what proof she had of her whereabouts when the captain's wife vanished."

"She was scary," Jacobs admitted. "She definitely fits the description of your mystery woman."

"We saw her at the funeral," said Barnes. "Jay Sumner said she dated Alex for a while in high school but her daddy didn't approve. Sumner also implied Alex was seeing an older woman. Maybe Whitney found out and killed him out of jealousy. If she did do something to Stevenson, I doubt she'd hesitate to off Phelps."

"Guess we'll find out soon enough," said Freeman.

"Good luck, man," said Mayhew. "Better you than me."

An hour later, they were looking at Whitney Benson from the observation room. "Damn, she is a looker," admitted Freeman. "You take this one Barnes. She won't mess with you."

"Sure, chicken shit," she said with a grin.

Barnes entered the interrogation room and introduced herself to the suspect. She got straight to the point.

"Miss Benson, we understand you've known Alex Phelps since high school."

"That's right."

"Were you involved with him again?"

"I don't know what you mean," said Whitney curling her lip.

"What I mean is, did you and Alex Phelps take up where you left off in high school?"

"I haven't seen Alex in years. My dad didn't like him."

"What if I were to tell you we have a witness who saw you and Alex together arm-in-arm this past July?"

"I'd say he's lying," Whitney said without looking Barnes in the eye.

"Funny. I didn't say the informant was a male." Barnes paused. "Why do you think someone would lie to us about seeing you and Alex together?"

"I don't know! You're the detective!" Whitney shouted, confirming Jacobs and Mayhew were correct about her quick, volatile temper.

Barnes fixed her gaze upon Whitney. "Look, Miss Benson. This is a very serious matter. Stop playing games with me!"

Whitney stared back at Barnes in a defiant manner.

"Okay, if you want to play it like this, I'll be glad to put you in a holding cell until your attitude becomes more cooperative."

Barnes rose from her chair and was about to grab the doorknob when Whitney cleared her throat. "Okay! I ran into Alex in the mall this summer. We hadn't seen each other since high school and were catching up. That's it — just old friends."

"That wasn't so hard now, was it? If you're *just* an *old friend* then why lie to me?"

"I don't want my dad to know. I'm sure he still wouldn't

approve."

"Unfortunately, now you and I have a problem. You've lied to me. How am I supposed to determine when you're telling me the truth?" asked Barnes.

"It's the truth! I swear!"

"We have a description of the woman who murdered Alex Phelps. Want to hear it?" Whitney did not respond, just crossed her arms over her chest, and sat back in her chair scowling at Barnes.

"She's Caucasian; approximately five feet, seven inches tall; slim, with blonde hair. You're white, blonde and slim. How tall are you, Miss Benson?"

"Five-seven. So what! There must be millions of women who fit that description!"

"Well, not all of them had a relationship with Alex Phelps. You can see why we might wonder about you. Where were you the day Alex Phelps was murdered?"

"I'm not answering any more of your fucking questions!" Whitney shouted as she slammed her hand on the table. "Are you going to charge me with something? If you are, then I want my damned lawyer."

"No, Miss Benson, I won't be arresting you — today," Barnes answered. "But I will tell you that you are a suspect in this investigation and in the Cassandra Stevenson case. You do remember your interview with Detective Jacobs and Detective Mayhew, don't you? You didn't give them a good alibi either."

"This is outrageous! Wait till my father hears about this!"

"Number one, little girl, your daddy is in no position to go around pissing off the cops since he's also a suspect in the Stevenson case. Number two, if you don't stop your fucking lying and smart ass attitude, *nobody* is going to be able to keep your ass out of jail! Now, get out of here before I change my mind about a holding cell."

Whitney jumped up so fast she knocked over her chair. Barnes held the door for her as she stomped out of the room like a spoiled child.

Freeman joined Barnes in the interrogation room finding her pacing. "Jacobs and Mayhew weren't kidding. What a bitch!" he said.

"I'm just glad you were on the other side of the glass so you could run in here and stop me from strangling her."

"Me!" he teased. "I figured on calling Mayhew down here. He's bigger than I am."

"Fuck off," she said as she left the room.

"I love you, too!" he shouted after her.

"Who you talking to?" asked Mandy watching Brent whip around surprised. "Am I to understand I have some competition?"

"I was talking to Barnes, or actually, annoying her," he said, rosy cheeked.

"I see," she responded. "Looks like you've ticked off more than one woman today. I was nearly run over by a pretty blonde as I got off of the elevator."

"Actually, it was Barnes who put Whitney Benson in a foul mood," he said. "She's the daughter of Paul Benson, your mother's boss. It seems she's the ex-high school sweetheart of Alex Phelps."

"So that's the Whitney Alex told me about. Interesting," she said looking toward the elevator. Whitney wasn't the type of girl she'd envisioned Alex dating.

"If you find hurricanes interesting," he commented. "If they haven't named one after her they should."

"Maybe I should talk to her."

"Please don't," he pleaded. "Your father would have my head for even telling you we spoke with her. I can't discuss Alex's case with you."

"All right, I understand," she declared, unhappy that no one trusted her to help. "Are we still on for tomorrow night?"

"Of course. Joe's Crab Shack sound good?"

"Sure," she replied coldly.

"Mandy, please don't be upset with me," he pleaded. "It's not because I don't want to tell you. I can't. It's regulations."

"Okay, Brent! I get it!" her patience running thin. "I'll see you tomorrow night at 6:00."

She turned and walked toward the elevators. She could feel his eyes on her as the guilt of taking her frustrations out on him surfaced. Before she even pushed the elevator button, Mandy had decided she'd make it up to Brent tomorrow, after she had her talk with Savannah Richmond.

Chapter 26

Leaving the house at around 10:00 Saturday morning, Mandy drove to a strip mall where her long-time friend, Marie, worked. Mandy needed to escape the reporters who had become more persistent since Alex died. She had arranged with Marie to come into the boutique as though she were shopping.

She could see a familiar car pulling into the parking lot right after her. The reporters were getting sneakier. Mandy got out of her car and walked quickly to the door. The bell tinkled and Marie was out from behind the counter in a flash.

"Mandy, you're late," said Marie, frowning. "I thought you said you'd be here when I opened at ten."

"I thought I said I'd leave the house at ten," Mandy said. "I guess it was just a misunderstanding, but I'm here now."

"I didn't mean to be ugly," said Marie, lips curling into a smile. "I worry about you. Having someone following you all the time — it's worse than having your cell phone distract you while you're driving. And how do you know which one's a reporter and who's a nut?"

"Okay, okay, Marie," she said, placing her hands on Marie's shoulders. "Let's get some clothes off the rack and put our plan in motion."

Marie took her to the back of the store with a few clothes to try on. "Here take my jacket and here's a hat," she said, helping Mandy pull her hair up, stuffing it under the hat. Marie gave Mandy a hug and the keys to her car.

"Follow me," said Marie. She took Mandy to a back door leading to a lot where employees always parked. Mandy simply slipped out and drove Marie's car the long way out at the opposite end of the mall.

She wanted to see Savannah Richmond without any reporters finding out. Of course, she kept checking her mirrors to make sure she wasn't being tailed. After driving through a couple of neighborhoods and stopping for coffee, she felt confident she'd gotten away.

Savannah Richmond and her family lived in a beautiful two-story brick home in the Kingsborough neighborhood in Carmel. When Mandy pulled up across the street from the house trying to muster the courage to pull into the driveway, she saw a young boy and girl climbing into the back seat of a black SUV. She saw Savannah and Jonathan Richmond walk out to the vehicle. He tried to kiss her, but she turned so he caught her cheek. He got in and drove off with the two children.

Mandy quickly realized the timing couldn't have been better. She would be able to speak with Savannah alone. Hopefully she wouldn't hold back answering Mandy's questions. She pulled into the driveway and found herself ringing the doorbell within seconds. She didn't want to give herself a chance to change her mind.

When Savannah Richmond answered the door, she didn't seem quite as together as when Mandy first met her. She was wearing an expensive sweat suit, her makeup slightly smudged and her hair disheveled.

"What can I do for you, Mandy?" she asked.

"Mrs. Richmond, I'd like to talk to you. May I come in?" Mandy asked.

"Oh. Yes. How rude of me," she said stepping aside.

Mandy entered a beautiful white foyer with a ceiling which reached up to the second floor. A sparkling crystal chandelier hung over a rich brown antique oak table with a huge bouquet of fresh white flowers in a cobalt blue vase.

Mandy noticed Savannah was just going through the motions. Her heart wasn't into anything right now.

"Mrs. Richmond…"

"Please, call me Savannah," she requested. "Being called Mrs. Richmond makes me feel ancient." She led Mandy to the living room, which was almost as big as Mandy's whole house. "May I offer you something to drink?"

"No, thank you," she answered feeling intrusive. "If you don't mind me saying, I noticed you seemed very upset the day of Alex's funeral. I'm sorry, but I was Alex's best friend and I don't remember him mentioning you."

"He wouldn't have, he was far too discreet," she said motioning for Mandy to take a seat on the couch. "But he certainly had a lot to say about you."

"Like I said, we've been...I mean we were the best of friends," Mandy repeated, trying not to lose control of her emotions. Breaking down would cause her to lose focus. She had to find out what kind of relationship Alex had with Savannah *and* what had gone on between her mom and Savannah's husband.

"Savannah," Mandy began again. "I'm not going to play games; I'm going to ask you straight. Were you and Alex lovers?"

"My, you are blunt," she said looking pleasantly surprised. "Alex always said you'd be a great social worker, because you wouldn't take any nonsense from anyone."

"So, were you lovers?" Mandy persisted. She was sure she knew the answer, but wanted to hear it from Savannah.

Savannah looked down at her hands which she had clenched tightly together. To Mandy's surprise, Savannah began to rock in her seat, face screwing up trying to hold back tears. Then the dam broke. Tears came running down Savannah's cheeks and she quickly covered her face with her hands and began to sob, obviously devastated by Alex's death. Alex had been involved with a married woman and had never trusted Mandy with his secret. She didn't know whether to be angry or sympathetic with this woman.

"Savannah," Mandy said gently. "Savannah, if you'd prefer, I can go. I can see this is very painful for you."

"No, Mandy," she said pulling a tissue from her pocket. "I already told all of this to those homicide detectives, so I'm surprised you don't already know."

Mandy's heart felt like it leapt to her throat. When were they going to bother to fill her in on this? She was sure her father knew, but wasn't surprised he'd kept silent. However, she was very disappointed Brent hadn't confided in her.

"I do want to tell you everything," said Savannah. "I think you of all people have a right to know. I want the police to find the person who did this. I want whoever shot Alex to pay!"

Mandy observed Savannah's sudden shift from vulnerable to angry. Vengeance was apparent in her eyes. Maybe they were more than lovers. Maybe Savannah Richmond had actually fallen in love with Alex.

"Alex was a wonderful person. He listened and empathized." Savannah paused to take a few deep breaths, looking at her hands as they twisted her tissue.

"It started last summer. Jonathan and I were at a cookout at the Phelps' house in early June. Gloria and I were sitting by the pool talking while the children swam. I glanced over to where Bradley was cooking and noticed Alex come out through the patio doors. I'd never quite noticed him in that manner before. He was bare-chested and buff; a young man had replaced the child. I made some silly comment about him. Gloria started admonishing me for lusting after a child, like she's never had an indecent thought about a younger man before."

Mandy knew precisely what she meant. Alex had made several comments about Gloria's flirtatious behavior.

"So, when exactly did the affair start?"

"July. As you may remember, Alex had taken a summer job with a landscaper his father knew. It just so happened we use that particular landscaper. I specifically asked for Alex to do our yard work."

Savannah rose. "Would you mind if we continue our conversation in the kitchen? I need to get something to drink."

Mandy followed her to a pristine kitchen. The walls were white with maple cabinets and brushed stainless appliances. The island in the center of the room contained a second smaller stainless steel sink and plenty of space to prepare food. There was a breakfast bar along the opposite side with six maple stools upholstered with tan leather, where Mandy sat watching Savannah.

"Are you sure I can't get you something? I have Perrier, bottled spring water, juice or I could make some coffee."

"Spring water would be great," Mandy responded, fearing a second refusal might offend her hostess.

"Now then, where was I?" Savannah appeared deep in thought as she handed one of the bottles to Mandy and stood on the opposite side of the island. Savannah took two long swigs of water before returning to the conversation.

"I flirted with him off and on through June. Many times I would offer him some refreshment — water, Gatorade, tea." She took another sip of her water.

"Then the children went to summer camp the last two weeks of July. By that time, my disgust for my husband had hit a peak. He had been seeing another woman for about three years at that point."

"I don't know if the detectives told you this, but Jonathan's mistress was your mother."

"Actually, I suspected it," said Mandy. "Her phone records showed a lot of calls to him."

"I had Jonathan followed by a private investigator. He gave me the proof I needed to confront my husband. Jonathan promised he'd stop seeing her. However, I discovered he was meeting her at a hotel. I told him not to go, and I went instead."

Savannah paused again, pacing back and forth the length of the island. Then she stopped, looking straight into Mandy's eyes. "The reason I'm a suspect in your mother's disappearance is because I pulled a gun on her in the hotel that day. It wasn't loaded, of course. I didn't want to kill her, just scare her into leaving my husband alone."

Mouth agape, Mandy shook her head in disbelief. No one had mentioned Savannah Richmond was a suspect. What else were they hiding from her?

"At any rate," Savannah continued. "I was angry with Jonathan and very attracted to Alex. So, one day while the children were away and Jonathan was at work, I seduced Alex. At first, he was upset with himself. He thought he was breaking up a happy home. Although I didn't tell Alex with whom, I did tell him about Jonathan's infidelity."

"So, did you start this affair with Alex to get back at your husband?"

"Subconsciously. Probably. But there was a real, deep attraction between us. Almost scary."

"What do you mean?"

"Have you ever been with someone you totally trusted? Someone who made you a whole person?"

"The only person I could ever totally trust was my brother."

"My point is I could feel myself falling in love with Alex. Even during the long period of separation when he was at school. It wasn't just an affair any more, not to me."

"So do you think your relationship with Alex had anything to do with his murder?"

"Are you asking me if my husband found out and went after him? I can't swear to it, but I don't think so. Besides, he'd prefer to rub it in my face, especially after I made such a fuss about his affair with Cassandra."

"Alex told me he went to their summer home in Michigan with his father the second week of August. Mr. Phelps said he never went there with Alex."

"Actually, he met me near Lake Shafer early that week. We camped and talked about the future. I had to return on Thursday. Alex told me he would be heading for Diamond Lake Friday morning to surprise his father and get in some last minute fishing before classes started. I don't understand why Bradley would lie to you about it."

"Are you sure Mr. Phelps is the one who's lying?"

"Yes, I am. Jonathan needed him to sign some papers. Bradley's secretary said he'd gone to the lake house for some last minute fishing and to store the boat. She said he'd been there since Tuesday."

"The day my mother disappeared," muttered Mandy.

"What did you say?" Savannah asked.

"Nothing important. Did you see Alex when he came back from Michigan?"

"Yes," Savannah said frowning. "He was acting very strangely."

"In what way?"

"He seemed agitated, but didn't want to talk about it. He even suggested we stop seeing each other for a while. I was so hurt and angry." Tears began to well in her eyes once more. "I said *"Fine"* and stormed out. I never really got a chance to tell him I was sorry or ask him why. I was too stubborn and now it's too late."

"I've taken up enough of your time," said Mandy. "Thank you for talking to me."

Mandy's head was spinning as she pulled out of the Richmond's driveway. Alex didn't lie to her after all, Mr. Phelps had. Why? Alex was dead. What was there to gain by making Mandy think Alex had lied to her?

Worse, why weren't Detective Jacobs and Detective Mayhew telling her everything related to her mother's case? Why is her Uncle Mel holding back? She's the one who filed the report. Shouldn't they keep her in the loop? Then there's Brent. Savannah had told him and his partner about the affair days ago.

"I'll have a little talk with him tonight," she said to herself aloud. She had to return Marie's car before she could go home.

Chapter 27

Brent arrived on Mandy's doorstep at 6:00 precisely. Mandy answered the door within seconds of hearing the doorbell ring.

"Hi Brent. It's good to see you *off duty*."

She was wearing an emerald green cashmere sweater which made her green eyes sparkle and a pair of skintight jeans that showed off every curve of her hips and legs. She noticed his mouth gaping and knew she'd accomplished the desired effect. She'd distract him enough to throw him off guard. Then she'd find out why he didn't tell her about Savannah and Alex.

"It's good to be off duty. I wish I could have sat with you at the funeral, but it was good your dad was there."

"Yeah," she said with a sweet smile remembering her dad's rare gentleness that day. "Dad's been more supportive lately."

"Ready to go?" he asked.

"You bet," she said as she pulled a heavy denim jacket out of the closet. Although it had been beautiful and sunny all day, she knew the temperature had dropped significantly since the sun set.

They snapped their seatbelts in place before Mandy spoke. "Brent, I found out something which doesn't make sense."

He glanced at her to let her know he was listening.

"After the burial, I went to the Phelps' house," she paused a moment, touching the pendant she was wearing. "While I was talking to Mr. Phelps, I mentioned the fishing trip in August. He told me he had not gone up there."

"And?"

"And, in August Alex was gone for a week. He said he was going to their lake house in Michigan to surprise his father and get in one more week of fishing before school started. On the other hand, Mr.

Phelps told me his business had kept him too busy to get away. *He said the last time they went fishing together was in June.*"

"Do you think Alex planned to go with his dad and Mr. Phelps backed out at the last minute?"

Mandy shook her head. "No, I'm not sure. This is where things get confusing. In my conversation with Mr. Phelps, he was adamant there were no plans made for August. When Alex returned, he said he'd had a huge fight with his dad so he came home early. Somebody's lied to me, Brent, and I think it's Mr. Phelps."

Brent's brow furrowed. "What makes you say that?"

"Alex had a girlfriend. I spoke with her today."

"What?" Brent exclaimed. "You knew he had a girlfriend and didn't tell me."

"Don't get shitty with me, Mister!" she retorted. "I just figured it out myself!"

"Please tell me you didn't go talk to Whitney Benson after I specifically asked you not to."

"No, I didn't talk to Whitney." Mandy's temper was rising. He hadn't given her the courtesy of keeping her informed, but expected her to call him the moment she found a clue. She crossed her arms in front of her and stared out the passenger window.

Brent drove along 86th Street and the silence became tension between them. He turned on the radio to an 80's and 90's station and tapped his fingers on the steering wheel with the rhythm of the music.

Shifting uncomfortably in her seat, she wondered if she should tell him to turn around and take her home. She didn't feel much like going out to eat right now.

Brent turned off the radio. "Mandy, I'm sorry. I guess the cop in me takes over when it shouldn't. Please don't be mad."

"I wish you could tell me what's going on. I know I'm going to have to tell you who she is, even if I don't want to, but why can't you help me understand what happened to Alex." Mandy continued to stare out the window. Her feelings for Savannah Richmond were confused in the morality of the situation. "She's married."

"Married?"

"I think you know perfectly well who she is because you've already talked to her."

"You mean Savannah Richmond?" Brent asked, looking horrified.

She turned her head, glaring at him. "That's right. I thought she'd appeared a little too broken up about Alex's death to just be a friend of the family so I went to see her this morning."

"I wish you hadn't done that."

"Well, maybe if you and your partner had been more forthcoming with the information I wouldn't have deemed it necessary," she spewed.

Brent didn't say a word to this. He appeared to be thinking of some way to save the evening.

"I don't believe she's the one who killed him," Mandy offered. "She's too devastated. She's not really sure if her husband knows it was going on. You might want to take a closer look at him. Seems to me he had motive to kill Alex and did you know he was screwing my mom? What about her? Did you ever think *he* might be responsible for both crimes?"

"Don't worry. We're competent enough to do our jobs," he sniped.

"Maybe he has a new girlfriend. He got rid of Mom because she wouldn't want to be shoved aside. Then his new girlfriend uses Savannah's name to get into Alex's apartment," she said, ignoring his sarcasm. "He would have trusted Savannah. He wouldn't have thought twice when the guard told him who was there."

"That's pretty farfetched," said Brent. "How do you know she didn't go and kill Alex in some sort of jealous rage?"

"I can't be one-hundred percent sure," said Mandy emphatically. "But my gut tells me she didn't murder Alex. The question is who else knew about the affair?"

"Gloria Phelps is a blonde. Do you think she knew?" he asked.

"I have no idea." The mention of Gloria seemed to diffuse her anger. She hadn't really thought about shallow, self-centered Gloria as a suspect.

"How was she with Alex?" asked Brent.

Mandy thought about it for a moment. "Well, I didn't see it happen, but Alex told me a couple of times he thought she was coming on to him. I just thought it was his male ego." She paused. "Of course, now I wonder."

"So you never actually witnessed Mrs. Phelps flirting with Alex?"

he asked.

"Not that I remember. I tried to avoid her if I could. She always acted like she wanted to be friends or something. I just wasn't into the whole let's go shopping, vanity thing like she was."

They sat quietly for a moment as he pulled into the restaurant's driveway. Then Mandy remembered the other tidbit Mr. Phelps had disclosed. "Brent, Gloria wasn't in town the first three weeks in August."

"How do you know?" he asked.

"Mr. Phelps told me," she paused, realization dawning on her face. "She took Lana to Ohio to visit her parents. As a matter of fact, Lana mentioned it to me a few weeks ago, but I didn't make the connection. That would have been during the time Mr. Phelps was supposedly in Michigan. Oh, yeah. Savannah also told me she and Alex were together in Monticello at Lake Shafer at the beginning of week and he didn't head for Michigan until Friday morning. I was shocked when Alex was home a day early, on Saturday."

"Sounds like you got more information out of her than we did. Is there more?"

Mandy finished telling Brent about the conversation and about Savannah's suspicions in regards to Gloria.

"I guess my partner and I will have to check out Mrs. Gloria Phelps' story A.S.A.P.," he said.

"Here we are talking about the case when I really just wanted to have a nice, quiet dinner with you," he said. "You too mad at me to eat or do you want to go in and forget the rest of the world for a while?"

"I'm okay," she conceded. "No point letting a little tiff spoil a good meal." She smiled as she got out of the car. From now on, she wasn't going to let Brent or anyone else discourage her from talking to whomever she pleased. Tomorrow she'd start with Bradley Phelps.

Chapter 28

Mandy had given a great deal of thought to Brent's 'cop attitude' and his lack of confidence in her. Maybe it was her lack of confidence in police procedure that was really at issue here. It seemed to her the procedures and rules were bogging down these investigations. She'd been able to glean more information from Savannah Richmond in a couple of hours than the police had in the past two weeks.

It was very unusual for Mandy to bend the rules, but she'd never been in such desperate, frustrating circumstances before. She was determined to find out why Alex's father would lie to her about going to the lake house.

Mandy would use her own car today since it wouldn't look strange for her to visit the grieving family of her best friend. Although her switch with Marie had worked out great, she didn't want to do it too often for fear the reporters would catch on. When she returned Marie's car late in the afternoon, Marie told her the reporters sent in a representative about a half an hour after Mandy's escape. The woman pretended to be shopping and picked out a couple of things to try on. Of course, she discovered very quickly no one else was in the dressing rooms and was out of there like a shot. They'd had a good laugh over it.

Since it was Sunday, Mandy was sure Mr. Phelps would be home. This time of year, he would normally be relaxing in an easy chair, watching the Colts play football. When she arrived, she saw a group of reporters lining the street in front of the Phelps house.

"Crap!" she said aloud. Honking as she pulled into the driveway, she'd hoped someone would hear it and come to the door before reporters rushed her. No such luck, of course.

"Miss Stevenson. Jake Cramden here. Have there been any new

developments in the Phelps case? Are you here to give them some new information?"

"I'm here to comfort Alex's family. I'm not a police officer. If there were any new developments, it wouldn't be *me* delivering the information."

"Oh, but surely you have the inside scoop, your father being the head of homicide."

"Sorry," she said smiling, pressing the doorbell again. "My father is a 'by the book' kind of guy. I'm no different than anyone else when it comes to his job."

The door opened and Gloria's mouth dropped at the sight of all the reporters. "Hurry up and get in here, Mandy."

"That's all I've got for you today." Mandy quickly went inside and shut the door behind her hearing their muffled shouts.

"Sorry, Gloria. Is Mr. Phelps home? I need to ask him something."

"I'm the only one here right now. Lana spent the weekend at Sally's and Bradley went up to the lake to close up the house and put the boat into storage."

"Really?" Mandy asked in surprise. That's what he was supposed to be doing in August. "Is he coming back this evening?"

"He should be back around 5:00 tonight," Gloria said, pacing and wringing her hands. "Shall I have him call you?"

"Yes, please. Are you all right? You seem nervous."

"Of course, I'm nervous. Every time I walk out the door, reporters jump out of the bushes. They're a bunch of vultures. Don't they know we're in mourning? My daughter isn't sleeping or eating right. Wouldn't you be nervous?"

"Yes, I'm sure I would." She couldn't believe Gloria could be so oblivious to the fact Mandy had been going through this for weeks. "Speaking of reporters, do you think I could slip out the back gate and sneak around the other side of the garage?"

"Sure, but make sure you shut the gate properly. I don't want that riff-raff coming into my back yard."

"Thanks, Gloria." Mandy went through the back yard, opened the gate slightly to see if anyone was near her car, then as quietly as possible moved towards it. No one saw her until she opened her car door giving her just enough time to slide into the driver's seat before they surrounded her. She backed out slowly, trying not to run anyone over.

Five o'clock came and went. No call from Mr. Phelps. Mandy had decided to make dinner to keep busy. She was trying to decide whether or not to tell her father about her conversation with Savannah and her suspicions about Mr. Phelps. Would he take her seriously or would she receive the same attitude Brent had given her?

Six o'clock came and went. No call from Mr. Phelps. Had Gloria remembered to give him the message? She'd call the house after dinner.

"Dad! Dinner!" she shouted at him over the sound of the television. She'd made Swiss steak, mashed potatoes and green beans, her father's favorite. He came to the table and wasted no time digging in. They sat quietly consuming their food, although Mandy mostly stirred and picked at hers trying to muster the courage to talk to him.

"Dad. I found out a couple of things I think you should know."

"Really?" He looked up at her curiously. "About what?"

"Some things people have told me regarding Alex. I think they might be important."

Now she knew she definitely had his full attention. He had laid down his knife and fork and was looking at her intently.

"What is it, Mandy?"

"When I went to the Phelps house after the funeral, I was talking to Mr. Phelps and mentioned Alex meeting him at the lake in August. He claims he didn't go to the lake. Then, I found out Alex was having a fling with Savannah Richmond and she knew Alex was going there that weekend to surprise his father. It was that weekend when Alex and his dad had a big blow up, but if I'm to believe Mr. Phelps, it never happened."

Her father leaned back in his chair, rubbing his chin as though deep in thought. He looked off in the distance, not meeting her eyes. It was all she could do to keep herself from asking what he thought, but it was never wise to push him. When he was ready to speak, he leaned forward with his hands clasped on the table in front of him.

"I'm glad you followed Mel's advice and decided to tell me what you've learned. Everything is significant in a case like this. How did you find out about Mrs. Richmond and Alex?"

"She told me." She could see him stiffen. "I'd noticed how upset she was when I met her at the Phelps' house. I couldn't understand why their lawyer's wife would be so upset over Alex's death. I just put two and two together."

"So you approached her?"

"Yes. I also found out from her that her husband definitely was having an affair with Mom for three years. Did you know?"

"Let's just say it doesn't surprise me. However, you should have told Barnes or Freeman about your suspicions and let them talk to her. What you've got is hearsay and wouldn't be allowed in court. *You* are not a cop. You need to stand back and let the professionals handle it."

"Oh, well that's good. Like Jacobs and Mayhew handled her. She brought her attorney with her and didn't tell them a damn thing. She spilled her guts to me. She even told me about pulling the gun on Mom in the hotel. I'm sure she didn't kill Alex, but I'm not so sure about her husband."

"Like I said, Mandy, let the professionals handle it."

"So what are the *professionals* going to do about Alex's dad? I told Brent about this last night. He didn't say anything about what he plans to do."

"That's because Brent is a good cop. Just because you're my daughter and you're dating him doesn't mean he can disclose something to you he wouldn't disclose to every other family member or friend of a victim. When we catch whoever's done this, we want everything in a nice neat package so the prosecutor can get a conviction. Otherwise, defense attorneys will have a field day."

"Okay, Dad. I get it!" she said, upset now. She stood and started clearing the table.

"I don't think you do," he shouted in response. "You don't have any idea what it's like to be out there day after day! To see the most horrendous things people do to one another. And then when you arrest somebody who you're one-hundred percent positive did it, some asshole defense attorney comes along and gets the guy off on some technicality. Then who do you think gets the blame? Not the prosecutor. It always falls back on the cops. Did we read him his rights, when did we read him his rights, how long was he being interrogated before you offered him a drink of water? Bullshit, all bullshit!"

"I said I get it, Dad," she repeated.

This only served to anger him more. He shook his head, rolling his eyes, and had to get in the last word. "I mean it, Mandy! Stay out of it!"

"Like hell I will," she mumbled when he was out of earshot. She grabbed the phone and called the Phelps house. Lana answered. "Hello Mandy. I miss you."

"I miss you, too, sweetie. Is your dad home yet?"

"No. Mom says she thinks he must have decided to stay in Cassopolis for another day. We can't get him on his cell. If he's out on the lake he's probably out of range."

"When you see your dad, tell him it's important I speak to him, okay?"

"Well." Lana hesitated. "Oh, I could leave a note on the refrigerator. I might be in school when he gets home so this way I won't forget."

"Thanks, sweetie. Try to get a good night's sleep."

"I will. Bye."

Mandy had made up her mind. If she didn't hear from Mr. Phelps by 10:00 tomorrow morning, she'd drive to Cassopolis, Michigan, herself. She'd ask some of the locals if they'd seen Alex or his dad there the second week of August. If she were lucky, she'd also find Alex's father before he headed back to Carmel. With or without her dad's help, she would uncover the truth.

Chapter 29

Monday morning, Freeman filled Barnes in on all of the information Mandy had given him on Saturday night. He told her the full story about Savannah Richmond's involvement with Alex and the facts she hadn't disclosed to them when they interviewed her. He also updated her on the discrepancies between Alex's and his father's versions of where they were the second weekend of August.

"Why the hell would a guy lie about his son? Or, visa versa?" Barnes questioned.

"I have no idea, but Mandy seems to think Bradley Phelps is the one who isn't telling the truth. Jonathan Richmond told his wife Bradley Phelps was at the lake house that week."

"Did Richmond try to call Phelps at the lake house?"

"Mandy didn't say."

"Something's screwy here, Freeman. What's up with the Richmond broad confessing everything to Mandy all of a sudden? You sure she's not using Mandy to try to deflect suspicion?"

"Right now, I'm not sure of anything. She may have confessed to Mandy because she'd already told us about it." Freeman let out a long stream of air, showing his exasperation. "Everything's all discombobulated."

"What?" Barnes said staring at him with an *'are you nuts'* look.

"Thing is," said Freeman. "We're starting to find the suspects in the Stevenson case are also appearing in the Phelps case. How did these people get so intertwined?"

"Do you think Phelps would have helped Savannah Richmond get rid of Stevenson?"

"Wouldn't be the first time we've seen a young love sick guy help his older lady friend *get rid of a problem*. Remember the Donaldson case a couple of years back?" he recalled. "Barry Sheets helped his lover Phillis Donaldson kill and dismember her husband and then throw his remains in the White River."

"No way I'd forget that one. We never did find all the pieces of the poor bastard. She claimed he abused her but we never found a record of any domestic calls."

"She was an upstanding citizen. Member of the PTA, involved in her church, a real pillar of the community." Freeman paused. "To answer your question, I think anyone's capable of anything if there's a strong enough emotion behind it. If Alex was in love with Savannah, he probably would have done anything for her and she hated Cassandra Stevenson. I doubt Mandy would see it this way. I hate to keep it from her. She already thinks we're hiding things."

"She's just going to have to get over it, partner. Maybe this wasn't such a hot time for you to start romancing her. Maybe you should cool it for a while."

"You're probably right. I'll think about it. In the meantime, we'd better get our butts over to the campus. We can talk to the Captain about our theories when we get back."

They arrived at the IUPUI campus at approximately 10:00 a.m. They headed straight to the Registrar's office. The Registrar had heard about Alex's death and was sorry to hear it. However, she didn't have much to say about him. She had never heard any complaints about him nor were there any reports of incidents involving him.

Barnes asked if they could see the professors of his classes. The Registrar provided the detectives with a list of classes. One of Alex's classes was about to end in ten minutes just across the street. They got to the classroom just as the class was letting out. They asked a few of the students if they knew Alex. No one remembered him. Of course, it was a huge lecture hall and he had only been in classes for a few weeks when he died.

The professor was of no help either. He wasn't even sure he'd recognize Alex. Feeling this was a dead end, Freeman convinced Barnes they should return to the station and call the remaining professors.

As Freeman pulled into the parking lot at the City-County Building, he turned to his partner and said, "We should see if we can sit down with Captain Stevenson. Let him know what Mandy said and what our theories are. Maybe we should ask for permission to go up to Michigan. We could quiz the folks in Cassopolis and we might find out who's telling the truth — Alex or Bradley Phelps."

When Freeman and Barnes entered the Homicide Department, they didn't have to ask to see Captain Stevenson. He was standing near their desks. When he spotted them, he gestured for them to come to his office.

"Mandy tells me she divulged some important information to you," he said staring directly at Freeman as Barnes shut the office door.

"Yes, sir," Freeman answered. "I've briefed Detective Barnes and we were just about to ask you for your permission to go to Cassopolis to investigate this new information."

"I think it's an excellent next step," Captain Stevenson agreed. "You can find out whether one or both men were in Cassopolis that week. It's a small town. Bradley Phelps bought the house when he was married to Alex's mother. There's no way either of them could have been there without being recognized."

"This is the information we got from the IUPUI campus," said Freeman handing the list of Alex's classes they'd acquired from the Registrar's office to the captain.

"I see you've marked off Professor Bland. While you're gone, I'll take care of interviewing the rest of Alex's professors. I doubt it's going to get us anywhere, but you never know."

"I'll call Gloria Phelps before we leave," mentioned Barnes. "I'll set up something for the end of the week so we can interview her as soon as we get back."

"Good thinking, Barnes," said the captain. "You two may want to think about another official interview with the Richmond woman, too. See if she gives you the same story she gave my daughter. Hopefully she won't bring her lawyer this time."

"Will do, sir," she said.

"It's a three hour trip, so make sure you take an overnight case. Matter of fact, Barnes, you may want to make the call to Mrs. Phelps from your cell while you're traveling. As long as you aren't driving, of course."

Barnes grabbed the notebook with Gloria's phone number in it.

Freeman told her he'd go to his place and pack then pick her up at her place.

An hour later they were heading north on US 31. The lake house was located near Cassopolis, Michigan, approximately fifteen miles north of the Indiana-Michigan state line. They were on the road for a little over two hours when a sign appeared — South Bend 5.

"Hey, can we stop here for something to eat," Barnes asked. "I'm starving, and I have to go to the bathroom."

"Okay. I'm sure there's a restaurant or truck stop close by. We can talk some strategy while we're at it."

"Well, the only strategy I'm interested in right now is how I'm gonna move without peeing my pants, so less talk and more action please."

Chapter 30

Mandy reached Cassopolis at 1:00 in the afternoon. She was pretty hungry by then and decided to stop at the Jensen Brothers Café. Gus Jenson, owner of the café, was standing near the cash register. Mandy took a seat at the counter and waved at him.

"Well, as I live and breathe. If it ain't Mandy Stevenson," he said.

"Hey Gus. How's business?"

Gus walked over to her and took her order himself. He gave it to the cook and came back with a diet soda for her. "What brings you up here now? I figured you'd be back at school?"

"I need to ask a few questions about Alex and his dad. Do you remember seeing them up here during the second week of August?"

"Let me think a sec. Come to think of it I did see Bradley driving through in early August. Him and his wife."

"You sure Gloria was with him?"

"I saw them from a distance, but I'm pretty sure it was her. Blonde for sure. She was wearing a white tee shirt and sunglasses, but it was pretty far away. I mean, who else could it be?"

"You're probably right, Gus."

"What's this all about?"

"Do you remember seeing Alex back then?"

"No. Can't say I do. That don't mean he wasn't here. Sometimes they go on up without eating here. They usually only eat in town when they have company, like when you used to come up with them."

The cook rang the bell signaling Mandy's food was prepared. Gus retrieved it for her. "There you go, Mandy. Best Rueben you'll find in Michigan."

"Probably the only Rueben I'll find in Michigan."

Gus guffawed. "You never did answer my question. What's this all about?"

"I've got some bad news. Alex was murdered a couple of weeks ago."

"Ah, no!" He turned for a moment, walking back and forth with his hand across his mouth. Then he stopped in front of Mandy who was picking at the meat in her sandwich. "What happened?"

"Somebody shot him. Since then I've heard some conflicting stories. My mother disappeared the same week. Strange thing is, some of the suspects in her case are also suspects in Alex's case."

"No kidding? You sure have been through the ringer. And Bradley must be devastated. He was heartbroken when Alex's mama died. Now he's lost his only son."

"I don't know if the two cases are connected," she said, "but I'm determined to find out."

Gus shook his head and walked away to collect money at the register, leaving Mandy to her thick, luscious Rueben which she wasn't sure she could eat. The conversation had caused her to lose her appetite. She gave it a shot though, knowing she'd need her strength. After managing to eat half the sandwich and a few of the chips, she paid her bill and thanked Gus for his help. Then she promised she'd keep him informed of how the investigation was progressing.

Getting back in her car, Mandy drove down East State Street until she found the old drug store. Mandy loved the fact the old drug store had kept its original look. There was a dark oak counter with a pearly white marble top where you could purchase a real fountain soda or shake. The woodwork trim was dark-stained oak and the floor was black and white tile. The owner, Cole Wright, was tall, blond, and good looking for his age. He recognized her right away and motioned for her to come over and have a seat at the counter.

"Mandy Stevenson, long time no see."

"Not since last summer, Mr. Wright. I couldn't manage to come up this summer. I've been looking for a job."

"Alex come with ya?"

Mandy looked down at the counter bracing herself to answer. "No, Mr. Wright. I'm afraid Alex died a couple of weeks ago."

"Oh, my," Mr. Wright said, taken aback. "I suppose he wrapped that fancy truck of his around a tree or somethin'. I told him he'd better slow down his drivin'."

"No, Mr. Wright, it wasn't a car accident. Alex was shot. We believe a woman who's about five-foot, seven inches tall, with blonde hair, murdered him. Did you ever see him up here with anyone who might fit this description?"

Mr. Wright contemplated what she had said before speaking. "No. The only one I'd ever seen with a blonde was Bradley. 'Course his wife's a blonde."

"When was the last time you saw Mr. Phelps?"

"Be back in August. Heard him and his wife was here to close up the house for the winter. Ya know, everybody 'round here thought there was somethin' odd goin' on with them two though. The Lathams, next house west of the Phelps, they said they never saw those two out durin' the day. Not even on the boat. Oh, except they said they heard the boat go out on the lake at about 11:30 one night and come back around 12:30 in the mornin'. Mrs. Latham didn't much like bein' woke up that time a night," he said with a grin. "Couple a days later, the Lathams went back to Ohio so I never heard anythin' else about it."

"Did Alex come in to the drug store during that time period?" Mandy inquired.

"Oh, yeah," Mr. Wright exclaimed as though a light bulb just lit up over his head. "He stopped here on his way out to the house. Said he was here to surprise his dad. Told me he'd decided to get in one more day of fishin' before he went back to school. It was strange though."

"What do you mean?" Mandy asked.

"A couple of hours after he was in here, I saw him tearin' down the street headin' outta town. No way he could have got in any fishin' in that length of time."

It took Mandy a moment to process this. That was very strange. "So this was the last time you saw Alex?"

"Yeah. Never saw him come back into town that day or any other. I hear everythin' in here, so I'm sure I'd have heard somebody say they saw him."

"Thanks, Mr. Wright. You've given me a lot to think about."

Mr. Wright winked at her and tapped the side of his nose with his index finger. "Want a root beer float, Mandy," he offered. "I remembered it's your favorite!"

"Thanks, Mr. Wright, but I have to talk to a couple more people and try to get to the house before it gets too dark. I do have one more question though. Mr. Phelps is supposed to be here now. Have you seen him?"

"No, I haven't seen him, but I heard he was out at the house."

"Thanks for your help, Mr. Wright," Mandy said.

He smiled at her. "Anythin' for you and Bradley. This must be really hard on him, losin' his boy like that."

Mandy nodded and smiled at Mr. Wright as she left.

Across the street was Craig's Hardware Store. Mr. Craig was behind the counter as usual with a broad smile on his chubby face.

"Mandy," Mr. Craig said cheerfully. "What brings you here?"

Mandy was dreading giving yet another person this terrible news, but she had no choice. She told him of Alex's death and got the usual response. Then she asked if he'd seen Alex or his father in August.

"Matter of fact, Bradley stopped in here about mid-week during the second week of August. I sold him a tarp and some rope. Not sure what he wanted it for though. Kind of funny, because he's usually more talkative than he was that day."

"So he didn't say anything about what he was doing or whether or not Alex or Gloria was out at the house with him?"

"Nope. He didn't say a word about anyone else. I didn't hear about her being here until later in the week when I stopped by Barney's place to gas up my truck." Mr. Craig paused momentarily. "Strange. I thought maybe he was buying the tarp for the boat. You know, like maybe the old one had ripped."

"What's strange about that?" Mandy asked.

"Well, the tarp I sold to him was black. When I saw him driving through town hauling the boat towards Jason's, the tarp on the boat was bright blue."

"So he put the boat in storage back in August," she stated.

"That's right. You can check with Jason, but I'm sure he did. Saw him driving her through town in that direction."

Mandy thanked Mr. Craig for his time, writing some notes as she walked out the door. Although her conversation with Mr. Craig was short, it was full of information. Information which made Mr.

Phelps' little stay at the lake appear more mysterious. It also confirmed her suspicions Mr. Phelps was the one who wasn't telling the truth. Mandy's brain reeled with questions. Why did Mr. Phelps say he wasn't here when he was? What caused Alex to leave so quickly? What were the two of them hiding? And Gloria was supposed to be visiting her family in Toledo. Did she decide to come to Cassopolis and leave Lana with her parents?

Next stop would be the Hardy's Friendly Market. While they were here, they had to eat and this was the best place in town to buy groceries. As she entered the market, she saw Iris Perkins running one of the checkout lines. If anyone had noticed anything out of the ordinary, it would be Iris.

"Hey, Iris, how are you doing?" Mandy called. "Do you have a minute to talk?"

"For you, honey, sure thing. Hey Al," she shouted towards the office. "Time for my break. Be back in fifteen." Al waved her off and she walked outside with Mandy.

Mandy told Iris what happened to Alex instead of waiting for the inevitable question of his whereabouts.

"I'm real sorry to hear it. Mr. Phelps and his kids are real good people. Terrible. But what can I do for you, Mandy?"

Iris lit up a cigarette while Mandy explained why she was there. She asked Iris the same questions she had asked all of the others.

"Come to think of it," Iris began after taking another puff. "Bradley Phelps came in here a couple of times early in August and bought enough food for an army. I thought his whole family was up here. He was acting kind of weird though. Not quite his usual cheery self, he was kind of quiet."

"Did you see any of the other family members?" asked Mandy.

"You know, that was really strange, too. Don't know if I've ever actually seen the wife, but Alex and his sweet little sister were regulars when they were here. Didn't see any of them once that whole week.

"I hope they catch whoever did this," Iris snorted as she stamped out her cigarette. "Got to get back to work, but I'll let you know if I hear anything more."

"You're the best, Iris! Thanks," said Mandy, giving Iris a big hug.

Mandy drove past the bait shop and River's Boat Storage. Both were closed. Small towns like this one rolled up their sidewalks just before suppertime. Checking her fuel gauge, she decided she'd better fill up before driving around the lake to the Phelps summer home.

Tony's Garage was the last place on the way out of town to get gasoline. Of course, Tony died ten years ago. Barney Anderson now owned the place. Barney had once told her he hadn't seen any reason to change the name of the place because everyone around already knew it as Tony's. It was also the only service station in town which actually had service. When Mandy pulled up to the pump, Barney came bounding out of the place.

Barney had graying hair and a bright smile which spelled small town friendly. Mandy had always had a soft spot in her heart for him.

"Mandy. Look at you! You get prettier every time I see you."

"Thanks, Barney. It's good to see you. Fill 'er up please.

Barney grabbed the hose and began to fill her tank. "So how's Alex doin'? Haven't seen him in ages."

"Didn't you see his dad come through here over the weekend?"

"Nope. Haven't seen him since early August. Somethin' goin' on, sugar?"

Mandy looked at Barney, frowning. Mr. Phelps had always stopped to say hi to Barney, even if he didn't need gas. "You're sure you didn't see him this weekend? I was told he came up here and he hasn't returned Indianapolis."

"Course I'm sure. I've known Bradley for over twenty years. I 'spect I'd know if I saw him."

"No offense."

"Shucks, girl. I'm just jerkin' your chain. You goin' out to the house?" He replaced the hose on the pump.

"That's the plan." She looked up at the darkening late afternoon sky.

"You never answered my question about Alex. He comin' up to join you?"

A stab of pain pierced her heart. She wished she hadn't had to repeat the story again, but she'd told everyone else, so she gave Barney the bad news.

"I thought Mr. Phelps came up here to get away for a while. You know, to mourn without interruption."

"Ah, no. Geez. Poor Bradley."

"It's been pretty rough. Mr. Phelps and Alex had been angry with each other and hadn't made up so I think it's extra tough for him right now."

"I can see why. What about you? God, this must be awful for you, too."

"It has been and to top it off, my mother disappeared in early August. We haven't heard a word from her," she said uncomfortably, avoiding eye-contact. "Look, Barney. I've gotta go. The sun's going down and you know how dark it gets around the lake this time of year. What do I owe you?"

"Forty-five dollars and eighty-five cents."

Mandy paid him and accepted his thanks. She headed towards the north side of the lake with more questions than ever. Why didn't Mr. Phelps stop in town? And, why hadn't he told anyone about Alex?

Chapter 31

"Cassopolis, Michigan is a lot larger than I expected," stated Barnes. "It says in this brochure I picked up at the restaurant Cassopolis is a scenic historic town established around 1829. It was named for Territorial Governor Lewis Cass. And get this," she said half-laughing, "one of their greatest claims to fame is being known as the home of Edward Lowe, the inventor of kitty litter."

"I'll have to remember that the next time I need to come up with a bit of trivia," Freeman huffed. "Anything else of interest?"

"The usual small town stuff. There are several quaint shops and churches, as well as a limestone courthouse built in 1899. There are several lakes in the area with fishing, boating, and camping. Lots of relaxing outdoor activities. No wonder so many people come here to get away from it all."

Freeman and Barnes stopped at the police station to introduce themselves. It's always a good idea to check in with the locals. When they entered, Police Chief Kaleb Matthews rose from the chair behind his desk to greet them.

The chief was tall with a stocky, muscular build. From the size of his pecks, Chief Matthews obviously lifted weights. He looked to be about Captain Stevenson's age and sported a cropped cut of light brown hair and a neatly trimmed mustache and beard.

"Hey there, folks. What can I do for you?"

The detectives introduced themselves showing him their IDs. Then they told him about the Phelps case. He was shocked to hear about Alex's death.

"Chief Matthews, we want to look around the Phelps house," said Freeman. "However, we couldn't get a hold of Bradley Phelps. We were told he was already up here."

"Bradley Phelps has been a friend of mine for over twenty years now. I'll personally meet you out there in about twenty minutes," the chief replied. "Thing is, I'm not sure we'll find him out there."

"Why?" asked Barnes.

"I saw Bradley on Friday, but not since. I figured he'd shut her up and went on home." The chief looked perplexed. "I wonder why he didn't tell me what had happened to his son. That's not like Bradley. Not one bit."

"The man's very upset," commented Barnes. "Maybe he just couldn't face telling anyone about it yet."

"Maybe," Chief Matthews said, stroking his beard and walking over to a map on the wall. "If you want to come over here, I'll show you the best way to get out to the house."

Barnes wrote down the specifics. It appeared to be pretty straightforward. On their way to the house, they decided to stop for gasoline.

Freeman got out of the car ready to pump his own gas when a gray-haired gentleman came toward them wearing a one-piece mechanic's coverall.

"Hey there," he shouted. "This is a *real* service station. Nobody pumps their own gas here."

"Oh, sorry…Barney," Freeman said reading Barney's name stitched just above his left breast pocket. "You don't find any of these back in Indianapolis anymore."

"Didn't think you guys were from these parts," he said congenially, as he started to pump their gas. "You've got a Hoosier accent. What brings you up?"

"This is Detective Erica Barnes and my name is Detective Brent Freeman. We are homicide detectives from Indianapolis."

"We're investigating the death of Alex Phelps," Barnes interjected.

"I heard," Barney said shaking his head. "I just saw him not too long ago. He was kind of upset mind you, but perfectly healthy."

"Alex? Do you know why he was upset?" Barnes inquired as she pulled out her writing tablet and pen.

"Not really, but I could tell he wasn't happy," Barney assured her. "He was here the second week of August. He stopped here to get gas. I asked him if he was going fishing. He said no. I took the hint and didn't ask any more questions."

"Did you see his father that week?" asked Freeman.

"Yep," answered Barney. "The wife was with him."

Freeman and Barnes exchanged significant looks. "Are you sure his *wife* was with him?"

"I'm pretty sure. Course she hardly ever talks to anyone in town. Kind of the snooty type. I saw a blonde, wearing sunglasses and a white shirt. Kept her face turned away most of the time."

"Thanks. How much do we owe you Barney?" asked Freeman pulling out his wallet to pay the man.

Barnes started to put her notebook away then remembered she didn't have Barney's last name.

"Fife," he said in response to her question. Then he and Freeman laughed at the look on Barnes' face. "Just kidding," he chortled. "My last name's Anderson."

Erica smiled, wrote it down, and got into the car. She jumped as Barney tapped on her window. Rolling it down, she gave him a quizzical look.

"You guys going out to the Phelps place, too?"

"What do you mean, *too?*" asked Freeman leaning over to see out of the passenger window.

"Mandy was just here getting gas…oh, about twenty or thirty minutes ago. Told me the same thing about Bradley supposed to be here, but she didn't mention you."

"Thanks, Mr. Anderson," said Freeman, furrowing his brow. "We'd better get going."

"Thanks for stopping in," Barney said as they drove off.

"Damn it!" Freeman shouted hitting the steering wheel with is open hands. "The captain told her *not* to interfere."

"Like father, like daughter, from what I see."

"He may be stubborn, but Captain Stevenson plays by the rules. He doesn't pull stupid stunts like this."

"Better not let her hear you say that. Otherwise, the last date you had with her, *will be* the last date you have with her."

"And what about Gloria Phelps?" Brent continued his voice getting even louder. "I thought Gloria Phelps was in Ohio with her parents and daughter in August. Do you think she changed her mind and came here to spend a couple of days with her husband? And what would be wrong with that? Why lie about it?"

"Don't know partner," said Barnes calmly. "Let's just get out to the house, in one piece please, so we can find out what Miss Mandy's up to."

The Phelps' house was on the north side of the lake about eight miles from town. "The road should be coming up soon," Mandy said aloud. It was always more difficult to find the road at dusk. She slowed looking for the road sign, which at times was obscured by long branches until the leaves fell. There it was. She made her turn heading for the second driveway on the right.

The driveway was long and spooky in the late afternoon light. There were pine trees lining the driveway and she could see the beautiful three-story house and the lake. As she got closer to the house, something chilled her, like a ghost flowing through her. She saw Mr. Phelps' truck parked in its usual spot.

But everything was quiet. Too quiet. Even the crunching of the driveway beneath her tires seemed loud and intrusive. She couldn't shake the feeling something was wrong. Maybe she should go back into town. "No," she said to herself. "I've come this far, I may as well go in."

Mandy took a deep breath and opened her car door. She slowly got out and stood there with the door open for what seemed like several minutes. It was ominously quiet here and very strange that Mr. Phelps hadn't turned on any lights in the house yet. She wondered if he was sitting on one of the decks out back waiting for the sun to set completely.

Ringing the doorbell, Mandy waited on the front porch for an answer. Nothing. She rang the bell a second time. She knew it was working, because she could hear it ringing. Deciding he might not be able to hear the doorbell if he were out on the boat dock, Mandy walked around to the back of the house.

The lake was getting dark and no one was on the boat dock. She could see the island where she and Alex used to go to be alone when his family was getting on their nerves. She felt a sudden sadness take over as she remembered how they'd laughed and talked out there. All gone now. Just like Charlie.

She jumped as she heard a noise behind her, breaking the vast silence and pulling her from her thoughts. Heart thumping, she scanned the area. Then she saw a raccoon scrambling across the deck. The patio door on the deck was not closed.

Looking around once more to see if Mr. Phelps was anywhere near, she decided to go into the house. Once inside, she called, "Mr. Phelps! Mr. Phelps are you here?"

No answer.

Again, the cold chill of dread seeped in. His truck was here. The door was open. What was going on? Where was he?

Flipping the light switch on, Mandy looked around the kitchen. Everything seemed to be in place. As a matter of fact, everything looked too neat. Knowing Mr. Phelps as she did, she couldn't imagine there wouldn't be at least one dish in the sink or a coffee pot with an inch of old coffee in it. She called his name again.

She walked through a small hallway towards the great room, heart throbbing in her ears. Why wasn't he answering her? Was he upstairs sleeping already? Maybe he'd taken a sleeping pill or something. In the great room she turned on the lights. Nothing. She let out a long nervous breath. Walking through the great room she again noticed the neatness of the room as though Mr. Phelps had a cleaning lady in today.

As much as she hated to disturb him if he were sleeping, Mandy decided to go upstairs to see if he was in his bedroom. Alex's death had taken quite a toll on him. She approached the stairway with more urgency, frightened that Mr. Phelps could be ill. Quickly ascending to the top, she went left towards the master suite.

The door to the master suite was open just a crack. Mandy knocked and waited. No answer. She knocked again and called out. "Mr. Phelps. Mr. Phelps, are you in there?" Still no answer.

Again, Mandy felt the icy sharpness of fear. She pushed the door open slowly. She could see a figure on the bed in the near darkness. "Mr. Phelps. It's me, Mandy. Are you okay?" No response. Now she was trembling. She reached for the light switch terrified at what she was about to discover. "Mr. Phelps, please wake up." No response. She turned on the light.

Looking at Mr. Phelps in horror, she saw the blood. It was everywhere and he was in a pool of it on his bed. "No, no! Not again! Not again!" she screamed. She turned and ran down the stairs crying hysterically; barely able to see where she was going. She wrenched open the door and ran straight into the arms of a large man. She screamed again and then everything went black.

Chapter 32

Mayhew had interviewed Savannah Richmond a second time early that morning. Her attorney was present as before, however, Mrs. Richmond seemed to want to be more cooperative this time. She told Mayhew of the affair with Alex. Admitting to the gun incident with Mrs. Stevenson, she explained the gun wasn't loaded. She just wanted to scare her.

"Jacobs!" Mayhew shouted at his partner as he saw him enter the department. He motioned for him to hurry over. "Testimony go okay?"

"Yeah. But you've got to feel sorry for the kid. Parents can't get along. Now Dad's probably going to go to jail for a while for taking off with him. Then there'll probably be a period of supervised visitation. Kid's only six. He just thought he was going on a little vacation with Dad."

"There's no parental manual that can take the stupid out of people. His father sure wasn't thinkin' when he decided to kidnap him."

"So, what's going on? You talk to Savannah Richmond this morning?"

"Sure did. She admitted to the affair with Phelps. Said she quit frettin' about her husband's fling with Miss Stevenson when she had her own extramarital activity goin'." Mayhew got the sour look of disgust on his face that he often did when people fooled around on their spouses. "Doesn't anybody pay attention to their vows anymore?"

"Not in this tangled web we've come upon," said Jacobs.

"There's more. Miss Richmond told me we should be lookin' at Miss Phelps as a suspect in the Stevenson disappearance."

"Really?"

"Miss Richmond hinted she thought Miss Phelps might have had her eye on young Alex, too. Made it sound like she ought to be questioned about Alex's murder."

"Why would Mrs. Phelps want to kill Alex?"

"Jealousy is a mighty powerful thing, Jacobs. Don't ever think it isn't."

"Should we bring her in for questioning?"

"In my opinion, I think you should get hold of Barnes and Freeman. See if they want in on it, too. Then she doesn't have to be called in here twice. Doesn't seem like the type of lady that'd like it much."

"Aren't Barnes and Freeman in Michigan today?"

"Yeah, but they'll probably be back tomorrow. We should give them a call. If they find Bradley Phelps we'll need to talk to him, too."

"All right," said Jacobs sighing. "I'll give Barnes a call."

The inside of the house was breathtaking with rich cedar paneled walls and floors, beautiful leather furnishings, and floor to ceiling windows looking out onto the lake. There was a sunroom downstairs, a deck on each upper level facing the lake, and seven bedrooms. It was a shame there was crime scene tape all around it and it was being trampled through by paramedics and police officers.

"So, Detectives," said Chief Matthews. "Have you had a chance to speak with Mandy yet? Poor thing came running out the door right smack into me and fainted dead away."

"No, we haven't spoken to her since the paramedics revived her," said Freeman. "They have her outside in the ambulance checking her vitals."

"They can take her to Borgess-Lee Memorial in Dowagiac if she needs attention," said the chief. "I think she'll be fine though. She was just scared real bad."

"She's the one who found Alex," Barnes told the chief.

"Holy Mother…no wonder she's so terrified," said Chief Matthews. Then he walked toward one of his deputies shaking his head.

"You know," Freeman said to his partner. "We're going to have to call Captain Stevenson about this. He's going to be so pissed that Mandy is here."

"You don't look any too happy yourself," Barnes said to him. "I'll call Stevenson, you go look after Mandy. And, be easy on her Freeman."

"Alright already," he said.

Barnes pulled out her cell phone to make the call when it started ringing. "Barnes," she answered. "Hey, Jacobs."

She listened then said, "I'll drive back tonight. Mandy was here when we arrived. Freeman will *escort* her back to Indy. I'll meet you in the morning." She paused again to listen.

"Yeah, well. Looks like she's linked to another death as well. Bradley Phelps is dead." She nodded as though Jacobs could see her. "See you in the morning."

"That your captain?" asked the chief after she hung up.

"No, it was one of our colleagues. He's requesting our assistance on an interview of a suspect."

"The crime lab folks from Kalamazoo should be here pretty soon. County Medical Examiner should be here shortly, too."

"Thanks, Chief. Will you need to question Mandy tonight?"

"Nah. My deputy was out there asking her what happened and she told him everything I think she can. I've known Mandy for a few years now. She was a good friend to Alex. I know she wouldn't do anything to hurt Alex's father. You can take her back home far as I'm concerned."

"Thanks," Barnes said, walking outside to make her phone call to the captain.

After listening to Captain Stevenson rant about his daughter's disobedience and ignorance for about fifteen minutes, Barnes finally assured him Freeman would escort her home as soon as possible. She walked over to the ambulance in time to see Freeman helping Mandy out of it.

"You talk to the captain," he asked.

"Oh, yeah," she replied looking at Mandy. "He's not too happy about your little escapade. I think I got him calmed down though. Told him Brent would have you home by noon tomorrow."

She then focused her attention on her partner. "Nothing more we can do here. M. E. and forensics will be here pretty soon. Chief Matthews said it's okay for Mandy to leave."

"Where's the nearest hotel?" asked Freeman.

"Chief says Dowagiac is about ten miles northwest of here. Or, you can head southwest to Niles, Michigan, fifteen miles away."

The whole time they were talking, Mandy stood quiet next to Freeman with a blanket across her shoulders. Still stunned by the discovery, Mandy's mind drifted off into another world. She heard what the detectives were saying, but didn't care. Looking at the house, she could see the yellow crime scene tape draped across the steps to the deck.

"What's going on?" Mandy asked suddenly.

"What do you mean, Mandy?" asked Barnes.

"What's going on?" she repeated frantically. "Why is everyone around me disappearing or dying?"

Barnes and Freeman looked at one another. "Mandy," he said softly, "we'd better get going. I'll drive your car and Barnes can drive mine. We'll find a hotel in Niles and I'll have you back home before noon tomorrow. Okay?"

"Okay," she said.

Freeman took Mandy's keys. He opened the door for her to slide into the passenger's seat. He turned to Barnes. "Anything else I should know?"

"Jacobs called. He wants one of us there in the morning to have a little talk with Mrs. Phelps. I'm thinking I'll just go on home tonight. Mandy needs to get some rest *away* from her father. Believe me; he needs a cooling off period."

"Okay," said Freeman. "Maybe she can drop me off at headquarters when we get back."

"Keys please," she said, hand extended. He gave her the keys to his car. "See you tomorrow. Oh, and don't forget, take it easy on her. She'll be getting enough crap when she gets home."

"Don't worry. All she had to do was look at me with those big green eyes and I melted."

"I should have known," she said, heading for Freeman's car.

He watched his partner walk away. He got into the car with Mandy and they drove to Niles where they found the Copperfeld Hotel. Before Brent could open the door, Mandy grabbed his right arm.

"Brent. Can we get one room? I don't want to be alone tonight."

"I guess so. I'll get a room with two beds. Do you want to come in with me?"

"Yes, I would," she said trembling.

They went in and Brent completed their registration. The clerk gave him a funny look when he requested two double beds. Mandy was grateful Brent was willing to stay with her. She'd pictured their first stay in a hotel as being a much more romantic event. Now all she had were images in her mind of two men she'd had the misfortune of finding murdered.

"Okay, Mandy. All set," Brent announced, bringing Mandy out of her revelry. "Room 220. Will you be okay here while I get our overnight bags?"

"Yes, I'm fine," she said. Of course, she wasn't sure she'd ever really be fine again.

Waiting in the hotel lobby, Mandy looked around at the rich brown cabinetry, forest green and tan checked carpets, comfortable wing backed chairs, and floral couch. Beyond the lobby was an area where a continental breakfast is served in the mornings.

Brent gently touched her shoulder and she forced herself to smile. Then they walked in silence toward the elevator. She could smell the faint chemical odor of the swimming pool, which was just around the corner. The scent lost its strength as the elevator doors shut and they ascended to the second floor.

Once in their room, Brent pulled down the blankets on one of the beds. "Here Mandy. You need some rest."

"Thanks. Would you lay here and hold me, at least until I'm able to fall sleep?"

"Sure," he said.

It had been a long day and they were both exhausted. They lay on the bed, both of them asleep within minutes fully clothed with the lights on.

Chapter 33

Captain Stevenson had one of his patrol officers call upon Gloria Phelps the night her husband's body was found in their summer home. He'd sent a message for her to stop by headquarters the following morning to answer some more questions. Although offended by his request, especially in light of the news she'd just received, she agreed to come by.

Gloria showed up at 10:00 and had been placed in an interrogation room. Barnes was waiting outside of the room for Jacobs to arrive.

"There you are," she said with a smile. "Ready for hurricane Gloria?"

He chuckled. "I guess we'll see how long she'll try to fool us into thinking she was just another loving wife and step-mother before she cracks."

"Something doesn't feel right here, Jacobs," Barnes said, her brow furrowed. "I know she's a snooty bitch, and Alex told Mandy about the flirtation. But I just don't see her killing Alex or kidnapping Cassandra Stevenson. What would she gain?"

"People kill over the most ridiculous things sometimes," Jacobs retorted. "Maybe Alex was going to tell Dad about Gloria's come-ons. Mrs. Stevenson's done some pretty shady things. She could have been blackmailing Gloria."

"I see your point. Ready?" asked Barnes, reaching for the door handle. "Here we go!"

Gloria Phelps was dressed like a widow in a black suit with a light blue silk blouse, pearl earrings, and black high heels adding three inches to her five foot, seven inch frame.

"Thank you so much for taking the time to come by this morning,

Mrs. Phelps," stated Jacobs. "We just have a few questions for you so it shouldn't take too long."

Gloria looked directly into Jacobs' eyes, flirtatiously batting her lashes. "I'm not sure I can tell you anything more than I told her right after Alex passed," Gloria replied, pointing at Barnes. "And now my dear husband is dead. I will do whatever it takes to bring their killers to justice."

"Mrs. Phelps, how would you describe your relationship with Alex?" asked Jacobs.

"I've known Alex since he was eight years old," she answered in a nauseating, sweet voice. "I believe we'd established a very amicable mother-son relationship."

"Amicable is an interesting choice of words," Jacobs noted. "Do you mean there was a time when things weren't so friendly?"

"Well, losing one's mother at such a young age is a very traumatic experience. I could tell he resented me at first. Bradley remarrying so quickly after Victoria's death must have been very hard on him." She paused, adjusting her position in the chair. "Of course, after about $10,000 worth of therapy, he seemed to calm down."

"I see," said Barnes as she made some notes. "Mrs. Phelps did you ever harbor any affection for Alex which might be more than…let's say…motherly love?"

Suddenly, Gloria's face turned red and the detectives could see it coming — zero to bitch in less than ten seconds. "How dare you!" she shouted, shooting up from her chair, smacking her hands on top of the table and leaning forward in a threatening manner.

Barnes and Jacobs both regarded her placidly. Then Jacobs stood up slowly, not taking his eyes off Gloria's. "Mrs. Phelps, you will please take your seat," he said firmly.

Gloria sat down again still angry. "Are you accusing me of something? Do I need to call my lawyer?" she raged.

"You have every right to call your attorney and have him or her present during questioning if you wish, Mrs. Phelps," said Jacobs staying calm as he sat down in his chair again. "However, you haven't been arrested or accused of anything. We just want to get to the truth so we can find out who murdered Alex and your husband. You gave us the impression you wanted that, too."

"Of course I do."

"Back to my question," interjected Barnes. "Alex apparently told people you had been flirting with him."

"People!" snapped Gloria. "You mean Mandy Stevenson. That little bitch was stringing poor Alex along, telling him she just wanted to be pals. Whatever!"

"Mrs. Phelps, please answer my question," Barnes politely commanded. "Did you have a sexual relationship with Alex Phelps?"

"Absolutely not!" Gloria bellowed. "I loved Bradley. I would never cheat on him with anyone, and definitely not with his own son! How can you do this to me? I've just lost two members of my family."

"All right, Mrs. Phelps," Barnes said. "We need for you to tone down your voice. I know these are tough questions, but we need for you to show some restraint."

Barnes continued, "We need to know your whereabouts between August 2nd and August 20th."

Still glaring at the detectives, Gloria pushed her glossy blonde hair off of her face. Then sitting up taller in her chair, she said, "My daughter and I went to Toledo, Ohio to visit my parents. Lana wanted to see them one more time before school started. But I don't understand what any of this has to do with these murders."

Barnes scratched more notes as Jacobs sat silently watching Gloria Phelps fidget in her chair, apparently unable to decide whether to put her hands on the table or in her lap. Then Barnes said bluntly, "There were some things that may have happened during that period of time which may be related to Alex's demise."

Again, they sat quietly forcing Gloria to wait several minutes for the next question. They stared at her then looked at one another trying to rattle her nerves.

"And you stayed with your parents the entire time from August 2nd through August 20th?" asked Barnes staring straight at her.

"Well, no," said Gloria, her eyes shifting. "I needed some alone time, so I drove to Nappanee, Indiana, to do some shopping at Amish Acres. They make lovely furniture and quilts, you know."

"When was that?" Barnes asked.

"I left my parent's house on August 12th, returning on the 19th," Gloria replied. "And you still haven't told me how exactly this relates to Alex."

"Why are you so nervous, Mrs. Phelps?" Barnes asked. "You do want to be ruled out as a suspect, don't you?"

"Suspect?" Gloria sputtered.

"Yes," Jacobs responded. "Everyone is a suspect, especially those who have a history with the victim." After a short pause, he continued, "Of course, we will need the names of your parents and their contact information. Also the name and contact information of the place where you stayed in Nappanee. Credit card receipts would help. Then we can confirm your story more easily."

"But I never keep receipts," she whined.

"It would also be helpful to you, if we had the names of any restaurants or shops you visited while there," Jacobs added. "They should have a record of the use of your credit card. They might even remember seeing you there."

Gloria nodded, lips pursed.

"One more question in regards to Alex," said Barnes. "Where were you between the hours of 2:00 p.m. and 6:00 p.m. on the day Alex Phelps was shot?"

"Shopping," she said caustically.

Jacobs raised an eyebrow.

"Yes, Detective," she said in response to Jacob's expression. "I went to Castleton Square Mall. I arrived at the mall around 1:00 p.m. and left at 5:00 p.m., arriving home at 6:00 p.m."

"Can anyone verify you were there?" asked Barnes. "Do you have receipts from purchases, witnesses such as store clerks or anyone else who knows you?"

"Well, no," Gloria answered rocking in her chair. "Maybe when the credit card bill comes, it will show my purchases. Then you will know I am telling the truth."

"Excellent," said Jacobs. "Make sure we get copies as soon as it arrives. Now, in regards to your husband, when did he leave to go up to the house in Cassopolis?"

"He left early on Friday. Said he had to close up the house and store the boat."

"I just returned from Cassopolis," said Barnes. "Your husband had already stored the boat when he was there in August."

"All I know is that's what he'd said he was doing," growled Gloria.

"Did you go with him over the weekend?" asked Barnes.

"No," she sputtered. "There wasn't any need for me to run up there. Besides, he'd been in such a crappy mood. I had no desire to be around him."

"Well, he *had* just lost his only son," said Barnes.

"Alex isn't his only child. He really should have been more concerned with Lana. Losing Alex was horrendous for her. She's going to be devastated by her father's death."

"Going to be?" said Jacobs. "You mean you haven't told her yet?"

"Look," said Gloria leaning on the table. "Lana was staying with her friend Sally all weekend. She came home Sunday night and went to school Monday morning. She was exhausted and already in bed when the policeman came by last night."

"Today is Tuesday," said Barnes gritting her teeth. "You mean to tell me you sent your daughter off to school this morning without telling her about her father. What if somebody else tells her first?"

"He died in Michigan," retorted Gloria. "How's she going to find out?"

Barnes rolled her eyes, taking a deep breath. Jacobs responded to Gloria's question. "The news media, Mrs. Phelps. Mr. Phelps was a very well known local businessman and he just lost his son. They could very easily find out and it would be all over the news before lunch."

"Oh, well." Gloria looked perplexed. "I didn't think about that."

Barnes glared at her before speaking. "So what did you do all weekend with your husband and daughter away?"

"Nothing much," said Gloria examining her nails. "It had been a very exhausting week with Alex's funeral and all. I sat out by the pool during the warmer part of the day, read a book, and relaxed."

"Can anyone corroborate your whereabouts this weekend?" asked Jacobs.

Gloria breathed a sigh of disgust. "I just told you I didn't do anything. I was home alone the entire weekend."

"How much do you stand to inherit, Mrs. Phelps?" Barnes asked.

Gloria glared at Barnes with a look of utmost contempt. "First you imply I might be involved in what happened to Alex, and now the two of you make it sound like I murdered my husband."

"You can either answer the question or we can subpoena the will, insurance records, and business records to determine his assets and how they were to be distributed," said Jacobs. "Course it'd be to your advantage to be cooperative. Otherwise, we might wonder what you're hiding."

"Talk to my attorney," she said, enunciating each word boldly. "I have no idea."

"The hard way it is?" said Jacobs slamming his folder shut. "We will need your fingerprints and a DNA sample."

"What the hell for?" she retorted.

"Again, Mrs. Phelps," Jacobs said exasperated, "to eliminate you as a suspect. Of course, if you don't volunteer we can officially label you a suspect, get a warrant, and collect it anyway."

"This is ridiculous," Gloria snapped. "I'm sure my lawyer will see this differently."

"Like I said before," said Jacobs, "you have every right to contact your attorney. However, you would save a lot of time by cooperating."

Barnes stood up and leaned on the table glaring into Gloria's eyes. "You should take Detective Jacobs' advice. You can do it now or you can sit in a holding cell for three or four hours until your lawyer gets down here. By then, we'll have a warrant from the judge and your lawyer will tell you to comply or be held in contempt. A contempt charge would mean you get to stay in our lovely facilities across the street in the Marion County Jail until you agree to cooperate. It's up to you, Gloria. What's it going to be?"

"Fine!" she said, eyes flaming. "But only to get you people off my back. I know I didn't do anything wrong. If all of this testing crap proves it, then I'll do it."

Jacobs left the room to call a lab tech from Forensics to collect the sample and the prints. While he waited, he watched the room through the two-way mirror. He saw Barnes writing notes as Gloria gave her the information they needed to check her August alibi. Once the lab tech arrived, it only took a couple of minutes for him to collect the fingerprints and the DNA swab. Jacobs returned to the interrogation room.

"Do you have anything else you want to tell us?" asked Barnes.

"I don't intend to answer *any* more questions without my attorney present!"

"Okay then, you're free to go, Mrs. Phelps," she said. "Just don't leave town without notifying us first."

"Oh, by the way," Gloria said as she rose from her chair, "you might want to talk to Savannah Richmond."

"Why?" asked Barnes.

"The Richmonds used to come to our house for parties and the occasional dinner. Savannah and I were friends for a time. I decided to stop asking her over after she made a despicable remark about Alex. She said, quote, 'I sure would like to have some of that beef,' unquote."

"So you think Savannah wanted to have an affair with your stepson?" asked Barnes.

"When Savannah *Gladstone* Richmond, Gladstone as in the R. J. Gladstone family, wants something, she gets it. She's a spoiled little rich girl whose father has always made sure she gets whatever she wants, including Jonathan. If she wanted a boy toy like Alex, she'd just flash some cash in his face. I always wondered where he got the cash to pay for his apartment because Bradley sure wasn't paying for it."

"Interesting, thanks for the information. We'll check it out," said Barnes as she held the door open for Gloria. Jacobs came out of the observation room to join her.

Barnes wiped her brow. "Whew, we survived it!"

"Thanks to you, Barnes," Jacobs said. "You handled her brilliantly."

"Thanks, Ben," she said. "So, what do you think?"

"She had a lot of nerve calling Savannah Richmond a spoiled brat. I think she's definitely hiding something," he said. "Want a cup of coffee before we start checking Gloria's alibis?"

"A recharge of the old battery sounds real good right about now," she laughed.

Chapter 34

Mandy had awakened in the morning with Brent's arms around her, giving her a stiff neck. She was, however, very grateful he'd stayed with her and hadn't taken her back to Indianapolis the night before. A lecture from her father was the last thing she needed. She was of age and could make her own decisions.

She and Brent sat in the breakfast area of the hotel having a continental breakfast. Watching him sip his coffee, she wondered how he was going to handle what she was about to suggest. Would he react like her father and tell her no? She decided she really didn't have anything to lose. Besides, they were in *her* car and she could leave him behind if he didn't choose to cooperate.

"Brent?" she began cautiously.

"Yes," he replied.

"I want to go back."

"We're going back in just a few minutes. Do you think you could drop me off at the station before you go home?"

"You don't understand," she said. "I want to go back to Cassopolis. I want to know what they found and talk to Chief Matthews."

"Please don't ask me to do that," Brent pleaded. "Your father is already ticked at me for not bringing you straight home last night."

"I talked to several people yesterday," she said, ignoring his request. "I found out Mr. Phelps was lying about Alex coming up here. I also discovered he was here with some blonde. No one who saw her got a good look at her, but they all thought it was Gloria."

She stared at Brent hopefully, but he didn't say anything. "I think we should talk to some of the other folks in town, like the guys at the bait and tackle shop and Mr. Rivers at the boat storage place." Mandy could feel her adrenaline pumping. She needed to know what happened the weekend when Alex and his father argued.

"You're afraid of my father, aren't you?" she asked.

"He *is* my boss. I promised him I'd bring you home first thing this morning."

"You shouldn't make promises unless you're sure you can keep them. I'm going to call him and tell him we're going back. I'll also tell him we've got my car and if you try to take it I'll call the police and tell them you're trying to steal it."

"You wouldn't!" he exclaimed. She could see the panic in his face.

"I would. This is important to me. Alex was my best friend," she said.

She called her dad, who was very upset, as she knew he would be. She told him she and Brent would leave as soon as he was finished asking questions.

"Dad, I have to know what was going on. I have a feeling it all ties in together. And Brent doesn't know these people like I do. He'll get more information out of them if I'm with him."

"Long as you stick with Freeman, I won't come running up there to drag you back home," her dad told her. "But, if I get wind you're interfering in this investigation, I'll have the Chief lock you up. Understand?"

"Yes, Dad," she said rolling her eyes. Hanging up she turned to Brent. "It's all set. He did say he wants you to stick with me. I guess I'm your assignment today."

"I've had worse." He smiled.

"Not sure if I should take that as an insult or a compliment."

"Come on. Let's get out of here so you can introduce me to the locals."

Mandy had suggested their first stop be the bait and tackle shop. It was stereotypical in its style, a bit run down and located at the edge of town right on the lake. There was a pier where boaters could stop to purchase gasoline. Next to the door stood a rumbling ice machine and a chalkboard advertising today's sale items.

As they walked inside the building, they saw nets and taxidermy fish of varying types and sizes on the walls. A young man came from the back of the shop asking what he could do for them. Mandy introduced Brent to Kameron Taylor, who ran the shop with his father-in-law. She quickly told him why they were there.

"Oh yeah, I heard about that," he said. "What a shame. He just graduated from college and all. They found his daddy up at the house last night, dead. Heard it was you who found him, Mandy. That true?"

"Yes, Kameron," she replied. "I'm afraid so."

"Sorry, you doing okay?" he asked.

"I'm okay," she replied. "Thanks for asking."

"Mr. Taylor, when was the last time you saw Alex Phelps?" asked Brent.

"Let me think," Kameron paused, looking at the ceiling tapping his chin. "I believe it was June."

"Not August?" asked Brent.

"No sir. I heard he was in town for a few hours back in August, but I didn't see him. Guess he was in a hurry. Alex sure did love fishing."

"Do you remember seeing his father back in August?" said Mandy.

"Oh, yeah. He came by and bought some bait and a couple of flies," said Kameron. "I remember seeing his wife waiting in the car. She didn't look too happy."

"Are you sure it was her, did you get a good look at her?" asked Brent.

"No, I didn't, but who else could it have been?" asked Kameron.

"Do you have surveillance cameras outside," asked Brent.

"Around these parts?" laughed Kameron. "I got one up there behind the counter. Those cameras are expensive and the father-in-law doesn't see any reason to have one outside. Most of the locals don't even lock their doors."

"Thanks for your help, Mr. Taylor," said Brent. "If you can think of anything else, please give us a call." Brent handed his card to Kameron.

"This is really getting complicated," Mandy said as they drove in the direction of Rivers Boat Storage.

"Yeah, sometimes these cases get this way. We're going to have to do a timeline just to figure out where and when Alex and Bradley were here."

Jason Rivers was in his early forties, tall and tan with dark brown hair and hazel eyes. He was just opening the doors to his place of business when Mandy and Brent arrived. "Mr. Rivers," Mandy said.

"Well hello there, Mandy. What brings you here?" he said.

Mandy introduced Mr. Rivers to Brent and told him they were here to ask questions about Alex and his father. "Terrible news. What can I do to help?" Jason asked.

"Is the Phelps' boat being stored here currently? Who brought it in and when?" Brent asked.

"It's in the third building, slot number 89. Bradley brought it in here the second or third weekend in August. I can look it up if you need the exact date. He said he was bringing her in because no one else was coming up this fall."

"Do you remember anything odd about Mr. Phelps' behavior?" asked Brent.

"The only thing I thought was odd was the boat wreaked of bleach," Mr. Rivers answered. "I mean, everybody cleans their boats and dries them out before storing them here, but the smell was so strong it gagged me. I told him I thought he got a bit carried away. He just laughed it off. Said he'd dropped the bottle while he was cleaning."

"Do you remember seeing Mrs. Phelps in town in August?" Mandy asked.

"No," he said. "Of course, I've only seen her from a distance. She mostly stayed out at the house when she was here, sunbathing I suppose. Saw the kids and Bradley a lot, but not her. Just know she's blonde, tan, and skinny. Not sure I'd know her if she were standing right in front of me."

Brent called Chief Matthews and asked him to bring a couple of his men to the boatyard, as there was some potential evidence there. When the chief arrived, Brent told him about the excessive cleaning and suggested the boat be turned over to the crime lab.

The chief instructed his men to seal off the boat slip where the Phelps' boat was kept. He then assigned one of them to guard it until someone from the Kalamazoo Crime Lab came to look at it for evidence.

"Don't let anyone near Phelps' boat," Chief Matthews advised Jason. "Not until the Kalamazoo lab rats get a chance to look it over."

Chief Matthews asked Mandy and Brent if they could meet him back at the station. He had a few questions of his own to ask and some information they might be interested in.

"Have a seat kids," he said as he pointed to two chairs sitting in front of his desk. "Oh, sorry," he said at the look on Brent's face. "At my age I call everyone under the age of 35 a kid. Didn't mean to insult you."

"I'm sure someday we'll learn to appreciate it," Mandy quipped.

"Mandy," the chief began. "Why'd you come up here all by yourself?"

"After Alex's funeral, Mr. Phelps had told me some things which didn't add up. I wanted to talk to him about it."

"So why not just wait until he came home?" Matthews asked while Brent looked on silently.

"My impatience got the better of me. His wife told me he was supposed to be back already. I really needed answers."

"So what were you so all-fired up to ask him?"

Mandy took a few minutes to give Chief Matthews a brief scenario of what Bradley Phelps had told her and how he'd lied about coming to the summerhouse in August. She told him about the fight Alex had with his father, but she wasn't sure what the argument was about.

"Strange," said Chief Matthews as he stroked his beard. "Bradley and his son always got along real well. Maybe that's why he wrote the suicide note."

"What?" Mandy and Brent shouted simultaneously.

"Sorry, didn't mean to spring it on you that way." Chief Matthews shuffled some paperwork on his desk and came up with a file. "Yep. The lab techs found a suicide note wedged between the bed and nightstand. Basically, it said he was sorry for everything. Guess being angry with his son and then having him die suddenly was more than Bradley could take."

"I don't believe it!" Mandy said standing. She paced back and forth in the small office, feeling like the walls were closing in. Mandy didn't believe for one second Bradley Phelps would kill himself and leave his daughter fatherless, no matter how bad he felt about Alex.

"Now, Mandy. Sit down and listen." The chief motioned for her to sit. "I should have said it looks like he killed himself. Just because there was a suicide note, doesn't mean he did himself in. He definitely took the shot in his mouth like most suicides committed by men. Problem is the gun is missing."

"The gun's missing?" Brent said, finally breaking his silence.

"That's right, son. Don't know if he went up intending to do it or not. Maybe he changed his mind then somebody else decided it was a bad idea."

"Did you call anyone at IMPD with this information," asked Brent.

"Well, no," said the chief. "Since the idea of suicide was questionable, I didn't think it was necessary to pass it along. I just figured since you're here, I may as well tell you about it."

"Was it a handwritten note, Chief?" asked Brent.

"No. Matter of fact it was typed. The lab should be able to discover what sort of printer it was. They may be calling on your lab guys to help them collect printers Bradley used. Work, home, wherever. They'll want to determine if he typed the note or could someone else have typed it."

"I'm sure Mark Chatham and his team will be glad to help," stated Brent. "If Bradley Phelps was murdered, it may be linked to his son's murder."

"You said the woman who murdered Alex Phelps was a blonde, right?" asked Chief Matthews.

"That's right, we believe so," said Brent.

"Then we very well may be looking at the same killer since people up here seen him with a blonde last month," replied the chief. "Best thing you can do," now he was looking straight at Mandy, "is be patient and let the boys in the lab tell us what they think went down. I think you know it takes several weeks for lab results, but the autopsy should be done in a couple of days."

"Yes, Chief Matthews. We just received the results from my mother's car. She's been missing for a little over a month."

"Which reminds me. There was one strange thing he wrote in his note," he said. Mandy noticed the frown on his face as he returned his gaze to Brent. "Bradley said something in this note about being sorry about Mandy's mom. Does this mean anything to you, Mandy?"

"My mom?"

Brent interceded, "Chief, did he say anything specific?"

"Not really. Did Bradley Phelps know your mom, Mandy?"

"As far as I knew they only saw one another a couple of times. His company built houses and I think I remember her saying one of her clients was interested in looking at them," she answered stunned by this news. Racking her brain, she could not think of any other time they had seen one another since she and Alex met.

"Maybe it's nothing," said Chief Matthews. "Maybe he felt bad for you and wanted to send you a message. Who knows what goes through people's minds."

"What if he knew something about Alex's death or what if they'd both found out something about my mom? Maybe they were killed because of it."

"Whoa there, girl," said the chief. "You sure are jumping the gun. We don't even know exactly what happened yet. Could be these cases don't connect at all."

Mandy turned to Brent, the volume of her voice increasing with every word. "Don't you think it's weird? My mom disappears, Alex has a fight with his dad then gets murdered, and *then* his dad winds up dead writing a suicide note which includes an apology for what happened to my mom?"

"We don't know that it's an apology, Mandy," said Brent. "We only know it was part of the note. I know this is hard, but you have to be patient and wait until we get the results from the crime lab. Barnes and I will put our heads together and include Mayhew and Jacobs and find out if there is a connection. Don't forget what your dad told you?"

"I won't," she sniped. "How can I with his puppet tagging along to make sure I behave?"

The moment the words came out of her mouth, she knew she'd gone too far. She could see the momentary pain on Brent's face. Being the consummate professional, he rallied.

"Well, Chief Matthews, I think we've taken up enough of your time. Here is my card if you need to get in touch. I'll have Mark Chatham from our lab call you when I get back to my office."

"Thanks, Detective."

Realizing it was time to go and she dare not push Brent any further, she got up and thanked Chief Matthews as well. The guilt over her nasty comment to Brent was giving her a headache.

"Mandy," Brent said gently touching her arm. "Let's go home."

Then he opened the car door for her.

When Brent slid into the driver's seat, she looked at him, throat tight with nerves. "I'm so sorry for what I said back there. I feel like an ass."

"You are an ass," he said giving her a sideways glance and a grin. "Besides, I know you're upset. Who wouldn't be after what you've been through?"

"That's still no reason to take it out on you."

"Maybe not, but I can take it," he said.

"Thanks, Brent," she said rubbing his right shoulder and eliciting another smile from him. He started the car and they headed south.

Mandy leaned back in her seat desperately searching her mind for some clue as to who would kill Alex and his father. Were they the same killer? Did Savannah blame Mr. Phelps for Alex's death somehow? Did she come up here and get her revenge? Then there's Gloria. All she cares about is money. Did Alex discover something about Gloria and she killed him for it? And how did any of this connect with her mother?

Chapter 35

Robert Stevenson was sitting at his desk going over his interviews with Alex's professors. School had only been in session for four weeks when Alex died. Most of Alex's professors barely had a chance to learn his name; they certainly didn't know him by sight. Those who did remember him hadn't seen him with a woman matching his assailant's description nor had they noticed him having any disagreements with anyone.

There was a knock on the office door. Lieutenant Melrose was looking at him through the glass. He smiled and gestured for Mel to come in.

"I could tell by the look on your face you're getting as frustrated with this whole thing as am I," Mel said. "Do you think Cassandra's disappearance and the murders of the two Phelps men are connected?"

"I haven't found any concrete evidence to link them, just lots of conjecture."

"We're still monitoring Cassandra's financial accounts. No money has been taken from your joint accounts. Neither her credit cards nor debit card have been used. There's still no cell phone activity. This case is getting colder by the minute. I'm sorry, Robert."

Stevenson shook his head. "I know. I was just sitting here thinking about how some of the suspects overlap in these two cases."

"What did you come up with?" asked Mel.

"As you know, Jonathan Richmond is Bradley Phelps' attorney. Mandy met the Richmonds at Alex's funeral and the next thing we know, Mrs. Richmond is confessing to her about the affair with Alex. Mandy seems to think Savannah Richmond was in love with Alex. Was she or was she fooling around with him to get back at her husband for screwing around with Cassandra?"

"My guys have those notes from Rosini stating he'd heard Mrs. Richmond threaten to kill Cassandra. It also appears she didn't care much for Mrs. Phelps either. Maybe she killed Alex and his father to frame her."

"Gloria Phelps is the one who really intrigues me," said Robert. "Mandy said Mrs. Phelps had been flirting with Alex. Maybe *she* was the jealous one. Perhaps she decided if she couldn't have Alex, no one could. In her interview, she implied it was Savannah Richmond doing the killing. She could be the one trying to frame somebody."

Robert leaned back in his chair. "Mandy called to tell me there was a suicide note. In it, Bradley Phelps stated he was sorry about Cassandra. Mandy and Freeman confirmed Phelps was up there in August with someone the locals thought was Gloria."

"We may want to consider that there's more than one person involved in all this, Robert. Maybe Phelps was trying to protect the person who caused Cassandra's disappearance. That secret and his son's death may have put him over the edge, especially if he suspected Blondie of killing Alex. His grief would have been overshadowed by guilt."

"Poor Mandy," Robert said, rising from his chair. "This whole thing is really tearing her apart."

"You know I love you like a brother and I don't want to interfere, but don't you think it might be time to talk to Mandy about — you know?"

"Absolutely not!" Robert said, glaring at Mel. "She's been through enough. Until we find out what happened to Cassandra, I can't see any reason to say anything to her about it."

"Okay," said Mel. "I just thought it might help her to understand things."

Robert rubbed his temples, closing his eyes.

"Sorry, Robert, I didn't mean to make things worse."

Robert turned, patting Mel on the shoulder. "You didn't bring on this headache, old friend," he said. "I've had one of these almost every day since Charlie died."

"Well, I just wanted to check on you. I'd better get back to my own headaches. See you later," Mel said. He opened the door and nearly ran into Mandy.

"Oh," Mandy said. "Hi, Uncle Mel, I'm glad you're here. I just dropped Brent off and wanted to talk to you and Dad for a few minutes."

"Sure," he said, allowing her to pass then closing the door.

Her dad stepped forward, but instead of yelling at her, threw his arms around her. "Thank God you're okay," he said, overwhelmed by emotion.

"Don't worry, Dad," she said. "Can we talk about these cases? I'm very confused."

"Join the club," he said, glancing at Mel. "I'll listen to what you have to say, but I can't guarantee I can tell you everything you want to know."

"I've got a gut feeling Mom's disappearance is somehow connected to these two deaths. I can't imagine why Alex or his father would have had anything to do with Mom's disappearance. I didn't even think Mom knew Mr. Phelps very well. Of course as many new lovers as we keep discovering, we could have 200 male suspects by now," Mandy spat.

"Come on Mandy," said her dad. "Don't exaggerate."

"You think it isn't possible, Dad." she said, her voice getting louder.

"Lower your voice," he said. "We can hear you."

"Don't tell me this doesn't frustrate the hell out of you! Come on, Dad! Doesn't this piss you off?"

"Of course it pisses me off!" he shouted, causing her to jump. "I've done everything I could to make that woman happy and all she's done is shit on me. About the time you turned five, I gave up and dove into my work. Work has always been faithful to me and has never let me down. I work hard and I get rewarded. If that makes me a horrible husband and father then I'm sorry. But you're twenty-two now and shouldn't need to be coddled anymore."

"Maybe I wouldn't if I'd ever experienced it as a child," she said. "Charlie's the only one who ever really loved me."

"Mandy, that isn't fair," said Mel. "Losing your temper and making cutting remarks isn't helping."

Mandy didn't say a word. Her dad noticed she was pursing her lips like she always did when she was trying not to cry.

"I know everyone's patience is wearing thin. Both of you not only have to deal with Cassandra's whereabouts, but Mandy has discovered two dead bodies, one of whom was her best friend. It's more than any one person should have to experience in a lifetime and she's experienced it in just a few weeks."

Robert looked down at the floor. He knew he could always count on Mel to bring things back around to common sense. He looked up into his daughter's glistening pale green eyes, seeing so much of her mother in them.

"I'm sorry, Dad," she finally said. "I was only thinking about myself and wasn't listening to your pain."

He stroked her cheek, and her tears began to flow. She turned to Mel. "Something's going on here, Uncle Mel. These cases are connected. I can feel it."

"You've got natural instincts for the job just like your dad and brother," said Mel. "You sure you don't want to go to the academy?"

"NO!" Robert and Mandy said in unison. Then they all started laughing.

"It's like a thousand-piece jigsaw puzzle, isn't it?" said Mandy.

"How so?" asked Robert.

"We've got this box full of tiny pieces we know connect together somehow, but with everything so scattered, we can't see how they fit just yet."

"Good analogy," said Mel. "We do have several pieces fitting together right now, but unfortunately, not enough to be able to see the whole picture."

"I wonder if Mr. Phelps was having an affair like everyone else was," said Mandy.

"In this group…it wouldn't surprise me," said Robert.

"Gloria was supposed to be in Ohio, what if she changed her mind and caught him with someone?" said Mandy. "Maybe Alex found his dad with this woman. That would explain why Alex was so angry with him."

"Interesting theories," Uncle Mel commented. "What do you think of Whitney Benson?" he asked.

"I'm not sure where she fits. I know she hated my mom because of the affair she had with Whitney's father. But why would she do anything to Alex or his dad?"

"Wouldn't be the first time Bradley Phelps fell for a younger woman, would it?" said Robert.

"No, it wouldn't," Mandy said, her eyes flashing with realization. "Do you think Whitney could have manipulated Mr. Phelps into helping her do away with Mom? That *was* the week Mom vanished. Then Alex went up the following weekend and caught Whitney and his dad together. Whitney would have wanted to shut him up. If her father didn't approve of Alex, he sure wouldn't approve of her seeing Mr. Phelps. Once Alex was dead, Mr. Phelps realized it had to be Whitney, he confronted her, and she got rid of him, too."

"Good job fitting those pieces together," said Mel, "but this scenario could also fit Savannah Richmond."

"Yeah, but her killing Alex doesn't fit. You know, like some puzzle pieces appear to have the same shape until you try them. She just seemed so sincerely in love with him."

"We're keeping a close eye on all three women for now," said Robert.

"If you come up with any new theories, run them past one of us first," said Mel.

"However, leave interviewing suspects to us," Robert interjected. "Alex and his father are dead, because they may have known too much. I don't want you to be next."

Mandy hadn't thought of that. "Okay, you two. I'll try."

Chapter 36

On a hunch, Barnes checked the database to see if Bradley or Gloria Phelps owned a Glock 23. She discovered there was a registration for a Phelps, but not for Bradley or Gloria.

Freeman walked up to her. "What's up, partner?" he asked causing her to jump. "You find something you want to share with me?"

"Maybe," she said, glancing at him. "I was just going through the gun registration database and found something very interesting." She turned the computer screen so Freeman could see it.

"Alex owned a Glock 23," he said. "Why the hell would he need a gun like that?"

"No idea," said Barnes. "Maybe he collected guns. He liked to fish, maybe he liked to hunt, too."

"Wouldn't doubt it. But that gun's for hunting humans, not wild game."

"We didn't find a gun in Alex's apartment. I think we need to visit Mrs. Phelps with a warrant and see if the gun is in her house."

"I'll find a judge who can help us out," Freeman said as he walked towards his desk.

They had their warrant in a couple of hours and headed for the Phelps' house with a couple of patrol officers for back up. They rang the doorbell and a young, lanky girl with long blonde hair and red, puffy eyes answered.

"Hi," she said. "Are you here to see my mom?"

Barnes pulled out her badge. "Yes. This is Detective Freeman and my name's Detective Barnes. Are you Lana?"

Lana nodded and stepped back allowing all four of them to enter the foyer. "I'll tell her you're here."

"Ah, Detective Barnes. Always a pleasure," Gloria said

sarcastically as she entered the foyer. "And you brought the troops with you, I see."

"It seems Alex owned a gun similar to the one that killed him. Did Alex keep his guns here?" asked Barnes.

"How am I supposed to know?"

"The gun wasn't in his apartment when we searched it after his death. We thought maybe he kept it here," said Barnes.

"We have a gun cabinet in our basement," said Mrs. Phelps. "What do Alex's guns have to do with this case?"

"He has more than one?" asked Freeman.

"Yes. He and my husband liked to hunt."

"The gun used to kill Alex was a Glock 23," Barnes explained. "We also received a report from Kalamazoo the gun used to kill your husband was also a Glock 23."

"I was told Bradley may have committed suicide," Gloria said, an edge of delight in her voice.

"That pleases you?" Freeman asked raising a suspicious eyebrow.

"Well, if he killed himself his insurance policy would be null and void," she said in a matter-of-fact tone. "Oh, don't look at me so hungrily, Detectives. Alex and Lana were his beneficiaries. Well, Lana is now."

"You said the gun cabinet is in your basement," stated Barnes. "Is it locked?"

"Yes, I certainly wouldn't want my daughter or any of her friends to get their hands on them."

"Get your keys then," Barnes said handing the warrant to Mrs. Phelps.

"What's this?" she asked.

"A warrant to search the premises," explained Barnes. "Now get the keys or we'll have to bust the lock. We're looking in the gun cabinet and in every nook and cranny of this house until we're satisfied this gun is not here."

"You and your daughter will have to have a seat in the living room with Officer Davis from the Carmel Police Department while we conduct the search," instructed Freeman.

"Nobody's searching my house until my attorney arrives!" she shouted.

"Mrs. Phelps," said Officer Davis. "This warrant was issued by a judge in the state court, which means these detectives can cross county lines to conduct this search. Your cooperation would show good faith. Your refusal will put you in jail."

"That's ridiculous!" Gloria shouted.

"The keys, Mrs. Phelps," stated Barnes.

Officer Davis followed Mrs. Phelps as she huffed into the kitchen. She opened a drawer and handed the keys to him. Officer Davis in turn gave the keys to Barnes and told Mrs. Phelps to call her daughter.

"What's going on, Mom?" asked Lana.

"These officers are going to look through our house to try to find one of Alex's guns."

"They're in the gun cabinet, aren't they," Lana said, looking frightened.

"Don't worry. They'll be finished in a few minutes," Mrs. Phelps told her daughter. "We just have to sit in the living room with Officer Davis while they do their search."

Barnes, Freeman, and the other officer headed for the basement. It was a finished family room and very masculine. Pool table, dartboard, bar, a buck's head mounted on the wall and in the corner near the gun cabinet. Pulling latex gloves from their pockets, Barnes unlocked the cabinet and searched it, opening drawers and finding only rifles and bullets, but no Glock.

"Looks like we're going to have to search the whole freakin' place," spouted Barnes.

"This could take some time," said Freeman. "Glove up, Officer West. We're going to need some help. You start in the opposite corner. Inspect the pool table to see if there's been any repair work done to it. I'll start with the bar area and Barnes can start with the lovely theatre couch."

"Why can't I do the bar?" she said. "These freakin' couches are a pain."

"That's why," he said smugly.

Barnes excused herself and went to the car. She came back with a small metal detector.

"What good's it going to do?" asked Freeman. "There's a ton of metal in those things."

"It will show me if there's a heavy concentration of metal in an area where there shouldn't be. It might keep me from ripping it to shreds unnecessarily."

It took the three of them approximately an hour to search the entire basement. This included looking in the room where the furnace, hot water heater, and water softener were located.

"I say we search the bedrooms next, starting with Gloria's," said Barnes. "Most stupid criminals hide their weapons in the bedroom closet thinking we won't think to look there."

"You believe this lady killed somebody?" asked Officer West.

"Yes, I'm afraid it's looking like it," said Freeman. "She may be involved in a missing person case, too."

"She doesn't look like the type," said West.

"How long you been on the job, West?" asked Barnes.

"About three months," he said, blushing.

"Give yourself about three years and you'll find out there is no such thing as someone who looks the type," said Barnes. "Motivation, West. That's what drives someone to kill another person. What are they going to gain by doing it? Is it worth it? Even psychos have motivation. Might be something sick like they enjoy eating human liver, but still, motivation."

"Got it," West said, looking a little green.

Barnes started going through Gloria's closet while the guys pulled the mattress off of the bed. There it was. In a plastic bag in the middle of the box springs. A Glock 23.

"Barnes, photo op," shouted Freeman. "We found it. You got an evidence bag?"

"You've got to be kidding," she said. "Why would someone hide a murder weapon under their mattress? West, you better go down to your squad and call Social Services. We're going to have to take her in and someone needs to take care of Lana until we can find a friend or relative to take care of her."

Officer West left the room. Barnes took photos from every angle. Freeman lifted the bag and rotated it so he and his partner could give it a preliminary exam.

"Hey look at this," he said pointing to the gun barrel. "This could be a speck of blood. Probably spatter from one of our victims." Barnes took more photos then held the evidence bag open so Freeman could insert the plastic bag and gun into it.

"I'll be glad to get the ballistics and the DNA tests completed," said Barnes. "I either want to put this bitch away or never see her again."

Chapter 37

While waiting for Gloria's attorney to show up, Barnes and Freeman had a conversation about Savannah Richmond with Jacobs and Mayhew. Mayhew said his second interview with her was much more forthcoming since she was ready to tell him about the affair with Alex. Although the police might have the weapon used to kill Alex and his father, Jacobs and Mayhew still weren't sure the Phelps murders were connected to the Stevenson case.

Since she was a suspect, it wasn't difficult for Captain Stevenson to compel a judge to grant a warrant for Mrs. Richmond's DNA and fingerprints. If nothing else, it might eliminate her as a suspect so they could focus on Mrs. Phelps and Miss Benson.

Jacobs had also taken most of the previous afternoon to investigate where Mrs. Richmond might have been during the week Alex told Mandy he was in Michigan. They were able to find several witnesses who placed Alex and Mrs. Richmond in the Monticello area at the beginning of that week and in Cincinnati with her family the following weekend.

Mrs. Richmond showed up right on time for her appointment with the homicide detectives with Mr. Van Gordon in tow. As they stepped into the interrogation room, Mr. Van Gordon spouted, "This is outrageous. I demand an explanation for dragging my client down here again."

"First of all, Mr. Van Gordon, no one dragged Mrs. Richmond anywhere," said Barnes. "Secondly, there have been some incidents which have come to our attention involving your client and our murder victim, Alex Phelps, which also may pertain to the death of his father, Bradley Phelps."

"You people accuse her of doing away with Mrs. Stevenson and now you think she murdered one or both of the Phelps!" he bellowed. His stout figure along with his white hair and beard made him look like an angry Santa Claus.

"Mr. Van Gordon, Mrs. Richmond," Freeman began, "please have a seat." They sat and he handed a copy of the warrant to Mr. Van Gordon to read. "This is a warrant for DNA and fingerprints from your client. It also gives us the right to search her purse, automobile and home if we deem it necessary. This includes the confiscation of any personal computers, laptops and printers in the home. We will also be checking her cell phone and credit card records."

As Mr. Van Gordon started to puff up like a blowfish again, Mrs. Richmond gently touched his arm and he abruptly deflated. "I have no reason not to cooperate with these officers, Percy. I had nothing to do with the disappearance of Mrs. Stevenson or with these murders, but I'm sure I know why they may think I did."

"And why would that be?" asked Barnes.

"Gloria," she said. "I said something about Alex which upset her. It was just a passing remark which wasn't meant to be taken seriously — at the time."

"Exactly what did you say?" asked Barnes.

"When Alex came out in his Speedo all trim and buff, I just said I'd like some of that. Don't we all fantasize now and then about good looking members of the opposite sex?" She grinned and said, "I'm married, but I'm not dead."

"I understand, but one doesn't normally verbalize such fantasies to the young man's mother," Freeman pointed out.

"Step-mother," Mrs. Richmond corrected him. "Believe me; I caught her giving him *the eye* more than once. Gloria doesn't like to share."

"Did Gloria or Bradley Phelps ever find out about your relationship with Alex?" Barnes inquired.

"Not to my knowledge," Mrs. Richmond simply stated. "I doubt Gloria would have kept it to herself. She's rather confrontational."

"We spoke with your husband. He told us you had been visiting in New York City during the week when Bradley Phelps was killed," stated Freeman. "When we contacted those people, they said they hadn't seen you since June of this year. So where did you go?"

"Okay, you've got me," Mrs. Richmond countered.

"Savannah, I must advise you not to go any further with this conversation," her lawyer advised. "They don't have anything but a bunch of circumstantial garbage or they'd be arresting you already."

"It's okay, Percy. This will get me *off the hook*," she said to him in a cavalier tone. "I was staying in the cabin Alex and I shared the last time we were together. I thought it would be therapeutic."

"We will need to contact the rental office to corroborate your story," said Barnes.

"The only time period we haven't covered, Mrs. Richmond," Freeman began, "is the week when Alex Phelps died."

Closing her eyes momentarily, she sighed and paused before responding. "Alex had just told me he thought we should stop seeing one another. So I decided to meet a friend in the Catskills. Someone who I've seen from time-to-time who I thought might help me get over Alex."

"And, who was this friend?" asked Barnes.

"I'd prefer not to say," she answered.

"We have to talk to him," stated Freeman. "That's how we clear suspects."

Mrs. Richmond sighed heavily. "It was Andre Marks." There were stunned looks all around the table. "Yes, *the* Andre Marks, the point guard for the Indiana Pacers."

"You're joking!" blurted Van Gordon rather unprofessionally.

Mrs. Richmond rolled her eyes and gave Van Gordon a look of disgust. "No, I'm not joking. At least I have better taste than Jonathan does. He goes screwing around with a bed hopper who's fifteen years older than he is. All she was after was money. At least, I chose a handsome, viral basketball player who is five years my junior and richer than sin."

"We'll try to be as discreet as possible when checking out your story, Mrs. Richmond," said Barnes. "However, the news media is all over this case and the Stevenson case, so I can't guarantee it won't leak out. It just won't be through me or my partner."

"Thank you, but I'm sure my father can help keep this quiet," she said. "Now can we get the fingerprint and DNA thing over with? I'd like to go home."

"Great," said Freeman. "I'll have our lab tech to come in."

Freeman knew Captain Stevenson and Lieutenant Melrose were in the observation room and the lab tech was waiting. He sent her in to do the collections while he spoke with the others.

"Good job in there," Captain Stevenson told him.

"Doubt she would have said anything to you about Andre Marks if it wasn't true," commented the lieutenant.

"Did Kendall go over to the Richmond's house to pick up the computer equipment?" asked Freeman.

"Yeah," said the captain. "Let's give her a quick call to see how it's going?" He called her on the speakerphone so all could hear.

"Captain, we've got two laptops, one which the Mister wasn't too keen to let go of, and one which supposedly belongs to his wife. I told Richmond he could have them back as soon as our lab geek finishes with them. Also took two printers."

"Were there any guns in the house?" asked the lieutenant.

"Affirmative. The same Glock test fired by our lab. The one that didn't match the bullet taken from Alex Phelps."

"Did the husband have anything to say?"

"Not much," she replied. "He's been pretty cooperative."

"So, you guys about done?" asked Freeman.

"Yeah," she answered. "I'm finishing up the husband's car as we speak. We should be out of here in about fifteen minutes."

"Thanks, Detective," said the captain. "I'll be waiting for your report."

"Yes, sir," she said. Then the line went dead.

"Of course, if the story about Marks pans out, I think we can eliminate her as a suspect," said the lieutenant. "Especially with the ballistics evidence."

"With her money and connections, she could have had someone else do it." Captain Stevenson said. "I know. I'm grasping for answers. Her other alibis have checked out. Freeman, check out her story about the cabin and about Marks. Keep an eye on her."

Chapter 38

Barnes returned to the office after dropping off the evidence she and Kendall had collected at the Richmond house. "Is Gloria Phelps ready to talk to us yet?" she asked her partner.

"They put her into Interrogation Room One with her lawyer," Freeman responded. "Guess who her lawyer is."

"Who?"

"Jonathan Richmond."

"You're kidding. He didn't mention it to me when he said he had to get down here to see a client."

"No, I'm serious."

"You'd think it would be some sort of conflict of interest or something. Especially since we're investigating his wife in conjunction with these same cases."

Freeman made a screwed up face. "I don't know. All I do know is that's who she called and that's who's in there with her now. I've got the ballistics report right here. It's a match for both murders. We also received the autopsy report from Kalamazoo. At least we can safely say Bradley Phelps was indeed murdered. Not sure we'll get much out of questioning her today though."

"I don't know. With her temperament, we just might get her to say something she doesn't intend to share."

"You're way too anxious, Barnes," Freeman said as he started to open the door.

Jonathan Richmond was just finishing with some last minute instructions when Barnes and Freeman entered the interrogation room. Gloria had an air of confidence about her which said 'I'm going to get out of here and then I'm going to sue your ass.'

The detectives took their seats to begin the questioning. "Mr.

Richmond. I'm sure you are aware my partner and I served a search warrant on your client's property this morning to locate a Glock 23 registered to her step-son, Alex Phelps," said Freeman. "During the search, we found a Glock 23 in a Ziploc freezer bag hidden between the mattress and box spring of your client's bed in the master bedroom."

"I am aware of this, Detective," answered Mr. Richmond.

Brent pulled photos and a report from his file folder. "These are photos of the evidence collected and the ballistics report on this evidence. It appears this was not only the gun used to kill Bradley Phelps, but it was also used to murder Alex Phelps."

The smirk Gloria had earlier had just turned to astonishment. Barnes caught this change of expression immediately. "What's wrong, Mrs. Phelps?" she asked.

"Nothing," Gloria said, looking over at her attorney. Apparently, he'd told her to keep her mouth shut.

"I'm a little confused, Mrs. Phelps," Barnes continued. "Why would this weapon be hidden in your bedroom?"

"I've advised my client not to answer any questions concerning the gun, Detectives," said Richmond.

"Frankly, Mr. Richmond," said Freeman. "I don't understand how you can in good conscience represent Mrs. Phelps. She has on more than one occasion implied your wife may have had something to do with not only the death of Alex Phelps, but the disappearance of Cassandra Stevenson. Isn't this a conflict of interest?"

"Bradley and Gloria Phelps have been clients and friends of ours for several years. Gloria needed someone right away, so here I am. I have a call into the law firm of Taylor and Smith to find permanent legal counsel for her."

"What?" cried Gloria. "You're not going to represent me?"

"Look, Gloria. Not only is my wife knee deep in these investigations, because as Detective Freeman pointed out, you have implicated her. I'm a corporate attorney. I represented Bradley in his business dealings. I'm not a criminal defense attorney. Now we're being told his death was not a suicide, but a murder. This does create a conflict of interest for me. I can advise you to keep your mouth shut, but I cannot represent you if this goes any further."

"Wonderful! Why should I take the advice of someone who

doesn't even intend to represent me? Besides, I thought Bradley killed himself," Mrs. Phelps said switching her attention to the detectives. "Monday, I was told Bradley died in what *appeared to be* a suicide. Then you two come to my home this morning to search for Alex's gun and tell me he may not have committed suicide. Now you say he was definitely murdered. How on Earth do you know for sure?"

"The autopsy report from Kalamazoo came today," said Freeman, pulling the paperwork out of the file. "Your husband's toxicology screens came back and showed an excessive dose of Lorazepam in his system. Not enough to kill him, but plenty enough to put him into a deep slumber. We called the local pharmacies and discover you have been using Lorazepam for a couple of years, and just renewed your prescription two days before your husband was murdered."

"I get nervous sometimes," said Gloria. "I'm sure lots of other people use that particular drug."

"Gloria," said Richmond in a warning tone.

"Shut up, Jonathan," she lashed back.

Jonathan Richmond shook his head. It was apparent he'd rather be anywhere than here.

"So, Mrs. Phelps," said Barnes. "Where *is* your prescription?"

"None of your business," she answered.

"Really," Barnes said with a sly grin. "The thing is, Mrs. Phelps, it is very much my business. For you see, now that we've found the murder weapon in your home, and we know you recently filled a prescription for the drug found in your dead husband's system, we now have probable cause to search your premises, cars, and your person for this prescription. According to the pharmacist, you received 30 capsules. How many have you taken since you picked up your prescription?"

"A couple, I guess."

"Then your bottle should have at least twenty-eight capsules in it, right?" asked Barnes.

"I'm sure it does since I didn't go up there and drug my husband," Mrs. Phelps said angrily. "You still haven't told me what makes you think my husband didn't kill himself."

"Well, Mrs. Phelps," Barnes said leaning toward her, "people who commit suicide usually have a problem shooting themselves in the mouth and then ditching their gun under a mattress that's three hours away."

"According to the autopsy," said Freeman, "Mr. Phelps had enough Lorazepam in his system to render him unconscious. Stomach contents indicated his last meal was some cheese and crackers with white wine. Although there is gunshot residue on his right hand, it isn't in the right place. There's an area on his hand which does not have GSR on it, indicating someone held his hand trying to make it look like he shot himself. Also, the angle of the gunshot wound is off. He definitely didn't do this himself."

"Gloria, please," Richmond implored. "You need to stop talking and consult with your new lawyer."

"I don't have anything else to say to you people," said Mrs. Phelps. "Now, when can I get out of here?"

"I'm afraid I can't tell you that. In lieu of this evidence, we are placing you under arrest on suspicion of the murder of Alex Phelps. Once we are finished trying you, the folks in Cassopolis, Michigan will take their turn for the murder of Bradley Phelps."

"This is outrageous!" she screamed.

"Gloria!" Richmond said smacking his hand on the table. "Now would be an excellent time to shut your mouth."

"You should probably listen to him, Mrs. Phelps," stated Freeman and then he read her the Miranda Rights.

"Surely you can't keep me here," Gloria stated. "What about bail?"

"That depends on when your new attorney shows up. You won't get a bail hearing before tomorrow afternoon. If not then, you'll be here all weekend," said Barnes.

"All weekend!" she shouted. "Jonathan, can't you do something?"

"I'll make some calls and make sure someone is here in the morning to talk to you. In the meantime, should I call your parents so they can come down and take temporary guardianship of Lana?"

"Oh, yeah. I forgot about her."

Barnes and Freeman looked at one another.

"Yes, please call my parents. Lana has been through enough. She shouldn't be staying with strangers."

"Okay, Detectives," said Richmond in a tone of finality. "This interview is over until Mrs. Phelps has been able to consult with her new attorney."

Barnes stood up and tapped on the glass of the two-way mirror. A female county officer unlocked the door and came in ready to cuff and escort Mrs. Phelps to the Marion County jail.

"Is this really necessary?" Mrs. Phelps asked.

"Afraid so ma'am," said the officer who promptly completed the task and escorted her out of the interrogation room. Jonathan Richmond had gotten to his feet and left without even looking at the two detectives.

"How rude," said Barnes.

"You'd think he'd at least be happy the suspicion is focused on Gloria now instead of on his wife."

"He ought to be jumping for joy that he doesn't have to defend her."

"How do you think Mandy will take this?" asked Barnes.

"Guess I'll find out tomorrow. I'm making dinner for her."

"You can cook?" she teased.

"I have my specialties."

"All Italian, I suppose."

"How did you know?"

"Lucky guess," she quipped. "Think I'm going to call it a day. I've got court in the morning."

"See you tomorrow," he said. "I'm going to go ahead and finish my write ups tonight."

"As you wish, hot stuff."

"Can it, Barnes."

Chapter 39

Brent had waited a few days after they had returned from Michigan to give Mandy a call. She had reluctantly accepted his invitation. Not because she didn't think the man could cook, but because she was still miffed at him for being such a *cop*. She wasn't sure whether this relationship really had a chance of taking off. She liked Brent, but the timing was off.

She rapped three times on the apartment door. She could hear the sounds of clanging cooking instruments, the shuffle of feet and then music — soft jazz. He must have turned on his CD player on his way to the door.

When he opened it, she held up the Chianti and smiled. She watched as he looked her up and down before he said, "You look great."

"Thanks," she said, waiting for him to move aside. When he didn't, she asked, "May I come in?"

Brent blushed. "Of course. May I take your coat?"

She walked past him and set the bottle of Chianti on the table then slipped off her coat. Mandy looked at the setting while Brent put her coat in the closet. He was actually quite the romantic. The table was set with snow-white dishes, shiny silverware, white linen napkins, and crystal wine goblets. In the center, a single red rose in a crystal vase and two white tapered candles in silver candlesticks. Very impressive, she thought.

"Is there anything I can do for you?" she asked.

"What?" Brent answered, causing Mandy's smile to widen at the affect she'd had.

"In the kitchen," she teased.

"Oh, yeah," he said, blinking. "Salad is already prepared. I was putting garlic butter on the bread when you knocked. We're having lasagna. It should be ready in about ten minutes."

"I remembered you said you planned to make something Italian, so I chose Chianti."

"You're brilliant," he said turning to finish the bread.

She could see Brent was nervous. She couldn't remember ever having that affect on a man before. It was empowering. So many of the men in her life had been the ones in control, but for once, she felt in control.

Mandy walked through the living area. There was a brown leather couch with reclining features on each end. Forest green and dark blue plaid throw pillows and forest green lamps accented the room. Two dark wood end tables and matching coffee table completed his furnishings. Simple and masculine. Of course, there was a large HDTV on the opposite wall. In her opinion, no man could retain his sanity unless he had a television of 52 inches or larger.

The oven buzzer caught her attention. She turned to see Brent removing a large casserole dish from the oven and putting the bread in its place.

"I've got to let this cool for a few minutes. It and the bread will be ready at the same time. Want to get started on the salad?"

"Sure. I'll open the Chianti." She poured the wine while Brent served their salads.

"How have you been, Mandy?" he asked.

"I've been behaving myself, if that's what you mean," she said more sharply than she'd intended.

"That's not what I meant," he said, his brow furrowed.

"Sorry," she said. "I guess I'm a bit touchy. Let's not talk about any of that right now. Tell me more about you."

"Okay by me," he said, sounding relieved by this suggestion.

"You haven't told me much about your family or where you were born," she said.

"Charlie never told you? Never mind, I don't suppose he'd have had any reason to at the time."

"I was still in high school if you recall," she said laughing. "He was very protective of me and probably wouldn't have let an older man like you anywhere near me."

Brent laughed. "I was born and raised in Kokomo, Indiana. My dad worked in a factory and my mom was a stay-at-home mom. I have three older sisters. The eldest, Janell, is married with two kids and lives in Swayzee. Patty is on her second marriage and has three kids. She lives on the south side of Indianapolis. Brenda is my twin sister, but she was born first making her older than me. She decided to go to Indiana University in Kokomo for a teaching degree. Then she changed her mind and transferred to Purdue University where she studied veterinary medicine. She has her own practice in Sharpsville, just a few miles south of Kokomo."

"Wow. A twin. I gather she's not married."

"No. She's very much into her work right now. I don't even think she's dating. She says her animals are her babies."

"I can't say I blame her. That's why I didn't date much in college. I didn't want to become one of those women who find a man and forget their own education."

"You're a wise woman, Mandy Stevenson," he said with a twinkle in his eye.

"Thanks for the compliment," she volleyed. "Do your parents still live in Kokomo?"

"Mom does. My father died when I was seventeen." Brent hesitated for a moment as though trying to decide whether to divulge any more information concerning his father. Mandy thought about changing the subject, but then Brent continued.

"Dad died from cirrhosis of the liver. He was a drunk. He worked second shift, 11:00 in the morning to 7:00 at night. When he got off work, he'd go to the bars with his buddies. Sometimes he came home, sometimes he didn't."

"I'm so sorry," Mandy said, reaching for his hand.

"It's okay. We managed. He always paid the bills and put food on the table. We just didn't have any extras or go on any vacations because he spent the remainder of his checks on booze. He didn't hit any of us, like some drunks do, but wasn't there much as a dad."

"That must have been hard."

"The toughest part was hearing my mom cry," he said gulping. "I decided I would always do my best not to cause any woman I knew that much pain. The woman I marry will be treated like a queen."

"I understand how you feel, but be careful. Being good to someone doesn't include letting them step all over you."

"I'll work on it," he said, grinning.

The buzzer went off again. Brent went to the kitchen to retrieve the bread from the oven and serve up the lasagna. Mandy grabbed their dinner plates and took them to the kitchen.

"I thought maybe you'd want to dish it out in here since the casserole dish is probably still too hot."

"Thanks, Mandy."

"It must have been tough growing up with three sisters."

"The two older sisters were pretty mean to me, but Brenda and I always stuck together. She was my best friend growing up. Still is actually."

"That's great. My friend, Marie, is my best friend from high school, but growing up I'd have to say Charlie was always my very best friend. I really miss him sometimes. You know?"

"I know, Mandy. I miss him, too."

"And then there's Alex, of course," she said, looking down at her plate. She looked up and saw him watching her. "But, I promised myself I wouldn't talk about Alex or his dad, or Mom tonight. This is our night, so let's talk about more fond memories of our childhood."

They continued talking all through dinner about their childhoods and their experiences in high school. They laughed enjoying each other's company, then Brent made coffee and served it with a light, fluffy piece of Tiramisu. After dessert, they took the remainder of their coffee to the living room and sat next to one another on the couch.

"I'm stuffed!" exclaimed Mandy. "That was fantastic. I must confess, Detective, I did not expect such a spectacular home cooked meal."

"You were expecting spaghetti from a box?" he laughed.

"Something like that."

"It's good to see you laugh. Since Gloria's in custody, I'm sure you're feeling much better about things."

Mandy sat upright nearly spilling her coffee. "What did you just say?"

Brent looked at her, his eyes wide in surprise.

"Never mind," she said. "I believe I heard you say Gloria is in custody. Why?"

"Are you telling me your father didn't say anything to you about this?"

"I thought I'd made it quite clear my father doesn't confide anything in me, especially when it has to do with his work."

"I hope you know I'd never just spring something like that on you. I honestly thought he'd tell you. It's been on the news all day."

"I haven't watched the news today. Now tell me what happened."

Brent told Mandy all the details he was allowed to divulge. The discovery of the murder weapon in Gloria's bedroom, the fact she has no alibi for the period of time either of the Phelps men was murdered.

"The gun was wiped down; however, a spot of blood was missed. It will take a week or two to get the DNA results back, but we think it's probably blood spatter from one of our victims. That will pretty much seal it up."

"Do you honestly think Gloria is clever enough to have done this?"

"I don't think hiding the murder weapon in a freezer bag between the mattress and box spring of her own bed was exactly bright, do you?"

"I've never liked Gloria much, but I just can't see her doing this."

"Mandy. We found the weapon which was not only used to kill her husband, but her step-son. Alex. Your best friend."

"I understand, but couldn't someone else have planted it there? Someone who wanted to frame her?"

"And who would that be?" Mandy could hear the irritation in his voice.

"Savannah Richmond hates her."

"I thought you said you didn't believe Savannah Richmond could have killed Alex."

"I did, but...."

"Look, Mandy. I've been a homicide detective for five years now. I think I know what I'm doing."

"But...."

"Gloria is the best suspect we have in these murders. Everything points to her. We still don't have a link between these murders and your mother's disappearance, and I'm beginning to think there isn't one. Mrs. Richmond's alibis check out and the Benson girl didn't have a beef with Alex or his dad that we can see. Benson might still be a good suspect in your mom's case, but not the Phelps cases."

"Well, it's getting late. I think I should probably head home."

"Come on, Mandy. Don't leave like this."

"I'm not leaving like anything, I'm just tired. I'm not used to eating such a large meal and it's made me sleepy. You don't want me to have an accident on my way home, do you?"

"Of course not. Let me get your coat."

She watched as he strode over to the closet to get her coat. Still not convinced Gloria could have had anything to do with these murders, Mandy decided it was about time she had a little conversation with Miss Whitney Benson.

Chapter 40

Jay Sumner was more than happy to give Mandy the contact information for Whitney Benson. He'd told Mandy he'd never trusted Whitney. He'd found her to be manipulative and snobbish. From some of Alex's descriptions and having met her father, Mandy had to agree with Jay's assessment.

Mandy was hoping to speak with Whitney, but Mrs. Benson told Mandy that Whitney was staying with friends for the weekend. She told Mandy to call Whitney on Monday after 10:00 in the morning.

Although it was Saturday, her father had gone into the office to check on a few things. She wasn't sure he knew how to do anything but work. She vowed she would never let work take over her life.

The telephone rang and Mandy was shocked to hear Gloria's voice on the other end of the line.

"Mandy," she said. "I know you and I haven't always been friendly, but I need your help."

"What on Earth could I possibly do for you, Gloria?"

"Mandy, please! I need someone to listen to me. I didn't do this!"

"I still don't see what I can do, or even why I should help you."

"Can you come visit me this morning? My new attorney will be here before the bail hearing on Monday, but I don't even know this guy."

Mandy sat in silence contemplating her options. She could refuse and always wonder if Gloria was telling the truth. On the other hand, why help the woman accused of murdering her best friend. Then again, she'd been the first one to say she didn't believe Gloria capable of murdering anyone.

"Okay, Gloria. I can be there in about forty-five minutes."

"Thank you," Gloria said sounding relieved.

Mandy arrived at the county jail fifty minutes later anxious to find out what this was all about. To her dismay, a half dozen reporters were waiting near the front entrance. She was hoping to slip by without being noticed, but no such luck. They rushed her, good old Jack Flack in the lead.

"Miss Stevenson, are you here to see Mrs. Phelps?" came one voice. She tried to move to the door but suddenly found herself engulfed in a sea of microphones and cameras.

"Miss Stevenson. Do you have any comment on whether or not Mrs. Phelps may have killed your mother?" shouted another voice.

"No comment," Mandy shouted.

"Why are you coming to see the woman who killed your best friend?"

"NO COMMENT," she shouted louder.

"Clear out people," she heard a familiar voice shouting. The next thing she knew there was someone pulling her close, helping her move through the crowd. Through all of the confusion, she hadn't realized who her hero was until they entered the building.

"Miss Mandy, are you okay?" said the kind voice of Detective Mayhew.

"Yeah, I guess so," she said shaking. "You'd think I'd be used to this by now."

"I don't reckon any of us ever really gets used to it," he responded. "By the way, why are you here?"

"Gloria wants to see me."

"Huh, now isn't that strange. Why do you suppose she wants to talk to you?"

"I think she wants to convince me she didn't kill Alex and his father. She probably thinks I can influence my father to drop the charges or some such nonsense."

"Well, I won't tell anybody I saw you here, but I wouldn't count on it not makin' the evenin' news. Those reporters will want to make a big deal out of you comin' to visit Miss Phelps."

"Thanks. If she tells me anything I think is relevant to the case, I'll let you know."

"Good girl. You want me to stick around to make sure you get to your car okay when you're done?"

"No. I'll just ask someone to walk with me to my car when I'm finished. I don't want to be a bother."

"Okay, if you're sure. You take care now."

Mandy watched Detective Mayhew walk out the doors. Then she turned to start the tedious process of visitor check-in. She had never actually visited anyone in the jail before, but knew there were several checkpoints and searches before she would actually be able to see Gloria. By the time she saw her, it had been well over an hour since she'd spoken to her on the phone.

"I thought you said you'd be here in forty-five minutes," Gloria said impatiently.

"You're lucky I'm here at all," Mandy snapped, irritated. After all, she'd been through to get in here; she didn't intend to take any crap from Gloria.

"Okay, I'm sorry. It's just that every minute in here seems like hours."

"You said you had something you needed to tell me, Gloria. Spit it out, I don't have all day."

"Mandy, you've known me now for how long?"

"Four years."

"You know I wouldn't do any physical harm to anyone, don't you?"

"Well, no. I can't really say I know that," said Mandy. She was pretty confident, but she didn't want to leave Gloria any room to con her.

"I loved Bradley. I would never hurt him and I certainly wouldn't kill him. I couldn't do that to my daughter. And why would I kill Alex?"

"Alex knew something. Maybe you needed to shut him up."

"No, no. You have to believe me. I didn't kill anyone."

"Gloria! The murder weapon was found hidden under your mattress. What are people supposed to think?"

"I can explain," Gloria said, beads of sweat forming on her brow.

"Go ahead. Explain." Mandy leaned back in her chair, arms crossed waiting.

"I did go up to the cabin on Saturday afternoon. Lana was at a friend's house for the weekend and I knew Bradley had been upset and depressed. I wanted to check on him. When I got there, he was already dead."

"Why didn't you call the police?"

"I saw the gun in his hand and thought he'd killed himself. I panicked and took the gun. I was afraid the life insurance wouldn't pay if he'd committed suicide. So I wiped the gun down because I had touched it. I put it in the freezer bag and took it back home with me. I was planning to do a missing person report mid-week, but you found him before I could do it."

Mandy blinked a few times shaking her head in disbelief. She couldn't believe this woman would have done something so stupid. Of course, knowing Gloria, she knew it was feasible that she thought about the money before anything else.

"So, let me get this straight. You decided to take the gun because you thought Mr. Phelps had committed suicide. Why the hell did you hide it in your house?"

"I don't know. Like I said, I panicked."

"Why tell me? Why not just tell the police your story?"

"You don't honestly believe any of them are going to accept my explanation, do you?"

Gloria looked like a frightened rabbit. Although Mandy's logical self could hardly grasp how this could have happened, her instincts told her Gloria was probably telling her the truth. And, this meant the killer was still out there.

"Even if I believe you, and I'm not saying I do, what is it you think I can do to help you? I've already told my father I'm not convinced you could have done this. I'm certainly not a lawyer."

"I knew you'd...."

"Hold on," Mandy interrupted. "Just because I think you could be innocent doesn't mean anyone will listen to me. The gun is what has you in so much trouble, Gloria. You should have left it and called the police."

"I know that now, Mandy. I wasn't thinking straight. He'd been so depressed and distant since Alex's murder. I honestly thought he'd killed himself."

Mandy looked at Gloria's desperate face. Then she thought of poor Lana. In two weeks time her brother and father had been killed and now her mother was in jail accused of committing the crimes.

"Have you seen Lana?" asked Gloria.

"No, but I heard your parents made it into town early afternoon yesterday. They were given temporary custody and they're back at your house."

"Visiting time's up," said the guard.

"I'll try to go by the house this weekend and see how she's doing. Good luck with your bail hearing on Monday."

"Thanks for coming, Mandy," Gloria said. "Please help me," she said, looking completely defeated.

"I'll do my best to try to figure out what happened. I'll wait to share your information about the gun with the detectives until you've talked to your lawyer."

"Thanks."

"Come on Mrs. Phelps," said the guard again. "Time's up."

Gloria Phelps stood and turned toward the guard. She definitely didn't have any of that spring in her step or *look at me attitude* she normally displayed. Perhaps deep down she was mourning her husband and the way of life she'd become accustomed to leading. But Mandy could not imagine how she was going to save Gloria from herself.

Chapter 41

Early Monday morning Freeman and Barnes met DNA expert Dr. Brian Palmer to go over the reports from the Kalamazoo Crime Lab on the evidence they found at the Phelps' lake house. Captain Stevenson said he would meet them in their conference room with Lieutenant Melrose and his detectives in an hour so they could share the test results.

As they waited in the Dr. Palmer's office, Freeman could not sit still. He paced and sat, then jumped up and paced again. After Freeman's fourth lap around the room, Barnes stood up with her hands gripping the edge of the small office table, clenching her teeth. "Will you please sit down? He'll be here any minute now and your pacing is making me crazy."

"Okay," he said plopping back down in his chair. "I didn't realize I was disturbing you."

Before Barnes could give him a clever retort, Dr. Palmer came through the door, reports in hand.

"Good morning," he said cheerfully as he placed his load of paperwork onto the table, pushing his glasses back up on the bridge of his nose.

"Good to see you, Dr. Palmer," said Freeman rising from his chair again. "What do you have for us?"

"Confusion," Dr. Palmer responded. "First, the lab in Kalamazoo said there wasn't enough DNA in the food or on the containers to get a usable sample."

Dr. Palmer smiled and sorted through his files. He found the report for which he was searching. "Oh, it gets better. There was some auburn hair found on a pillow in the guest room, along with some blood drops someone missed when cleaning up. The DNA matches a missing person who is in the system — Cassandra Stevenson."

"Are you sure?" Barnes and Freeman said in unison.

"Take a look," he said pointing to the two DNA reports. "Even a ten year old could see the two DNA samples tested are exactly the same. No doubt in my mind."

"What the hell would Mrs. Stevenson's hair and blood be doing in the Phelps' summer house?" Freeman asked.

"Oh, but there's more," said Dr. Palmer. "The lab sent us a copy of prints they took from Bradley Phelps. We ran them against our database and found a match." Dr. Palmer took a dramatic pause then said, "They match the John Doe prints from the Stevenson case. The ones Chatham found in her vehicle."

Freeman glanced at Barnes realizing she was as surprised as he was.

Dr. Palmer continued. He had the enthusiasm of a child discovering candy for the first time. "With this new evidence, we decided to compare the DNA profile for Mr. Phelps to the DNA from the hair found in Mrs. Stevenson's car. They also match. The John Doe from the Stevenson case is Bradley Phelps."

They all stood in momentary silence. It was broken by another pronouncement by Dr. Palmer. "I know this is a big shock, but there's more. Kalamazoo also found some blood in the boat. Of course, the bleach ruined most of the blood for DNA testing, but whoever cleaned it missed some things. In particular, there was rope with human blood on it. When their forensics lab tested it, they again found it matched Cassandra Stevenson."

"I can't believe this," said Barnes.

"I'm not a detective," Dr. Palmer commented, "but it seems to me a huge lake would be a great place to get rid of evidence."

"Good Lord, Freeman," said Barnes. "Do you think that's what Bradley Phelps meant in his note when he said he was sorry about Cassandra?"

"It would seem so," he answered. "But what reason would Bradley Phelps have for kidnapping Cassandra Stevenson and keeping her in his house up there?"

"I told you this was confusing," said Dr. Palmer.

"Yes, you did Brian," Freeman scowled. "So, what do you think,

Barnes?"

"According to Mandy, Bradley Phelps went up there in August during the week her mother disappeared," she stated. "Alex didn't go up to the house until the end of the week. What did he see that made him angry with his father?"

"Well, Detectives," interrupted Dr. Palmer, "if you're finished with me, I need to get back to the lab."

"Thanks, Dr. Palmer," said Barnes, as the man left the detectives alone in his office.

"What about this, Barnes? We know Cassandra Stevenson fooled around. What if she was having an affair with Bradley Phelps and Gloria Phelps found out."

"That could be, but where does Alex fit in?"

"Alex didn't go up there until the weekend. Maybe he caught them together. He could have decided to tell Gloria. Gloria goes up there and kills Cassandra in a jealous rage. Bradley helps her get rid of the body by dumping it in the lake. Then they cleaned up, but missed the hair and those few blood drops."

"So why did she kill Alex?" asked Barnes.

Freeman took a moment tapping his fingers on the table. "Let's say Alex caught his dad and Cassandra Stevenson together. He's pissed because his dad is screwing around with his best friend's mom. However, his loyalty to his dad overrides his loyalty to Mandy no matter how ticked off he is. He decides to keep his mouth shut until he hears Cassandra's car is found and there's blood in it which belongs to her. He confronts his father and Gloria overhears. Now she has to shut him up so nobody discovers what she's done."

"So," interjected Barnes, "Bradley Phelps probably figured out his wife was responsible for Alex's death, but felt responsible for what happened. He decides to go up to the lake house and do himself in, but Gloria doesn't know about the suicide note. So, she decides to go up there and...."

"She dopes up his wine, gets him in bed and as soon as he goes to sleep — BOOM!"

"From Mandy's information in talking to the locals, the neighbors heard the Phelps' boat go out in the middle of the night back in August," Barnes noted. "The hardware store owner said he sold Bradley Phelps a black tarp that he didn't use to cover his boat.

Maybe he and Gloria wrapped Cassandra in it before throwing her into the lake."

"I wonder if the captain will want to involve the FBI now," Freeman said.

"Let's go give him the news."

Captain Stevenson, Lieutenant Melrose, Detective Jacobs, and Detective Mayhew were in the conference room when Freeman and Barnes arrived. Freeman briefed everyone on the DNA reports received from the Kalamazoo lab. He and Barnes recited their theories about what may have happened to the captain's wife. Everyone, including the captain, appeared stunned by these latest developments.

"I'm sorry, Captain Stevenson," said Freeman. "We need to know if you want the locals to drag the lake before the FBI is brought in."

Robert shook his head, his eyes closing momentarily. "That lake is huge. We should call Chief Matthews and leave it up to him. I'm sure he'll call in the FBI since the potential victim may have been driven across state lines. Besides, I doubt Chief Matthews has the manpower and equipment to take on such a huge task. The neighbors said they heard the boat leaving in the middle of the night. It was gone for approximately an hour, correct?"

"That's correct, Captain," stated Freeman.

"This might give them a good idea of where to start searching," said the captain. "Since Cassandra's blood was in the house and on the boat, it would appear someone dumped her in the lake and then tried to clean up. However, it's hard to prove she is dead without finding her body."

Captain Stevenson turned to Lieutenant Melrose. "Well, Lieutenant, with this new evidence it looks like you and I need to meet with Major Lewis. I don't feel I should be involved in the Alex Phelps murder investigation any longer."

"Now that we've found a link, I would concur," the lieutenant replied. "I would like to volunteer to head up these investigations until Major Lewis decides who should permanently take charge."

"Agreed," said the captain. "I'm going home for a few hours so I can break this news to Mandy in private." He then left the room.

Lieutenant Melrose smiled bleakly at the assembly. "I suggest we get this team organized quickly. The major will want to be briefed as soon as possible on our plan of action."

After a few moments of silence, Lieutenant Melrose continued. "We need to look at things with new eyes. Let's tie up any loose ends and come together tomorrow afternoon to brainstorm."

He turned to Barnes. "Barnes, since the captain has removed himself from this case, I need for you to call Chief Matthews. Let him know what we have so far and ask him if he plans to drag the lake or bring in the FBI to do it. We don't want them to think we're taking over their investigation. Also, make sure he has all the information we do on Gloria Phelps."

Turning his attention to Jacobs, he instructed, "With the arrest and mounting evidence against Gloria Phelps, I don't believe the others are viable suspects any longer. Make sure anyone conducting surveillance in this case is pulled off the assignment."

The lieutenant then instructed Mayhew to gather all of the evidence and files regarding the Stevenson case and take them to his office A.S.A.P. "I also want you and Jacobs to sit down with the computer geek, what's his name?" Melrose inquired.

"Kodey Marshall," said Mayhew.

"Yeah, that's right," the lieutenant nodded. "Find out if he's making any progress on the computer equipment confiscated from the Phelps and Richmond homes and offices. People think they can just erase emails and they disappear. We also need to find out whether Bradley Phelps wrote the suicide note on his computer and whether or not one of his printers was used to print it. This should also tie up any loose ends with the Richmonds' involvement."

"Freeman, Barnes, have you completed the confirmation of Gloria Phelps' alibis?"

"Yes," responded Barnes. "We can't corroborate that she's told the truth about her whereabouts during any of these crimes."

"The afternoon Alex Phelps died," interjected Freeman, "Gloria Phelps said she was shopping at Castleton Square Mall. She made no purchases and no one can verify seeing her there. The weekend her husband was murdered, she claims to have been home alone all day on Saturday. Plenty of time to drive to Cassopolis and back."

"Sounds like we've got our killer," said Melrose.

Chapter 42

At 10:15 Monday morning, Mandy called the Benson home. She spoke with Whitney Benson, asking to meet her and talk. Whitney reluctantly agreed to meet Mandy at Kona's Bar and Grill at 1:00 in the afternoon.

A few pangs of doubt had crossed Mandy's mind as she drove to her destination. She wished she'd called Marie for back up. From what she'd heard, Whitney had a very nasty temper. She wondered if Whitney had ever actually become violent or if she was all talk and no action.

She immediately recognized Whitney, because she'd seen her at the police station. Mandy stood and gave Whitney a quick wave.

"Ah, so you're Mandy," Whitney said as she approached the table. "Alex certainly had a lot of good things to say about you."

"Thanks, I guess. Let's sit."

"So why were you so anxious to talk to me?" asked Whitney, staring at Mandy intently.

"You certainly get to the point."

"Why waste time playing games?" said Whitney. "You obviously want to talk to me about Alex or your mother. What do you want to know?"

Although Mandy had rehearsed this in her mind several times, she wasn't sure what to ask first. She decided to ask about her mother first. "Did you have anything to do with my mother's disappearance?"

"No," said Whitney, maintaining a peculiar almost stoic look on her face. "I hated her for confirming my father was an unfaithful asshole. Now that I've had the indignity of being dragged in for questioning by the police, I've been rethinking my attitude."

"In what way?" asked Mandy.

"I'm sure you've heard I slapped her and threatened her last year. She's the only one I've actually caught him with, so I guess I took my anger out on her. The thing is I'm really pissed at my dad. He's the one who demanded I split up with Alex, you know."

"Jay told me. So you really cared for Alex?"

"I was crazy about Alex, but my dad threatened to send me to a state college if I didn't drop him."

Mandy saw tears forming in Whitney's eyes. Whitney quickly took a deep breath and turned her head, wiping her face. When she turned back to face Mandy, she had regained her previous demeanor.

"Mandy, please don't take offense to this, but I was so angry with my father when I found him with a woman who was not only married, but one of his employees. Someone *he* would have told me was not in my social class."

"I'm not offended. Sounds like a case of do as I say, not as I do."

"Exactly. He's pounded the social status thing into my head so often that when the detectives had the *audacity* to question me, I lost it."

"When you saw Alex again, did you have hopes of getting back together?"

"I saw him at the mall not too long after I was questioned about your mom. He told me he was seeing someone, so I never even considered it," said Whitney, a glint of sadness in her eyes. "We did sit down and have a long talk though. That's when I told him about your mom and my dad and how angry I was. He suggested I see a counselor."

"Did you?"

"Yeah. He told me about going to counseling after his dad married Gloria. Said it helped him straighten out his life and get control of his anger."

Mandy couldn't believe this was the same person she'd heard about. A server came by and took their drink orders.

"From what Jay says, Alex put all of his energy into school instead of being angry," Mandy said.

"So I figure if Alex can do it, I can."

"Sounds like a good attitude to me," Mandy said, evoking a smile from Whitney. "Did you know Alex and his father were both shot with a gun Alex owned?"

"No, I hadn't heard. I don't understand why men think they have to own guns. Statistically, more people are killed with their own guns than by people on the street. I've never touched a gun and don't intend to ever have one in any home of mine."

"You knew they arrested Gloria for the murders, didn't you?"

"Yes," Whitney responded. "I heard it on the radio, seems hard to believe."

"She had hidden the gun under her mattress."

"She is as stupid as I thought," Whitney sniggered. "I'm just baffled by the idea that she had the balls to do it. She didn't seem the type."

"She asked me to come see her on Saturday, so I did," said Mandy. "She claims she went to the lake house but Mr. Phelps was already dead. She took the gun because it was in his hand, so she thought he committed suicide. If he had, the life insurance would be null and void."

"What an idiot!" exclaimed Whitney. "Can I ask you something?"

"Sure."

"What makes you think your mother didn't just take off with some guy?"

"She didn't take any of her things. They found her car abandoned with her blood in it."

"I'm sorry, Mandy. Really, the cops didn't tell me any of that information," said Whitney. "Alex thought the world of you and I loved him, so I hate seeing you in so much pain. What do you say we order some lunch? My treat."

"That would be great. I think Alex would have approved of us becoming friends."

Mandy returned home from her lunch with Whitney and saw her father and Aunt Karen's cars in the driveway. Rushing through the garage, she expected to see her Aunt Karen and father sitting at the kitchen table, however, they were not there.

Walking into the foyer, she stopped to listen hearing her aunt and father speaking to one another in very agitated voices.

"Karen, she can't find out. She'd never forgive us," her dad said.

"She's going to find out what we did eventually," retorted Karen.

"No she won't," he said. "I've covered our tracks well."

Mandy was listening intently wondering if the "she" they were referring to was her. She couldn't imagine what type of secret could be so awful her father wouldn't want her to know. As she edged closer, she accidentally bumped the side table knocking over a picture frame. The conversation between her aunt and dad ceased immediately.

"Mandy, is that you?" he called.

Darn it, she thought. "Yes, Dad. Is Aunt Karen here?" she inquired hoping they wouldn't realize she had been listening. The last time she spied on her father, they didn't speak for days.

"She is," he said and they both came out into the foyer. "Let's go sit down at the kitchen table. I have some news to share with the two of you."

When her father finished telling them about the DNA results and fingerprint evidence, Mandy sat there in shock trying to absorb the immensity of what this evidence implied. She knew her mother could be dead, but Bradley and Gloria Phelps being involved was more than she could fathom.

She was glad her Aunt Karen was there with her to hear this latest news. Mandy had even forgotten all about the conversation she'd overheard between them just minutes before. Aunt Karen always seemed to be the one who held everyone together in a crisis, and Mandy needed her now more than ever.

"Dad, are they absolutely sure?" Mandy asked, desperately hoping for another answer.

"I'm afraid so. I'm sorry, Mandy, I know this isn't easy to hear," he said looking at her, his forehead wrinkled with worry.

"This just keeps getting worse," said Mandy, standing up and bursting into tears. She couldn't help herself. "When will it stop?"

After all of these weeks of hoping for the best it appeared her mother may have been murdered by her best friend's father and step-mother. But why? What did they have against her mother?

Realizing Aunt Karen was touching her shoulder; she turned seeking comfort in Karen's brilliant green eyes, then fell into her waiting arms. Karen and Mandy held one another and cried.

Mandy pulled away from Karen when she heard the clinking of

dishes and the whistle of a teakettle. Her father had apparently decided to make tea, which was always Gran's cure when people were upset. Mandy thought it probably gave him something to do to get past this horribly awkward moment. She knew it must have been just as hard for him as it was for her, although he would never admit it.

Mandy walked to the kitchen sink, splashing cold water on her face then patting it dry with a paper towel. She turned to see her father standing beside her with a cup of tea in his hand. She smiled at him as she took it.

"Thanks, Dad. I appreciate being told the whole truth and being treated like an adult." She paused to take a sip of her tea. "What's next?" she asked.

"The local authorities will be called," he said. "They will decide whether or not to bring in the FBI. From the evidence collected and from what the local residents told you, if they killed your mother they may have dumped the body in the lake. I've decided to take myself completely off the investigation of Alex's death."

Mandy looked at him in disbelief. He explained to her that he and Mel met with Major Lewis. The major decided to put Mel in charge of both cases.

"At least we know someone's in charge we can trust. Mel will put every effort into discovering what happened," he said.

"We're sure the Cassopolis police will have the FBI come in. They have more resources for this type of search," he said. He took a deep breath before continuing. "If they find her, then it will definitely be considered an interstate kidnapping and murder."

"And to think I let Gloria talk me into coming to visit her on Saturday."

"You visited her in jail?" asked her dad.

"Yeah," Mandy said, half chuckling. "She gave me some bull shit story about taking the gun because she thought her husband had killed himself. She was afraid she wouldn't be able to collect on his life insurance."

"Mandy," he retorted. "You should have told me about this."

"I promised I'd wait until she talked to her new lawyer," Mandy said. "Do you know if she was able to post bail?"

"No, I haven't heard," he said, sounding disgusted.

Mandy knew a lecture usually followed when he used that tone.

"When you talk to people in regards to this case, you need to disclose the information to us. You shouldn't be making those kinds of promises to suspects. I hope you realize now that she's told you this cock 'n bull story, you may be called as a witness in her trial."

"No, I didn't," she said feeling foolish. "So if I tell you I just had an interesting lunch with Whitney Benson, you won't freak on me."

"Of course he won't," said Aunt Karen who had been rather quiet up to now.

Mandy could see Aunt Karen raise an eyebrow at her dad. He took a deep breath before speaking again.

"Did she have anything to say pertaining to these cases?"

"Not really. She explained why she thought she hated Mom, but it's really her dad she's angry with. Alex talked her into seeking therapy. I don't think she had anything to do with what happened to Mom."

"So she didn't say anything incriminating."

"No, Dad. As a matter of fact, she claims she's never touched a gun in her life. She said she'd never allow one anywhere near her."

Mandy walked to the sink with her teacup. She then turned to her dad. "I need to know why. What on Earth could have pushed Gloria to murder Alex and her husband? I don't think she ever met Mom. What reason would she have for hurting her?"

Her father and aunt both looked down, apparently not able to keep eye contact. Mandy rolled her eyes and shook her head in disbelief.

"One theory they're checking out is the possibility your mother and Bradley Phelps were having an affair," he said.

"Is there any man in this city she hasn't slept with?" asked Mandy in frustration. "I just want this to be over. What if they don't find her in the lake?"

"Mandy, this will take some time," he told her. "That's a huge lake. If they don't find anything by the end of October they will probably have to wait and search again in spring when the water warms up again."

Mandy felt her Aunt Karen touch her shoulder. "Don't worry, they'll find out what happened to your mother. The truth will come out." Then Mandy saw her aunt give her dad a strange look before saying, "It always does."

Chapter 43

Lieutenant Melrose was sitting in his office looking at the box of evidence collected by his detectives on the Cassandra Stevenson missing person case. Of course, now it looked more and more like a homicide. "I'm sorry I let you down Mandy," he said aloud. "Maybe if I'd pushed harder we would have found Cassandra before the situation became so dire."

He grabbed the box and headed for the Homicide Department conference room which was already set up with the Alex Phelps murder case evidence. He set the box on one of the empty tables, closing his eyes momentarily. He slipped on latex gloves, and lifted the lid from the box.

Pulling out the DNA reports and physical evidence found in Cassandra's car, he read each report one more time. This was undeniable scientific evidence. However, when he read the Bradley Phelps case reports from Kalamazoo, something caught his attention.

Lab techs had gone through the lake house with luminal to find any blood someone may have attempted to clean up. There was very little found. If Cassandra had been killed in the house, then there should have been more evidence of her blood in other parts of the house. The blood evidence found on the rope could indicate strangulation. However, her epithelial skin cells were only found on the area of the rope where the blood was found. Her skin cells should have shown up all along the length of the rope. Plus why not leave it around her neck and dispose of it with her body?

There was a knock on the door, and his assistant entered the conference room. "Yes, Mary," he said.

"Lieutenant, I have a message for you. A woman called just now claiming to have information on the Stevenson case. She said she would only talk to you and gave me this address. You're to meet her there at noon, which is only forty-five minutes from now. She told me if you don't show up alone, she'll leave and she won't call again."

"Okay, Mary. Let's just keep this between you and me for now. I'll go check it out. It may be somebody's idea of a joke. I should be back in time for the 3:00 briefing this afternoon."

The address was for a storage facility in Fishers. Lieutenant Melrose arrived at the storage facility at five minutes to noon. He spoke with the attendant briefly, identifying himself as a police officer and telling him he was meeting someone at Unit 307. "Do you know who rents that unit?" Mel asked.

"By sight, yeah. When I first met her, she had long blonde hair and now it's short and black. I guess women are never satisfied with the way they look, eh?"

The lieutenant nodded.

"The lady is somewhere around five-seven, skinny, always wore sunglasses, even when it's cloudy. 'Course I can't remember everybody's name, I think it started with a 'B'. I'd look it up for you, but the computers are down right now. Danged thing should be up in a few minutes, if you want to wait."

"That's okay. Did you happen to see what type of car she drives?" Mel asked.

"White sedan with Indiana plates," he replied. "Sometimes she comes in here on a blue scooter. Damndest thing I ever saw, but with the price of gas these days."

"When was the last time you saw her?"

"She's here right now," said the attendant. "Saw her pull in on her scooter about five minutes ago. It seems mighty chilly to be riding a scooter today, but she was all decked out like a she was riding a motorcycle — lots of black leather."

"Thanks for answering my questions. Seems I have a young lady waiting for me. Where is Unit 307?" Mel asked.

"You just follow the road back to the third row and turn left. Each unit is labeled with the number. It will be the fourth one on your left."

"Thanks, again," Lieutenant Melrose said as he drove away and down the narrow little road. As he turned the corner, he saw a blue scooter parked in front of the fourth unit on the left, just as the attendant had said.

He hesitated for a moment before exiting his vehicle. "You probably shouldn't have come here alone," he said, admonishing himself. When he got out of the car, he unsnapped his holster and approached the storage unit.

The woman was as the attendant described and was standing in the unit with her back to him. Hand on his weapon, he said, "Hello. I'm Lieutenant Melrose, IMPD Missing Persons. You said you had some information on Cassandra Stevenson."

"Yes, I do," she said. Then before he could say another word, she turned abruptly.

He looked straight into her eyes. "What the hell is this?" he said. Then there was a ping and the lieutenant went down on his knees. He was only able to utter one more word, "Why?" before he collapsed.

"One more to go," she said. "Then Robert Stevenson can live the rest of his miserable life in the same pain I've been suffering all these years."

She pushed her scooter into the storage unit. Searching his pockets, she found Lieutenant Melrose's car keys. She grabbed a suitcase, closed and locked the door, and used Mel's car for her getaway.

Chapter 44

Mark Chatham was walking down the hallway with Dr. Brian Palmer. They were discussing the forensic evidence each had tested in regards to the Stevenson-Phelps investigations. They were about to attend a briefing with the investigating team to go over everything and make sure they had all the evidence they needed for the prosecutor to take Gloria Phelps to trial for the murder of her step-son.

In the conference room, Detective Mayhew had added the Stevenson crime scene photos, and all of the forensic reports onto a board next to all of the Phelps evidence. Chatham and Dr. Palmer entered the conference room to find the team going over the reports.

"It's 3:10 so we'd probably better get started. Barnes did you hear from Chief Matthews regarding their search of the lake?" asked Jacobs.

Barnes responded, "Cassopolis doesn't have the personnel to search the lake. The state could do it, but not until spring — too many lakes and not enough personnel. Since this is an interstate crime, they called in the FBI. They started this morning."

He then turned his attention to Forensics Computer Specialist, Kodey Marshall. Kodey was six foot tall with sandy blonde hair and blue eyes, not your stereotypical computer geek.

"Marshall, what did you find out about the files on Phelps' computers?"

"Alex's computer was pretty standard stuff. No strange emails. No porn sites. Lots of school papers. Research that seemed to follow his work. Nothing incriminating."

"What about Bradley Phelps' computer?" Freeman asked.

"His work computer was mostly stuff to do with his job. However, I found some emails from a BMason on his home computer. I've provided all of you with copies, and as you can see, several are signed 'Love, Beth'. It's a yahoo.com address so it could be accessed anywhere. The address was created at the public library in Fishers using one of the library's computers. The Head Librarian is preparing a report for us containing the names of all the users on the specific times and dates in question. This should narrow things down for us. My investigation also revealed some of these emails originated from the Lawrence, Nora, and Marion County libraries. Their librarians are cooperating as well."

"Shouldn't we wait for Lieutenant Melrose?" inquired Freeman. "I thought he'd be here by now."

"Let me give Mary a call," said Jacobs. He hit the speakerphone button and punched in her extension.

"Lieutenant Melrose's office, Mary speaking," she answered.

"Mary, this is Detective Jacobs. Is Lieutenant Melrose on his way down to the briefing?"

"I haven't seen him since he got that mysterious message today. He left at around 11:30 this morning and hasn't returned. I thought he'd gone straight to the meeting. It's not like him not to at least call to let me know he's running late. He was so sure he'd be back in time to meet with you."

"Do you know who this woman was or what she wanted?" asked Jacobs.

"She wouldn't give her name, but said she had information on the Cassandra Stevenson case. She said she wouldn't talk to anyone but Lieutenant Melrose about it and would leave if she saw he wasn't alone. I still have a copy of the message with the address on it."

Jacobs wrote down the address.

"It's a storage facility in Fishers," Mary said. "He was to meet her at Unit 307."

Standing and directing his attention to Freeman and Barnes, Jacobs said, "I'm going to give Major Lewis a call and see if he can get Judge Pritchard to rush through a search warrant for this storage unit. A missing cop should give us enough probable cause to rush it through. I want you to go over to the courthouse and wait for it." He paused tapping his chin with his pen, pacing.

"Mayhew and I will head over to the storage unit," said Jacobs. "We'll talk to the attendant to see if the lieutenant was seen coming and going. Maybe he'll give us access to the unit before you get there with the warrant."

The Major had no problem getting Judge Anthony Pritchard to push through the search warrant. Major Frederick Lewis and Judge Pritchard had been friends for many years and the fact a police officer might be in danger sparked him to prepare it immediately. By the time Barnes and Freeman got to the courthouse, the warrant was waiting for them.

In the meantime, Detectives Jacobs and Mayhew were pulling up to the storage facility. Jacobs had tried several times and failed to reach Lieutenant Melrose by cell phone. It wasn't going directly to voicemail, indicating he was unable to answer for some reason.

"I got a bad feelin' about this," Mayhew said to his partner as they walked towards the attendant's booth.

"Me, too," Jacobs responded as he and Mayhew pulled out their badges.

"More cops!" said the attendant. "This Mason chick rob a bank or something?"

"So you've seen another police officer come through here today?" asked Jacobs.

"That's what I just said, ain't it?"

"Look chump!" Mayhew spouted angrily. "We're in no mood for smart mouthin'. You saw him come in, did you see him leave?"

"I just caught a glimpse of the car as it left," said the attendant. "I didn't really pay much attention. I just figured it was him because it was the only car in the place."

"So what about this Mason chick as you called her? Did she ever show?" inquired Jacobs.

"Oh, yeah. She got here before the lieutenant."

"I thought you just said his car was the only one here," Mayhew said giving the attendant his most intimidating look.

"She wasn't in a car. She rode a scooter."

"I don't suppose you saw her leave," Mayhew said, raising one eyebrow.

"Matter of fact, I didn't," said the attendant. "I assumed she left with him."

"The problem we have here," Jacobs began, "is that our lieutenant never made it back to the station. We cannot raise him on his cell phone and we're becoming very concerned about his whereabouts. You are the last person to see him so we need for you to give us access to Unit 307."

"I can't do that," the attendant exclaimed in a panic. "I'll lose my job."

"You're liable to lose more than that if somethin' happened to Lieutenant Melrose and you're bein' uncooperative," said Mayhew, glaring at him.

"I can't let you into our units without a search warrant," said the attendant defiantly, starting to sweat.

Mayhew and Jacobs turned as they heard another car pull up. It was Barnes and Freeman. "Here's the fucking warrant," sneered Mayhew. "Now get your lock cutters and let's get going."

The attendant grudgingly took the group to Unit 307. The attendant broke the padlock and stepped aside. Freeman pushed the door up and heard his partner gasp. The attendant turned and gagged. Looking down Freeman saw the body of a man, face down in a pool of blood. He and Barnes carefully approached the victim. As he reached down to try to find a pulse in the man's neck, he recognized the face.

"Barnes, this is Lieutenant Melrose!" Freeman declared.

"Oh my God," she gasped. "Is he alive?"

"Is it him?" asked Jacobs.

Mayhew pushed past Barnes and then cursed as he saw his fallen leader.

Jacobs hadn't moved his eyes, still locked on Barnes' face. Once he was able to pull himself together, he looked down and said, "I'll go to the car and call for the DI, and uh," he paused trying to maintain a professional demeanor. "I'll grab some crime scene tape."

"No, wait!" shouted Freeman. "Jacobs, call the paramedics! He still has a faint pulse! Hurry!"

"Where's he bleedin' from?" asked Mayhew.

"Looks like his head. There's an entrance wound in the front, but I don't see an exit wound," said Freeman. "I think he bled more from his nose than the gunshot wound. Probably broke it when he fell on his face."

The attendant was still standing outside of the unit looking pale and shocked. Freeman asked Barnes to take him to the office and wait there with him. "When he gets past this initial shock, see if you can't get a description and an address for this woman," Brent suggested.

Jacobs returned crime scene tape in hand. "Paramedics and forensics are on their way. Do you think he'll make it?"

"Depends on whether or not the bullet bounced around in there before it stopped. We won't know until he gets to the hospital and they do their tests."

"Scooter's still here, so I bet *she* took his car," said Jacobs.

"You better call headquarters and put out an APB on the lieutenant's car. Make sure they check the airport, train station, and bus station in case she's planning to flee the state."

"Ambulance is here," Jacobs said. "He's over here you guys! Hurry, he's in bad shape!"

As Freeman stepped aside to let the EMTs do their work, Barnes came running up to him. "I got a name," she said. "It's the same as on Bradley Phelps' computer. Beth Mason. Address belongs to the local library."

"So maybe Gloria Phelps wasn't the one involved in Mrs. Stevenson's disappearance. I'd better tell Captain Stevenson what's going on," he said as he pulled his cell phone from his pocket and hit one of his speed dial buttons and put it on speakerphone so his partner could hear.

"Captain Stevenson," said Freeman. "When Lieutenant Melrose didn't show up for our briefing we found out he was meeting someone who claimed to know something about the disappearance of your wife."

"And did she?" asked the captain.

"I don't know sir," Brent paused momentarily. "I'm sorry to have to give you this news, but Lieutenant Melrose was shot and left in the storage unit."

There was silence on the other end of the line. Then Captain Stevenson asked, "What's his condition?"

"He's weak and unconscious. They're transporting him to St. Vincent Hospital. He'll definitely need surgery. It appears there may be a small caliber bullet lodged in his head."

"Ah, Christ," Captain Stevenson said, voice cracking.

"Detective Jacobs called in requesting an APB on Lieutenant

Melrose's car since it looks like the shooter took it. They'll be looking at all transport out of the city as well."

"Good. Any ID on the renter of the unit?"

"Yes, Captain. Her name is Beth Mason. We'd just been discussing her earlier in our briefing. She was apparently sending love emails to Bradley Phelps."

"Beth Mason. That name sounds familiar, but I can't place it at the moment," the captain noted. "Did you find the weapon?"

"No, sir," Freeman replied. "But from the entrance wound and lack of an exit wound, I think it was at most a .22."

"Notify the Fishers Police," instructed the captain. "This is their jurisdiction so they'll need to be involved. I'll call Lewis to let him know Mel's out of commission. He'll be hotter than a bonfire. Mel never should have gone down there alone."

Chapter 45

She knew she had to complete her unfinished business today and then get out of the country. Calling Mandy Stevenson and pretending to be one of Lieutenant Melrose's detectives, she convinced Mandy that Lieutenant Melrose wanted to meet her in a warehouse on the near northwest side in one hour. There might be some new evidence there regarding her mother's disappearance and he wanted to show it to her.

She relished the fact that Mandy was so naïve and vulnerable. It made what she had to do so much easier. As far as she was concerned, Robert Stevenson had ruined her life and he had to pay.

It was a shame Alex Phelps had to interfere with her plans. If he'd just stayed home that weekend, he never would have found out what his daddy was up to and he'd still be alive. Alex had promised his father he wouldn't tell. Unfortunately for him, he had a soft spot in his heart, or maybe it was in his head, for that wretched girl. He had planned to tell Mandy everything. She couldn't have that now, could she?

Then of course, Bradley figured out what she'd done to keep Alex quiet and had come up to the summerhouse looking for her. Being the great actress she was, she easily convinced him it had to have been someone else. Then she talked him into drinking a lovely, relaxing cocktail she'd mixed for him. Too bad. He was an excellent lover. They could have had so much fun together in the Caymans.

Of course, she hadn't disclosed her whole plan to Bradley. She didn't tell him about her plans for Mandy. How she was going to watch Mandy take her last breath then bask in the knowledge of how painful this would be for her father.

"Poor Mandy, you've suffered enough," she said aloud. "Tonight I will put you out of your misery. Too bad I won't be able to stick around to see the look on Daddy's face when he finds you and realizes everyone he ever cared for is gone. Sweet revenge at last."

With a smile of satisfaction on her face, she pulled up to the warehouse. Getting out of the car, she opened the dock doors where the loading equipment used to move in and out. She didn't want anyone to find the dear lieutenant's car before she enacted her plan. Mandy would expect to see it out in the parking lot when she arrived.

She walked around Mel's car and there sat the rental car Bradley had so generously provided for her. She deduced by the time they found it in the airport parking lot she'd be drinking some lovely fruity rum drink on the beach on Grand Cayman Island.

After pulling Lieutenant Melrose's car into the warehouse, she strode over to the rental car and opened the trunk. She'd kept a packed bag in case of some hitch, like killing a cop, and now added the second bag she'd taken from the storage unit.

She checked her carry-on to make sure her new passport was there. Ah, yes, there it was. Her new identity would be Sara Rose Fletcher. She had opened the bank account in the Caymans under this name and had been putting cash into it for several years. All was set and perfectly executed. No one would ever find her.

Mandy had just finished speaking with a Detective Sims. She said she worked with Lieutenant Melrose and the lieutenant wanted her to meet him in a warehouse on New Augusta Road in about an hour. Detective Sims made it sound very urgent. Apparently, some new evidence regarding her mother's disappearance had surfaced and Uncle Mel wanted her to check it out.

Mandy wasn't comfortable with this meeting place. She wondered why Uncle Mel had asked this detective to call her instead of making the call himself. She tried to call him earlier, but his phone kept going straight to voicemail. He must have turned it off or run the battery down. However, her anxiety prompted her to try to find someone who would be willing to go with her.

She tried to call Brent to ask him to come, but it went straight to voicemail. "Hey, Brent, it's Mandy. A Detective Sims just called to tell me Uncle Mel wants to meet me at a warehouse on the northwest side near 7500 New Augusta Road in an hour. If I remember correctly, she described the building as having blue siding and white doors. Actually, I'm supposed to be there in about 45 minutes now. If you get this message, please come. I'm not really very familiar with the area and would feel safer if you were there. Later."

She hung up the phone and decided to try her dad. Same result, so she left a similar message, deciding she'd better leave now if she was going to make it to the rendezvous at the appointed time.

Mandy found the warehouse more easily than she had anticipated. It was about 500 feet off the road and surrounded by mature oak trees giving it a rather spooky feel. The sun had set and it was starting to get dark, but there was a security light turned on right outside the front door. She saw Uncle Mel's car in the parking lot but he wasn't in it. She didn't understand. It wasn't like Uncle Mel not to be waiting for her outside the building, but she did see some lights inside, so she decided to go in and look for him.

The first thing she saw as she walked into the building was an office which was the source of the light. When she approached the office, she noticed there was a woman standing near the door wearing a black leather trench coat, black jeans and boots. She had short black hair and was about Mandy's height and build.

Feeling apprehensive, Mandy said, "Hello, I'm looking for a friend of mine."

The woman turned and moved into the light to face Mandy.

"Oh, my God!"

Chapter 46

Earlier, Captain Stevenson asked Detective Chennelle Kendall to research the name Beth Mason..Since the name sounded familiar, he thought Beth Mason might be someone he arrested in the past who might have revenge on her mind.

He was on his cell phone with another one of his detectives, when Kendall knocked on his office door. The captain motioned for her to come in and sit down.

"Yeah, I know that Perkins," Robert said gruffly. "Just make sure the evidence is given to Chatham A.S.A.P." He closed his cell phone, placed it in its case, and turned to Detective Kendall. "You find anything?"

"Yes, sir," she began, handing him an old file folder. "It took a while, because there wasn't anything referring directly to Beth Mason."

Captain Stevenson stood up and paced back and forth a few times as he skimmed the file. "Darren Mason!" he exclaimed. "About twenty years ago. Lieutenant Melrose had just joined the IMPD and was assigned to me as a rookie. We got a call out on a robbery in progress at the bank on 82nd and Allisonville Road. When we got there, the suspect had just come out, gun in hand pointing at Melrose. I told him to drop his weapon and he made a move. I thought he was going to shoot my partner. He died at the hospital."

"So was this woman his wife?" Kendall asked.

"Sister," said the captain. "She found out who I was and waited outside the building one day. Her name was Beth. I wrote a report on her because she told me I'd ruined her life. Said her brother was all she had left and now she had nothing."

"Did she threaten you?"

"Yes, as a matter of fact she said she'd be around to watch while everyone I loved disappeared. I remember it as clear as day now. Why didn't I think of her sooner?" the captain said, running his fingers through his hair.

"Like you said, Captain, it was twenty years ago. No one would have guessed a person would hold a grudge so long. Usually threats such as these are carried out right away."

"This is too much," said the captain. "I should call Mandy and let her know what's going on before she hears it on the news, or one of those news hounds corners her and asks her about it."

"Don't you think you should go home and tell her?" asked Kendall. "You've had a blow, too. Maybe you should take the rest of the day."

"No, Detective. That's not my style," he said abruptly. "I should call her Aunt Karen and ask her to go over to the house. Then Mandy won't be alone when she gets the news."

He took his cell phone from its case and noticed the message indicator light was blinking. "I wonder when this call came in." He looked at the missed call record. "I missed a call from Mandy."

He continued to pace as he listened to Mandy's message. He stopped abruptly, a look of panic on his face.

"What's wrong, Captain?" asked Kendall.

"It's Mandy," said the captain. "She said a Detective Sims called her this afternoon and said Mel wanted her to meet him at some warehouse."

Kendall stood up. "That's not possible," she said. "I was told the lieutenant was shot at around noon today. Besides, I've never heard of a Detective Sims."

"Neither have I, Kendall. I think my daughter is in big trouble." Kendall and the captain jumped when they heard the knock on his office door. Kodey Marshall was standing there his hands full of reports.

"Since the majority of the team on the Stevenson-Phelps case is in the field, I was told to bring these to you," Kodey began. "We received these reports from the librarians. Beth Mason's name pops up on all of them."

"Now I know Mandy is in deep trouble. If she can trick Lieutenant Melrose into meeting her, Mandy is a prime target," the captain groaned. "That bitch has my daughter in that warehouse. It's near 7500 New August Road. Blue siding. My daughter's red Mustang should be somewhere nearby. Have Jacobs and Mayhew meet you at Mason's current address to check it out."

"Yes, sir," she said. "I'll get a couple of patrol officers to go with us as backup."

"I'll contact Bresslin from SWAT and tell him we've got a potential hostage situation," Captain Stevenson said in torment. "Holy Mother of God. I don't want Mandy to be Mason's next victim."

She sat in her living room sipping a beer, munching on popcorn and enjoying the news. "I've been waiting for this for twenty years," she said.

"There's only one hostage," reported Andrea Atkins, "Mandy Stevenson, daughter of Captain Robert Stevenson, Commander of the IMPD's Homicide and Robbery Division."

"Glorious, simply glorious!" she exclaimed, giddy with happiness. "He's finally getting what he deserves!"

Her evening was suddenly interrupted by a knock at the door.

"Who the hell's here?" The knock came even harder. "Hold your horses, I'm coming!" she shouted. "Who's there?"

"Indianapolis Police. Open the door, please," boomed a deep male voice.

"Priceless," she said quietly giggling to herself. "Hold on! I'm coming as fast as I can!"

She opened the door to see three plain clothed detectives and two uniformed patrol officers. "Come in ladies and gentleman. Let's all watch the mayhem together."

Seeing the woman was in a wheelchair, Mayhew turned to Sanchez and Lloyd and asked them to wait outside. He, Jacobs, and Kendall followed the dark haired woman into her living room.

"Are you Beth Mason?" asked Kendall.

"Course I am. You're in my house, ain't you?"

"Miss Mason," said Jacobs, "there's somebody out there killing people and trying to make it look as though you're doing it. Do you have any idea who it might be?"

"No, idea," she said laughing, "but I want to shake the bitch's hand when you catch her — if you catch her!"

"Miss Mason, you do realize all the evidence points to you," said Kendall.

"Yeah right! And how the fuck did I get around to do all these folks in. In case you didn't notice, I'm slightly *incapacitated*."

"We noticed you're in a wheelchair, ma'am if that's what you mean," growled Mayhew. "We also know you love seein' the captain suffer, and we know why. Maybe you hired somebody to do the job and loaned them your name."

"Yeah, I'm sure my disability check is real attractive to all the hit men in town," she said sarcastically. "That son of a bitch murdered my brother! He's getting what he deserves!"

"The captain shot your brother because he was goin' to shoot another police officer while committin' a bank robbery," spat Mayhew. "*He* got what *he* deserved!"

"Get the hell out of my house!" she shouted. "You got no right to be here! I don't know who's doin' this, but more power to her."

"Let's go," Mayhew suggested. "It stinks in here!"

"Get out! *Get the fuck out!*" Beth screamed.

The three detectives left, and as Mayhew pulled the door closed, he heard something hit the door and shatter.

"What a waste of beer," Mayhew sniggered. "I'd better call Captain Stevenson and let him know what we found here. Looks like we're back to square one on this bitch's ID."

"Kendall and I'll wait in the car for you," said Jacobs.

As he watched them walk away, he pulled out his cell phone to make the call. Before dialing, he closed his eyes for a moment and prayed quietly. "Dear Lord almighty, please watch over sweet, innocent Mandy and keep her safe. Amen."

Chapter 47

Freeman was racing down the 465 Bypass to the northwest side of the city. He would use their siren until they were close to the scene and then go in silent. They didn't want Beth Mason to hear them coming.

Adrenaline rushed through Freeman's veins as he accelerated. He turned to his partner. "If anything happens to her, I don't know if I can forgive myself."

"Look, Freeman, you missed her call while you were in the middle of an investigation. It's not your fault."

"Then whose fault is it?" he asked bitterly. "If I'd just checked my messages sooner I might have gotten there before she did."

"There was only a twenty minute lapse between the time she called and the time Kendall called us," Barnes tried to reassure him. "She was further away than we were, so she probably hasn't been there long. We'll get there in time."

Barnes looked at him, biting her lip slightly, and then added, "I just hope the captain doesn't kick our asses for coming down there without his permission."

"He knows Mandy and I are dating," said Freeman. "I'll just tell him I got her voicemail and we decided we should meet her."

"When I called the station, dispatch told me SWAT had been deployed, so I'm sure they'll find a way to stop this bitch before she's had a chance to touch one hair on Mandy's head. Believe me; they're all just as pissed as we are about Mason shooting Lieutenant Melrose so they'll be extra hyped to get her."

"You don't look confident," he said.

"I'm more worried about whether we're going to get there in one piece," she said, deflecting the comment. "You need to slow down before you get us both killed. We can't help Mandy if we're out here on 465 in a junk heap."

Freeman slowed the vehicle, knowing his partner was correct. His emotions were in turmoil, climbing to the edge of insanity. His stomach rumbled from fear, not hunger. He glanced over at his partner, who was now looking out the passenger side window, avoiding his stare.

They finally arrived at the South Michigan Road off ramp, and in one piece. Brent cut the sirens as he turned west onto 71st Street, then the lights when they approached New Augusta Road. Spotting the SWAT truck, he pulled in behind it.

Captain Stevenson had already arrived, and was pacing near Lieutenant Bresslin, head of the SWAT Team.

"Here is a photo of my daughter. She has long wavy auburn hair," the captain was telling Bresslin as they approached. "According to the description the attendant at the storage facility gave us, Beth Mason has short dark hair. Miss Mason is armed and dangerous. This woman has already killed two people and attempted to kill a police officer," he paused. "My daughter must *not* be her next victim."

"From the looks of the building schematics, it only has one office," said Bresslin as he showed it to Captain Stevenson. "There's a door on the north side of the building, another on the west, with the large garage door on the south. The door on the north side has a window in it, and there is a window in the wall next to it. I'll have officers posted near each door to prevent her escape.

"There is a smaller building about 500 feet north of this one which will give us a great vantage point of the door and window I showed you. If that cop shooter comes anywhere near the area, we should be able to get a good shot."

"When you get the shot, take it," Captain Stevenson said roughly.

Bresslin nodded.

Captain Stevenson turned to see Barnes and Freeman. "What are you doing here," he growled at them. "Why aren't you at the storage facility processing the scene?"

"The Fishers Police are handling it," said Barnes.

"What can we do to help?" Freeman asked anxiously.

"Since you're already here, put your vests on. I don't intend to lose any officers today." Robert said with utmost authority. "Stay back and let SWAT do their job. I know you want to get Mandy out of there as badly as I do, Freeman, but you have to stand down until you're needed."

"But, Captain," Freeman said firmly. "I want to help. I know I can help."

"You heard me, Freeman. I said stand down!" Robert shouted. "I will not have some love sick puppy putting my daughter in danger. You *will* let SWAT do their jobs or you will get in your car and go back to the station."

"Yes, sir," Freeman said angrily flushing.

"Captain Stevenson, over here!" He turned to see several representatives from the news media calling him asking for a statement.

"That's something else you can do, Freeman. Get over there and tell those news hounds we have a hostage situation, and we don't want any more hostages. We have no further comments until Major Lewis arrives," commanded Captain Stevenson. "Barnes go with him and make sure those reporters stay safely out of the way and don't break through the barriers."

"Captain Stevenson," Robert said as he answered his cell phone. "You're on speaker. What you got for me, Mayhew?"

"We were just at Beth Mason's house, Captain. She's there. She's sittin' in a wheelchair in front of her television enjoyin' a beer and the breakin' news."

"She's what?" Captain Stevenson shouted. "If Mason's at home, then who the hell has my daughter?"

Chapter 48

Those were the same beautiful blue eyes Mandy knew so well. Mandy gasped in shock as she realized she was face-to-face with her mother. She had cut and dyed her hair, but it was her.

It took a minute for Mandy to recover from the shock. "Where have *you* been?"

Cassandra looked at Mandy with a half grin and crinkled brow making Mandy feel like she was five years old again. "Does it really matter?" Cassandra asked.

"Of course, it matters!" cried Mandy. "Dad and I've gone through hell. We thought you'd been murdered! They found your car and your blood, but not you. It doesn't make sense!"

With a sudden wave of fury Cassandra shouted, "It makes perfect sense to me! I hate your father! It's his fault Charlie decided to be a cop! He's responsible for my son's death. You don't know what hell is until you've lost your only child."

Mandy froze speechless. Shock pulsated through her body. What did she just say? She knew she didn't hear her right.

Heartsick, Mandy stared into Cassandra's eyes. "What do you mean Charlie's your only child? Why would you say that? I'm your child."

Cassandra looked at her with more contempt in her eyes than Mandy had ever seen. It made Mandy tremble with fear. "Don't you get it, you little fool? You are not *my* child," Cassandra hissed through clenched teeth. "Charlie was my only child."

Mouth agape, Mandy stood rooted to the spot unable to comprehend what she was hearing. She closed her eyes for a moment, unable to focus. Then she opened them again staring at her mother, "Am I adopted? Who are my parents, and how did I end up with you if you didn't want me?"

"Not too bright for a college graduate, are you?" taunted Cassandra. "The reason should be clear. Robert *is* your father. He had an affair and they produced you. Your mommy decided she didn't want you, so I got stuck with you!"

"What? What do you mean? Who is she?" Mandy asked shaking uncontrollably, trying to hold back her tears.

"Mandy, Mandy," Cassandra said in a softer, more sinister voice. "I thought you would have guessed by now." She paused, obviously enjoying this psychological torture. Drawing closer she pointed at Mandy's face. "When you look in the mirror, who do you see when you look into your own eyes?" Cassandra walked slowly around Mandy, smiling like a cat playing with its prey. "Perhaps Auntie Karen?"

She seemed to relish the look of pain on Mandy's face as she came around to face her once more. She stopped abruptly, pouting at Mandy.

"Oh, so you don't believe me? Didn't you ever wonder why you are the only one in our little family with green eyes?"

Cassandra paused. "Yes, my dear, it was Karen, my own sister. You know, the one who didn't want any children, but was always around to take you to the park, or give you advice, or take you for ice cream. She wanted all the fun, but none of the responsibility.

"Of course, your father thought it would be good for Charlie to have a sister. And then there was my dear mother who kept droning on and on about how the girl should at least be raised by one of her natural parents.

"Charlie wasn't hard to fool. He was very young at the time. He loved the idea of having a baby sister, and I couldn't refuse my Charlie anything.

"It was quite fortunate that your hair was the same shade of auburn as mine, but those damned green eyes of yours. It was like having Karen looking at me every day, reminding me of her betrayal."

"You're lying!" Mandy shouted no longer able to hold back the tears. "Aunt Karen would never do that! Gran would never lie to me!"

She approached Mandy stroking her hair. Mandy jerked away.

"Poor Mandy, I know it's a shock, but you're a big girl. Get over it!"

Mandy's face boiled with anger. Thoughts flooded her mind. Scream! Hit her! Make her take it back. How could Dad keep this from me? I have to pull myself together.

"So why bring me here and tell me all of this now?" Mandy asked. "Why didn't you just take off and leave us to our misery?"

Cassandra calmly reached into her coat pocket pulling out a gun. It looked like one of the guns she'd seen in her father's gun cabinet. "I thought you should know the truth before you die," Cassandra said as she raised the gun pointing it at Mandy. "Let's go into the office over there and chat some more."

Mandy did as she was told, walking into the office with Cassandra right behind her.

"Where's Uncle Mel?" Mandy asked to distract Cassandra and buy more time.

"Oh, yes that's right. You were expecting to see Mel here. Actually, I'm the one who called you pretending to be Detective Sims. A good performance if I do say so myself. But I'm afraid your dear godfather won't be joining us this evening." Cassandra grinned malevolently.

"His car is here. Where is he? What did you do to him?" Mandy shouted, fearing her mother's answer.

"I called his assistant and told her I wanted him to meet me at a storage unit in Fishers I've been renting. Mel's almost as precious to your father as you are. When he showed, I merely eliminated him."

Mandy gasped. Cassandra gave a dramatic pause to allow Mandy time to absorb this new information. "They'll find him in Unit 307 when the smell gets bad enough. Of course, by then I'll be out of the country never to be heard from again, and your father? Well, he'll be grieving for you looking to exact revenge on the real Beth Mason."

Oh, God, she killed Uncle Mel. This can't be happening, she thought. Trying to stall for more time, Mandy kept talking. "Who's Beth Mason and why would you want to frame her?"

"Your daddy killed her brother, who was robbing a bank and drew his gun on Mel. She publicly threatened to get rid of everyone he loved, so I just thought I'd borrow her identity for a while to distract them. I'm sure she won't mind."

"Clever," Mandy said.

"Why, thank you. Polite even in the face of death."

"I thought you hated guns," Mandy said, changing the subject. "I didn't think you knew how to use one."

"While you were in college, I took lessons. After what happened to Charlie I wasn't going to go around feeling vulnerable. I was top in my class," Cassandra gloated while pointing the gun at various vital areas of Mandy's body. "Always hit the bull's eye.

"Your father always had plenty of guns around for me to borrow for the practice range, so I didn't have to worry about buying one. He's so busy with his career he never realized what I was doing."

"But why kill me?" Mandy said appealing to Cassandra's motherly instincts. "It shouldn't matter that you're not my biological mother. You still raised me like any good mother would."

"Weren't you listening?" Cassandra said with mounting irritation. "I was *forced* to raise you. I didn't have a choice in the matter. Charlie loved you from the moment he laid eyes on you. It would have broken his heart if I had refused," she paused looking maniacal. "No, no, no, no, no, I could never, never, never disappoint my son."

"Do you honestly think Charlie would approve of what you're doing now?" Mandy asked desperately.

Cassandra's face contorted with rage. "Well, we'll never know, will we? He isn't here to express his opinion. Can you think of a better way to repay your father for Charlie's absence? Once you're dead, he and his whore will suffer the same way I suffer every day."

Now Mandy knew what all the whispering was about between her Aunt Karen and her dad. She knew what they were keeping from her, but Aunt Karen thought she should know. She now understood what had brought on all this bitterness between her parents, and why her mother and Aunt Karen had never been close. However, she couldn't understand why her mother would hate her for it. The circumstances of her birth certainly weren't her fault.

Before her eyes, Cassandra's demeanor changed again. She couldn't believe this woman could switch personas in the blink of an eye. Cassandra now looked softer and almost regretful. "I do bemoan the necessity of ridding myself of poor Bradley. I was hoping I could take him with me. He did help me a great deal with my disappearance."

Mandy shook her head in disbelief. Cassandra laughed. "Oh, poor

Mandy. You didn't know Bradley Phelps lusted for your mommy. Jonathan Richmond introduced us. Bradley was so sweet and that wife of his was such a bitch. It wasn't hard to seduce him into helping me." She grinned, giving Mandy a sideways glance. "I told him my marriage was a sham, and he told me his marital woes. It wasn't long before we became lovers.

"Once I had him hooked, I told him I needed to get away. I pleaded with him not to tell Alex even though you would be upset. I sported a blonde wig so people would think I was Gloria. Then Bradley took me to his summer home at the lake. He said no one was planning to use it anymore this season so it would be a safe place for me to hide."

Cassandra watched Mandy's expression then continued. "Unfortunately, Alex showed up and caught us in bed together. Bradley told me Alex had sworn he wouldn't tell anyone, not even you. However, after we drove to Hamilton County and dumped my car, Alex started having second thoughts. He didn't like the idea we'd made it look like there was foul play when I left those smears of blood on the door handles. Of course, it's *your* fault he's dead."

"What?" said Mandy.

"You're the one who told him about the blood in the car. He started feeling guilty and wanted me to come back and simply leave Robert instead of putting you through the pain of thinking I was dead."

"So why didn't you? Why not just get a divorce and then there wouldn't have been any reason for anyone to die?"

"That would have ruined my ultimate plan. When Bradley told me Alex was going to tell you everything, I came back to Indianapolis and simply eliminated the problem."

Trying not to lose her cool, Mandy stared at Cassandra. "*You…killed Alex?*"

"Yes, Mandy. Once I had killed him with the gun his father had given me to use for protection," she said nonchalantly, "I knew Bradley would figure out it was I who killed his son. I couldn't stay at the summer home any longer, but Bradley showed up before I could get away. At first, he threatened to kill me and then himself. He'd even brought a suicide note with him.

"I told him if he was going to do it we should at least have one more drink together. I prepared two glasses of wine and we went up to the bedroom. He was out before the glass was even empty, since I'd spiked it with some of Gloria's pills. So I thought I'd help him finish the job. I used the Glock to make it look like he was committing suicide, and then took the smaller gun he'd brought to use on me — this one. I used it on Mel this afternoon and will finish tonight by killing you with it."

"So Gloria was telling me the truth when she said she'd taken the gun so it wouldn't look like suicide."

"Really?" Cassandra sniggered. "God, she's stupid."

"Money hungry. Sort of like you."

"Touché. Of course, my dear boss was very helpful as well," she bragged. "Paul helped me open some accounts in the Caymans where I could hide money. Your father let me handle our finances, so he never knew about the extra cash I was getting from Paul."

Mandy was reeling from this painful information. "But you didn't just hurt us. What could have been so insurmountable that you would damage so many people who had nothing to do with your pain?"

"People create their own pain. These men cheated on their wives without batting an eye. I just took advantage of their stupidity for my own gain," noted Cassandra. "I thought I had a cash cow in Jonathan Richmond, too. It might have worked, but his bride became suspicious and put a private dick on our tails. The gun in my face convinced me to move in a different direction."

Turning in a circle Cassandra said, "This place is a piece of property I had been trying to sell. I still had the keys from the last time I showed it. Paul probably doesn't even know they're missing. Seemed like the perfect place for our parting moments."

As Cassandra completed her turn, she tripped on an extension cord someone had left strung across the floor. Mandy didn't hesitate. Cassandra's attention diverted, Mandy ran out of the office turning off the light, fleeing for her life.

Chapter 49

"We're good here, Mayhew. Take Jacobs and Kendall to St. Vincent with you and check on your lieutenant," Captain Stevenson ordered. "We've got plenty of people here to take care of this situation. Report back to me if there are any significant changes in his condition."

Major Lewis had arrived and was handling the press. Freeman and Barnes came back to the front lines.

"What's going on, Captain?" asked Freeman.

"It appears the suspect is sitting at home reveling in this circus," Captain Stevenson said, pointing at the news reporters. "Not only that, but just before we started focusing on Beth Mason, I was told Gloria Phelps made bail this morning."

"Shit!" exclaimed Barnes. "This is a fucking set up. Maybe she thought Alex told Mandy something before she wacked him and that's why she took her."

"Captain Stevenson! Tina Jackson, Channel 13. If I could just have a minute of your time, the people want to know what's going on."

"How the hell did she get past the barrier?" shouted the captain. "We have a crisis here, Miss Jackson. The barrier is there for a reason."

"Come on, move back behind the barrier with everyone else," said Major Lewis. "I'm getting ready to give you all an update."

"Just answer me this," she said breaking free and running back to the captain. "Is it true your daughter is the hostage?"

"I have no comment at this time! Now get back behind the barrier before I have you arrested for interfering with a police officer!"

This time Barnes and the nearest patrol officer each took one of her arms and escorted Miss Jackson away. They then stood guard to make sure no one else crossed the line while Major Lewis gave his statement.

"Captain," said Lieutenant Bresslin as he approached. "The owner of the building is here. He saw the news coverage and was hoping he could help by bringing us the keys to the building. He said this one is for a door in the back. Since the lights we see are on near the front, we figure that's the best way to get in."

"I'll take those keys," Captain Stevenson demanded as he snatched them from the lieutenant's hand.

"Captain!" protested Bresslin.

"I'm not having a whole troupe of your men storming the place and getting my daughter killed. Is your sniper in position?"

"Yes, Captain."

"Freeman, you need to get over there and assist your partner. I want no more reporters getting in here."

"What are you going to do?"

"Get my daughter out of there."

Mandy ran toward the door where she had entered, but found it had automatically locked behind her when she'd come in. This door was too close to the office. She was trembling too hard to unlock it before Cassandra would be able to catch up with her. She heard Cassandra's voice coming from the office.

"Mandy," she said in her sweetest motherly voice. "Mandy, come back. You can't get away. Come back and meet your fate bravely, honey."

Mandy was too vulnerable here. She scanned the area for another escape route. Thoughts swirled in her head making her dizzy. She had to get out of sight — but where?

She saw some crates across the room, and moved as quickly and quietly as possible to hide behind them. She heard Cassandra step out of the office, her footsteps echoing through the quiet warehouse.

"Mandy, Mommy doesn't have time to play hide and seek right now. We need to take care of this so Mommy can go catch her plane."

Mandy crouched; barely breathing for fear she would betray her hiding place.

"Come out, come out wherever you are," said Cassandra playfully.

Please, God, please help me, Mandy pleaded in her head. Don't let her find me. I don't want to die.

"Mandy, you're going to make Mommy late. Mommy is getting very angry."

When Cassandra's footsteps were distant, Mandy frantically scanned the area for another way out. Where was Brent? Where was Dad? Wasn't anyone going to help her?

Deafening quiet ensued. Cassandra had stopped calling for her and she could no longer hear any footsteps. Mandy crawled along the floor, trying to stay low and hidden. Then she saw it. There was a window and door to her right. She stood, but she lost her balance and fell against the crates, sending one crashing to the floor.

Panicked, Mandy ran to the door and tried to open it. "No, no, no!" she said aloud. "This can't be happening." The door was locked. With her right hand, she finally turned the deadbolt lock. Freedom at last!

Just as she was about to turn the knob she felt a searing pain in her left arm. She released the knob, screaming in pain, and looked down to find her arm was bleeding. Instinctively, she pulled it up against her chest to try to get the bleeding under control. She was defeated. It was over. Soon she'd be just another one of Cassandra's victims.

Mandy turned to see Cassandra, mouth curled up in an evil grin, holding her shoes in her left hand, pointing the gun at Mandy with her right. When Cassandra advanced on her, Mandy backed away, but kept looking her straight in the eye.

"Well, we come to the end my dear. Do you have any last words?"

"Yes," Mandy said defiantly. "I love you! I trusted you as my mother. Biology doesn't change our relationship. You are and always will be my mom. You can get help, Mom. I'll be there for you."

"Oh, how very touching," sneered Cassandra. "Nice try, but it isn't going to change things. Do you want to open or close your eyes when I do it? They say you don't hear the bullet coming anyway."

"Open," Mandy stated boldly.

"Drop the gun!" Robert shouted. "Miss Mason or whoever the hell you really are. Drop the gun or I'll have to shoot you."

Mandy shouted, "No, Dad. Don't shoot!"

Her dad frowned at Mandy's plea, but did not take his eyes or aim off of the woman who was pointing a gun at his daughter.

Cassandra smiled and keeping the gun aimed at Mandy turned her head so Robert could see her face.

"Cassandra!" exclaimed Robert in surprise.

"Yes, Robert. It's me," she said in disappointment. "How did you know we'd be here?"

"Mandy is a smart young woman. She left messages for me and Detective Freeman," he said, keeping his cool-headed police persona intact.

"Damn it!" she screeched as she brought her full attention back to Mandy, pointing the gun at Mandy's face. "You always ruin everything!"

Mandy stood there looking into those beautiful blue eyes which glistened with ice-cold hatred. The gun was now level with Mandy's face. Cassandra was going to kill her the same way Charlie and Alex had been killed.

Robert took another step toward Cassandra. "Cassandra, drop your weapon! You surely don't think I came here alone. The place is surrounded. If you don't put down the gun, SWAT will shoot you, even if I don't."

"You'd love that, wouldn't you, Robert?" she sneered. "To be the one who takes me down! To be the big hero!"

"No, Cassandra," he said. "I don't want you, or anyone else to die."

"Liar!" she shouted. "You want me out of the way so you can be with your true love. You and your bitch ruined my life. You took my son from me, now I take your only living child from you!"

Then Mandy saw it, a red dot shining on Cassandra's chest. Her eyes instinctively followed the beam of light to the warehouse window. Then she looked at her dad suddenly aware of what was about to happen. If her dad hadn't realized Cassandra was holding her, SWAT certainly wouldn't know.

Mandy looked back at Cassandra desperately pleading, "Mom, please, please put the gun down. I don't want you to die."

Cassandra glared at her, anger rising again. "I told you I'm not your mother, stop calling me that!" she screamed.

Everything seemed to happen as if in slow motion — the breaking glass, the gun dropping to the floor, and the expression on Cassandra's face as she tumbled sideways from the force of the blast. Mandy screamed, "No, no! Mom!" and ran to her, forgetting about her own injury. Mandy pulled Cassandra close, cradling her like a baby. She wailed as tears streaked down her face. Her mother's blue eyes were open now, empty and lifeless. All Mandy could do was rock back and forth holding Cassandra tightly, sobbing, repeating over and over, "No! No! No! Why? Why couldn't you just love me?"

The door burst open and Mandy heard voices shouting and saw someone kick the gun away as she continued to hold Cassandra in her arms. She felt hands pulling her and heard voices asking her to let go. The EMTs had arrived wanting to look at Cassandra, but Mandy resisted, knowing her mother was beyond help.

A gentle male voice finally convinced Mandy to release Cassandra. He helped her stand and move away. She turned to see Brent standing there with a look of worry on his face.

"Did she hurt you?"

Mandy started to shake and presented her injured arm to him. He saw the bullet hole and the blood-drenched coat sleeve. Mandy suddenly felt weak then faltered, not knowing if she was swooning because of the blood, or from emotional loss. As Brent caught her, she saw her dad looking at her with tears in his eyes.

"I found her Dad, I found my mother." Then she gave into her dizziness and collapsed into Brent's arms.

Chapter 50

When Mandy opened her eyes, she felt a chill as she realized she was lying on the concrete warehouse floor and her coat had been removed. She looked up to see a lovely red-haired woman with warm hazel eyes. The woman was cleaning Mandy's wounded arm and examining it carefully.

As Mandy's eyes began to focus, she became more aware of her surroundings. Looking to her right, she saw her dad kneeling close by. He saw she was awake and began stroking her hair.

"Hi, honey. How are you feeling?" he asked his voice choking with emotion.

"Not so good, Dad," she said as her face screwed up with grief as realization flooded in. Tears trickled down her cheeks. Her dad took her right hand, kissed it, and then held it to his cheek.

"Mandy, I didn't know it was her. I swear I didn't," he said looking down at her with sadness in his eyes. "I don't know what I would have done if anything had happened to you."

Mandy looked at her father and nodded, trying to show him she understood. She was too exhausted to speak.

The paramedic attending Mandy's injury touched Captain Stevenson's arm. "Captain, we need to get your daughter to the hospital," she said gently. "She's lost a lot of blood and this wound may require surgery. Bullet went in and out, but we need to make sure it doesn't get infected and check for nerve and muscle damage."

"You're right, O'Hara," he replied, tenderly laying Mandy's arm down across her abdomen. "I've got to finish up here, but I'll be there when you get out of surgery," he assured his daughter. "This is Kathleen O'Hara and she's one of our best EMTs so you'll be in good hands."

Kathleen smiled at him as she motioned for one of her colleagues to bring the gurney.

"St. Vincent Hospital, O'Hara," instructed her dad. O'Hara nodded, smiling at him.

"She told me everything, Dad," Mandy said, choking on her tears.

He looked at her with new tears forming in his eyes, aware she now knew his secret. Mandy started to sob, all of the pain of the last few months flowing from her eyes.

"I'm so sorry, Mandy. I love you," he said. He kissed her on the forehead and wiped his eyes. "Take good care of her, O'Hara," he said before getting up and walking away.

"Like he said," Kathleen told her, wiping Mandy's face with a soft piece of gauze, "we'll take good care of you."

The EMT with the gurney pulled up to Mandy's right side, lowered it and locked it into place. He and Kathleen lifted Mandy with ease. Kathleen told her partner she needed to start an IV in the ambulance before transport.

When they pulled the gurney out into the parking lot, Mandy saw all of the flashing blues and reds of lights from several police cars and ambulances. She saw Uncle Mel's car sitting next to hers in the parking lot feeling another pang of grief as she remembered Cassandra bragging about killing her godfather.

Before they put her into the ambulance, Mandy saw another gurney coming out of the building, transporting a dark vinyl body bag. It was Cassandra. The woman she had known as her mother for 22 years, now a stranger, a criminal, a lunatic. Cassandra had died on that cold, dirty warehouse floor where she had planned to leave Mandy to die.

Mandy felt overwhelming sadness and anger grip her. It didn't have to be this way. How could she harbor such hatred for someone who loved her? How could Alex's father have been so stupid? Why would he choose to follow her scheme? Damn him! Dad, Aunt Karen, Gran…it's perfidy! All the lies, the infidelity, the disloyalty! Who could she trust now? The only people in the world she could fully trust — Uncle Mel and Charlie — are dead.

Mandy bit her lower lip as the thoughts ran through her mind. She really wanted to stop crying, but wondered if she ever would.

Kathleen was preparing the IV when Mandy heard someone

entering the ambulance. It was Brent. He stood there looking at her tenderly.

"I don't know what to say," he began. "When I got your message, I was terrified." Mandy looked into his golden eyes and felt his sincerity.

"It's over, Brent," she sniffed. "It's finally over."

He took her right hand and kissed it gently before Kathleen told him she needed that arm for the IV. "Of course." He smiled. He stroked her auburn tresses gently. "Mandy, I'm so glad you left those messages for your dad and me, otherwise...," his voice broke off and he gulped.

"What about Uncle Mel? Did you find him?"

Surprised, he answered, "Yes. He's in St. Vincent Hospital. Mayhew called a while ago and told us he's in surgery."

"He's alive! But she bragged about killing him and...," she paused trying not to start crying again.

"I'm sure she intended to kill him, but she failed," Brent said. "That's not to say he isn't in serious condition, but he's a fighter. I think he's got a good chance."

Her voice cracked with the pain of her next words. "Alex. She killed Alex. He was going to tell me she was still alive and she killed him to keep him quiet."

Kathleen interrupted them indicating it was vital they transport Mandy now. Brent kissed her lightly on the lips, told her he would see her later, and exited the vehicle. Kathleen told the driver the patient was secure and they were ready to go.

Mandy heard the siren screaming, trying to relax by closing her eyes, but that only brought unwanted images. She knew she would have to relive it all by making a statement, but for now, she just wanted to remember Brent's sweet kiss.

When they arrived at the hospital, the emergency room personnel were ready for her. After close examination of the wound, they prepared her for surgery. As she faded off into her anesthetically induced slumber, she wondered how she would be able to face her Aunt Karen. Should she start calling her mom? Could she forgive her for the deceit, and worse, for giving her to someone who didn't want her? Just before giving in to the drugs, she decided to take one thing at a time. Heal the body then take on the task of healing the heart.

Chapter 51

Mandy woke the next morning in a semi-private room. She looked to her left noting she had no roommate. Then she looked to the right seeing her dad in the hallway talking to a man wearing green scrubs. Her vision was still blurry from the anesthetic, but she could see her dad shake hands with the man and then turn towards the door.

"Hey, Dad," she said in a groggy, almost drunken voice. For the second time in less than 24 hours, she saw her strong stoic father burst into tears and cover his face, sobbing. If anything was going to bring her around, it was this. "Dad, don't cry. I'm okay."

He gently touched her right arm, stroking it carefully, trying not to disturb the IV tubing. He continued to stroke her as he sobbed. "Oh, Mandy, this whole thing is my fault. How can you ever forgive me?"

"To be honest, I don't know, Dad," Mandy said unable to look him in the eye. "Having her blurt it out like that. It broke my heart." Mandy couldn't avoid tears, but tried to continue. "It's hard to believe this was kept secret from me for 22 years. Didn't anyone realize what this would do to me when it came out?"

"That's what made it so hard to tell you," he said, wiping his face on his sleeve. "The longer we waited, the harder it became. I'm so sorry, Mandy. I don't know what I would have done if she had killed you. You're my whole life."

This was certainly more than Mandy ever expected to hear from her father. She'd never seen him break down like this, not even when Charlie died. "Look Dad, no matter what she said, she had a choice. She chose to let the circumstances of my birth eat at her until it festered into hate. Then when Charlie died, she snapped."

"Everyone pressured her," he said, "even her own mother."

"Stop making excuses for her. I was just a baby!" Mandy retorted with bitterness in her voice. "She may have been pressured, but she didn't have to do it. She could have *chosen* to accept and love me like Charlie did. She could have told me about it a long time ago, when I was old enough to understand. But no, she *chose* to keep it bottled up inside her, and then *chose* revenge. Even divorce would have been a better option. Then she would have been free of me, and you could have raised me on your own."

Adrenaline pumping, Mandy took a deep breath to calm her pounding heart. Tears poured from her eyes. Anesthesia could not mask this type of pain.

"Exposing my birth mother wasn't the only confession Mo ..., Cassandra made," said Mandy. "She told me she was having an affair with Alex's father."

"What?" he said, wiping his tears.

"Yeah, like I said, she confessed *everything*. She killed Alex because he'd seen her after she went missing. That's what he wanted to tell me the day he died. He couldn't handle watching me suffer. Then when Mr. Phelps figured out she'd killed his son, she decided he had to go, too."

Her dad sat aghast as Mandy told him every detail of what Cassandra had planned, anger showing on his face at times. "I thought she loved me, but when Charlie died she became so distant. I made excuses for her like; 'Oh, she's just depressed. She'll come around some day.' "

"Oh, Mandy," her father said, squeezing her hand. "I don't know how I could have lived with her for twenty-five years and not seen this coming."

"I know, Dad," she said sharply. "She fooled us all."

After a short silence, Mandy continued, "Does Aunt Karen know that I know?"

"I called her," he said. "As a matter of fact, she and Gran are waiting to see you."

"Gran flew up from Florida? Is she healthy enough for this?" asked Mandy.

"She's been doing better lately," he said. "But the one thing you must understand, Gran just lost her daughter. No matter what Cassandra has done, Gran had to be here to put her to rest."

Mandy hadn't thought about the fact her grandmother would be mourning the death of her child. "Just do me one favor, Dad. Stay with me while they're here."

She saw an expression of relief on her dad's face. He must have taken this last statement as implied forgiveness. She was still very angry with him, yet something tugged at her heart. A bond not to be broken by anything or anyone. Look what holding onto years of anger did to Cassandra.

"I'll let them know you're awake and we'll be right back," he said.

Mandy looked around the sterile room. How was she going to handle this? These are the two women who pressured Cassandra to take her. If they'd made different choices, maybe things wouldn't have turned out this way.

Gran walked in first sporting a cane. She approached Mandy slowly. There was so much pain in Gran's face, her eyes puffy and red, and her body shaking slightly. When she reached the bed, Mandy smiled as best she could and the old woman leaned against Mandy's shoulder. She started crying, trembling. Mandy rubbed Gran's bony back, tears burning her eyes. Suddenly, her anger towards her grandmother diminished.

Gran stood, pulled a tissue from her pocket, and wiped her face. "Can you ever forgive an old woman for making such a terrible mistake?" she asked.

"Gran, I love you, but this is really hard. This is something which isn't going to go away easily," Mandy answered.

"I know," said Gran. "This is all my fault. If only I hadn't pushed Cassandra to adopt you. Granddad and I should have taken you. I honestly thought Cassandra would forgive Robert and would love you as much as she loved Charlie. She was such a good mother to that boy."

"Instead, I was a constant reminder of Dad's infidelity," Mandy said.

"I just can't believe a child of mine could do such a thing. Murder two people and then try to kill you and Mel," Gran anguished. "Where did I go wrong?"

Mandy took a moment to look into Gran's glistening, deep blue eyes. "It's not your fault. She wasn't in her right mind. She let Charlie's death turn her into a bitter, vengeful person, Gran. We can try to place blame, but what's the point?"

"If Charlie hadn't become a police officer and been killed doing his job, maybe she wouldn't have snapped," said Gran.

"But what if he'd become a veterinarian and was killed by a car while crossing the street," said Mandy. "Would her grief and resentment have been any less? We'll never know. What's happened is her fault. She's the one who chose to hate rather than love."

"That's right, Mom," said Karen.

Mandy had focused on her grandmother so intently; she didn't hear her dad and Karen come in.

"Hi, Aunt Karen," Mandy said as she tried to sit up. She grimaced and groaned as a pain shot through her injured left arm.

Karen moved quickly to Mandy's side. "Are you okay, sweetheart? Are you in pain?"

"Should I call the nurse?" asked her dad.

Mandy smiled at first at the attention, but then winced as she recovered from her foolish attempt at rising. She decided to send her dad for the nurse, while her grandmother and Karen fussed over her. Karen tried to help her into a sitting position, and Gran positioned the pillows.

A very short, blonde woman in a nurse's uniform entered with her dad, who was very pale with concern. "Hi, Mandy. My name is Alice," said the very pleasant young woman. "I'll be your nurse today until about 3:00 this afternoon. How are you feeling?" Alice asked as she checked Mandy's bandage and IV.

"Okay," said Mandy. "Guess I tried sitting up too fast."

"No harm done," she said, taking Mandy's pulse. "Actually, we'll probably get you up and out of bed for a little walk later this morning. I'll show you the best way to get out of bed with minimal pain. However, don't get up on your own; even to go to the bathroom, while you are on the pain medication. You might get dizzy and fall. Do you need to go now?" Alice asked pointing toward the bathroom.

"No," said Mandy.

The nurse took her blood pressure and temperature. As soon as she made sure Mandy was comfortable, the nurse produced a syringe, explaining it was a pain reliever she could ask for every four hours. Once Alice had administered the medication, she left Mandy alone with her family.

282 M. E. May

"You sure you're okay now?" asked Karen, worry lines creasing her forehead.

"I will be as soon as these drugs kick in," Mandy said, a little too harshly from the look on Gran's face.

"Mandy, I wish I had handled this better," Gran said shaking and wiping the tears from her cheeks. "I only wanted to make sure you didn't go to strangers. I couldn't stand the idea of having a grandchild I would never see. I know it was selfish, and I'm sorry."

"You did the best you could at the time," said Mandy. "Nobody could have predicted things would turn out the way they did."

Mandy looked at her dad. "I think Gran could use a cup of tea, don't you? I'd like to speak with Aunt Karen alone."

"Sure," he said, taking Gran by the arm. "Be back in about twenty minutes, okay?"

"That should do it," said Mandy.

Karen turned and walked back to the window. In the awkward silence which followed, Mandy struggled with herself. She loved Karen, but at the same time, anger ebbed and flowed through her as everything Cassandra told her came rushing back. Why should she care how Karen feels? She obviously didn't think about her actions leaving Mandy vulnerable to Cassandra's wrath.

Karen's deep sigh broke the silence. She turned to look at Mandy, walking slowly towards her with arms crossed. "Mandy, I know you may never be able to forgive me," she said choking on the last two words. "However, I do hope you'll let me explain what happened."

"I've heard Mom's side, or should I call her Aunt Cassandra?" said Mandy. "So yes, I think you and Dad owe me that much."

"You're right, we do. I'm not going to make excuses for my actions. But believe me, I would never have allowed Cassandra to adopt you if I'd known she'd take her hatred for me out on you."

"Start from the beginning, please," Mandy requested irritably. "I want to know everything, like why you would screw around with your sister's husband."

"It wasn't like that," Karen said, but Mandy eyed her in disbelief. "It started about a year after Charlie was born. I'd just finished graduate school. Although Cassandra and I weren't close, I spent some time with her, Robert and Charlie when I returned from school. I hadn't gotten to know your father very well before I went away, but found him to be very pleasant and charming."

"I bet you did."

"Please let me finish before you pass judgment," Karen pleaded. Mandy nodded but didn't change her angry expression.

"Robert and I became friends. He called me one day needing someone to talk to and I met him at the local coffee shop. I think he was hoping for some insight on Cassandra, because he started confiding very intimate details of their lives to me. They hadn't had sexual relations since just before Charlie was born. I felt badly for him, but Cassandra wouldn't listen to me, so all I could do was listen to Robert when he needed to talk.

"I found a position at Clarian and lived with my parents until I had enough money to move into my own place. Charlie was about two and a half at the time. I was still meeting your dad occasionally for a cup of coffee or lunch so he could blow off some steam."

Karen paused, looking away from Mandy. She walked towards the window. "Then I made a huge mistake. I allowed Robert to come by my apartment to talk.

"My day had been pretty rough, so I had opened a bottle of wine. We drank and talked. I guess it loosened us both up a little *too* much. I hadn't realized until then I had feelings for your father which were deeper than just friendship. The next thing I knew we were in my bed."

"Well. Now I know how I was conceived," said Mandy crisply. "So if Dad was so unhappy with his marriage, why didn't he just get a divorce and marry you?"

"That night was the only time he and I were intimate. As a matter of fact, I cut off the bitching sessions," said Karen as she turned to face Mandy again. "I didn't want anyone to find out about it. I didn't want Charlie to be without a father."

"That was noble of you," Mandy said, seeing the pain in Karen's face as the comment stung her. Immediately she recognized she had gone too far. "Sorry, please continue," she said.

"After a couple of months, I realized I hadn't had a period and went to see my doctor. I don't know why, but I was shocked when he told me I was pregnant. I was so busy getting my career going I hadn't dated at all in the year and a half since grad school. Well, except for the one night with Robert.

"I was young and stupid and terrified. At first, I thought about an abortion, but it didn't take me long to nix the idea. I just couldn't do it. Then I considered putting my baby up for adoption, because I didn't have the money to take care of a child."

"There are lots of single moms out there," Mandy retorted.

"Like I said, I was young, stupid, and scared to death," Karen interjected. "I wanted to do what was best for my child. I decided to do what most young girls do in these situations. I went to my mother."

"Cassandra told me Gran instigated this whole thing," said Mandy.

"It depends on how you look at it," Karen said. "When I told her about my pregnancy and I was thinking about giving you up for adoption, she was very upset. Like she told you, she didn't want you going to strangers. She told me the father should take responsibility. I finally confessed that he was married and I didn't want to break up his family.

"She kept badgering me about the father's identity until one day I blurted out the truth." Karen paused, looking at the ceiling shaking her head. "I thought she was going to have a heart attack right then and there."

"I'm sure it was quite a shock for her," said Mandy. "So how did she come up with the idea of Cassandra adopting me?"

"Like I said, she thought the father should take responsibility for his own child. Your granddad took care of Charlie while Mother met with me, Robert and Cassandra. I felt awful. I knew this would only deepen the wedge between them. In the end, Cassandra gave in. She even agreed to give me visitation with you as long as I never told you the truth. I was so happy. Even if I couldn't keep you, I could still have you in my life."

Tears streamed from Karen's eyes. "From what I could see, Cassandra always treated you like her own daughter. And Charlie, he loved you from the moment he set eyes on you. Maybe that's what softened her heart towards you."

"Then when he died, all of the resentment she had buried destroyed her," commented Mandy sadly. "She lost her son then she lost her mind."

"My only hope for you is, no matter what you think of me, you don't let what happened to Cassandra happen to you." Tears continued to roll down Karen's cheeks.

Mandy nodded, hot tears welling in her own eyes now. "After everything I've been through these past few months, you don't have to worry. I won't allow myself to turn into a hate driven monster. It's going to take some time for me to work through this. Just don't push, okay?"

"I won't," Karen said, wiping her tears. "I don't really have any right to expect anything from you. But I do love you."

"We're back," announced Gran. Mandy's father was following slowly, a tray with four cups of tea in hand. "I had your dad bring tea for everybody. It's the best thing in times like these."

"Good idea," Mandy said softening.

Gran stroked Mandy's cheek, wiping away her tears. "Your brother would be very proud to see what a wonderful young woman you've become," said Gran.

"I miss him every day," said Mandy. "I'm just glad I had the opportunity to know him, even for such a short time. Charlie taught me everything about unconditional love."

Gran smiled. "He was very special," she said. "I miss him, too. I have a feeling he is your special guardian angel."

"I believe you're right, Gran. I believe he's still watching over of me."

She watched as everyone became more relaxed sipping their tea. Her dad had sweetened her tea to perfection. Of course, this almost made her believe things could be normal again. It would take a long time for the anger to subside completely and the wounds to heal. All she knew was this was her family — her grandmother, her father and her real mother. Hadn't Karen always been the one who showed her the affection she needed? Wasn't Karen the one who was there to help her mourn for Charlie? She had always been there for her, whenever Mandy needed her. Yes, they had deceived her, but she knew no matter what storms would come, they all loved her.

Chapter 52

Mandy and Brent walked slowly through Oaklawn Cemetery toward his car. She watched as her Uncle Frank and Karen helped Gran into the limousine. It had been very difficult to see Gran's pain as she said goodbye to her youngest daughter. It was good to know Uncle Frank would be taking Gran back to Chicago with him for a few weeks. Mandy couldn't bear the idea of Gran going back to Tampa alone.

Mandy gave the police her formal statement yesterday. She had also met with the team of detectives who worked so hard to find her mother and Alex's killer. Unfortunately, finding Cassandra and Alex's killer were one and the same.

She was so deep in her thoughts she didn't hear what Brent was saying until he tapped her good arm. She looked up to see him smiling at her.

"I asked you how you're feeling."

"I'm doing all right," she said. "I'm not saying it wasn't hard, but I needed to be here for Gran. It was sweet of you to ask."

She stopped walking for a moment, looking straight ahead. "Brent," she said.

"What is it?" he asked.

She turned to him, an overwhelming feeling of gratitude swelling in her chest. "I really appreciate that you came with me today. I don't know if I could have done it without you."

He reached in his pocket and pulled out a packet of tissues. He took one out and gently wiped the tears from her cheeks. "I'm glad I could be here for you, Mandy." He paused. "I care very much for you, you know."

All she could do was nod. She had been so caught up in the recent drama in her life she hadn't given much thought to how she truly felt about Brent. She knew she liked him and was physically attracted to him. Of course, isn't this the way a relationship should begin, with good feelings and physical attraction? She couldn't think about this now, so she changed the subject.

"I'm glad to be out of the hospital," she said. "I've got another week to wear this sling. It's such an annoyance."

"Did you get a chance to visit Lieutenant Melrose?" he asked.

"Yes," she smiled at the memory. "He was wide awake and complaining, so that's a good sign. However, the doctors aren't sure if he'll be the same mentally. It's all so complicated."

"That's too bad, he's a great guy," said Brent. "Did you get to see Gloria and Lana yesterday?"

"Oh, yeah," said Mandy. "At first Gloria was ranting and raving about wanting to sue the police department, but her attorney advised her to forget it for Lana's sake."

"Well, the part about the attorney is half right. Gloria did it for Gloria," said Brent. "We simply reminded her about the little problem of her removing evidence from a crime scene and her attorney told her not to make a fuss. I don't know what the Cassopolis police will do to her."

"At least Lana has her grandparents if Gloria has to go to jail again," said Mandy. "Oh, and she couldn't help but tell me Savannah Richmond threw her husband out and filed for divorce."

"It doesn't surprise me," he said. "They were making each other miserable, so I'm sure it was just a matter of time before they parted ways. I just hope they try to remain civil for the sake of their children."

"Me, too," said Mandy, slipping her hand in Brent's. "Lana seems to be doing all right, but I'm going to keep checking on her. Sometimes people seem all right when they aren't. I don't want her bottling her feelings up to the point of exploding some day."

They reached the car and Brent opened the passenger door. He helped her slide into the seat since it was difficult for her to do so with the sling.

When he slipped into the driver's seat, he said, "I forgot to tell you something. It appears Paul Benson was skimming money from the business to keep Cassandra from going public with the affair. Now he's under investigation."

"Don't expect me to feel sorry for him," said Mandy. "I know you and the other detectives thought Whitney was a bitch, but her father created her dark side. She's really very sweet and really cared for Alex. If it weren't for her dad, she and Alex might have been together instead of him fooling around with Savannah Richmond."

"But then the two of you might never have met," said Brent.

Mandy's heart skipped a beat in remembrance of her friend. "Did the FBI ever find anything in the lake?" asked Mandy, changing the subject.

"The divers found a black tarp tied with rope at both ends which was really heavy — much heavier than a body. They pulled it out of the lake finding a bag of cement, or at this point a large block of cement, and a trash bag with Cassandra's purse, identification, and the clothing you told us she was wearing when she disappeared."

"Unbelievable!" Mandy exclaimed. "So she must have planted her own blood in the boat like she did in her car."

"Exactly," he said. "Are things going okay with your dad?"

"Dad's been great," she said. "Actually, more than great. He's free, Brent. He's almost a different person now that Cassandra isn't making his life miserable. Of course, don't expect him to be different at work."

"Hey, I can hope," he said, grinning. "I noticed you and Karen are getting along. How's it going?"

"Better than I expected," said Mandy. "Each day seems to be easier. I don't want to waste my time or energy being angry, but sometimes I just can't help it. After witnessing the damage first-hand, I would never allow these types of secrets under my roof. Like Karen said not long ago, the truth will come out, it always does."

"She's right, Mandy. It does," said Brent.

"Thanks, Brent, for being there for me."

"Hey, that's what friends are for," said Brent, squeezing her hand.

Mandy met Brent's eyes, smiling and thinking fondly of another friend. "That sounds just like something Alex would say."

About the Author

M. E. (Michele) May lives in the Far Northwest Suburbs of Chicago with her husband, Paul, and their white Husky, Iris. She was born in Indianapolis, Indiana, the fourth of five children to working class parents. She has a son and daughter still living in Indiana, and four wonderful grandsons, the eldest of whom she gives the credit for inspiring her to pursue her dream of writing novels.

She attended classes at Indiana University in Kokomo, Indiana, studying Social and Behavioral Sciences. Her interest in the psychology of humans sparked the curiosity to ask why they commit such heinous acts upon one another. Other interests in such areas as criminology and forensics have moved her to put her vast imagination to work writing fiction that is as accurate as possible. In doing so, she depicts societal struggles which pit those who understand humanity with those who are lost in a strange and dangerous world of their own making.

CPSIA information can be obtained at www.ICGtesting.com
Printed in the USA
LVOW082347091112

306720LV00001B/2/P

9 781937 148201